STORIES OF
PEOPLE & CIVILIZATION
MESOAMERICA
ANCIENT ORIGINS

FLAME TREE PUBLISHING
6 Melbray Mews, Fulham,
London SW6 3NS, United Kingdom
www.flametreepublishing.com

First published and copyright © 2023
Flame Tree Publishing Ltd

23 25 27 26 24
1 3 5 7 9 10 8 6 4 2

ISBN: 978–1–80417–614–6

Cover and pattern art was created by Flame Tree Studio, with elements courtesy of
Shutterstock.com/svekloid/Zvereva Yana. Additional interior decoration courtesy
of Shutterstock.com/Drawlab19.

Judith John (lists of Ancient Kings & Leaders) is a writer and editor specializing in
literature and history. A former secondary school English Language and Literature
teacher, she has subsequently worked as an editor on major educational projects, including
English A: Literature for the Pearson International Baccalaureate series. Judith's major
research interests include Romantic and Gothic literature, and Renaissance drama.

The text in this book is compiled and edited, with a new introduction, from
extracts fom the following sources: *True History of the Profound Mexico* (2010)
by Guillermo Marín Ruiz, *Yucatan Before and After the Conquest* by Diego de Landa,
translated by William Gates, published by the Maya Society (Baltimore, 1937);
Ancient Cities of the New World by Désiré Charnay, translated by J. Gonino and
Helen S. Conant, published by Chapman & Hall (London, 1887); *History of the
Conquest of Mexico* by William Hickling Prescott, published by J.B. Lippincott
Company (1904).

A copy of the CIP data for this book is available
from the British Library.

Designed and created in the UK | Printed and bound in China

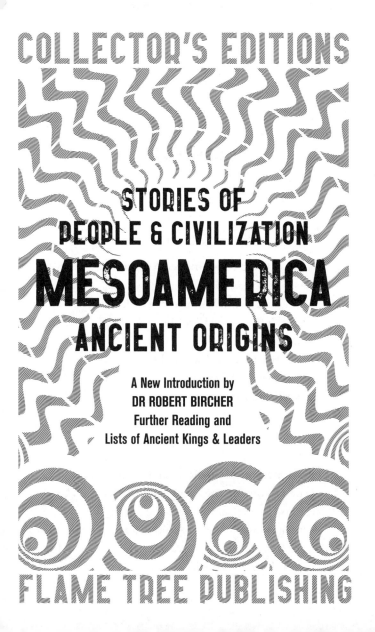

COLLECTOR'S EDITIONS

STORIES OF
PEOPLE & CIVILIZATION
MESOAMERICA
ANCIENT ORIGINS

A New Introduction by
DR ROBERT BIRCHER
Further Reading and
Lists of Ancient Kings & Leaders

FLAME TREE PUBLISHING

CONTENTS

4

CONTENTS

CONTENTS

CONTENTS

STORIES OF
PEOPLE & CIVILIZATION
MESOAMERICA
ANCIENT ORIGINS

SERIES FOREWORD

Stretching back to the oral traditions of thousands of years ago, tales of heroes and disaster, creation and conquest have been told by many different civilizations, in ways unique to their landscape and language. Their impact sits deep within our own culture even though the detail in the stories themselves are a loose mix of historical record, the latest archaeological evidence, transformed narrative and the unwitting distortions of generations of storytellers.

Today the language of mythology lives around us: our mood is jovial, our countenance is saturnine, we are narcissistic and our modern life is hermetically sealed from others. The nuances of the ancient world form part of our daily routines and help us navigate the information overload of our interconnected lives.

The nature of a myth is that its stories are already known by most of those who hear or read them. Every era brings a new emphasis, but the fundamentals remain the same: a desire to understand and describe the events and relationships of the world. Many of the great stories are archetypes that help us find our own place, equipping us with tools for self-understanding, both individually and as part of a broader culture.

For Western societies it is Greek mythology that speaks to us most clearly. It greatly influenced the mythological heritage of the ancient Roman civilization and is the lens through which we still see the Celts, the Norse and many of the other great peoples and religions. The Greeks themselves inherited much from their neighbours, the Egyptians, an older culture that became weary with the mantle of civilization.

Of course, what we perceive now as mythology had its own origins in perceptions of the divine and the rituals of the sacred. The earliest civilizations, in the crucible of the Middle East, in the Sumer of the third millennium BCE, are the source to which many of the mythic archetypes can be traced. Over five thousand years ago, as humankind collected together in cities for the first time, developed writing and industrial scale agriculture, started to irrigate the rivers and attempted to control rather than be at the mercy of its environment, humanity began to write down its tentative explanations of natural events, of floods and plagues, of disease.

Early stories tell of gods or god-like animals who are crafty and use their wits to survive, and it is not unreasonable to suggest that these were the first rulers of the gathering peoples of the earth, later elevated to god-like status with the distance of time. Such tales became more political as cities vied with each other for supremacy, creating new gods, new hierarchies for their pantheons. The older gods took on primordial roles and became the preserve of creation and destruction, leaving the new gods to deal with more current, everyday affairs. Empires rose and fell, with Babylon assuming the mantle from Sumeria in the 1800s BCE, in turn to be swept away by the Assyrians of the 1200s BCE; then the Assyrians and the Egyptians were subjugated by the Greeks, the Greeks by the Romans and so on, leading to the spread and assimilation of common themes, ideas and stories throughout the world.

The survival of history is dependent on the telling of good tales, but each one must have the 'feeling' of truth, otherwise it will be ignored. Around the firesides, or embedded in a book or a computer, the myths and legends of the past are still the living materials of retold myth, not restricted to an exploration of historical origins. Now we have devices and global communications that give us unparalleled access to a diversity of traditions. We can find out about Indigenous American, Indian, Chinese and tribal African mythology in a way that was denied to our ancestors, we can find connections, plot the archaeology, religion and the mythologies of the world to build a comprehensive image of the human experience that is both humbling and fascinating.

The books in this series introduce the many cultures of ancient humankind to the modern reader. From the earliest migrations across the globe to settlements along rivers, from the landscapes of mountains to the vast Steppes, from woodlands to deserts, humanity has adapted to its environments, nurturing languages and observations and expressing itself through records, mythmaking stories and living traditions. There is still so much to explore, but this is a great place to start.

Jake Jackson
General Editor

STORIES OF
PEOPLE & CIVILIZATION
MESOAMERICA
ANCIENT ORIGINS

INTRODUCTION
& FURTHER READING

INTRODUCTION TO MESOAMERICA ANCIENT ORIGINS

In 1952, Mexican archaeologist Alberto Ruz Lhuillier made one of the most remarkable discoveries of modern archaeology – the remains of K'inich Janaab' Pakal, or Pakal the Great. Ruz Lhuillier had been investigating the Temple of Inscriptions in Palenque, the site of a city-state of the Maya, one of the great civilizations of Mesoamerica. Noticing an unusual floor slab, Ruz Lhuillier discovered steps leading down beneath the temple's main platform. But this tunnel was packed with rubble, and it took four years of work before Ruz Lhuillier stood in the burial chamber, deep beneath the temple, where K'inich Janaab' Pakal had lain undisturbed since his death, aged eighty, on 9.12.11.5.18 by the Maya calendar (August 683 CE). Over his face was a death mask made of intricate jade pieces, and the body was dressed with elaborate jewellery. Perhaps of greatest significance, however, was the lid of the sarcophagus – a seven-tonne block of limestone that Ruz Lhuillier's team needed four car jacks to lift. The lid was covered with carvings, those on the sides showing Pakal's ancestors being reborn as trees, and those on the top depicting the rebirth of Pakal as a god.

The discovery was remarkable in many ways, not least in highlighting how slowly the secrets of Mesoamerica's ancient civilizations have been revealed, and how much there is still to discover. For example, the first account of Palenque was published in 1567 by a Spanish priest, who named it after a Spanish word for 'fortification', and yet it took another 400 years to establish that the pyramidal Temple of Inscriptions had the dual use of temple and tomb. Even today, it is estimated that less than five per cent of the ruins of Palenque have been uncovered.

Another example: the structure at the top of the Temple of Inscriptions is covered in the hieroglyphic script of the Maya which as recently as sixty years ago was generally agreed to be largely abstract and undecipherable. And yet by the 1960s it was established beyond doubt that in fact it listed, together with the astronomical events that fascinated the ancient Mesoamericans, the rulers and great events of the city state of Ba'aakal, of which Palenque, or Lakam Ha as the Maya called it, was the capital. Indeed, it wasn't until 2015 that Mexican researchers finally decoded the name given to Pakal's burial chamber: the House of the Nine Sharpened Spears.

Many more examples could be given: when Europeans first encountered Palenque in the sixteenth century, it had already lain abandoned by the Maya for 600 years, and yet the reasons for the collapse of the great Maya civilization are still a mystery, as are its origins. Was Palenque in fact originally an Olmec city? Why is it, too, that the deciphered descriptions say that Pakal reigned for sixty-eight years and died aged eighty, when his teeth appear to be those of a forty-year-old?

Even these few questions are too many for an introduction such as this to explore in any depth, though they provide some starting points and some context for the four extracts that make up this book. Each of these extracts come from a key document in the historiography of ancient Mesoamerica and cover, in turn, the Olmec, Maya, Toltec and Aztec civilizations. Let us begin with a brief introduction to Mesoamerica itself, and then consider some key features of each of these four civilizations.

WHAT IS MESOAMERICA?

Mesoamerica stretches from present-day Mexico in the north, down through Central America to the western parts of Costa Rica, with its heart being the Middle American isthmus. It was home to some of the most advanced and complex civilizations of the ancient world, including the Olmecs, Maya, Toltecs and Aztecs – the four civilizations featured in this book. Mesoamerica is not what these civilizations would have called their domains. Like much to do with writings about Mesoamerica's ancient origins, the term comes from outside the indigenous peoples of the region. Mesoamerica was coined from the Greek for 'middle America' in the mid-twentieth century by Paul Kirchhoff, a German ethnologist and anthropologist, who observed shared characteristics of the indigenous cultures of this region: advanced agricultural practices that included the cultivation of maize and cacao, hieroglyphic and pictographic writing systems, complex social and political organizations, sophisticated religions with intricate mythologies and rituals, and monumental architecture – including the vast temple complexes, ball courts and stepped pyramids such as the Temple of Inscriptions in Palenque, under which K'inich Janaab' Pakal was entombed.

In the first section of this book, from his *True History of the Profound Mexico*, Guillermo Marín Ruiz attempts to unpick the centuries of colonial exploitation, appropriation and reinterpretation of Mesoamerica's ancient origins. He uses for Mexico the term Cem Anahuac, 'the land surrounded by waters' in the Nahuatl language of the Aztec people, referring to the waters of the Caribbean Sea, the Gulf of Mexico and the Pacific Ocean. And he talks of the Anahuac civilization as the ancient core of what became Mexico, which developed the technological, social and spiritual innovations that Kirchhoff identified as linking the ancient civilizations of Mesoamerica. For Marín Ruiz, the history of Mesoamerica is the history of 'our Old Grandfathers', the birthplace of one of the world's six oldest civilizations that independently produced 'the highest human development for its population in the history of mankind' (page 45). These ancient civilizations at their Classical period peak (about 250 to 900 CE) reached a level of sophistication that rivalled anything in Europe at the time. This sophistication has continued to trouble Europeans ever since their first contact with the indigenous cultures of Mesoamerica at the start of the sixteenth century: a theme we will return to later in this introduction.

INTRODUCING ANCIENT MESOAMERICAN CIVILIZATIONS

The four sections of this book each have as their focus one of the great ancient Mesoamerican civilizations: the Olmecs, the Maya, the Toltecs and the Aztecs. The Further Reading list on page 39 has recommendations for finding out more about each of these rich and fascinating cultures, and you can find details of the leaders of each civilization, as far as they are known, on page 358.

The Olmecs

Humans have inhabited the Americas since at least 11000 BCE, with some archaeologists dating this much further back: to human habitation of Mesoamerica in 21000 BCE. Around 7000 BCE, climate changes prompted a move towards more settled habitation. By 5300 BCE, maize cultivation was under way, together with the domestication of other key crops such as beans and squashes. In some areas where maize cultivation was particularly successful, food surpluses permitted higher levels of cultural development by about 2500 BCE, along with an elite landowning class: the building blocks for ancient civilizations.

The Olmecs, known as the 'mother culture' of Mesoamerica, emerged around 1400 BCE in the rich agricultural lands of the modern Mexican states of Veracruz and Tabasco. Our understanding of the Olmecs has significantly evolved over the years, but there are still many ongoing debates and mysteries about this ancient culture. We can be confident that their social structure was a complex one, with a hereditary elite. Sophisticated farming techniques included irrigation systems, terracing and raised fields. There is evidence for a system of markets and a trading network. The Olmecs had a hieroglyphic writing system, though our understanding of it is imperfect, especially in its earliest forms. While the earliest Mesoamerican calendar so far discovered is from the Maya period, it is considered likely that the Olmecs were deeply interested in astronomy – as evidenced by the specific orientation of buildings in Olmec temple complexes – and in mathematics. These are features of all the ancient Mesoamerican cultures; the buildings (including pyramids and earthen mounds), together with ceramics, intricate jade carvings and monumental statues (including colossal stone heads), are all characteristic of the other Mesoamerican civilizations, too. A final two examples: the Mesoamerican ballgame (a sport with religious significance played with a rubber ball in a stone-built court) and sacrificial rituals involving bloodletting are both believed to have originated with the Olmecs.

The decline of the Olmec civilization is not fully understood, but by 350 BCE a population crash occurred and cities were abandoned, perhaps as a result of changes to river flows or volcanic activity. Within a century, non-Olmecs were living in the old Olmec heartlands.

For Marín Ruiz, in the first section of this book, the significance of the Olmecs extends far beyond the ancient Mesoamerican civilizations that followed. He references an Olmec heritage – 'an optimism for life, capable of performing immeasurable spiritual projects' and 'a mystical and spiritual sense of existence and the universe' (pages 69 and 70) – which has persisted and is 'an intrinsic part' of what Mexicans are today.

The Maya

The ancient Maya civilization emerged around 2000 BCE, reaching its peak between 250 and 900 CE, and was renowned for its advances in astronomy, mathematics, art, architecture and written language. Spanning a third of Mesoamerica: present-day Mexico, Guatemala, Belize, Honduras and El Salvador, the Maya peoples created an intricate network of city-states (including Ba'aakal, where K'inich Janaab' Pakal ruled for sixty-eight years), each with their own distinct culture and political structure, although interconnected through alliances and conflicts. The largest cities had populations of up to 120,000 people. The Maya's hieroglyphic script is considered one of the most sophisticated writing systems of the ancient world and, since its decipherment, has provided a unique window into their religious beliefs, political affairs and everyday life.

The ninth century CE began a period of collapse of the Classical period Maya civilization, with the abandonment of cities, possibly due to warfare and/or rulership structures that were not able to respond quickly enough to environmental changes. During the Postclassical period, Maya peoples retreated to the Yucatan Peninsula and, especially, the city of Mayapan. By the mid-fifteenth century, Mayapan had itself been abandoned, but the Maya peoples were still able to successfully resist Spanish colonization for several decades between the first contact in 1511 and the 1540s.

This is context for Diego de Landa's *Yucatan Before and After the Conquest* – in the second section of this book – written around 1566. Landa speaks of the 'various calamities felt in Yucatan in the period before the conquest' – storms, wars and disease – and concludes that considering these, and the many other calamities suffered by the Maya after the Spanish began their colonization, 'that it is a marvel there is any of the population left, small as it is' (page 90). Despite this narrative of decline, and the reality of the calamities that devastated this culture, the Maya did not disappear – far from it. Today there are an estimated seven million Maya people living in the region, many of whom speak Mayan languages as their primary vernacular, and who retain strong links to their cultural heritage.

The Toltecs

The Toltec civilization, emerging around 900 CE and lasting until the twelfth century, began in the central Mexican highlands, with their capital at Tula (also known as Tollan). The Aztecs considered the Toltecs as their predecessors and the origin of many key Aztec customs, religious practices and artistic styles. For the Aztecs, the Toltecs were the epitome of civilization, and Aztec elites would make claims to having Toltec ancestry. Their influence is debated, not least because most of the written information about the Toltecs comes from Aztec sources, and archaeological evidence for the Toltecs is limited. Archaeologists have established that Tula had a population of up to 40,000 people, a much smaller settlement than some of the great Maya and Aztec cities. Some scholars today have concluded from this, and from the smaller scale and quality of its monumental architecture, that Tula was a regional capital and not the centre of a large and dominant empire as Aztec sources describe. That said, Toltec artifacts are found across Mesoamerica, so perhaps the Toltec empire was extensive but was more of a loose confederation than a dominant, centrally controlled empire on the Aztec model.

Tula shares similarities in layout and architectural styles with the great Maya city of Chichen Itza. These similarities were first identified by Désiré Charnay, whose *Ancient Cities of the New World* (1883) is the source of the third section of this book. Charnay was the first archaeologist to work on the site of Tula. His explanation of the similarities he observed between Tula and Chichen Itza was that the Toltecs were the builders of both cities, 'which they reared by their mighty word, in accordance with their pacific and civilizing character, as described by Herrera and Landa' (page 234). Although Charnay accepted that he had no scientific basis for his conjecture, others took up the idea and argued for a Toltec empire across most of present-day central Mexico.

As with the Olmecs, historians and archaeologists are not certain of the reasons for the decline of the Toltecs in the twelfth century. Military campaigns against the Toltecs by the neighbouring Chichimecs and other nomadic peoples may have been the reason, or perhaps attacks by the Chichimecs exacerbated the significance of other factors: environmental changes such as prolonged drought, large-scale population movements and internal conflicts and rivalries that destabilized rigid political and social structures.

The Aztecs

The Aztecs, who dominated Mesoamerica from the fourteenth to the early sixteenth centuries, constructed their magnificent capital, Tenochtitlan, on an island in Lake Texcoco. This city was colonized and reconfigured by the Spanish after 1521 as their colonial capital: Mexico City.

As we have seen, the Aztecs considered the Toltecs to be their cultural and intellectual predecessors, adopting elements of Toltec religion, art, architecture and political organization. The Aztecs revered the Toltec capital of Tula and incorporated Toltec traditions and myths into their own society. However, the Aztecs emerged as a distinct civilization 200 years after the decline of the Toltecs, and experts are divided about the extent of actual Toltec influence. There is also debate about the origins of the Aztecs – they themselves claimed to have migrated from a northern mythical homeland called Aztlan; historians tend to agree that a migration southwards to Mexico is likely.

Alliances with other small city-states enabled the Aztecs to dominate the region, and their civilization expanded thanks to the highly productive chinampas system – artificial islands of rich farmland created on the lakes of the Anahuac region. Trade was extensive (how extensive is another area of debate), record-keeping for trade and tribute was sophisticated and their military prowess unrivalled in the region, so that by the height of their power, the Aztec empire stretched over 200,000 square kilometres (77,000 square miles) and exacted tribute from 371 city-states.

The Aztec empire's military conquests were frequently met by fierce resistance, and the Aztecs used a variety of strategies to maintain control over such a huge area. A dedicated administrative system was a key part of this, with a bureaucracy controlling the tribute system and ensuring laws and regulations were enforced. Efficient communication infrastructure spread across the empire, and political alliances and puppet rulers were used to enable local elites to retain some element of power, as long as the calpixqui, the complex Aztec tribute system, was maintained. Human sacrificial victims were part of that tribute system, and part of the mechanism of social control of the Aztec empire.

Debate continues about the precise role of human sacrifice in Aztec civilization – and in other ancient Mesoamerican cultures – and its extent. The traditional view is set out in the fourth section of this book, an extract from *History of the Conquest of Mexico* by William Hickling Prescott, published in 1843. For Prescott, Aztec sacrifices were, as the Spanish saw them, a 'cruel abomination' (page 294) and justified the Spanish conquest:

In this state of things, it was beneficently ordered by Providence that the land should be delivered over to another race, who would

27

rescue it from the brutish superstitions that daily extended wider and wider with extent of empire. (page 301)

Prescott's account relies heavily on Spanish sources – not least perhaps because in his time Aztec writing systems were undeciphered (he refers to the 'dubious language of hieroglyphics' page 280). Our view of the Aztecs – and other ancient Mesoamerican cultures – continues to be influenced by the lens of the Spanish conquest and the centuries of Spanish colonization that followed it. Marín Ruiz, in the first section of this book, names this 'cultural colonialism' as 'a contaminated, confusing and complex cloud that prevents us from knowing the history of our ancient past' (page 44). Today, there is an increasing focus on challenging this bias through a more careful reading of the accounts of the Spanish colonizers, and by incorporating indigenous perspectives. Indigenous sources, including oral traditions, are being re-evaluated and given more prominence in the historiography of Mesoamerica. This is a welcome development that will perhaps finally end a long-established feature of the Western historiography of Mesoamerica – the assumption of external influences.

EXTERNAL INFLUENCES AND ANCIENT MESOAMERICAN CIVILIZATIONS

While historians and archaeologists today endeavour to put new and old discoveries about the ancient civilizations of Mesoamerica into their own indigenous context, European and Euro-American encounters with Mesoamerica have, for centuries, been deeply affected by Eurocentric bias. We can see this in the modern era, with the 1968 publication of the book *Chariots of the Gods? Unsolved Mysteries of the Past*, by Erich von Däniken. Following the discovery of K'inich Janaab' Pakal's tomb, von Däniken interpreted the main inscription of the tomb lid as showing Pakal at the controls of a spaceship. Like many previous commentators, Von Däniken could not accept that Mesoamerican civilizations could have reached such spectacular levels of sophistication independently of others. Instead, external influences must have been responsible. In his case, the external influence was an extraterrestrial one: alien beings who, von Däniken imagined, built the great temples themselves, or gave the ancient Maya elite the technology to do so. The book was, inevitably, a bestseller.

This tradition regarding the necessity of external influences was notable from the first encounter by the Spanish of Maya monumental architecture, which, by the sixteenth century, was often in abandoned city complexes. Some conquistadors believed that the Maya ruins were the work of a different, more ancient and advanced civilization, possibly associated with the mythical 'Seven Cities of Gold' or the lost civilization of Atlantis. Early scholars sought to find connections between the Mesoamerican civilizations and the lost tribes of Israel, or to Egypt (again, via the myth of Atlantis), noting similarities such as pyramids and hieroglyphics. This led to misguided attempts to connect Mesoamerican chronologies to the timelines of ancient Egypt. The extract from *Yucatan Before and After the Conquest* in section two has Diego de Landa stating, after hearing local legends of ancestors who came from the east, 'if this is true, all the inhabitants of the Indies must be of Jewish descent' (page 79) – though he goes on to note that the temples of each Maya town 'are not the work of other peoples, but the Indians themselves', as the carvings show figures wearing the typical dress of the region.

The nineteenth-century explorations of ancient Mesoamerican ruins by European and Euro-American explorers raised awareness about these ancient cultures, but understanding remained limited and hampered by Eurocentric bias. Most nineteenth-century scholars believed in a linear and unidirectional progression of cultural development, with their own European civilization as the pinnacle of human achievement. By the 1840s, when John Lloyd Stephens and Frederick Catherwood visited key Maya sites such as Copan and Palenque, there was less regard for arguments that Mesoamerican civilizations could only have been the result of Old World external influences. Stephens and Catherwood were prepared to accept the ruins they explored as being the product of civilizations that had developed independently of and in parallel with European civilization. But even then, it seemed impossible that such sophisticated cities had been built by the ancestors of the indigenous people they saw around them, and must have been constructed instead by an ancient and superior race that had then disappeared.

DECIPHERING THE MAYA HIEROGLYPHS

The key to understanding Mesoamerican civilizations on their own terms came with the decipherment of Maya hieroglyphs, which has in turn inspired and influenced the decipherment of other ancient Mesoamerican scripts. This decipherment has enabled scholars to study inscriptions on monuments (especially tablets and stelae – upright stone slabs or pillars that are carved or inscribed to commemorate events, individuals and beliefs), ceramics and codices (Maya books), revealing information about historical events, rulers and calendar systems spanning thousands of years. For example, it was the decipherment of the Tablet of the 96 Glyphs at Palenque that allowed scholars to establish the reign of the ruler K'inich Janaab' Pakal with certainty and shed light on the political history of the site.

The story of how Maya hieroglyphs were deciphered is a fascinating one that spans centuries. A very similar story can be told about the decipherment of the Aztec writing system, known as Nahuatl hieroglyphs (after the Aztec language), which involves codices described and copied by Spanish colonizers, attempts at decipherment by sixteenth-century Spanish scholars, partial successes led by European scholars, the recognition of a phonetic system based on syllables in the twentieth century and a key set of inscriptions, the Aztec Calendar Stone, which allowed scholars to match known dates and identify the names of rulers and significant historical events. Within the confines of this introduction, however, let us outline the history of the Maya hieroglyphs, since that story involves Diego de Landa and connects to K'inich Janaab' Pakal and the Temple of Inscriptions, and let that stand in for both Aztec decipherment and recent work on the writing systems of other Mesoamerican cultures, including, most tantalizingly, the Olmecs.

Spanish Chroniclers of the Maya

This process of decipherment began with the Spanish conquest and colonization, ironically at the very same time

as the Spanish were engaged in a programme of wholesale
destruction of Maya cultural artifacts, including almost all of
the Maya codices. Foremost among the chroniclers was Bishop
Diego de Landa, who documented Mayan language and culture
in the Yucatan Peninsula, recording Maya hieroglyphs and
attempting to create a key for their translation. At the same
time, Landa led the campaign to burn all the Maya codices,
destroying, he says, twenty-seven of these priceless repositories
of Maya knowledge. Landa's method of decipherment was to
ask two Maya individuals with ancestors from the Maya elite
to write down glyphs as they corresponded to the letters of
the Spanish alphabet – creating in this way the 'de Landa
alphabet': an unsuccessful attempt at decipherment since the
Maya script was not based on letters. His informants gave
him glyphs corresponding to the sounds they heard, a very
small part of the Maya syllabary, but one that, much later, was
involved in the decipherment breakthrough.

The Dresden Codex

Interest in deciphering the Maya script re-emerged in the
eighteenth century, when explorers such as Antonio del Río
and José Antonio Calderón discovered ancient Maya ruins
in the Petén region of present-day Guatemala. However, it
wasn't until the nineteenth century that the scientific study
of Maya hieroglyphs truly began. A major breakthrough came
after the rediscovery of the Dresden Codex. This was one of
four Maya codices that had survived the Spanish conquest,
and had been stored, largely forgotten about, in the Royal
Library of Dresden. Ernst Förstemann, chief librarian at the
Royal Library, began to study the Codex, and identified

glyphs relating to dates from calendars in the document. The Maya system, found in other Mesoamerican cultures too, calculated dates by counting from the starting date of the Maya creation myth. His work allowed a correlation to be made to the Western calendar, which set the date of the Maya creation at August 11, 3114 BCE. This provided the basis for understanding the Maya Long Count calendar, and for enabling archaeologists to decipher the dates on Maya stelae and other carvings.

Breakthroughs in Decipherment

Yuri Knorosov, a Russian linguist, made ground-breaking progress on decipherment in the 1950s. He proposed that the Maya hieroglyphs were phonetic, meaning they represented sounds. Knorosov recognized that Landa's alphabet, while not working as an alphabet, had recorded the sounds represented by a number of the Maya glyphs. This idea, though initially strongly disputed, ultimately laid the foundation for further progress in decipherment.

In the 1960s and 1970s, American scholars Tatiana Proskouriakoff and Michael D. Coe built upon Knorosov's ideas. Proskouriakoff saw that many of the dates on Maya stelae did not relate to astronomical events or religious ceremonies, and then demonstrated that these hieroglyphs were used instead to record historical events, such as the reigns of rulers and important battles. Coe supported Knorosov's phonetic hypothesis and made significant contributions to the decipherment of the script. He published a book, *Breaking the Maya Code*, in 1992, which provided a comprehensive account of the decipherment process.

Collaborative Efforts and Final Decipherment

In the late twentieth century, the collaborative efforts of various scholars led to significant advances in the understanding of Maya hieroglyphs. Key figures in this period include Linda Schele, David Stuart and Stephen Houston.

These scholars, along with many others, participated in a collaborative approach to deciphering the Maya script, using digital imaging and computer databases to facilitate the sharing of information and ideas among researchers. The Maya Hieroglyphic Database Project became an essential resource for epigraphers studying Maya script.

By the early twenty-first century, this collaborative approach had led to the decipherment of some eighty-five per cent of the Maya script. Today, the Maya hieroglyphs are understood well enough that researchers can read and interpret texts on a wide range of topics, including history, religion, astronomy and daily life.

DEVELOPMENTS IN MESOAMERICAN ARCHAEOLOGY

Archaeology and epigraphy have, in most cases, gone hand in hand in the gradual process of developing our understanding of ancient Mesoamerica. In the mid-twentieth century, the field of Mesoamerican archaeology matured, and systematic excavations and interdisciplinary research began to yield more accurate and detailed results. Radiocarbon dating, introduced in the late 1940s, revolutionized the dating of ancient sites and artifacts. It was, for example, the dating of Olmec artifacts, such as the colossal stone heads found at the site of La Venta, that helped to establish the Olmec civilization's timeline of circa 1400–400 BCE, confirming its status as the earliest complex culture in Mesoamerica.

A key discovery for establishing the chronology of the Olmecs was that of the Tres Zapotes Stela C: a two-metre-tall basalt slab, the lower half of which was discovered in 1939 by archaeologist Matthew W. Stirling at the site of Tres Zapotes, an important Olmec centre, in the present-day Mexican state of Veracruz. Stela C is an anchor point for Olmec chronology as it is inscribed with a date in the Long Count calendar system that corresponds to September 3, 32 BCE in the Gregorian calendar. As well as providing evidence of a sophisticated Olmec understanding of timekeeping, mathematics and astronomy, Stela C implies cultural and intellectual connections between the Olmecs and the Maya, who also, as we have seen, used the Long Count calendar system.

In the 1960s and 1970s, the archaeological excavation of the ancient city of Teotihuacan, near modern Mexico City, revealed the grandeur and complexity of this pre-Aztec city which was once the largest city of the Americas. Once thought to be a Toltec settlement, following the theories of Spanish colonizer-chroniclers, archaeology has since shown that the ruins are centuries older than the Toltec civilization, with Teotihuacan reaching its peak around 450 CE. Instead, academics believe Teotihuacan may have been a multi-ethnic city, perhaps populated by migrants fleeing a natural disaster. Evidence of burning confined to elite areas of the city suggest the city's sixth-century CE decline followed a popular uprising. Skeletons from this time showing signs of malnutrition also point to environmental crises, perhaps drought.

In recent years, advancements in technology have revolutionized archaeological investigations. Remote sensing techniques such as LiDAR (Light Detection and Ranging) have allowed researchers to map vast landscapes and reveal hidden features beneath the surface. The use of LiDAR in the Maya region, for example, has uncovered thousands of previously unknown structures, including ancient causeways, canals and complex irrigation and terracing systems, providing valuable insights into the extent and complexity of Maya urban centres and, in particular, their highly connected nature. Studies of the alignment of buildings suggest that Mesoamerican cultures had developed a calendar long before the development of writing systems to record it, since the buildings are positioned to align with the sunrise on specific days. Buildings are often grouped in twenties, with twenty being the base of the later Mesoamerican calendar and numerical systems.

CONTINUING CONTROVERSIES

Contemporary debates among historians and archaeologists often revolve around the interpretation of new findings and reassessments of existing evidence. For example, the recent discoveries of early Maya settlements using LiDAR have prompted debate about the origins and development of Maya civilization. Some scholars argue that these early settlements represent a much more complex and advanced society than previously believed.

Another area of debate is a familiar one, concerning the role of external influences in the development of Mesoamerican civilizations. Some scholars argue that interregional contacts, such as trade and migration, played a significant role in shaping Mesoamerican cultures, while others emphasize the importance of local, independent development. The external influence of South American civilizations is a factor in this debate. Others are interested in the interactions between Mesoamerican civilizations and the Spanish and other European powers.

The importance of religion has been long recognized in Mesoamerican cultures. However, there has been ongoing debate about the extent to which religious beliefs influenced social and political structures. There is also debate about how central human sacrifice was to Mesoamerican religious practices and social structures. Some scholars argue that it was a fundamental part of Mesoamerican belief systems, while others suggest that it was a more marginal practice that was used for specific political and social purposes. Historians have also, belatedly, started to focus on the role of women in Mesoamerican societies. This has involved a re-evaluation of traditional gender roles, as well as the examination of ways in which women participated in religious and political life in the region.

Another area of controversy is over how important writing was in these cultures. Was it a central component of political and social organization, or primarily a tool for elite communication that had limited impact on the lives of most people? Chronology, too, is under scrutiny: the dating of Mesoamerican archaeological sites and cultural artifacts is challenging, and there is debate over the accuracy of various dating methods. Certain cultural developments may have occurred earlier, or indeed later, than traditionally thought, which can have significant implications for our understanding of Mesoamerican history and civilization.

As ever, therefore, studies of Mesoamerica's ancient origins continue to be a fascinating and richly rewarding area of study. It is hoped that the Further Reading suggestions that follow will provide a suitable starting point for learning more, while the four texts that make up this book, from Landa to Marín Ruiz, offer remarkable insights into both the ancient civilizations themselves and those who study them.

FURTHER READING

Benson, Elizabeth P., *The Olmec and Their Neighbours* (Harvard University Press, 1981)

Berdan, Frances F., *The Essential Codex Mendoza* (University of California Press, 1997)

Carlson, William, *Jungle of Stone: The Extraordinary Journey of John L. Stephens and Frederick Catherwood, and the Discovery of the Lost Civilization of the Maya* (Mariner Books, 2017)

Carmack, Robert M. *The Legacy of Mesoamerica: History and Culture of a Native American Civilization* (Routledge, 2017)

Carrasco, David, *The Aztecs: A Very Short Introduction* (Oxford University Press, 2012)

Cervantes, Fernando, *Conquistadores* (Allen Lane, 2020)

Christenson, Allen J., *Popol Vuh: Sacred Book of the Maya* (Oklahoma University press 2019)

Clendinnen, Inga, *Aztecs: An Interpretation* (Cambridge University Press, 1995)

Coe, Michael D., Rex Koontz and Javier Urcid, *Mexico: From the Olmecs to the Aztecs* (Thames & Hudson, 2019)

Coe, Michael D. and Stephen Houston, *The Maya* (Thames & Hudson, 2015, 9th edition)

Diaz del Castillo, Bernal and John Cohen (translator), *The Conquest of New Spain* (Penguin Classics, 1973)

Diehl, Richard A. and Glyn Daniel, *The Olmecs: America's First Civilization* (Thames & Hudson, 2006)

Grove, David C., *Discovering the Olmecs: An Unconventional History* (University of Texas Press, 2014)

Leon-Portilla, Miguel and Lysander Kemp (translator), *The Broken Spears: The Aztec Account of the Conquest of Mexico* (Beacon Press, 2006)

Miller, Mary Ellen, *The Art of Mesoamerica: From Olmec to Aztec* (World of Art, 2019)

Miller, Mary Ellen and Karl Taube, *An Illustrated Dictionary of the Gods and Symbols of Ancient Mexico and the Maya* (Thames & Hudson, 1997)

Phillips, Charles and David M. Jones, *Aztec and Maya: An Illustrated History: The Definitive Chronicle of the Ancient Peoples of Central American and Mexico - Including the Aztec, Maya. Olmec, Mixtec, Toltec and Zapotec* (Lorenz Books, 2019)

Pool, Christopher, *Olmec Archaeology and Early Mesoamerica* (Cambridge University Press, 2007)

Ptroskouriakoff, Tatiana and Rosemary A. Joyce, *Maya History* (University of Texas Press, 2000)

Restall, Matthew, *Seven Myths of the Spanish Conquest* (Oxford University Press, 2021 (updated edition)

Restall, Matthew, *When Montezuma Met Cortés: The True Story of the Meeting that Changed History* (Ecco, 2018)

Restall, Matthew and Amara Solari, *The Maya: A Very Short Introduction* (Oxford University Press, 2020)

Schele, Linda and David Freidel, *A Forest of Kings: The Untold Story of the Ancient Maya* (WmMorrowPB, 1993)

Sharer, Robert J., *Daily Life in Maya Civilization* (Greenwood, 2009)

Smith, Michael E. and Marilyn A. Masson, *The Ancient Civilizations of Mesoamerica: A Reader* (Wiley-Blackwell, 2000)

Tiesler, Vera and Andrea Cucina, *Janaab' Pakal of Palenque: Reconstructing the Life and Death of a Maya Ruler* (The University of Arizona Press, 2006)

Townsend, Camilla, *Fifth Sun: A New History of the Aztecs* (Oxford University Press, 2019)

Townsend, Camilla, *Malintzin's Choices: An Indian Woman in the Conquest of Mexico* (Dialogos, 2006)

Townsend, Richard F., *The Aztecs* (Thames & Hudson, 2010)

Dr Robert Bircher is an author and consultant in the field of educational publishing. Since completing his doctorate (Oxon, 1998) in historical geography, Dr Bircher has dedicated his career to authoring, commissioning, developing and publishing high-quality educational materials for History and Geography courses in the UK and internationally. As a consultant, he has been involved in a wide range of projects, including training editors working on Kazakh-language primary textbooks, advising on diversity and decolonization of History publishing, editing a primary series of books on ancient civilizations and, most recently, a publishing project on Indigenous American history.

MESOAMERICA: A CRADLE OF CIVILIZATION

This chapter and the one that follows takes the form of extracts from Guillermo Marín Ruiz's *True History of the Profound Mexico* (2010), in which Marín locates the Olmecs as the culmination of millennia of cultural and technological development, and connects the deep history of Mesoamerica to indigenous Mexico today.

Guillermo Marín Ruiz is a writer, historian and advocate of indigenous Mexican history. He is a critic of Mexican government education policies towards indigenous peoples, arguing that Mexican indigenous people today have been systematically 'deindianized' as part of a state programme to base Mexican identity not on its indigenous roots, but on the European culture imported during the Spanish conquest and colonization. Influenced by the anthropologist Bonfil Batalia, Marín seeks to reconnect Mexicans with the cultures and histories of Cem Anahuac, 'the land between the waters' – the Aztec people's name for what we call Mesoamerica today – and of the ancient 'cultural philosophical matrix' which he argues connected and connects all indigenous peoples of the Americas.

TRUE HISTORY OF THE PROFOUND MEXICO

THE SIX CIVILIZATIONS WITH AUTONOMOUS ORIGIN

Earth's oldest civilizations originated about 10,000 years ago. Experts use the emergence date of a culture by the invention of agriculture, since humans ceased being nomadic hunter-gatherers to remain, for generations, in the same place. Thus, they were able to observe, experiment and discover the miracle of plant cultivation, philosophy, science, crafts, art and religion. In fact, Egypt and Mesopotamia began settlement processes and agricultural techniques approximately 8,000 years BCE; followed at about 6,000 years BCE by China, India, Mexico and the Andean region, according to Miguel Leon-Portilla in his book *Native Meso-American Spirituality*.

These six civilizations are the most ancient, but above all, they had an autonomous development; that is, none received external cultural contributions. They were able to access, invent and develop all their knowledge without external input. Thus, Mexico started its cultural development approximately 6000 BCE with the development of agriculture – but, above all, we must emphasize the hybridization of corn – and reached surprisingly high levels of knowledge until the European arrival in 1519. During approximately 7,500 years of independent development, the Mexican ancestors established the foundations of one of the oldest and most important world civilizations. Moreover, our Old Grandfathers bequeathed the sons of the sons of the ancient Mexicans 'a face of our own and a true heart', where it still lives on.

DIFFICULTIES IN LEARNING THE ANCIENT HISTORY OF MEXICO

There is a contaminated, confusing and complex cloud that prevents us from knowing the history of our ancient past. Among existing problems in this regard we can, at least, mention the following: the five-century-old cultural colonialism, which condemned the vanquished peoples to lose their historic memory, in order to completely and permanently dominate them. From 1521 onwards, those who have held power during this time period, whether conquerors, colonizers or creoles, have developed a complex and efficient system so that the children of the children of the invaded-defeated lose contact with their ancient origins and link their past to the arrival of the dominant culture. The dominant culture titled the 7,500 years of human development prior to the invasion 'Pre-Hispanic history'. That is, our Old Grandfathers were divested of their name and are now called 'before the Spaniards'. Because of the colonization processes we now do not know what they called themselves, or what they called this land.

Little is known of the first two most significant periods (Preclassic and Classic), because when the late Classic or pinnacle period ended, the knowledge centres and those who inhabited them mysteriously disappeared without a trace, and left no tangible evidence of their passing, for they destroyed and buried, not only their impressive buildings, but basically the wisdom and knowledge that allowed their apex.

The Aztecs in their expansion period ordered the destruction of all important codices, where the ancient Cem Anahuac [also spelled Cemanahuac] historical memory was kept, and they rewrote history, wherein they appear as the chosen people; in spite of the fact that, from the founding of México-Tenochtitlan (1325) until the arrival of the invaders (1519), only 194 years had elapsed since the Postclassic, which is already considered to be a decadent phase of Anahuac civilization; during which they degraded and transgressed the Quetzalcoatl's philosophy and religion.

When the conquerors arrived, they exterminated and destroyed almost all the men of knowledge and their codices, the knowledge centres, temples and all traces of their civilization until its apparent extinction from the new Spanish world.

THE ANAHUAC CIVILIZATION

What today comprises the territory of Mexico was the birthplace of one of the world's six oldest civilizations of independent origin that achieved the highest human development for its population in the history of mankind. Our Old Grandparents called themselves 'Anahuacas', because the continent was called in the Nahuatl language (which was the lingua franca), 'Cem Anahuac'. This civilization has had a single philosophical-cultural matrix through various cultures that expressed it at different times and locations, linked by a common thread in its three major periods.

The formative stage where all knowledge was developed began with agriculture and the hybridization of corn, which provided the basis of sustenance for a nation throughout its existence. Each of these six mother cultures had a crop as a food base; some had wheat, others had potatoes, rice or millet; but our ancestors hybridized corn, which was, originally, a type of grass that, through a process that we now call 'biogenetic engineering', was developed into this wonderful food that today nourishes many peoples on the five continents.

This effort was only made possible through research and scientific work that was passed from one generation to another, over thousands of years, until this wonderful food was developed.

Indeed, our ancestors walked by themselves, the long way, which led them from being nomads, wild hunters and gatherers, to slowly starting to develop knowledge about the world, life and nature, which would allow them not only to ensure their existence and physical survival, but perhaps, and most importantly, to reach the transcendence of their existence, both as individuals and as a people.

The history of these 7,500 years of cultural development of our peoples has been called the 'Pre-Hispanic' epoch by scholars. It is important to underline the colonial and Western vision of history, as it is seen through the eyes of the victors. Why call what is uniquely ours, that of our Old Grandfathers and their long history, by a name referring to the Spanish invader conqueror? Why not call it the Pre-Cuauhtemoc epoch? History is written by the victors, therefore we should remind ourselves: what kind of history do we know?

Well, then, the experts have divided our Old Grandparents' history before the European invasion into three major periods.

The first is called Preclassic and is chronologically placed by researchers between 6000 BCE and the year 200 BCE, approximately. The second period is the Classic, from about 200 BCE up to 850–900 CE. The third period starts around 850–900 CE and concludes with the European invasion and the taking of Tenochtitlan in 1521.

a) Preclassical: 6000 BCE–200 BCE, 5,800 years (73%)
b) Classical: 200 BCE–850 CE, 1,050 years (13%)
c) Postclassical: 850 CE–1521 CE, 671 years (8%)
d) Colonial: 1521 CE–2011 CE, 490 years (6%)

When this incredible time span of 7,500 years (almost four Christian eras) is compared with the last 500 years of history, which could accurately be called the 'Hispanic era', the reader will appreciate [based on the percentages indicated above] that the structural basis of what constitutes our nation today is unquestionably rooted in Mexico's indigenous past.

It is important to mention that those interested in Mexico's ancient history have mostly been foreigners. Therefore, they have 'studied and researched' Mexico's past, as noted by [classical scholar] Dr. Rubén Bonifaz Nuño, almost always with an attitude of superiority. One day, investigator Paul Kirchhoff thought about dividing the Anahuac into Mesoamerica (taken from the concept of Mesopotamia which means 'between two rivers' in the Sumerian culture) and Arid America. In other words, the 'cultured-dead-disappeared-Indians-of-the-past' who built pyramids and beautiful objects to worship their gods and who lived from the present states of Sinaloa, Zacatecas, San Luis Potosí and Tamaulipas to the south, and the 'savage-dead-disappeared-Indians-from-the-past' who lived in the northern region of Mexico.

However, the Anahuac cultural philosophical matrix was shared by all peoples, from Alaska to Nicaragua, creating a continental civilization that, starting with Columbus's mistake (of confusing this continent with India), Europeans have not wanted to know or understand, or have been unable to do so. Perhaps that is why, after 500 years of knowing that Christopher Columbus (1451–1506) was wrong, and did not reach India, they continue to call the people originating in the Anahuac 'Indian', the proper name for persons born in India.

The Anahuac civilization permeated everything that makes up our national territory today. We assume that this civilization has a *continental* nature. In fact, there are very similar 'cultural' elements between Kumeyaay natives from Baja California and Maya natives from Quintana Roo. At the same time, we can find these basic similarities between a native from Canada and one from Patagonia, passing through the Great Plains of North America, Mexico, Central America, the Andean zone to the Amazon. The core values of life, death, nature, the cosmos, the divine and the sacred are harmoniously and intimately shared by all the so-called 'indigenous' peoples of the American continent. What bonds and identifies peoples with indigenous roots is the philosophical-cultural matrix that gives us structure and not the alleged 'Latinity' ('Latin

ethnicity') which was invented by Napoleon III to seize the
non-Anglo-Saxon America in the nineteenth century, or the
'Hispanic ethnicity' with which English speakers catalogue us
in the twentieth century.

The contempt that we have inherited from the five centuries
of colonialism keeps us from valuing and respecting the
indigenous peoples, our Old Grandparents and even ourselves.
It is very clear when we disparagingly call them 'Indians'. For
many centuries, it has been known that Christopher Columbus
was wrong and never reached India while searching for a new
trade route; therefore, the 'found' peoples were not 'Indians'.
After so many years of colonization we are not even interested
in knowing what our ancestors called themselves. In other
words, we have lost our historic memory, interest and pride.
The ancient Mexicans called the continent Cem Anahuac and
they recognized themselves as Anahuacas, which is why there
were Maya Anahuacas, Zapotec Anahuacas, Mexica [an Aztec
people] Anahuacas and so on.

THE PRECLASSICAL OR FORMATIVE PERIOD

The first stage of the history of ancient Mexico is known
as the Preclassic or formative period, and lasted for
approximately 6,000 years; that is, it starts in the year 6000
BCE, and extends to about 200 BCE. This period is very long and
covers the great effort made by our ancestors to pass from being
nomadic hunter-gatherers, primitive savages, to forming small
villages and developing an efficient food system, an effective
health system, a complex educational system, a system of social

organization and a legal system. They had, moreover, a refined system of values and philosophical, ethical, moral, aesthetic and religious knowledge that allowed them to lay strong foundations over which one of the most important and ancient civilizations that remains alive to date, despite the aggression it has suffered over the past five centuries, was developed.

This valuable civilizing infrastructure that somehow remains alive and present today in contemporary Mexico turns out to be the most important heritage bequeathed to us by the Old Grandparents of the Anahuac and is the deep foundation for all that we are today.

The relationship with nature and working with the land, especially with the milpa invention, allowed the peoples of ancient Mexico to have a healthy diet. Knowledge about the human body, plants, animals and minerals was the base that allowed ancient Mexicans to enjoy incomparable good health. The development of an efficient educational system allowed the training and education of their children in order to develop a long-term civilizing process that maintained the 'social purpose' for centuries, while their scientific infrastructure allowed them to start their studies of mathematics, astronomy, medicine, engineering, linguistics, architecture, botany and zoology. They learned an artistic language which enabled them to express, aesthetically and universally, their perception of the immeasurable and marvellous in human existence, and its complex and wonderful relationships with nature and the cosmos. They possessed a sophisticated and effective system of social organization that allowed them to develop monumental works that spanned several generations to complete, and maintained their original purpose throughout. In short, they possessed a myriad of knowledge, which formed the foundations of what will later be known as the Classic or the flourishing period.

AGRICULTURE

*T*he 'invention' of agriculture was in fact a prolonged process, *which took place in the region in the course of several millennia, starting at about 8,000 to 10,000 years ago, according to recent dating technologies. Between 1500 and 1000 years BCE, the first permanent agricultural villages began appearing at various points of the future Mesoamerica. They domesticated over 70 local species of plants like pumpkins, corn, avocado, amaranth, beans, chili pepper, green tomato, century plants, prickly pear cactus and cotton, among others, totalling over 70 different species, in addition to others from other areas, which were all cultivated with good results (for example, tomato and gourds).*
Teresa Rojas Rabiela, 'Los sistemas hidráulicos Mesoamericanos en la transición de la Nueva Espana', 2001

The Preclassical period represented a millenary effort from our Old Grandfathers, not only to humanize themselves, but also to humanize the world around them; because human beings, according to ancient Mexicans, are the beginning and the end of creation, and are responsible for its preservation and development towards perfection.

This philosophical element is very important in order to understand the cultures of ancient Mexico. Indeed, while other civilizations seek to dominate, exploit and transform nature, ranking themselves at the apex of universal creation, for ancient Mexicans the objective of human beings was to support the gods' creative project and to humanize the world, while considering the planet as their 'beloved mother' Tonatzin.

'Man is the measure of all things,' said the Greek, giving people a sort of dominion over the world; 'Kill and eat', God says to man in the New Testament. Thus, the two aspects of Western culture, the Hellenistic and the Judeo-Christian, allotted man, for his subsistence, dominion over everything and the authority to destroy it.

Morally, far above such concept, the ancient Mesoamerican native, as attested by their images and texts, proclaimed their own idea: man is the beginning of the world's creation and is responsible for its surroundings. Thus is our culture constituted, of which we are exclusive heirs today.

Let us, therefore, understand its origins and accomplishments, in order to know what we are; and what we ought to become.

Bonifaz Nuño, *Olmecas Esencia y Fundación,* **1992**

While it is assumed that the Old Grandparents started agricultural practices and hybridized corn in the sixth millennium BCE, actually, the first cultural forms appeared, called Olmec by scholars, about 1500 years BCE, between the states of Tabasco and Veracruz; but indisputably, they were present in all cultures, in a phase that we shall call 'Olmecoid', or with an Olmec influence. In small villages all that vast and immeasurable knowledge about the universe, nature, life, death and man before the divine and the sacred began to be expressed.

In the approximately 4,500 years of endogenous cultural development, from the onset of agriculture until the formation of the Olmec culture, the Old Grandparents invented, discovered, produced, processed and systematized all that wisdom which appeared approximately 1500 years prior to the beginning of the splendour or flourishing of ancient Mexico, in the Classic period.

Foreign researchers have tried to erase these priceless 4,500 years from our ancient history by belittling it. Indeed, from the first agricultural practices until the emergence of the Mother Culture, they are barely given importance in research texts and are almost non-existent in the 'official story' that is recorded from the first appearance of the Olmec culture. But the Olmecs were not created by 'spontaneous generation'. There were 4,500 years of intense research and systematization of human life experience.

THE CORN INVENTION

The corn invention is perhaps one of the greatest achievements of the Preclassical or formative period, since, from wild grass, our Old Grandparents produced the splendid maize plant, which became the staple food of their civilization. It is important to stress that no other people on the planet made such an important discovery.

Agriculture accompanied the civilizing process itself, fully integrated with the rest of the cultural and social activities. The limits of its practice, as a basic activity, were also the limits of the cultural area; the presence of advanced agricultural cultures in central and southern Mexico and in Central America is no accident, given the possibility of rainy season cultivation.

However, the increase of potential productivity of this rain-dependent agriculture was made possible thanks to irrigation systems and remodelling of hillsides and other works on special terrains, like the improvement of domesticated plants (and those in the process of domestication) through natural growth promoters, and the transformation of social organization and economic structures. In fact the various farming systems, while being in part ecological adaptations, were social, demographic and economic adaptations.

Teresa Rojas Rabiela, 'Los sistemas hidráulicos Mesoamericanos en la transición de la Nueva España', 2001

The development of hydraulics for agriculture is yet another great foundation, because it allowed a greater number of people to have energy and time available to develop major civilizing projects; to perform scientific research and to explore art, as well as the construction of imposing buildings found in today's 'archaeological zones'; impressive material monuments to the spiritual project of this civilization.

The 'formative' era is so called because it is when the main crafts make their appearance – basketry, ceramics, weaving, metallurgy and construction – and the communal cultural patterns take form. The population grows, culture and settlements expand, there is peace, and a large cultural diffusion takes place from and amongst the civilization centres. Intensive agriculture begins; local irrigation takes place and the most important animals are domesticated.

Food production continues at subsistence levels, except for the portions destined to sustain the ruling class. But intensive agriculture

begins to provide free time for the satisfaction of social needs: the
production of luxury goods, construction of religious buildings, and
so on.
Ángel Palerm, *Introducción a la Teoría Etnológica*, 1990

THE MILPA INVENTION

The milpa was another valuable trigger for the development of
the Anahuac civilization, because by planting maize, chili,
squash and beans, intensively farming a very small piece of land
during four months, one man could feed his family for an entire
year. This is as if today, with four months of minimum wage
earnings, one could survive for one year. Hydraulic engineering
reached very advanced levels in Cem Anahuac, not only due to
extensive irrigation, but also because the use of the chinampa
was a very advanced concept, even by today's standards.

Irrigation agriculture was the only technological way to sustain
a sufficiently productive economy and to maintain a concentrated
population, stable and specialized in non-agricultural work and a
political organization to maintain the functioning of a productive
system and good distribution. Therefore, the use of irrigation would
have fostered urban life and, consequently, civilization.
Teresa Rojas Rabiela, 'Los sistemas hidráulicos
Mesoamericanos en la transición de la Nueva Espana', 2001

We definitely cannot imagine the wonders and magnificence of
Teotihuacan or Monte Alban in the Classical period without the
basis of an efficient food system, which was able to support the

challenges of building the various and numerous centres of knowledge that existed in our territory. Foreign researchers have not given Anahuac agriculture the place it deserves in the history of mankind.

In fact, the conclusion that we were compelled to reach was that in pre-Hispanic times farming systems had risen to levels of efficiency and productivity comparable to, if not higher than, the most advanced contemporary practices. The legend of mere subsistence farming, or of being only capable of generating a small surplus, was destroyed.
Ángel Palerm, *México Prehispánico*, 1990

The Preclassical period was the foundation for the development and subsequent splendour of ancient Mexico. It was almost six millennia of forging, by ourselves, one of the oldest and most important civilizations in the world, of which we are today the undisputed legitimate heirs.

THE OLMECS

TRUE HISTORY OF THE PROFOUND MEXICO CONTINUED

Regarding the Olmecs, Guillermo Marín Ruiz continues: Also called the 'Mother Culture', the Olmecs represent the final achievement of thousands of years, during which previously nomad peoples, hunter-gatherers, settled themselves for thousands of years in a given place and, there, generation after generation, investigated and observed nature, the skies, and explored their inner spiritual selves. This long Preclassical period that successfully culminates with the formation of the Olmec culture between 1500 and 1200 BCE is of great value to our civilization, as it helped define the early cultures of ancient Mexico, for our present; because part of what we are today is rooted in the early Olmecs; and especially for our future, because they remind us of our capabilities, our desire to be and transcend time, but above all, [this history] talks to us about continuity and direction.

The Olmecs should not be considered to be the 'beginning', but rather, the end of a very long period of cultural formation that took more than four millennia (two Christian eras) and is quite unknown to ordinary Mexicans.

One of the most controversial aspects about the Olmecs, in addition to their chronological position in relation to other Mesoamerican cultures, has been the elucidation of their ethnic, linguistic and racial affiliation of this culture that, in the south of Veracruz and east of Tabasco, experimented with new forms of social, economic, political and religious organization. This was completely different from the village and tribal life that preceded them, and which existed in most of the geographical space that, with the passage of time, would build the macro cultural area called Mesoamerica.

Tomás Pérez Suárez, 'Breve crónica de la arqueología olmeca' in *Los Olmecas en Mesoamérica*, 1994

However, it is necessary to point out that the philosophical synthesis which was embodied in the Olmec iconography will remain as a common thread throughout the entire developmental process of the Anahuac civilization. The Spanish invaders found the roots of the Olmec culture alive in the sixteenth century. This is how Quetzalcoatl, whose image was engraved in the stones of Chalcatzingo, Morelos, during the Preclassical period, is also found in Teotihuacan in the Classical period, with the Toltecs, and in Tenochtitlan, with the Aztecs, in the Postclassical. Rattlesnakes, felines, the Quincunx, and representations of Tlaloc through the use of two opposing snake faces in profile, talk to us about a knowledge, philosophy and religion which were alive and evolved for at least 3,000 consecutive years and which somehow survive in the mystical and spiritual being of native peoples and peasants of contemporary Mexico.

Neither warriors nor traders, but civilizing agents, the Olmecs fulfilled their self-assigned destiny. They reached as far as they could, and extended their knowledge over time, thus building what was to be the spiritual backbone of our ancient culture.

The concept of humanity they forged provided the foundation of the perpetual optimism of the men who succeeded them. Their heirs, whether Teotihuacan, Zapotecs, Maya, Mixtecs, Huastecs, Totonacs or Aztec, succeeded, thanks to the momentum provided by them, in the endless proliferation of happy cultural constructions whose vestiges still educate and dazzle.

Teotihuacan, Tula, Xochicalco, Cacaxtla, El Tajín, Tikal, Palenque, Toniná, Uxmal, Monte Alban, Mitla, Malinalco, Chichen Itza, Tenochtitlan, and many other similar cities, bear witness to this justified and enduring optimism.

Offensively, scholars still speak of primitive cultures, of totemism, of rain worship and of bloody rites, and focus their attention in the 'Guerra Florida' (flower war) and the so-called Aztec human sacrifices, in an attempt to legitimize the contempt with which they justify our exploitation.

Rubén Bonifaz Nuño, *Olmecas Esencia y Fundación*, 1992

When the Anahuac civilization managed to neatly produce what we call today the Olmec culture, the knowledge foundations were already in place, both the tangible kind: agriculture, engineering, architecture, medicine, etc., as well as intangible ones, like philosophy, mathematics, religion, art and astronomy, among others. They already had in operation the four basic systems which are the foundation of every society, regardless of the culture to which they belonged and which were developed and perfected, almost entirely, during the first 4,500 years of civilization, between the advent of agriculture and the appearance of the Olmec culture.

These four systems are: food, health, education and social organization and the rule of law. They represent the four indispensable foundations for the development of any culture.

THE FOOD SYSTEM

In those 4,500 years, our Old Grandparents not only came up with agriculture, the milpa, chinampa and the edible cactus, but also developed a sophisticated and complex nourishing system, which included tortillas, nachos, empanadas, tamales, sauces, chocolate, atole, aguas frescas, tejate, pulque, mezcal, alegría (amaranth candy), corn, the various types of chili peppers, pinole, the use of plants, meat of hunted animals and dried and salted fish, lots of vegetables including algae, the extensive use of insects, honey, seeds, as well as the turkey and Xoloitzcuintle dog domestication.

The food system consisted not only of food but delicious and very sophisticated dishes that perfectly balanced plant and animal proteins, sugars and fats. Altogether it provided ancient Mexicans with enough energy, health and time to develop their civilizing projects, both in construction and in research.

THE HEALTH SYSTEM

The health system is another of the great contributions to civilization. Our Old Grandparents developed a deep knowledge of the human body and its diseases. They investigated healing substances from plants, insects, animals and minerals. Doctors and Anahuaca medicine reached levels that until recently were unsuspected but have managed to survive history. In fact, this legacy of knowledge was able to survive the 300 years of persecution and in the last 200 years has been marginalized and disregarded by the dominant culture.

But without a doubt it has been a most valuable resource to maintain the health of the poorest Mexicans, neglected by the government and exploited by the dominant society. Native peoples and peasants have maintained this traditional knowledge. 'Home remedies', infusions, massage, the use of plants, animals, insects and minerals for the ancestral remedies remain amazingly alive, as do the rituals that have powerful results in the psyche of the patients, not to mention the 'power plants' that occupy a special place in the ancestral wisdom.

THE EDUCATION SYSTEM

The educational system was one of the major pillars of the Anahuac civilization. Because of its importance a special chapter on education is provided [not included here], but from the 'system' point of view we could point out that the ancient Mexicans, surely from 1500 BCE, with the appearance of the filtered Olmec culture, already had an education system that systematically reached every child and young person in society in the most advanced cultures, up to the arrival of the Spanish.

The educational system is a basic structural element in order to develop a civilization project, since education is the method to produce and reproduce knowledge within a society. Thanks to this system, we can understand the mega projects in the long term of the Anahuac cultures, knowledge centres that took centuries to build, such as Teotihuacan, Palenque, Monte Alban and Xochicalco, among the tens of thousands built in the country.

The education that generated the Anahuac civilization applies not only to the academic aspect, which was taught in the Telpochcalli, Cuicacalli and Calmécac [all types of schools], but education from a deeper point of view. We refer to the philosophical and spiritual spectrum, in fact, the foundations, so that the individual can understand himself, family, society, nature and the universe in an integral and comprehensive manner. The relationships that exist between each other of responsibilities, limits and possibilities, have given us an 'own face and a real heart', as individuals and as a civilization. This immense wealth of wisdom and experience is what makes us Anahuacas or 'Mexican' as we were 'baptized' by the Spanish Creoles as of 1821.

Education, as the rich experience that has been selected and systematized over hundreds of generation, is part of our 'cultural heritage'. For the Anahuac civilization the upper knowledge vertex is in the possibility of releasing the spirit from matter. This is what unites all the Anahuaca origin peoples and makes us culturally sensitive to the mystical and spiritual aspects of life. To understand our ancient culture, we must realize that our Old Grandparents lived in educational societies for more than thirty centuries.

The Olmecs had much to do with cultural development processes, from the development of agriculture until the formation of the first villages; and at the same time with later Olmec cultures and the Mexicans of today, with the 8,000 years of cultural development that human beings produced in what today is our territory.

In the Anahuac for at least 3,000 years a schooling system was maintained, in which our ancestors lived uninterrupted and systematically from generation to generation. And, although this was certainly truncated during the last five centuries by colonization, in the 'genetic bank of cultural information' or 'genetic memory', we Mexicans should find in education a valuable and powerful tool for human development. We are a civilization with an ancient educational experience like no other on the planet.

THE SOCIAL ORGANIZATION SYSTEM

The social organization system and legal regime is another of the fundamental foundations that were created in the first 4,500 years from the invention of agriculture up to the emergence of the Olmec culture. Indeed, we could not understand the construction of the so-called 'archaeological sites' without [knowledge of] the social organization and regulation of a legal order that would allow the regulation and harmonious and orderly interaction of individuals and peoples. The social organization and legal system allows the other three systems – food, health and education – to fully develop in harmony.

Just as the thinking and beliefs of peoples are the result of observation and human meditation, the political organization is in close relationship with the economic, scientific and religious thinking of peoples.

From the mathematical, astronomical, physical and biological concept that the Anahuacas had of the universe, Anahuacas, by observing nature, reflecting on what they saw, conforming to it, and also overcoming it, established a political and social order appropriate to the physical, economic and scientific conditions, with the fundamental purpose of promoting and preserving community life in the country, reaching thereby a high degree of culture and knowledge, both of nature and the universe.

Ignacio Romerovargas Yturbide, *Los Gobiernos Socialistas De Anáhuac,* **1978**

The concept of Tollan which has been translated as city or metropolis, was a daily reality in the Anahuac cultures. Whether in the Maya area, Nahuatl, Zapotec, Mixtec and Totonac, Tarascan or any other, the large human concentrations of the Classical and Postclassical period were impressive. As far as the city of Tenochtitlan, the most conservative estimates are of a population of half a million inhabitants. The concepts of Tlatócan, Calpulli, Hueytlahtocáyotl, Tequíyotl, Tetlatzontequilíca are intimately linked to the formidable social organization which was the fruit of wisdom accumulated and systematized by centuries and centuries of work in partnership to achieve human development.

Ancient Mexicans would have never been able to achieve the civilizing prodigies, both tangible and intangible, without a complex network of values, attitudes, principles, institutions, laws and authorities that would make them possible, to maintain not only its social order, but also its development. Each pyramid, every work of art, each codex, or stele, could not exist without the backing and support of the social organization system and legal regime that sustained them.

They established a type of federal and interstate superstructure in political, educational, scientific and cultural matters with a tax system, mentioned earlier, appropriate to the needs of both the government and the various federation entities, to cater for public expenditure or for product redistribution from some regions to others in combination with a special commercial organization.

Given these fundamental concepts, two classes of organization can be distinguished:

A. Territorial, which were: 1. The rural calpulli (autonomous and dispersed); 2. Urban calpulli (autonomous and concentrated in sorts of neighbourhoods); 3. The region or calpótin icniúhtli, brotherhood, fraternity, housing groups (autonomous regional entities) called Tlatocáyotl, government; 4. State Territories or Lordships (autonomous, but authority depended on the State) called tecúhyotl, lordships; 5. The State (independent) called hueytlahtocáyotl, great government; and 6. The State federation called Tlatacaicniuhyotl, brotherhood or governors friendship, or tecpíllotl, principals complexes or palaces.

B. The institutional, centralized government hierarchies, which could be: local (religious organizations, industrial groups, lords' societies) or federal (educational, administrative, fiscal, judicial, governmental or political hierarchies, the commercial and military).

The government of any group, both territorial and institutional, corresponded to an assembly of elders or subject experts, elected by the members of the group. 'Nothing was done, according to chroniclers, without assembly consultation'. This was invariably led by two heads, whose posts were usually lifelong; one was administrator and the other executor, almost always the first was an elder person with succession right, and the other younger, elected by the Assembly, depending on the particular circumstances of each group, the determination of rules and procedures for implementation. The Assembly was called 'in cohuáyotl', circle or as a snake.

Ignacio Romerovargas Yturbide, *Los Gobiernos Socialistas De Anáhuac*, 1978

This complex system of social organization took the Anahuac civilization several millennia to filter and perfect. The truth is that at the decline of the Olmec culture it was already formed and was the same found and even used by the Spanish invaders. Currently some structural elements of this system are still alive in the indigenous and farming communities. The 'charge system', communal lands, tequio [collective work for the community], work tasks, assembly, the council of elders, the stewardships, the temple committees, schools, drinking water, etc., bear witness of the survival to this ancient wisdom of social organization.

All those territorial autonomies were not isolated and abandoned to their own fate, but were articulated, harmonized, related and integrated to the State, through hierarchical institutions which together accounted for two great powers in each state: the administrative power, whose head was the Cihuacoátl, literally 'serpent woman', ideologically the Tlatoani's twin supreme administrator [...] who governed, with right to succession from father to son; and the Executive Branch, whose head was the Tlatoani, literally 'he who

speaks', ideologically he who performs, orders or governs, which was a post elected from the members of a family from earlier sovereigns, possessors of land; but which did not succeed from father to son.
Ignacio Romerovargas Yturbide, *Los Gobiernos Socialistas De Anáhuac*, 1978

At the time of the Spaniards' arrival, in the decadent period known as the Postclassical, the invaders did not find kings or queens, princes or princesses, much less European style kingdoms or empires. The Spaniards interpreted this democratic and sophisticated form of social organization as a decadent and vertical 'monarchy', such as they had in Europe.

Such was their inability to appreciate and understand this ancient form of government that Hernán Cortés (1485–1547), when he took Moctezuma (1502–20) prisoner in his house and after having ordered the killing of Templo Mayor, which led to the Aztec people's insurrection against the invaders, he ordered that Moctezuma be taken handcuffed to the roof, for to him to order the people to cease the insurrection.

To the Spaniards' surprise, the Tlatócan had already dismissed the Tlatoani Moctezuma and transferred power to Cuitláhuac. For the European culture the king was the representation of God on earth and his succession was hereditary through the royal houses. Cortés believed that by taking Moctezuma prisoner he had control of the Aztec people and didn't understand how the Aztecs could dismiss their ruler. To date, the system of social organization and the legal regime of ancient Mexico are still not understood and scholars continue to talk about 'kings, kingdoms and pre-Hispanic princesses'.

Considering in it all his hope of remedy, he determined one day to take Moctezuma out in public, in order for him to order and plead with the Mexicans to cease and stop mistreating them. And so it was, while Mexicans were bravely fighting, almost demolishing the houses with stones, the Marquis and one other, one with a cover and the other with a steel shield to protect themselves from the stones and lances, took [Moctezuma] to the roof of the House, that faced the place where the Indians were fighting, and taking him so covered, led him to the roof parapet and the good [Moctezuma] gave a hand sign to quiet down as he wanted to speak to them, they quieted a bit and ceased to beat the house, and removing the shields which had covered them, he begged them to stop causing evil to the Spanish and he ordered them to stop harming them.

The captains standing in front began to shout very nasty words, telling him that he was the woman of the Spanish and that, as such, he had confederated with them and agreed with them to have them killed, as they killed their great lords and brave men and that he was no longer recognized as King, nor he was their Lord.

Fray Diego Durán, *The History of the Indies of New Spain,* c. 1581

THE MOTHER CULTURE

The Olmec culture is the essence and foundation of our civilization. The most important cultural traits that were in force for at least three millennia of human development were implemented in what today makes up the national territory and of which we are the unique and legitimate heirs.

The iconography, architecture, the philosophical-religious symbols of the snake, the jaguar and the eagle, which appeared clearly defined in the testimonies of the Olmec culture, remained current during successive periods up to the time of invasion. Their optimism for life and capacity for performing immeasurable spiritual projects left an impressive footprint: whether pyramids – complex systems of rooms without any domestic or residential use – up to the formidable hydraulic systems, with dams and canals, or kilometers of paved roads.

And now judge for yourself the progress of the cultural phenomenon which occurred in the territory of Mesoamerica for nearly three millennia; thinking about the nature of the human energy that possessed the ability to build, among other things, the above cities, cities in which the arts and sciences fruitfully flourished; where wisdom served as root and crown of the huge material efforts required by such building.

It must be concluded that only a people that take a fully optimistic and happy moral view of themselves and the world could generate the core of such incalculable power: a joyful humanist conception of reverence for life in all its manifestations.

Rubén Bonifaz Nuño, *Olmecas Esencia y Fundación*, 1992

The truth is that the current and palpable Olmec heritage has been transmitted to subsequent cultures, which in turn developed and went on to create exquisite expressions of culture and art, each adding their touch and personal accent – undoubtedly [thanks to] their optimism for life and their mystical and spiritual sense of existence and the universe.

With them (the Olmecs) definitely begins what can rightfully be deemed the Mesoamerican culture in its fullness. Due to a reason which I will explain later, they were able to propagate the principles of the idea of man and of the world to their contemporary peoples, and what is even more significant, they managed to make people live with the integrity of cultural customs that arose in Mesoamerica, even when they had disappeared thousands of years earlier, ensuring that these customs were, through their common background, a unique culture.

Rubén Bonifaz Nuño, *Olmecas Esencia y Fundación*, 1992

Much more remains to be discovered about the ancient Olmec civilization. However, intelligent researches and un-colonialized publications free of prejudice are being now published in Mexico, such as that of Dr. Rubén Bonifaz Nuño, who points to a new path. But there are other ways, such as oral tradition, knowledge lineages or by the careful use of entheogens.

To understand our historical and cultural continuity throughout these 8,000 years is one of the most important challenges facing those who want to put an end to the [colonial perspective] and to build a just and harmonious society. The fruit of Olmec wisdom has not died, nor is it missing. It is an intrinsic part of what we are today. It is our own culture, not shared by any other people in the world.

Victorious over foreign insults and contempt, there are still signs of that spiritual lighting system that built our cities.

Urban planning, engineering, architecture, sculpture, metallurgy, painting, all arts, sciences, mathematics, astronomy, measurement of the time, flourished there, obedient to the same enthusiasm of the self-assured man, proud to be the source and ascending path to perfection of life.

Man lived and built happily, for about 30 centuries, the glorious testimony of his passage on earth.

The ideal foundation for the happiness of modern humanity, the Olmec creation that is the wonder of the Mesoamerican culture remains there, multiplied in works that provide examples without compromise.

And this wonder is our particular heritage that honours and distinguishes us among all.

Rubén Bonifaz Nuño, *Olmecas Esencia y Fundación*, 1992

All cultures subsequent to the Olmecs will bear its influence. The philosophical-cultural structure bequeathed by the Toltecs to the Anahuac is one of the testimonies that confirm the existence of a single civilization with many different cultures in time and space, but all born with Olmec roots, all sharing the same philosophical essence.

Hence, we affirm that there is a cultural and civilizing continuity, not only just before the invasion, but what colonizers refuse to accept, that there was a civilizing and cultural continuity during those 500 years of colonization. It cannot be denied that during this period there was a brutal 'cultural pruning', but the root has continued living. It can also not be denied that the cultural root has taken other external elements, not only from Western culture, but from other peoples of the world, which has enriched and strengthened it.

THE CLASSICAL PERIOD – THE LEGACY OF THE OLMECS

The **greatest period of splendour** of ancient Mexico was the so-called Classical period that approximately comprises the period between 200 BCE to 850 CE. During this period philosophy, wisdom and science reached its full development. The large knowledge centres led by Teotihuacan achieved their peak. Social life found a balance between meeting material subsistence needs and the needs of transcendental existence. Art has been the best testimony of this luminous period.

If the basis of human development occurred with the Olmecs in the Preclassical period, the upper vertex of the cultural development of ancient Mexico was reached during the Classical period. It covered more than 1,000 years of impressive humanist progress in the Anahuac. All 'Mother' world civilizations sought in the apogee of their development the spiritual significance of existence. Ancient Mexicans were not the exception. Their knowledge of the human spirit, of the conception of the world as energy fields, of the relationship between microcosmos and macrocosmos and of the responsibility of 'humanizing and balancing' interaction between nature and cosmos, is striking and astonishing.

In the Middle Ages, Europeans sought inspiration in their past to build a bridge to take them out of the Dark Ages. The question is, why can we not likewise look for a historical source of inspiration in the values, principles and attitudes created by our Old Grandparents, to reach the zenith of evolution and cultural development, and with these values design and build the future?

Currently we do not know the outreach of [these ancient peoples'] energy and spiritual achievements, but the truth is that the ruined material vestiges of their development leave us breathless and exalt our spirit. While visiting Teotihuacan, for example, we can't help thinking about their intangible achievements, while facing their impressive handling of materials. If their pyramid of knowledge was aimed at attaining spiritual consciousness and its significance, when we reflect with an uncolonial mind at the top of the Sun pyramid, we must think about the scope and achievements that they must have had on the intangible level of knowledge, especially in the field of energy.

When the conception of our Old Grandparents is decolonized, despite denial and destruction of their knowledge, we shall understand that they remain alive in our hearts. That the Anahuac civilization is not dead, as was preached by colonizers in the last five centuries. And that we are all their continuation in the cycle of time.

THE MAYA

Diego de Landa (1524–79), of whose work we present selected extracts here, was a Spanish Franciscan friar, missionary and bishop who played a crucial role in the early study and documentation of the Maya civilization, particularly in the Yucatan Peninsula. Born in Cifuentes, Spain, Landa joined the Franciscan Order and was sent to Spanish-controlled Yucatan in 1549 to aid in the conversion of the native Maya population to Christianity.

As a fervent missionary, Landa made zealous efforts to eradicate the religious practices of the Maya. In 1562, he led the 'auto de fé' in Mani, during which he ordered the burning of countless Maya artifacts, including hieroglyphic books and religious idols, believing them to be the work of the devil. This act of destruction led to the loss of a vast amount of irreplaceable knowledge.

Yet Landa also contributed significantly to the preservation of Maya history and culture. He spent many years learning the Mayan language and documenting Maya customs, beliefs and ways of life. His *Yucatan Before and After the Conquest* documented Maya social organization, religious practices, agriculture and architecture. He also attempted to create a key for translating the Maya script, known as the 'Landa Alphabet' (*see* Introduction, page 32) which was an early (flawed) attempt at deciphering Maya hieroglyphs.

Diego de Landa's legacy is therefore a complex one, strongly influenced by the cultural, religious and political climate of that time and deeply biased by his evident desire to portray the Maya civilization as being in need of conversion. Landa's understanding of the Maya script was limited and flawed, and so any descriptions and translations, and the 'Landa Alphabet' itself, must be approached with caution. Keeping these substantial biases and inaccuracies in mind, however, Landa's work provides a valuable first-hand account of Postclassical Maya civilization during the early period of European contact. His descriptions offer unique insights into the Maya way of life.

YUCATAN BEFORE AND AFTER THE CONQUEST

YUCATAN, ITS LANDSCAPE AND SEASONS

Yucatan is not an island, nor a point entering the sea, as some thought, but mainland. This error came about from the fact that the sea goes from Cape Cotoche along the Ascension passage to the Golfo Dulce on the one side, and on the other side facing Mexico, by the Desconocida before coming to Campeche, and then forming the lagoons by Puerto Real and Dos Bocas.

The land is very flat and clear of mountains, so that it is not seen from ships until they come very close,; with the exception that between Campeche and Champotón there are some low ranges and a headland that is called Los Diablos.

As one comes from Veracruz toward Cape Cotoche, one finds himself at less than twenty degrees, and at the mouth of Puerto Real it is more than twenty-three; from one point to the other it should be over 130 leagues, direct road. The coast is low-lying, so that large ships must stay at some distance from the shore.

The coast is very full of rocks and rough points that wear the ships' cables badly; there is however much mud, so that even if ships go ashore, they lose few people.

A small range crosses Yucatan from one corner to the other starting near Champotón and running to the town of Salamanca in the opposite angle. This range divides Yucatan into two parts, of which that to the south toward Lacandón and Taiza (Tah-Itza, the country of the Itzas, around Lake Petén) is uninhabited for lack of water, except when it rains. The northern part is inhabited.

This land is very hot and the sun burns fiercely, although there are fresh breezes like those from the north-east and east, which are frequent, together with an evening breeze from the sea. People live long in the country, and men of 140 years have been known.

The winter begins with St Francis Day, and lasts until the end of March; during this time the north winds prevail and cause severe colds and catarrh from the insufficient clothing the people wear. The end of January and February bring a short hot spell, when it does not rain except at the change of the moon. The rains come on from April until through September, during which time the crops are sown and mature despite the constant rain. There is also sown a certain kind of maize at St Francis, which is harvested early.

YUCATAN'S ETYMOLOGY AND SITUATION

This province is called, in the language of the indigenous people, *Ulumil cuz yetel ceh*, meaning 'the land of the turkey and the deer'. It is also called Petén, meaning 'island', an error arising from the gulfs and bays we have spoken of.

When Francisco Hernández de Córdoba came to this country and landed at the point he called Cape Cotoche, he met certain Indian fisherfolk whom he asked what country this was, and who answered *Cotoch*, which means 'our houses, our homeland', for which reason he gave that name to the cape. When he then by signs asked them how the land was theirs, they replied *Ci uthan*, meaning 'they say it', and from that the Spaniards gave the name Yucatan. This was learned from one of the early conquerors, Blas Hernández, who came here with the admiral on the first occasion.

In the southern part of Yucatan are the rivers of Taiza (Tah-Itzá) and the mountains of Lacandón, and between the south and west lies the province of Chiapas; to pass thither one must cross four streams that descend from the mountains and unite with others to form the San Pedro y San Pablo river discovered by Grijalva in Tabasco. To the west lie Xicalango and Tabasco, one and the same province.

Between this province of Tabasco and Yucatan there are two sea mouths breaking the coast; the largest of these forms a vast lagoon, while the other is of less extent. The sea enters these mouths with such fury as to create a great lake abounding in fish of all kinds, and so full of islets that the natives put signs on the trees to mark the way going or coming by boat from Tabasco to Yucatan. These islands with their shores and sandy beaches have so great a variety of seafowl as to be a matter of wonder and beauty; there is an infinite amount of game: deer, hare, the wild pigs of that country and monkeys as well, which are not found in Yucatan. The number of iguanas is astonishing. On one island is a town called Tixchel.

To the north is the island of Cuba, with Havana facing at a distance of sixty leagues; somewhat further on is a small island belonging to Cuba, which they call Isla de Pinos. At the cast lies Honduras, between which and Yucatan is a great arm of the sea that Grijalva called Ascension Bay.

In front of Yucatan, somewhat below Cape Cotoche, lies Cuzmil (Cozumel), across a 5-league channel where the sea runs with a strong current between the mainland and the island. Cozumel is an island 15 leagues long by five wide. The natives are few in number, and of the same language and customs as those of Yucatan. It lies at the twentieth degree of latitude. Thirteen leagues below Point Cotoch is the Isla de las Mugeres, two leagues off the coast opposite Ekab.

PROVINCES AND ANCIENT STRUCTURES OF YUCATAN

Some old men of Yucatan say that they have heard from their ancestors that this country was peopled by a certain race who came from the East, whom God delivered by opening for them twelve roads through the sea. If this is true, all the inhabitants of the Indies must be of Jewish descent because, the straits of Magellan having been passed, they must have spread over more than 2,000 leagues of territory now governed by Spain.

The language of this country is all one, a fact which aided greatly in its conversion, although along the coasts there are differences in words and accents. Those living on the coast are thus more polished in their behaviour and language.

There are in Yucatan many edifices of great beauty, this being the most outstanding of all things discovered in the Indies; they are all built of stone finely ornamented, though there is no metal found in the country for this cutting. These buildings are very close to each other and are temples, the reason for there being so many lying in the frequent changes of the population, and the fact that in each town they erected a temple, out of the abundance of stone and lime, and of a certain white earth excellent for buildings.

These edifices are not the work of other peoples, but of the natives themselves, as appears by stone figures of men, unclothed but with the middle covered by certain long fillets which in their language are called *ex*, together with other devices worn by the natives.

While the author of this work was in that country, there was found in a building that had been demolished a large urn with three handles, painted on the outside with silvered colours, and containing the ashes of a cremated body, together with some pieces of the arms and legs, of an unbelievable size, and with three fine beads or counters of the kind the natives use for money. At Izamal there were eleven or twelve of these buildings in all, with no memory of their builders; on the site of one of these, at the instance of the natives, there was established the monastery of San Antonio, in the year 1550.

The next most important edifices are those of Tikoch and of Chichen Itza, which will be described later. Chichen Itza is finely situated ten leagues from Izamal and eleven from Valladolid, and they tell that it was ruled by three lords, brothers who came to the country from the West. These were very devout, built very handsome temples, and lived unmarried and most honourably. One of them either died or went away, whereupon the others conducted themselves unjustly and wantonly, for which they were put to death.

CUCULCAN AND THE FOUNDATION OF MAYAPAN

The opinion of the natives is that with the Itza people who settled Chichen Itza there ruled a great lord named Cuculcan (Kukulkan), as an evidence of which the principal building is called Cuculcan.

They say that he came from the West, but are not agreed as to whether he came before or after the Itza, or with them. They say that he was well disposed, that he had no wife or children, and that after his return he was regarded in Mexico as one of their gods, and called Cezalcohuati [Quetzalcóatl]. In Yucatan also he was reverenced as a god, because of his great services to the State, as appeared in the order which he established in Yucatan after the death of the chiefs, to settle the discord caused in the land by their deaths.

This Cuculcan, having entered into an agreement with the native lords of the country, undertook the founding of another city wherein he and they might live, and to which all matters and business should be brought. To this end he chose a fine site eight leagues further inland from where Mérida now lies, and some fifteen or sixteen from the sea. They surrounded the place with a very broad wall of dry stone some eighth of a league in extent, leaving only two narrow doorways; the wall itself was low.

In the middle of the enclosure they built their temples, calling the largest Cuculcan, the same as at Chichen Itza. They built another circular temple, different from all others in the country, and with four entrances; also many others about them, connected one with the other. Within the enclosure they built houses for the lords alone, among whom the country was divided, assigning villages to each according to the antiquity of their lineage and their personal qualifications. Cuculcan did not call the city after himself, as was done by the Ah-Itzaes at Chichen Itza (which means the 'Well of the Ah-Itzaes'), but called it Mayapan, meaning the 'Standard of the Maya', the language of the country being known as Maya. The natives of today call it Ich-pa, meaning 'Within the Fortifications.'

Cuculcan lived for some years in this city with the chiefs, and then leaving them in full peace and amity returned by the same road to Mexico. On the way he stopped at Champotón, and there in memorial of himself and his departure he erected in the sea, at a good stone's throw from the shore, a fine edifice similar to those at Chichen Itza. Thus did Cuculcan leave a perpetual memory in Yucatan.

GOVERNMENT, PRIESTHOOD AND ACADEMIC SUBJECTS

On the departure of Cuculcan, the chiefs agreed that for the permanence of the State the house of the Cocoms should exercise the chief authority, it being the oldest and richest, or perhaps because its head was at that time a man of greater power. This done, they ordained that within the enclosure there should only be temples and residences of the chiefs, and of the High Priest; that they should build outside the walls dwellings where each of them might keep some serving people, and whither the people from the villages might come whenever they had business at the city. In these houses each one placed his mayordomo, who bore as his sign of authority a short thick baton, and who was called the Caluac. This officer held supervision over the villages and those in charge of them, to whom he sent advices as to the things needed in the chief's establishment, as birds, maize, honey, salt, fish, game, clothing and other things. The Caluac always attended in the chief's house, seeing what was needed and providing it promptly, his house standing as the office of his chief.

It was the custom to find the crippled and the blind in the villages, and give them their necessities. The chiefs appointed the governors and, if worthy, confirmed their offices to their sons. They enjoined upon them good treatment of the common people, the peace of the community, and that all should be diligent in their own support and that of the lords.

Upon all the lords rested the duty of honouring, visiting and entertaining Cocom, accompanying and making festivals for him, and of repairing to him in difficult affairs. They lived in peace with each other, and with much diversion according to their custom, in the way of dances, feasts and hunting.

The people of Yucatan were as attentive to matters of religion as of government, and had a High Priest whom they called Ahkin May, or also Ahaucan May, meaning the Priest May, or the High Priest May. He was held in great reverence by the chiefs, and had no allotment of natives for himself, the chiefs making presents to him in addition to the offerings, and all the local priests sending him contributions. He was succeeded in office by his sons or nearest kin. In him lay the key to their sciences, to which they most devoted themselves, giving counsel to the chiefs and answering their inquiries. With the matter of sacrifices he rarely took part, except on it festivals or business of much moment. He and his disciples appointed priests for the towns, examining them in their sciences and ceremonies; put in their charge the affairs of their office, and the setting of a good example to the people; he provided their books and sent them forth. They in turn attended to the service of the temples, teaching their sciences and writing books upon them.

They taught the sons of the other priests, and the second sons of the chiefs, who were brought to them very young for this purpose, if they found them inclined toward this office.

The sciences which they taught were the reckoning of the years, months and days, the festivals and ceremonies, the administration of their sacraments, the omens of the days, their methods of divination and prophecies, events, remedies for sicknesses, antiquities and the art of reading and writing by their letters and the characters wherewith they wrote, and by pictures that illustrated the writings.

They wrote their books on a long sheet doubled in folds, which was then enclosed between two boards finely ornamented; the writing was on one side and the other, according to the folds. The paper they made from the roots of a tree, and gave it a white finish excellent for writing upon. Some of the principal lords were learned in these sciences, from interest, and for the greater esteem they enjoyed thereby; yet they did not make use of them in public.

ARRIVAL OF THE TUTUL-XIUS

The natives relate that there came into Yucatan from the south many tribes with their chiefs, and it seems they came from Chiapas, although this the natives do not know; but the author so conjectures from the many words and verbal constructions that are the same in Chiapas and in Yucatan, and from the extensive indications of sites that have been abandoned. They say that these tribes wandered forty years through the wilderness of Yucatan, having in that time no water except from the rains; that at the end of that time they reached the Sierra that lies about opposite the city of Mayapan, ten leagues distant. Here they began to settle and erect many fine edifices in many places; that the inhabitants of Mayapan held most friendly relations with them, and were pleased that they worked the land as if they were native to it. In this manner the people of the Tutul-xiu subjected themselves to the laws of Mayapan, they intermarried, and thus the lord Xiu of the Tutul-xius came to find himself held in great esteem by all.

These tribes lived in such peace that they had no conflicts and used neither arms nor bows, even for the hunt, although now today they are excellent archers. They only used snares and traps, with which they took much game. They also had a certain art of throwing darts by the aid of a stick as thick as three fingers, hollowed out for a third of the way, and six palms long; with this and cords they threw with force and accuracy.

They had laws against delinquents which they executed rigorously, such as against an adulterer, whom they turned over to the injured party that he might either put him to death by throwing a great stone down upon his head, or he might forgive him if he chose. For the adulteress there was no penalty save the infamy, which was a very serious thing with them. One who ravished a maiden was stoned to death, and they relate a case of a chief of the Tutul-xiu who, having a brother accused of this crime, had him stoned and afterwards covered with a great heap of rocks. They also say that before the foundation of the city they had another law providing the punishment of adulterers by drawing out the intestines through the navel.

The governing Cocom began to covet riches, and to that end negotiated with the garrison kept by the kings of Mexico in Tabasco and Xicalango, that he would put the city in their charge.

In this way he introduced the Mexicans into Mayapan, oppressed the poor, and made slaves of many. The chiefs would have slain him but for fear of the Mexicans. The lord of the Tutul-xiu never gave his consent to this. Then those of Yucatan, seeing themselves so fixed, learned from the Mexicans the art of arms, and thus became masters of the bow and arrow, of the lance, the axe, the buckler and strong cuirasses made of quilted cotton together with other implements of war. Soon they no longer stood in awe of nor feared the Mexicans, but rather held them of slight moment. In this situation several years passed.

This Cocom was the first who made slaves; but out of this evil came the use of arms to defend themselves, that they might not all become slaves. Among the successors of the Cocom dynasty was another one, very haughty and an imitator of Cocom, who made another alliance with the Tabascans, placing more Mexicans within the city, and began to act the tyrant and to enslave the common people. The chiefs then attached themselves to the party of Tutul-xiu, a man patriotic like his ancestors, and they plotted to kill the Cocom. This they did, killing at the same time all of his sons save one who was absent; they sacked his dwelling and possessed themselves of all his property, his stores of cacao and other fruits, saying that thus they repaid themselves what had been stolen from them. The struggles between the Cocoms, who claimed that they had been unjustly expelled, and the Xius, went on to such an extent that after having been established in this city for more than 500 years, they abandoned and left it desolate, each going to his own country.

CHRONOLOGICAL MONUMENTS AND THE THREE PRINCIPAL KINGDOMS OF YUCATAN

On the site of Mayapan are to be found seven or eight stones each 10 feet in height, round on one side, well carved and bearing several lines of the characters they use, so worn away by the water as to be unreadable, although they are thought to be a monument of the foundation and destruction of the city. There are others like them at Zilán, a town on the coast, except that they are taller. The natives being asked what they were, answered that it was the custom to set up one of these stones every twenty years, that being the number by which they reckon their periods. This however seems to be without warrant, for in that event there must have been many others; besides that there are none of them in any other places than Mayapan and Zilán.

The most important thing that the chiefs who stripped Mayapan took away to their own countries were the books of their sciences, for they were always very subject to the counsels of their priests, for which reason there are so many temples in those provinces.

That son of Cocom who had escaped death through being away on a trading expedition to the Ulna country, which is beyond the city of Salamanca, on hearing of his father's death and the destruction of the city, returned in haste and gathered his relatives and vassals; they settled in a site which he called Tibulon (or Tibolon), meaning 'we have been played with.' They built many other towns in those forests, and many families have sprung from these Cocoms. The province where this chief ruled was called Sututa.

The lords of Mayapan took no vengeance on those Mexicans who gave aid to Cocom, seeing that they had been influenced by the governor of the country, and since they were strangers. They therefore left them undisturbed, granting them leave to settle in a place apart, or else to leave the country; in staying, however, they were not to intermarry with the natives, but only among themselves. These decided to remain in Yucatan and not return to the lagoons and mosquitos of Tabasco, and so settled in the province of Canul, which was assigned them, and where they remained until the second Spanish wars.

They say that among the twelve priests of Mayapan was one of great wisdom who had an only daughter, whom he had married to a young nobleman named Ah-Chel. This one had sons who were called the same as their father, according to the custom of the country. They say that this priest predicted the fall of the city to his son-in-law; they tell that on the broad part of his arm the old priest inscribed certain characters of great import in their estimation. With this distinction conferred on him he went to the coast and established a settlement at Tikoch, a great number of people following him. Thus arose the renowned families of the Chels, who peopled the most famous province of Yucatan, which they named after themselves the province of Ahkin-Chel. Here was Izamal, where the Chels resided; and they multiplied in Yucatan until the coming of the admiral Montejo.

Between these great princely houses of the Cocoms, Xius and Chels there was a constant feud and enmity, which still continues even though they have become Christians. The Cocoms call the Xius strangers and traitors, murdering their natural lord and plundering his possessions. The Xius say they are as good as the others, as ancient and as noble; that they were not traitors but liberators, having slain a tyrant. The Chel said that he was as good as the others in lineage, being the descendant of the most renowned priest in Mayapan; that as to himself he was greater than they, because he had known how to make himself as much a lord as they were. The quarrel extended even to their food supply, for the Chel, living on the coast, would not give fish or salt to the Cocom, making him go a long distance for it; and the Cocom would not permit the Chel to take any game or fruits.

VARIOUS CALAMITIES FELT IN YUCATAN IN THE PERIOD
BEFORE THE CONQUEST

These **tribes enjoyed** more than twenty years of abundance and health, and they multiplied so that the whole country seemed like a town. At that time they erected temples in great number, as is today seen everywhere; in going through the forests there can be seen in the groves the sites of houses and buildings marvellously worked.

Succeeding this prosperity, there came on one winter night at about six in the evening a storm that grew into a hurricane of the four winds. The storm blew down all the high trees, causing great slaughter of all kinds of game; it overthrew the high houses, which being thatched and having fires within for the cold, took fire and burned great numbers of the people, while those who escaped were crushed by the timbers.

The hurricane lasted until the next day at noon, and they found that those who lived in small houses had escaped, as well as the newly married couples. whose custom it was to live for a few years in cabins in front of their fathers or fathers-in-law. The land thus then lost the name it had borne, that 'of the turkeys and the deer', and was left so treeless that those of today look as if planted together and thus all grown of one size. To look at the country from heights it looks as if all trimmed with a pair of shears.

Those who escaped aroused themselves to building and cultivating the land, and multiplied greatly during fifteen years of health and abundance, the last year being the most fertile of all. Then as they were about to begin gathering the crops there came an epidemic of pestilential fevers that lasted for twenty-four hours; then on its abating the bodies of those attacked swelled and broke out full of maggoty sores, so that from this pestilence many people died and most of the crops remained ungathered.

After the passing of the pestilence they had sixteen other good years, wherein they renewed their passions and feuds to the end that 150,000 men were killed in battle. With this slaughter they ceased and made peace, and rested for twenty years. After that there came again a pestilence, with great pustules that rotted the body, fetid in odour, and so that the members fell in pieces within four or five days.

Since this last plague more than fifty years have now passed, the mortality of the wars was twenty years prior, the pestilence of the swelling was sixteen years before the wars, and twenty-two or twenty-three after the destruction of the city of Mayapan. Thus, according to this count, it has been 125 years since its overthrow, within which the people of this country have passed through the calamities described, besides many others after the Spaniards began to enter, both by wars and other afflictions sent by God; so that it is a marvel there is any of the population left, small as it is.

INDUSTRY AND COMMERCE, AGRICULTURE, JUSTICE AND HOSPITALITY

Among the occupations of the natives were pottery and woodworking; they made much profit from forming idols of clay and wood, in doing which they fasted much and followed many rites. There were also physicians, or better named, sorcerers, who healed by use of herbs and their superstitious practices. It was so also with all their other occupations.

Their favourite occupation was trading, whereby they brought in salt; also cloths and slaves from Tabasco and Ulúa. In their bartering they used cacao and stone counters which they had for money, and with which they bought slaves and other fine and beautiful stones, such as the chiefs wore as jewels on festal occasions. They had also certain red shells for use as money and jewels for wearing; these they carried in net-work purses. In their markets they dealt in all the products of the country; they gave credit, borrowed and paid promptly and without usury.

The commonest occupation was agriculture, the raising of maize and other seeds; these they kept in well-constructed places and in granaries for sale in due time. Their mules and oxen were the people themselves. For each married man and his wife it was their custom to plant a space of 400 feet, which was called *hun vinic* [one man], a plot measured with a 20-foot rod, twenty in breadth and twenty in length.

The natives have the excellent custom of helping each other in all their work. At the time of planting, those who have no people of their own to do it join together in bands of twenty, or more or less, and all labour together to complete the labour of each, all duly measured, and do not stop until all is finished. The lands today are in common, and whoever occupies a place first, holds it; they sow in different places, so that if the crop is short in one, another will make it up. When they work the land they do no more than gather the brush and burn it before sowing. From the middle of January to April they care for the land and then plant when the rains come. Then carrying a small sack on their shoulders they make a hole in the ground with a stick, dropping in five or six grains, and covering them with the same stick. When it rains, it is marvellous how they grow. In hunting also, they unite in bands of fifty, or more or less; the flesh of the deer they grill over rods to keep it from spoiling; then when they come back to the town they first make their presents to the chief and then distribute all as between friends. In fishing they do the same.

The Madrid Codex, which has chiefly to do with farm ceremonies, shows legends that explain farming: the growing plant springs from the head of the god Itzamna. The plant, springing from the earth, withers and is revived. The Corn deity holds forth the growing plant, springing from the sign *ik*, or Breath, Life. Itzamna plants the tree in the earth. Itzamna drops the seed in the earth and animals attack it. Worms attack the Corn-god, seated on the earth. Birds of prey feed on the dying Corn-god. The Fire-dog, or heat rays from the sun, burns the growth, while the Corn-god, with arms bound, is dying. Next, Itzamna waters the growing maize.

In making visits the natives always carry a gift, according to their quality, and the one visited returns the gifts with another. During these visits third persons present speak and listen attentively to those talking, having due regard for their rank; notwithstanding which all use the 'thou.' Those of less position must, however, in the course of the conversation, repeat the title or dignity of the one higher in rank. They have the custom of assisting one who delivers a message by responding with a cadence of the voice, a sort of aspirate in the throat, as if to say 'it is well', or 'be it so.' The women are brief in what they say, nor do they have the habit of negotiating on their own account, especially if poor; for this the chiefs scoffed at the friars for giving ear to poor and rich without distinction.

For offences committed by one against another the chief of the town required satisfaction to be made by the town of the aggressor; if this was refused it became the occasion of more trouble. If they were of the same town they laid it before the judge as arbitrator, and he ordered satisfaction given; if the offender lacked the means for this, his parents or friends helped him out. The cases in which they were accustomed to require such amends were in instances of involuntary homicide, the suicide of either husband or wife on the other's account, the accidental burning of houses, lands of inheritance, hives or granaries. Other offences committed with malice called for reparation through blood or blows.

The Yucatecans are very generous and hospitable; no one enters their houses without being offered food and drink, what drink they may have during the day, or food in the evening. If they have none, they seek it from a neighbour; if they unite together on the roads, all join in sharing even if they have little for their own need.

METHOD OF COUNTING, GENEALOGIES, INHERITANCES AND SUCCESSION

They count by fives up to twenty, by twenties to 100 and by hundreds to 400; then by 400s up to 8,000. This count is much used in merchandising the cacao. They have other very long counts, extended to infinity, counting twenty times 8,000, or 160,000; then they multiply this 160,000 again by twenty, and so on until they reach an uncountable figure. They do all their counting on the ground or a flat surface.

They make much of knowing the origin of their lineages, especially if they come from one of the houses of Mayapan; this they learn from their priests, it being one of their sciences, and they boast much about one of their lineage who has distinguished himself. The name of the father is transmitted to his sons, but not to his daughters. Both sons and daughters received the name of their father and their mother, the father's as the proper name, and the mother's as the given one; thus the son of Chel and Chan was called Na-Chan Chel, meaning the son of so and so. For this the natives consider all of the same name as related, and treat them accordingly; and thus when they go to a part of the country where they are unknown, and are in need, they make known their names, and if there are any of the same they are received and treated with good will and affection. Thus also no man or woman marries another of the same name, because this was for them would bring great disgrace. Today they use their baptismal names.

Daughters did not inherit equally with their brothers, except as a matter of favour or goodwill, in which case a part of the whole was given them. The rest was divided equally, except where one had helped more in the accumulation of the property, in which case he received an equivalent before the division. If the children were all daughters, then the cousins or other nearest kin inherited. Where the heir was not of sufficient age to receive the property, they entrusted it to the nearest relative as guardian or tutor, who supplied the mother with what she needed for his bringing up; for it was not their custom to place the property in the mother's control; or they even took the children from her care where the tutors were the brothers of the deceased. When the heirs reached their majority, the guardians rendered them the property; if this was not done it was held as in great dishonour, and became the cause of violent quarrels. The transfer was made in the presence of the chiefs and leading men, deducting what had been spent for their care; the heirs received nothing of the harvests, or the products of the hives or cacao trees, because of the labour involved in keeping them up.

When the chief died, if he left no sons to succeed him, but left brothers, the eldest or most capable became the ruler; meanwhile the heir was instructed in the customs, the ceremonies and everything he would need to know when he came of age. These brothers, even when the heir came to his position, still controlled affairs through their lives. In the case of there being no brothers of a deceased chief, the priests and leading men chose a man fitted for this position.

MAYA DIVORCE AND NUPTIAL CUSTOMS

In the olden times they married at the age of twenty, but now at that of twelve or thirteen. For this reason they divorce the more easily because they marry without love, and ignorant of married life and the duties of married people; and if their parents could not persuade them to return to their wives, they hunted them another, and others and others. With equal ease men with children left their wives with no anxiety lest another might take them as wives, or that they themselves might later return to them. Nevertheless, they are very jealous, and do not lightly suffer infidelity on their wives' part; and now that they see that the Spaniards kill their wives for this reason, they are beginning to maltreat and even to kill them. In cases of divorce, small children stayed with their mothers, while the grown-up went with their father and the girls with their mother.

Even though divorce was so common and familiar a thing, the old people and those of better customs condemned it, and there were many who never had but the single wife; nor did they ever marry one bearing their own name on the father's side, for this was considered a very bad thing. Equally wrong was it held that a man should marry his sister-in-law, the widow of a brother. Neither did they marry their stepmothers, their wives' sisters, nor their mothers' sisters, all these being regarded as wrong. But with all other kinsmen on their mothers' side, even first cousins, it was held legitimate.

The fathers were at great care to seek in good season wives for their sons, of equal rank and condition; and for the men to seek their wives themselves was regarded as undignified, as well as for the parents of the woman to make advances. In these matters they left the preparatory steps in the charge of other persons to care for; these then negotiated, dealt together, discussed the dowry or the settlement (which was not large). This the youth's father gave to the prospective father-in-law, while the girl's mother prepared garments for the bride and for the child.

The day of the marriage having arrived, they all gathered at the house of the fiancée's father, where a repast had been prepared. The guests met with the young couple and their relatives; the priest assured himself that the latter had given the matter all due consideration, gave the young man his wife, if it was settled for him to receive her that night; and after this the banquet took place. From that day the son-in-law remained in his father-in-law's house for five or six years, working for him; if he failed in this, he was driven from the house, but the mothers arranged always for the wife to supply her husband with his food, as a mark of the marriage.

The marriage of widowers and widows took place without any festival or ceremonies; the man simply went to the woman's house, was admitted and given to eat, and with this it was a marriage. The result of this was that they separated as easily as they came together. The Yucatecans never took more than a single wife, although in other places they frequently took a number together. At times the parents contracted marriages for their sons even when they were young children, and were regarded as their fathers-in-law until they came of age.

METHOD OF BAPTISM AND HOW IT WAS CELEBRATED

Baptism is not found anywhere in the Indies save here in Yucatan, and even with a word meaning to be born anew or a second time, the same as the Latin *renascer*. Thus in the language of Yucatan *sihil* means 'to be born anew', or a second time, but only however in composition; thus *caput-sihil* means to be reborn. (*Sihil* means 'to be born' simply; *caput-sihil* 'to be born a second time', and is the specific term in Maya for baptism, being distinct from *caput-cuxtal*, 'to come to life a second time.') Its origin we have been unable to learn, but it is something they have always used and for which they have had such devotion that no one fails to receive it; they had such reverence for it that those guilty of sins, or who knew they were about to sin, were obliged to confess to the priest, in order to receive it; and they had such faith in it that in no manner did they ever take it a second time. They believed that in receiving it they acquired a predisposition to good conduct and habits, protection against being harmed by the devils in their earthly affairs, and that through it and living a good life they would attain a beatitude hereafter which, like that of Mahomet, consisted in eating and drinking.

Their custom of preparing for baptism was as follows: the native women raised the children to the age of three, placing for the boys a small white plaquette, fastened to the head in the hair of the tonsure; the girls wore a thin cord tied very low about the waist, to which was attached a small shell over the private parts; to remove these two things was regarded among them as a sin and disgraceful, until the time of the baptism, which was given between the ages of three and twelve; until this ceremony was received they did not marry.

Whenever one desired to have his child baptized, he went to the priest and made his wish known to him, who then published this in the town, with the day chosen, which they took care should be of good omen. This being done, the solicitant, being thus charged with giving the fiesta, selected at his discretion some leading man of the town to assist him in the matter. Afterwards they chose four other old and honoured men to assist the priest on the day of the ceremony, these being chosen with the priest's cooperation. In these elections the fathers of all the eligible children took part, for the fiesta was a concern of all; those so chosen were called *chacs*. For the three days before the ceremony the parents of the children, as well as the officials, fasted and abstained from their wives.

On the day, all assembled at the house of the one giving the fiesta, and brought all the children who were to be baptized, and placed them in the patio or court of the house, all clean and scattered with fresh leaves; the boys together in a line, and the girls the same, with an aged woman as matron for the girls, and a man in charge of the boys.

When this was done the priest proceeded to the purification of the house, expelling the demon. To do this they placed four benches in the four corners of the patio, on which the four *chacs* seated themselves, with a long cord tied from one to the other, in such fashion as that the children were corralled in the middle, after which those parents who had fasted stepped over the cord, into the circuit. Afterwards, or previously, they placed in the middle another bench on which the priest seated himself, with a brazier and a little ground maize and incense. Then the boys and girls came to him in order, and he put a little of the ground maize and incense into the hand of each, and they threw it into the brazier. When all had done this, they took up the brazier and the cord held by the *chacs*; they also threw a little wine in a vase and then gave it all to an Indian to carry away from the village, enjoining him not to drink the wine or to look behind him on his return; and in this manner they said that the demon had been exorcised.

After this they swept the patio and took away the leaves that were scattered at the beginning, which were of a tree called *sihom*, and scattered others of a tree called *copó*, laying down mats while the priest changed his vestures. He next entered wearing a tunic of red feathers, worked with other varicoloured feathers, and with other long feathers pendant from the ends; on his head he wore a sort of mitre of the same feathers, while beneath the tunic there hung to the ground strips of cotton like tails. He carried a short, finely decorated stick of hyssop, and the tails of certain serpents like rattlesnakes; all this with neither

MESOAMERICA ANCIENT ORIGINS

more nor less gravity than that of a pope crowning an emperor, and a serenity that was a marvel to behold. The *chacs* then went to the children and placed on the heads of all white cloths which their mothers had brought for the purpose. They asked of the largest ones whether they had done any bad thing, or obscene conduct, and if any had done so, they confessed them and separated them from the others.

When this was done the priest called on all to be silent and seated, and began to bless the children, with many prayers, and to sanctify them with the hyssop, all with great serenity. After this benediction he seated himself, and the one elected by the parents as director of the fiesta took a bone given him by the priest, went to the children and menaced each one with the bone on the forehead, nine times. After this he wet the bone in a jar of water he carried, and with it anointed them on the forehead, the face and between the fingers of their hands and the bones of their feet, without saying a word. This liquor was confected out of certain flowers and ground cacao, dissolved in virgin water, as they call it, taken from the hollows of trees or of rocks in the forest.

After this unction the priest rose, removed the white cloths from their heads, as well as others they wore suspended from the shoulders containing a few feathers of very beautiful birds and some grains of cacao, all of which were collected by one of the *chacs*. Then with a stone knife the priest cut away the small bead or counter each had worn fastened to his head. After this the other assistants of the priest brought a bunch of flowers and a pipe such as the natives smoked; with these they menaced each child nine times, and then gave him the bouquet to smell and the pipe to smoke. After this they gathered the presents brought by the mothers, which were things to eat, and gave these to each child to eat there. Then they brought a fine chalice of wine and quickly offered it to the gods, invoking them with devout prayers to receive this small gift from the children; this chalice they then gave to another officiant called *cayom*, that he might empty it at a single draught; for him to stop to take breath in this was regarded as something sinful.

When this was over the girls took their leave first, their mothers removing the cord and shell they had worn about the girdle in sign of their chastity; this gave licence for them to be married, when such might seem best to their parents. Then the boys took their leave, and the fathers came bearing the heap of mantles they had brought, and gave them with their own hands to the assistants and the officiants. The fiesta then ended with long eating and drinking; and this fiesta was called *em-ku*, which means 'the descent of the god.' The one then who had instituted and borne the cost of the ceremony, in addition to his three previous days of abstinence and fast, was obliged to continue this for yet other nine days; this they did invariably.

CONFESSIONS, SUPERSTITIONS, IDOLS AND DUTIES OF THE PRIESTS

The Yucatecans naturally knew when they had done wrong, and they believed that death, disease and torments would come on them because of evildoing and sin, and thus they had the custom of confessing to their priests when such was the case. In this way, when for sickness or other cause they found themselves in danger of death, they made confession of their sin; if they neglected it, their near relatives or friends reminded them of it; thus they publicly confessed their sins to the priest if he was at hand; or if not, then to their parents, women to their husbands, and the men to their wives.

The sins of which they commonly accused themselves were theft, homicide, of the flesh and false testimony; in this way they considered themselves in safety. Many times, after they had recovered, there were difficulties over the disgrace they had caused, between the husband and wife, or with others who had been the cause thereof.

The men confessed their weaknesses. Sins of intention they did not confess, yet considered them as evil, and in their counsels and sermons advised against them.

Those widowed did not marry for a year thereafter, nor know [intimaely] one of the other sex for this time; those who infringed this rule were deemed intemperate, and they believed some ill would come on them.

In some of the fasts observed for their fiestas they neither ate meat nor knew their wives. They always fasted when receiving duties in connection with their festivals, and likewise on undertaking duties of the State, which at times lasted as long as three years; those who violated their abstinence were great sinners.

So given were they to their idolatrous practices that in times of necessity even the women and youths and maidens understood it as incumbent on them to burn incense and pray to God that he free them from evil and overcome the demon who was the cause of it.

Even travellers on the roads carried incense with them, and a little plate on which to burn it; and then wherever they arrived at night they erected three small stones, putting a little incense on each, and three flat stones in front of these, on which they burned incense, praying to the god they called Ekchuah that he bring them safely back home; this ceremony they performed every night until their return, unless there were some other who could do this, or even more, on their account.

The Yucatecans had a great number of temples, sumptuous in their style; besides these temples in common the chiefs, priests and principal men also had their oratories and idols in their houses their private offerings and prayers. They held Cozumel and the well at Chichen Itza in as great veneration as we have in our pilgrimages to Jerusalem and Rome; they visited them to offer gifts, especially at Cozumel, as we do at our holy places; and when they did not visit they sent offerings. When travelling also, and passing an abandoned temple, it was their custom to enter for prayers and burn incense.

So many idols did they have that their gods did not suffice them, there being no animal or reptile of which they did not make images, and these in the form of their gods and goddesses. They had idols of stone (though few in number), others more numerous of wood, but the greatest number of terracotta. The idols of wood were especially esteemed and reckoned among their inheritances as objects of great value. They had no metal statues, there being no metals in the country. As regards the images, they knew perfectly that they were made by human hands, perishable and not divine; but they honoured them because of what they represented and the ceremonies that had been performed during their fabrication, especially the wooden ones.

The most idolatrous of them were the priests, the *chilánes*, the sorcerers, the physicians, the *chacs* and the *nacónes*. It was the office of the priests to discourse and teach their sciences, to indicate calamities and the means of remedying them, preaching during the festivals, celebrating the sacrifices and administering their sacraments. The *chilánes* were charged with giving to all those in the locality the oracles of the demon, and the respect given them was so great that they did not ordinarily leave their houses except borne upon litters carried on the shoulders. The sorcerers and physicians cured by means of bleeding at the part afflicted, casting lots for divination in their work, and other matters. The *chacs* were four old men, specially elected on occasion to aid the priest in the proper and full celebration of the festivals. There were two of the *nacónes*; the position of one was permanent and carried little honour, since it was his office to open the breasts of those who were sacrificed; the other was chosen as a general for the wars, who held office for three years, and was held in great honour; he also presided at certain festivals.

MAYA SACRIFICES AND SELF-MORTIFICATION

At times they sacrificed their own blood, cutting all around the ears in strips which they let remain as a sign. At other times they perforated their cheeks or the lower lip; again they made cuts in parts of the body, or pierced the tongue crossways and passed stalks through, causing extreme pain; again they cut away the superfluous part of the member, leaving the flesh like the ears. It was this custom which led the historian of the Indies to say that they practised circumcision.

At other times they practised a filthy and grievous sacrifice, hereby they gathered in the temple in a line, and each made a pierced hole through the member, across from side to side, and then passed through as great a quantity of cord as they could stand; and thus all together fastened and strung together, they anointed the statue of the demon with the collected blood. The one able to endure the most was considered most valiant, and their sons of tender age began to accustom themselves to this suffering; it is frightful to see how much they were dedicated to this practice.

The women made no similar effusions of blood, although they were very devout. Of every kind of animal obtainable, birds of the sky, animals of the earth, fishes of the sea, they used the blood to anoint the face of the demon; they also gave as presents whatever other thing they had. Of some animals they took out the heart and offered that; others were offered whole, some living, some dead, some raw, some cooked. They also made large offerings of bread and wine, and of all the kinds of food and drink they possessed.

To make these sacrifices in the courts of the temples there were erected certain tall decorated posts; and near the stairway of the temple there was a broad, round pedestal, and in the middle a stone, somewhat slender and four or five palms in height, set up; at the top of the temple stairs there was another similar one.

Apart from the festivals which they solemnized by the sacrifices of animals, on occasions of great tribulation or need the priests or *chilánes* ordained the sacrifice of human beings. For this purpose all contributed, for the purchase of slaves. Some out of devotion gave their young sons. The victims were feted up to the day of the sacrifice, but carefully guarded that they might not run away, or defile themselves by any carnal acts; then while they went from town to town with dances, the priests, the *chilánes* and the celebrants fasted.

When the day of the ceremony arrived, they assembled in the court of the temple; if they were to be pierced with arrows their bodies were stripped and anointed with blue, with a mitre on the head. When they arrived before the demon, all the people went through a solemn dance with him around the wooden pillar, all with bows and arrows, and then dancing raised him upon it, tied him, all continuing to dance and took at him. The impure priest, ventured, ascended and whether it was mars or woman wounded the victim in the private parts with an arrow, and then descended and anointed the face of the demon with the blood he had drawn; then making a sign to the dancers, they began in order as they passed rapidly, dancing, to shoot an arrow to the victim's heart, shown by a white mark, and quickly made of his chest a single point, like a hedgehog of arrows.

If his heart was to be taken out, they conducted him with great display and concourse of people, painted blue and wearing his mitre, and placed him on the rounded sacrificial stone, after the priest and his officers had anointed the stone with blue and purified the temple to drive away the evil spirit. The *chacs* then seized the poor victim and swiftly laid him on his back across the stone, and the four took hold of his arms and legs, spreading them out. Then the *nacon* executioner came, with a flint knife in his hand, and with great skill made an incision between the ribs on the left side, below the nipple; then he plunged in his hand and like a ravenous tiger tore out the living heart, which he laid on a plate and gave to the priest; he then quickly went and anointed the faces of the idols with that fresh blood.

At times they performed this sacrifice on the stone situated on the top step of the temple, and then they threw the dead body rolling down the steps, where it was taken by the attendants, was stripped completely of the skin save only on the hands and feet; then the priest, stripped, clothed himself with this skin and danced with the rest. This was a ceremony with them of great solemnity. The victims sacrificed in this manner were usually buried in the court of the temple; but it occurred on occasions that they ate the flesh, distributing portions to the chiefs and those who succeeded in obtaining a part; the hands, feet and head want to the priests and celebrants; and these sacrificial victims they then regarded as sainted. If they were slaves captured in war, their masters kept the bones, and displayed them in the dances, as a mark of victory. At times they threw the victims alive into the well at Chichen Itza, believing that they would come forth on the third day, even though they never did see them reappear.

THE MILITARY AND CUSTOMS OF WAR

They had offensive and defensive arms. The offensive were bows and arrows carried in their quivers, tipped with flints and very sharp fishes' teeth, which they shot with great skill and force. The bows were of a beautiful yellowish wood, marvellously strong and more straight than curved, with cords of their hemp fibres. The length of the bow was always somewhat less than that of the one who carried it. The arrows were made of reeds that grow in the lagoons, and more than five palms long, in which was fixed a piece of thin wood, very strong, in which again was fastened the flint. They do not know or use poisons, though from no lack of them. They had hatchets of a certain metal and of this shape, fastened in a handle of wood. These served them both as arms in war, and then at home for working wood. The metal being soft, they gave it an edge by beating with a stone. They had short lances a man's height in length, pointed with very hard flint; besides these they had no other arms.

For defence they had shields made of split and woven reeds, and covered with deer hide. They wore protective jackets of cotton, quilted in double thickness, which were very strong. Some of the chiefs and captains wore helmets of wood, but these were not common. With these arms they went to war, adorned with feathers, and with skins of tigers and lions, when they possessed them. They had two captains, one perpetual and hereditary, the other elected for three years with a great deal of ceremony. This latter was selected to celebrate the festivals of the month Pax, which falls on the 12th of May; and during a war he commanded the second corps of the army.

This captain was called Nacon; during these three years he was forbidden to converse with women, even with his wife, or to eat meat. They held him in great respect, and supplied him with fish and iguanas, which are a sort of edible lizards; during this period he must not become drunk, and the vessels and household articles for his use were kept apart; he was not served by a woman, and mingled little with the townsfolk.

The three years passed as stated. These two captains arranged matters for wars, and put things in their order. In each district there were men chosen as the soldiery, and when the occasion came they presented themselves with their arms; these were called the *holcánes*, and if there were not enough of them, others were collected; they were then given instructions and divided. Marching led by a lofty banner they set out from the town in complete silence, and then taking their enemies by surprise, fell on them with great cries and fierceness.

On the roads and passages the enemy set defences manned by archers, barricades of stakes and trees, and more often of stone. After a victory they cut off the jawbones from the dead, and hung them clean of flesh on their arms. In these wars they made great offerings of the spoils, and if they captured some renowned man they promptly sacrificed him, not to leave alive those who could later inflict injury upon them. The rest became captives of war in the power of those who took them.

These *holcánes* received no pay except in time of war, and then they were given certain money by the captains, but not much, because it came from their own funds; or if they lacked the needful, the town helped them. The town also supplied their food, which the women prepared for them; this they carried on their backs for the lack of animals, and thus the wars were of short duration. After the war the soldiers harassed the people in the districts greatly, under colour of the war, while this lasted, requiring services and gifts; if any of them succeeded in killing some captain or chief he was greatly honoured and feted.

PENALTIES AND PUNISHMENTS

From Mayapan these people retained the custom of punishing adulterers in the following manner. The investigation having been made and the man convicted of adultery, the leading men gathered at the chief's house and brought the adulterer tied to a piece of wood, delivering him to the husband of the woman. If he pardoned him he went free; if not, he killed him by dropping a large stone on his head, from a height. For the woman a sufficient punishment was the infamy, which was great; and commonly for this he left her.

The penalty for homicide, even when involuntary, was death at the hands of the relatives, unless he paid himself off. A thief had to reimburse the value, and was besides enslaved, however small the theft, which was a reason why they had so many slaves, especially in times of hunger. Because of this the friars made special effort to baptize them, that they might be set at liberty. If the thief was one of the chiefs or leading men, they assembled and having seized him scarified both sides of his face from the beard to the forehead, which constitutes a major dishonour.

The young men respected the elders highly, and took their counsels and sought to pass as mature. The elders said to the younger ones that since they had witnessed more, what they said should be received with credit, so that the youths following this would gain more respect themselves. So much was the respect given to the elder men that the youths did not mingle with them, except in cases of necessity, such as marriages. Also they visited little among the married people; so that it was the custom to have in each town a large building, whitewashed and open on all sides, where the young men gathered for their pastimes. They played ball, and a certain game with beans like dice, and many others. Here they nearly always slept, all together, until they were married.

They painted their bodies black before marriage, but were not tattooed until after, except slightly. As to other things they always accompanied their fathers, and so became as great idolaters as they; and they helped them much in their labours.

The Indian women raised their children both harshly and wholly naked. Four or five days after the child was born they laid it on a small cot made of rods, face down, with the head between two pieces of wood, one on the occiput and the other on the forehead, tying them tightly, and leaving it suffering for several days until the head, thus squeezed, became permanently flattened, as is their custom. This however caused so great distress and risk for the poor infants that they were at times in danger of death; and the author hereof saw one where the cranium was pressed well behind the ears, which must have been happened to many.

They were brought up entirely naked, but at about four or five years of age they gave them a wrap for sleeping, and strips of cloth to cover themselves as their fathers did; the little girls also began to cover themselves from the girdle down. They suckled much, for the mothers never ceased to give them milk as long as they could, until three or four years old; from this there has resulted so many robust people in the country.

For the first two years they grew up marvellously pretty and fat; after that, due to the constant bathing by their mothers, and the heat of the sun, they became tanned. But during the whole of their childhood they were jolly and lively, always armed with bows and arrows, and playing with each other. Thus they grew up until they began to behave as youths, taking on more importance, and leaving children's things.

MAYA WOMEN'S CLOTHING

The Indian women of Yucatan who are beautiful are quite vain of it, and indeed they are not bad looking; they are dark-skinned, caused more by their constant bathing and by the sun, than naturally; they do not powder their faces as our women do, regarding this as immodest. They have a habit of filing their teeth, saw fashion, as a matter of elegance; this is done for them by the old women, using certain stones and water.

They pierce the cartilage of the nose within, to take a stone of amber for adornment. They also pierce the ears for rings, in the manner of their husbands; they tattoo the body from the waist up, leaving the breasts for nursing reasons, the patterns being more delicate and beautiful than those of the men. They bathe constantly, like the men, in cold water, but with little reserve, going stripped into the places where they go for water. They also bathe in hot water, heated by fire; this is however rather for sake of health than cleanliness.

Their custom is to rub themselves with a red ointment, like their husbands; those who can do so add an odoriferous and very sticky gum which I take to be liquidambar, and which they call *istahté*. This ointment they apply to a sort of briquet like soap, decorated with fancy designs, rubbing it on their breasts, arms and shoulders, until they are very gallant and odorous, as they feel; it lasts a long time without disappearing, according to the quality of the ointment.

They wear the hair very long, which they used to and still do arrange in very fine tresses, parted in two parts, and made use of to build up the coiffure. When the young girls go to be married, their mothers go to such pains in arranging their hair, and use such skill, as that I have seen many with their coiffures as fine as those of the most coquettish Spanish women. The little girls, not grown up, wear theirs in two or four plaits which become them well.

The Indian women of the coast, of the province of Bak-halal and of Campeche, are more modest in their costume; besides the skirt which they wear from the waist down, they cover the breasts with a double mantle fastened below the armpits. As to the others, their sole garment is a long wide sack, open at the sides, reaching to the thighs and there fastened by its own ends; besides this they have only the mantle in which they always sleep, and which when on the road they carry doubled and rolled, and wrapped up.

MAYA WOMEN'S EDUCATION AND CUSTOMS

The women vaunted themselves as chaste, and were in the habit of turning their shoulders toward the men in passing them, and of turning to the side on the roads; this also they did in giving a man drink, until he had finished it. They taught their daughters the things they knew, and raised them excellently in their mode; they reprimanded them, instructed them and made them work; if they misbehaved they punished them by boxing their ears or slapping their arms. If they raise their eyes they reprove them severely, and put pepper on them, which causes great pain; if they are immodest they whip them, and put pepper on the other part, as a punishment and affront. It is also a grave reproach to tell the young girls they are like women brought up without a mother.

They are very jealous and at times lay hands on those women that have aroused their suspicions; again they are quick to anger and irritation on this score, though in other ways very mild; so that they are wont to pull their husbands' hair for the least infidelity. They are great workers and good in all the domestic economies, for on them rest the most, and most important, work of alimentation, housekeeping and education of their children, and the payment of the tributes; with all this they bear heavier burdens if it is necessary, working the fields and harvesting the crops. They are great economists, watching at night in what time is left them after their domestic labours, attending the markets to buy and sell their things.

They raise both Spanish and native fowls for sale, and for eating. They raise birds for their pleasure and for the feathers for adornment on their finer clothes; also raising other domestic animals, among these even offering their breast to the deer, which they have so tame that they never run away into the woods, even when they take them there and back, and raise them there.

They help each other mutually in their working and spinning, paying for this work in the same way as do their husbands on their farms; and while at this they ever have their jokes and tell their stories, at times with a bit of grumbling. They hold it disgraceful to look at the men and laugh at them, so this fact alone is enough to cause trouble, and with no other grounds to bring them into disrepute.

The most of their dances they do by themselves, although in some they dance with the men; among these the naval dance, one not very modest. Their fecundity is great, and they bear the children in good time; they are excellent nurses, first because their hot morning drink produces plenty of milk, and again because their constant grinding of the maize without tying up the breasts causes them to grow large and thus to hold a great deal of milk.

They also become intoxicated in their banquets, which they have among themselves, but not so much as do the men. They desire many children, and she who lacks them invokes their idols with gifts and prayers; and today they pray to God for them. They are prudent and polite, and affable, with those who understand them; also extremely generous. They cannot keep a secret; and they are not as clean and proper in their persons and affairs as they should be, in spite of their washing like ermines.

They were very devout and pious, rendering many devotions to their idols, burning incense before them, offering gifts of cotton, food and drink; it was also their charge to prepare the offerings of food and drink to be made during the ceremonies; but they did not share the custom of drawing blood for the evil spirits, and never did so. Neither were they allowed to come to the temples at times of the sacrifices, except in a certain festival where certain old women were admitted to take part therein. At the time of accouchement they went to their sorceresses, who made them believe all sorts of lies, and also put under their couch the image of an evil spirit called Ixchel, whom they called the goddess of childbirth.

When the children were born, they bathed them at once, and then when the pain of pressing the foreheads and heads was over, they took them to the priest that he might cast their fate, declare the office the child was to fill, and give him the name he was to retain during his childhood; because they were accustomed to call the children by different names until they were baptized or somewhat grown up; afterwards they dropped these and called themselves after their fathers until they were married. Then they took the names of both father and mother.

MAYA FUNERALS AND THE AFTERLIFE

This people had a great and excessive fear of death, and this they showed in that in all their services they rendered to their gods were for no other end than that they should give them health and life and their subsistence. But when it came the time to die, it was a thing to see what were the grief and lamentations they displayed for their deceased, and the sadness they felt. They wept during the day in silence, and during the nights with loud and mournful cries that were grievous to hear. For many days they went about in deepest mourning. They kept abstinence and fasts for the deceased, especially a husband or wife. They declared it was the devil that had taken them off, because they thought all ills came from him, especially death.

At death they shrouded the body, filled the mouth with ground maize and a drink they call *koyem*, and with this certain stones they used for money, that food might not be lacking to him in the other life. They buried them in their houses or the vicinity, throwing some of their idols into the grave; if he was a priest they threw in some of his books; if a sorcerer his divining stones and other instruments of his office. They commonly abandoned the house after the funeral, except where many people were living there, in whose company they would lose some of their fear of death.

On the death of a chief or man of position they cremated the bodies and put the ashes in large urns, and built temples over them, as is seen to have been done in the old times in the cases there have been found at Izamal. Today it is found that they put the ashes of great chiefs in hollow clay statues.

The others of the upper classes made statues of wood, left hollow in the occiput, for their fathers; then they burned part of the body and put part of the ashes therein, and stoppered it; then they removed the skin from the occiput and fastened it there, burying the remainder in the usual fashion. These images they kept with much reverence, among their idols. Among the ancient lords of the house of the Cocoms they cut off the heads after death, boiled them so as to remove the flesh; then they sawed away the back part of the skull, leaving the front with the cheeks and teeth, replacing in these half sections of the head the removed flesh with a sort of bitumen, and gave them almost the perfection of what they had been in life. These they kept together with the images, and the ashes, all in the oratorios of their houses among their idols, with great reverence and affection. On all festivals and feast days they put before them offerings of food, that nothing might fail them in the other life, where they believed the souls rested and received their gifts.

These people have always believed in the immortality of the soul, in greater degree than many other nations, even though they were not so civilized; they believed that after death there was another life better than this, which the soul enjoyed after leaving the body. This future life they said was divided into good and evil, into pains and delights. The evil life of suffering they said was for the vicious, and the good and delectable for those whose mode of life had been good. The delights they said they would come into if they had been of good conduct, were by entering a place where nothing would give pain, where there would be abundance of food and delicious drinks, and a refreshing and shady tree they called Yaxché, the Ceiba tree, beneath whose branches and shade they might rest and be in peace for ever.

The torments of the evil life which they said awaited the wicked, lay in going to an evil place below the other, and which they called Mitnal, meaning hell, where they were tormented by demons, by great pains of cold and hunger and weariness and sadness. They said there was in this place a chief demon whom all the rest obeyed and whom in their language they called Hunhau; also they said that these good and evil afterlives had no end, because the soul itself had none. They also said, and held as quite certain, that those who had hung themselves went to this paradise; and there were many who in times of lesser troubles, labours or sickness, hung themselves to escape and go to that paradise, to which they were thought to be carried by the goddess of the scaffold whom they called Ixtab. They had no knowledge of the resurrection of the body; neither could they give account of whence had come to them these beliefs in this, their paradise and their hell.

COUNT OF THE YUCATECAN YEAR

The sun does not sink or go away far enough in this land of Yucatan for the nights to become longer than the days; thus in their full maximum, from San Andrés to Santa Lucia [Nov. 30 to Dec. 13] they are equal, and then they begin to lengthen.

To know the hour of the night the natives governed themselves by the planet Venus, the Pleiades and the Twins. During the day they had terms for midday, and for different sections from sunrise to sunset, according to which they recognized and regulated their hours for work.

They had their perfect year like ours, of 365 days and six hours, which they divided into months in two ways. In the first the months were of thirty days and were called *U*, which signifies the moon, and they counted from the rising of the new moon until it disappeared.

In the other method the months had twenty days, and were called *uinal hunekeh*; of these it took eighteen to complete the year, plus five days and six hours. Out of these six hours they made a day every four years, so that they had a 366-day year every fourth time.

For these 360 days they had twenty letters or characters by which to designate them, without assigning names to the five supplementary days, as being sinister and unlucky. The letters are as follows, each with its name above to understand their correlation with ours.

I have already related that the Indian method of counting was from five to five, and four fives making twenty; thus then from these twenty characters they take the first of each set of five, so that each of these serves for a year as do our Dominical letters, being the initials days of the various twenty-day months (or *uinals*).

Among the multitude of gods worshipped by these people were four whom they called by the name Bacab. These were, they say, four brothers placed by God when he created the world, at its four corners to sustain the heavens lest they fall. They also say that these Bacabs escaped when the world was destroyed by the deluge. To each of these they give other names, and they mark the four points of the world where God placed them holding up the sky, and also assigned one of the four Dominical letters to each, and to the place he occupies; also they signalize the misfortunes or blessings which are to happen in the year belonging to each of these, and the accompanying letters.

The evil one, who has in this as in many other cases deceived them, fixed for them the services and offerings hat had to be made in order to evade these misfortunes. Thus if they failed to occur, they said it was because of the ceremonies performed; but if they did come to pass, the priests made the people believe that it was because of some error or fault in the ceremonies,

The first of these Dominical letters, then, is Kan. The year served by this letter had as augury that Bacab who was otherwise called Hobnil, Kanal-bacab, Kan-pauahtun, Kan-xibchac. To him belonged the South.

The second letter, or Muluc, marked the East, and this year had as its augury the Bacab called Can-sicnal, Chacal-bacab, Chac-pauahtun, Chac-xibchac.

The third letter is Ix, and the augury for this year was the Bacab called Sac-sini, Sacal-bacab, Sac-pauahtun, Sac-xibchac, marking the North.

The fourth letter is Cauac, its augury for that year being the Bacab called Hosan-ek, Ekel-bacab, Ek-pauahtun, Ek-xibchac; this one marked the West.

In whatever ceremony or solemnity these people celebrated for their gods, they always began by driving away the evil spirit, in order the better to perform it. This exorcism was at times by prayers and benedictions they had for this purpose, and at other times by services, offerings and sacrifices which they performed for that end. In order to celebrate the solemnity of the New Year with the greatest rejoicing and dignity, these people, with their false ideas, made use of the five supplementary days, which they regarded as 'unlucky', and which preceded the first day of their new year, in order to put on a great fiesta for the above Bacabs and the evil one, to whom they gave four other names, as they had done to the Bacabs; these names were: Kan-uvayeyab, Chac-uvayeyab, Sac-uvayeyab, Ek-uvayeyab. These ceremonies and fetes being over, and the evil one driven away, as we shall see, they began their new year.

THE KAN NEW YEAR

In all the towns of Yucatan it was the custom to have at each of the four entrances to the town two heaps of stones, one in front of the other; that is, at the east, west, north and south; and here they celebrated the two festivals of the 'unlucky' days, in the following manner.

For the year whose Dominical letter was Kan, the augury was Hobnil, and they say that both of these ruled the South. In this year, then, they made an image or clay figure of the demon they called Kan-uvayeyab and carried it to the piles of stone they had erected at the South. They chose a leading man of the town, at whose house was celebrated this fiesta on these days, and then they made a statue of a demon whom they called Bolon-tz'acab, which they set at the house of the principal, erected in a public spot to which all might come.

This being done, the chiefs, the priest and the men of the town, assembled and having the road clean and prepared, with arches and green branches, as far as the two heaps of stone where the statue was, there they gathered most devoutly; on arriving there the priest incensed the statue with forty-nine grains of ground maize, mixed with incense; then the nobles put their incense into the brazier of the idol, and incensed it. The ground maize alone was called *sacah*, and that of the lords *chahalté*.

Thus incensing the image, they cut off the head of a fowl, and presented it as an offering. When all had done this, they placed the image on a wooden standard called *kanté*, placing on his shoulders an angel as a sign of water and of a good year, and these angels they painted so as to make them frightful in appearance. Then they carried it with much rejoicing and dancing to the house of the principal, where there was the other statue of Bolon-tz'acab.

From the house of this principal they brought out to the road, for the chiefs and the priest, a drink made of 415 grains of toasted maize (which they call *picula kakla*), of which all drank. On arrival at the house, they set the image they were carrying in front of the statue of the demon they had there, and then made many offerings of food and drink, of meat and fish; these offerings were given to whatever strangers there were there; and to the priest they gave a leg of venison.

Others drew blood by cutting their ears and anointing therewith a stone image they had there, of the demon Kanal-acantun. They moulded a heart of bread and another of calabash seeds, and offered those to the image of the demon Kan-uvayeyab. They kept this statue and image through those fateful days, and perfumed them with their incense, and with the ground maize and incense. They believed that if they did not perform these ceremonies, certain sicknesses would come on them in the ensuing year. When these fatal days were over they took the statue of Bolon-tz'acab to the temple, and the image to the eastern entrance where the next year they would go for it; there they left it and went to their houses to do what was their part in celebrating the new year.

These ceremonies over, and the evil spirit exorcised according to their deluded beliefs, they looked on the coming year as a good one, because it was ruled by the character Kan and the bacab Hobnil; and of him they said that in him there was no sin as in his brothers, and because of that no evils would come upon them. But since they often did so come, the evil one provided ceremonies therefor, so that when they happened they might throw the blame on the ceremonies or celebrants; and thus they continued always deluded and blind.

It was then commanded to make an idol called Itzamna-kauil, and place it in the temple. Then in the temple court they burned three balls of a milk or resin they called *kik* (rubber), while sacrificing a dog or a man; this they did keeping the same procedure I have described in a later chapter, except that in this case the method of the sacrifice differed. In the temple court they erected a great pile of stones, and then placed the dog or the man to be sacrificed on something much higher, from which they threw him, tied, upon the pile below; there the attendants seized him and with great swiftness drew out his heart, raised it to the new idol, and offered it between two plates. They offered other gifts of food, and in this festival there danced old women of the town, chosen therefor, clothed in certain vestures. They say that an angel descended and received this sacrifice.

THE MULUC NEW YEAR

In the year whose dominical letter was Muluc the augury was Cansicnal. On this occasion the chiefs and the priest selected a president to care for the festival, after which election they made an image of the demon as they had done in the previous year, and which they called Chac-uvayeyab, and carried this to the piles of stone at the East, where they had left the other one the year before. They also made a statue of the idol called Kinchahau, and placed it in the house of the president in a convenient place; from there, with the road all cleaned and dressed, they all proceeded together for their accustomed devotions before the god Chac-uvayeyab.

On arriving the priest perfumed it with fifty-three grains of the ground maize, with the incense, which they call *sacah*. The priest gave this to the chiefs, who put in the brazier more incense, of the kind called *chahalté*; then they cut off a fowl's head, as before, and taking the image on a wooden standard called *chacté*, they carried it very devoutly, while dancing certain war dances they call *holcan-okot*, *batel-okot*. During this they brought to the road for the chiefs and principal men their drink made from 380 grains of maize, toasted as before.

When they had arrived at the house of the president, they put this image in front of the statue of Kinch-ahau, and made all their offerings to it, which were then distributed like the rest. They offered to the image bread formed like the yolks of eggs, others like deer's hearts, and another made of dissolved peppers. Many of them drew blood from their ears, and with it anointed the stone they had there, of the god Chac-acantun. They took boys and forcibly drew blood from their ears, by blows. They kept this statue and the image until the fatal days were passed, meanwhile burning their incense. When the days were over, they took the image to the part of the North, where next year they had to go to seek it; the other they took to the temple, and then went to their houses to care for the works of the new year If they did not do all these things, they feared the coming especially of eye troubles.

The dominical letter of this year being Muluc, the Bacab Can-sicnal ruled, whence they held it a favourable year, for they said he was the best and greatest of these Bacab gods; for this they put him first in their prayers. Yet for all this the evil one caused them to make an idol called Yaxcoc-ahmut, which they placed in the temple and took away the old images; then they erected in the temple court a stone block on which they burned their incense, and a ball of the resin or milk *kik*, with a prayer there to the idol, asking relief for the ills they feared for the coming year; these were a scarcity of water, buds (*hijos*) on the maize, and the like. To gain this protection the evil one ordained offerings of squirrels and an unembroidered cloth, which was to be woven by old women whose office it was to appease Yaxcoc-ahmut.

In spite of this being held a good year, they were still menaced with many other evils and bad signs, if they did not perform the sacrifices ordained. These were having dances on tall stilts, with offerings of heads of turkeys, bread and drinks made of maize. They had to offer clay dogs with bread on their backs, the old women dancing with them in their hands, and sacrificing a virgin puppy with a black back.

The devotees had to draw their blood and anoint the stone of Chac-acantun with it. This ceremony and sacrifice they regarded as acceptable to their god Yaxcoc-ahmut.

THE IX NEW YEAR

In the year whose dominical letter was Ix and the augury Sac-sini, after the election of the president for the celebration of the festival, they made an image of the demon called Sac-uvayeyab, and carried it to the piles of stone at the North, where they had left the other one the year before. They then made a statue of the god Itzamna and set that in the president's house, then all together, with the roadway prepared, they went devoutly to the image of Sac-uvayeyab. On arrival they offered incense in the usual way, cut of the head of a fowl, and placed the image on a wooden stand called Sac-hia, and then carried it ceremoniously and with dances they called *alcab-tan kam-ahau*. They brought to the road the usual drinks, and on arriving at the house they set this image before the statue of Itzamna, and there made their offerings, and distributed them; to the statue of Sac-uvayeyab they offered the head of a turkey, patés of quail with other things, and their drink.

Others drew blood and with it anointed the stone of the demon Sac-acantun, and they then kept the idols as they had done the year before, offering them incense until the last day. Then they carried Itzamna to the temple and Sac-uvayeyab to the place of the West to leave him there to be gotten the next year.

The evils the natives feared for the ensuing year if they were negligent in these ceremonies were loss of strength, fainting and ailments of the eyes; it was held a bad year for bread and a good one for cotton. And this year bearing the dominical Ix, and which the Bacab Sac-sini ruled, they held an ill-omened, with many evils destined to occur; for they said there would be great shortage of water, many hot spells that would wither the maize fields, from which would follow great hunger, and from the hunger thefts, and from the thefts slavery for those who had incurred that penalty therefor. From this would come great discords, among themselves or with other towns. They also said that this year would bring changes in the rule of the chiefs or the priests, because of wars and discords.

Another prognostic was that some men who should seek to become chiefs would fail in their aim. They also said that the locusts would come, and depopulate many of their towns through famine. What the evil one ordained that they should do to avert these ills, some or all of which were due to fall on them, was to make an idol of Kinch-ahau Itzamna, which they should put in the temple, where they should burn incense and make many offerings and prayers to the god, together with the drawing of their blood for the anointing of the stone of the demon Sac-acantun. They danced much, and the old women danced as was their custom; in this festival they also built a new oratorio for the demon, or else renewed the old, and gathered there for sacrifices and offerings to him, all going through a solemn revel; for this festival was general and obligatory. There were some very devout persons who of their own volition made another idol like the above, and placed it in other temples, where they made offerings and revels. These revels and sacrifices were held to be very acceptable to the idols, and as remedial for freeing them from the ills indicated as to come.

THE CAUAC NEW YEAR

In the year whose dominical was Cauac and the augury Hosan-ek, after the election of the one to serve as president had been made, they made an image of the demon named Ek-uvayeyab, and carried this to the piles of stone on the West, where they had left the other the year before. They also made a statue of a demon called Vacmitun-ahau, which they put in the president's house in a convenient place, and from there went all together to where the image of Vacmitun-ahau stood, having the road thither all properly prepared. On arriving the priest and the chiefs offered incense, as they were accustomed, and cut off the head of a fowl. After this they took the image on a standard called *yax-ek*, placing on the back of the image a skull and a corpse, and on top a carnivorous bird called *kuch* [vulture], as a sign of great mortality, since they regarded this as a very evil year.

They then carried it thus with their sentiment and devotion, dancing various dances, among which was one like the *cazcarientas*, which they thus called the *xibalba-okot*, meaning the dance of the devil. The cupbearers brought to the road the drink of the chiefs, which they drank and came to the place of the statue Vacmitun-ahau, and then they placed before it the image they brought. Thereupon commenced the offerings, the incense and the prayers, while many drew blood from many parts of the body, to anoint the stone of the demon called Ekel-acantun; thus the fatal days passed, after which they carried Vacmitun-ahau to the temple, and Ek-uvayeyab to the place of the South, to receive it the next year.

This year whose sign is Cauac and which was ruled by the bacab Hosan-ek, they held as one of mortality and very bad, according to the omens; for they said that many hot spells would kill the maize fields, while multitudes of ants and birds would eat up the seeds that had been sown; but since this would not happen in all parts, in some places they would lack food, and in others have it, though with heavy labour. To avoid this the evil one caused them to make four demons called Chichac-chob, Ekbalam-chac, Ahcanuol-cab, Ahbuluc-balam, and set them in the temple where they should offer incense, and burn two balls of the milk or resin called *kik*, together with some iguanas, and bread, a mitre, a bunch of flowers and one of their precious stones. After this, to celebrate the festival, they made a great vault of wood, filling it aloft and on the sides with firewood, leaving doors to enter and go out. Then the most of the men took each two bundles of rods, very dry and long, tied together, and a singer standing on top of the firewood sang and made sound with one of their drums, while those below danced in complete unison and devotion, entering and leaving the doors of that wooden vault; dancing thus until the evening, each left there his bundle, and they then went home to rest and eat.

When the night came on they returned, and with them came a great crowd, because this ceremony was held in great regard. Each then took his bundle of rods, lit it, and each for himself put fire to the firewood, which burned high and quickly. When only the coals were left, they smoothed and spread them out; then those who had danced having come together, some of them began to walk unshod and naked from one side to the other across the hot coals; some of these came off with no lesions whatever, some came burned or half burned. In this way they believed to lie the remedy against the ills and bad auguries, and that this was the service most acceptable to their gods. After this they went off to drink and get intoxicated, for this was called for by the customs of the festival, and by the heat of the fire.

THE CALENDAR

Together **with the characters** of the natives shown above (page 130) they gave names to the days of their months, and from all the months together they made up a kind of calendar, by which they regulated their festivals, their counting and contracts as business, as we do ours; save that the first day of their calendar was not the first day of their year, but came much later; this being the result of the difficulty with which they counted the days of the months all together, as will be seen in the Calendar itself we shall give herein later. The reason is that although the signs and names of the days of their months are twenty, they used to count them from one to thirteen; after the thirteen they return to one again, thus dividing the days of the year into twenty-seven thirteens or triadecads, plus nine days, without the supplementary ones.

With these periodical returns and the complicated count, it is a marvel to see the freedom with which they know how to count and understand things. It is notable that the dominical always falls on the first day of their year, without fail or error, no other of the twenty ever taking that position. They also used this way of counting to bring out by the aid of these characters a certain other count they had for their ages; also other matters which, although they were important for them, do not concern us much here. We shall therefore be content with saying that the character or letter with which they began their count of the days or Calendar is called Hun Imix (One Imix), which is this: and which has no fixed day on which it must fall. For each modifies its own count, and with all this the dominical letter as they have it never fails to fall on the first day of the following year.

Among these people the first day of the year always fell upon our 16th of July, and was the first of their month Pop. Nor is it to be wondered at that this people, however simple as we have found them in many ways, also had ability in these matters and ideas such as other nations; for in the gloss on Ezekiel we find that according to the Romans January began the year, according to the Hebrews April, according to the Greeks March, and according to the Orientals October. But, although they began their year in July, I put their calendar here in the order of ours, and parallel, so that our letters and theirs will come noted, our months and theirs, together with their above-mentioned count of the thirteens, placed in the order of their progression.

And since there is no need for putting the calendar in one place and the festivals in another, I shall place in each of the months its festivals and the observances and ceremonies with which they celebrated it. Thus I shall do as I before promised, giving their calendar and with it telling of their fasts and ceremonies wherewith they made their idols of wood, and other things; all of these things and what else I have told of these people serving no other purpose than to praise the divine goodness which so has permitted and has seen well to remedy in our times. This in order that, in recording them, with Christian entreaties we pray Him for their preservation and progress in true Christianity; and that those whose charge this is may promote and aid this end, so that neither to this people for their sins, nor to ourselves, may there be lacking help; nor may they fail in what has been begun and so return to their misery and vomitings of errors, thus falling into worse a case than before, returning the evil ones we have been able to drive out of their souls, out of which with so laborious care we have been able to drive them, cleansing them and sweeping out their vices and evil customs of the past. And this is not a vain hope, when we see the perdition which after so many years is to he seen in great and very Christian Asia, in the good, Catholic and very august Africa, and the miseries and calamities which today our Europe suffers, and where in our nation and houses we might say that the evangelical prophecies over Jerusalem have been fulfilled, where her enemies encircle her and crowd her almost to the earth. All of this God already had permitted for us, as we stand, were it not that his Church cannot pass, neither that which is said concerning her: *Nisi Dominus reliquisset semen, sicut Sodoma fuissemus.*

MONTHS AND FESTIVALS OF THE MAYA CALENDAR

The first day of Pop (16 July or 12 Kan), which is the first month of the natives, was its New Year, a festival much celebrated among them, because it was general, and of all; thus the whole people together celebrated the festival for all their idols. To do this with the greater solemnity, on this day they renewed all the service things they used, as plates, vases, benches, mats and old garments, and the mantles around the idols. They swept their houses, and threw the sweepings and all these old utensils outside the city on the rubbish heap, where no one dared touch them, whatever his need.

For this festival the chiefs, the priest and the leading men, and those who wished to show their devoutness, began to fast and stay away from their wives for as long time before as seemed well to them. Thus some began three months before, some two, and others as they wished, but none for less than thirteen days. In these thirteen days then, to continence they added the further giving up of salt or pepper in their food; this was considered a grave penitential act among them. In this period they chose the *chacs*, the officials for helping the priest; on the small plaques which the priests had for the purpose, they prepared a great number of pellets of fresh incense for those in abstinence and fasting to burn to their idols. Those who began these fasts, did not dare to break them, for they believed it would bring evil upon them or their houses.

When the New Year came, all the men gathered, alone, in the court of the temple, since none of the women were present at any of the temple ceremonies, except the old women who performed the dances. The women were admitted to the festivals held in other places. Here all clean and gay with their red-coloured ointments, but cleansed of the black soot they put on while fasting, they came. When all were congregated, with the many presents of food and drink they had brought, and much wine they had made, the priest purified the temple, seated in pontifical garments in the middle of the court, at his side a brazier and tablets of incense. The *chacs* seated themselves in the four corners, and stretched from one to the other a new rope, inside of which all who had fasted had to enter, in order to drive out the evil spirit, as I related in 'Method of Baptism and How It Was Celebrated' (page 97). When the evil one had been driven out, all began their devout prayers, and the *chacs* made new fire and lit the brazier; because in the festivals celebrated by the whole community new fire was made wherewith to light the brazier. The priest began to throw in incense, and all came in their order, commencing with the chiefs, to receive incense from the hands of the priest, which he gave them with as much gravity as if he were giving them relics; then they threw it a little at a time into the brazier, waiting until it ceased to burn.

After this burning of the incense, all ate the gifts and presents, and the wine went about until they became very drunk. Such was the festival of the New Year, a ceremony very acceptable to their idols. Afterwards there were others who celebrated this festival, in this month Pop, among their friends, and with the chiefs and the priests, these latter being always first in their banquets and drinking.

In the month Uo (6 August, 6 Kan) the priests, and the physicians and sorcerers (who were one) began, with fasting and the rest, to prepare to celebrate another festival. The hunters and fishermen began to celebrate on the 7th of Sip, each celebrating for himself on his own day. First the priests celebrated their fete, which was called Pocam ['the washing']; gathered in their regalia in the house of the chief, they first cast out the evil spirit as was their custom; after that they brought out their books and spread them upon the fresh leaves they had prepared to receive them. Then with many prayers and very devoutly they invoked an idol they called Kinch-ahau Itzamna, who they said was the first priest, offered him their gifts and burned the pellets of incense upon new fire; meanwhile they dissolved in a vase a little verdigris and virgin water which they say was brought from the forests where no woman had been, and anointed with it the tablets of the books for their purification.

After this had been done, the most learned of the priests opened a book, and observed the predictions for that year, declared them to those present, preached to them a little enjoining the necessary observances, and then assigning this festival for the coming year to the priest or chief who should then perform it; if he should die within the year his sons were under obligation to carry it for the deceased. After this they ate the gifts and food that had been brought, and drank until they were filled; thus they ended this festival, in which at times they gave the dance *okot-uil*.

On the following day (Sip, 25 August, 13 Kan) the physicians and sorcerers gathered in the house of one of them, with their wives. The priest exorcised the evil spirit. After that they opened the wrappings of their medicines, in which they had brought foolish things, including (each of them) small idols of the goddess of medicine whom they called Ixchel, from whom this festival was called Ihcil-Ixchel, as well as certain little stones called am, and with which it was their custom to cast the lots. Then with great devotion they invoked the gods of medicine by their prayers, these being called Itzamna, Cit-bolontun and Ahau-chamahes, the priests offering the incense, burned in braziers with new fire; meanwhile the *chacs* covered the idols and the small stones with a blue bitumen like that of the books of the priests.

After this each one wrapped up the implements of his office, and taking the pouch on his back all danced a dance they called Chantuniah. After the dance the men sat by themselves, and the women by themselves; and after putting over the festival until the next year, they ate the presents, and became drunk without regard; except the priests, who as they say refrained from the wine, to drink it when alone and at their pleasure.

The next day the hunters gathered in the house of one of them, bringing their wives, like the others; the priests came and exorcised the evil spirit in their manner. Then they placed in the centre the materials prepared for the sacrifice of the incense and the new fire, and the blue bitumen. Then with worship the hunters invoked the gods of the chase, Acanum, Suhuy-sib, Sipitabai and others; they distributed the incense, which they then threw in the brazier; while it burned each one took an arrow and the skull of a deer, which the *chacs* anointed with the blue pitch; some then danced with these, as anointed, in their hands, while others pierced their ears and others their tongues, and passed seven leaves of a broadish plant called ac, through the holes. When this was done, the priest first and then the officers of the festival at once made their offerings, and thus dancing they served the wine and became drunk.

Immediately on the following day the fishermen celebrated their festival in the same order as the others, except that what was anointed was the fishing tackle, and they did not pierce the ears but tore them on the sides; they danced a dance called *chohom*, and when all this was done they blessed a tall thick tree trunk and set it up erect. After this festival had been celebrated in the towns, it was the custom for the chiefs to go with many of the people to the coast, where they had great fishing and sport, having taken with them a great quantity of dragnets, hooks and other fishing equipment. The gods who were the patrons of this festival were: Ahkakne-xoi, Ahpua, Ahcitz-amalcum.

In the month Sotz (14 September, 7 Kan) the proprietors of the beehives prepared themselves to celebrate their festival in Tzec (4 October, 1 Kan), and although the chief preparation here was fasting, there was no obligation save on the priest and the officers who assisted therein, and it was voluntary on the part of the rest.

When the day of the festival had come, they all gathered in the appointed house, and did as in the others, except that there was no drawing of blood, since the patrons were the Bacabs, and especially Hobnil. They made many offerings, and especially to the four *chacs* they gave four platters with balls of incense in the middle of each, and painted on the rims with figures of honey, to bring abundance of which was the purpose of the ceremony. They ended it with wine as usual, in plenty, the hive owners giving honey for it in abundance.

In Cuculcan and the Foundation of Mayapan (page 80) was related the departure of Kukulcán from Yucatan, after which some of the natives said he had departed to heaven with the gods, wherefore they regarded him as a god and appointed, a time when they should celebrate a festival for him as such; this the whole country did until the destruction of Mayapan. After that destruction only the province of Maní kept this up, while the other provinces in recognition of what they owed to Kukulcán made presents, one each year, turn and turn about, of four or sometimes five magnificent banners of feathers, sent to Maní; with which they kept this festival in that manner, and not in the former ways.

On the 16th of Xul (24 October, 8 Kan), all the chiefs and priests assembled at Maní, and with them a great multitude from the towns, all of them after preparing themselves by their fasts and abstinences. On the evening of that day they set out in a great procession, with many comedians, from the house of the chief where they had gathered, and marched slowly to the temple of Kukulcán, all duly decorated. On arriving, and offering their prayers, they set the banners on the top of the temple, and below in the court set each of them his idols on leaves of trees brought for this purpose; then making the new fire they began to burn their incense at many points, and to make offerings of viands cooked without salt or pepper, and drinks made from their beans and calabash seeds. There the chiefs and those who had fasted stayed for five days and nights, always burning copal and making their offerings, without returning to their homes, but continuing in prayers and certain sacred dances. Until the first day of Yaxkin these comedians frequented the principal houses, giving their plays and receiving the presents bestowed on them, and then taking all to the temple. Finally, when the five days were passed, they divided the gifts among the chiefs, priests and dancers, collected the banners and idols, returning them to the house of the chief, and thence each one to his home. They said and believed that Kukulcán descended on the last of those days from heaven and received their sacrifices, penances and offerings. This festival they called Chicc-kaban.

In this month of Yaxkin (13 November, 2 Kan) they began to get ready, as usual, for the general festival they would celebrate in Mol, on the day appointed by the priest for all the gods; they called it Olob-sab-kamyax. After they were gathered in the temple and the same ceremonies and incense burning as in the previous festivals had been gone through with, they anointed with the blue pitch all the instruments of all the various occupations, from that of the priest to the spindles of the women, and even the posts of their houses. For this festival they assembled all the boys and girls, and in place of the painting and the ceremonies they gave to each nine little blows on the knuckles of their hands, outside; for the girls this was done by an old woman, vestured in a robe of feathers, who brought them there; from this she was called Ixmol, meaning 'the bringer together'. These blows they gave them that they might grow up expert craftsmen in their fathers' and mothers' occupations. The conclusion was a fine drinking affair, with eating of the offerings, except that we must not believe that the devout old woman was allowed to become so drunk as to lose the feathers of her robe on the road.

In this month the beekeepers held another festival like they did in the month Tzec, to the end that the gods might provide flowers for the bees.

One of the most arduous and difficult things these poor people had to do was the making of images of wood, which they called the gods. Thus they had a particular month designated for this work, and this was the month Mol (3 December, 9 Kan), or some other if the priest said it was right. Those then who wished to make them first consulted the priest, and after taking his counsel went to the artisans; they say that the artisans always excused themselves, believing that either they or someone of their household would die or would suffer heart attacks or strokes; when however they had accepted, the *chacs* whom they had chosen to serve in the matter, together with the priest and the artisan, began their fasts. While they were fasting, he who was to have the idols went himself or else sent to the woods for the material, which was always cedar. When the wood arrived they built a small fenced-in hut of thatch, in which they put the wood and a large urn into which to put the idols, and to keep them covered up while they were working. They put incense to be burned to the four deities called the Acantuns, which they brought and placed at the four cardinal points. They also brought the instruments with which to scarify themselves or draw blood from their ears; and also the tools for carving their black gods. When all these were ready in the hut, the priest, the *chacs* and the artisan shut themselves in the hut, and they began their making the gods, from time to time cutting their ears and anointing the statues herewith, and burning the incense. Thus they worked until they were finished, their families bringing to them their food and needs; during the period they were not to consort with their wives, even in thought; nor could anyone enter that place where they worked.

They worked in much reverence and fear, as they say, making the gods. When they were finished and the idols perfected, the owner made them the finest present he was able, of birds, game and their money, to pay for the labour of those who had made them. Then they removed them from the hut and set them in another enclosure of branches prepared for them in the court. where the priest blessed them with great solemnity, and an abundance of devout prayers; but first the priest and the artisans removed the soot with which they had covered themselves during their fasting. Then having exorcised the evil one and burned the sanctified incense, they put the images wrapped in a cloth in a chest and delivered them to their owner, who very devotedly received them. Afterwards the good priest preached a little on the excellence of the artisans' profession, or making new images of the gods, and on the ills that would have attended them had they not been faithful to the precepts of abstinence and fasting. After that they ate much and drank more.

In whichever of the months Ch'en (23 December, 3 Kan) or Yax (12 January, 10 Kan) were designated by the priest, and on the day set by him, they celebrated a festival they called Oc-na, meaning the 'renovation of the temple', in honour of the *Chacs*, regarded as the gods of the maize fields. In this festival they consulted the predictions of the Bacabs, as we have told at more length in earlier chapters (pages 121–26), and in conformity with the order there given. Each year they celebrated this festival and renewed the idols of terracotta, and their braziers, since it was the custom for each idol to have his own little brazier for burning his incense; and if it was necessary they built a new house, or repaired the old one, placing on the wall the record of these things, with their characters.

January 29: 1 Imix. Here begins the calendar of the natives, saying in their language, Hun Imix.

The hunters, who had celebrated one festival in the month Sip, now celebrated another in the month Sac (1 February, 4 Kan), on a day set by the priest, doing this to appease the anger of the gods against them and their fields because of the blood they shed in their hunting; for they regarded with abhorrence any shedding of blood except in their sacrifices. For this reason, whenever they went to the hunt, they invoked the god and burned incense to him; and if possible later they anointed the faces with blood from the heart of the game.

February 17: 7 Ahau. On whatever day of the year 7 Ahau fell they celebrated a very great festival with incense and offerings, and restrained drinking; and since this was a movable feast it was in the care of the priests to publish it in sufficient time ahead, that they might fast in due manner.

On some one of the days of this month Mac (13 March, 5 Kan) the oldest people celebrated a festival to the *Chacs*, the gods of sustenance, and Itzamna. One or two days ahead of this they performed the following ceremony, which they called tupp-kak ('fire-quenching'). They hunted for as many animals and creatures of the fields as they could, and as there were in the country. With these they gathered in the temple court, where the *chacs* and the priest placed themselves in the corners to exorcise the evil spirit according to custom, and each with a jar of water, as brought there to him. In the middle they placed, set up erect, a large bundle of dry sticks, tied together; then first burning the incense in the braziers they set fire to the sticks, and as they burned they drew out the hearts of the birds and animals, liberally, and threw them into the flames. If they had been unable to get any of the larger animals, such as tigers, lions or caimans, they made hearts out of incense instead. If they had killed any, they brought their hearts for the fire. Then when the hearts were all consumed, the *chacs* extinguished the fire with their jars of water. This and the coining festival were to obtain the needed rains for their maize crops in the ensuing year; they thereupon celebrated the fiesta.

This was done in a different manner from the others, since for this they did not fast, except that the provider of the festival did his fast. When the time arrived, all the townsfolk, the priest and the officials assembled in the temple court, where they had a pyramid of stones, with stairways, all clean and dressed with green branches. The priest then gave the prepared incense to the one providing, and he burned it in the brazier, whereby they said the evil spirit was exorcised. This being done with their accustomed reverence, they spread the lower step of the pyramid with mud from the well, and the other steps with blue pitch.

They used much incense and invoked Itzamna and the *chacs* with prayers and rituals, and made their offerings. When this had been done they took their comfort in eating and drinking what had been offered, confident that their service and invocations would bring a prosperous new year.

During the month Muan (22 April, 6 Kan) the owners of cacao plantations made a festival for the gods Ekchuah, Chac and Hobnil, who were their protectors. To do this they went to the property of one of them, where they sacrificed a dog spotted with the colours of the cacao, burned incense to their idols, and offered up iguanas of the blue sort, with certain bird's feathers, and other game; then they gave to each one of the officers a branch of the cacao fruit. After the sacrifice and the prayers they ate the gifts and drank, but (as they tell) no more than three draughts of wine, no more than this having been brought. After this they went to the house of him who had provided the fiesta, for various diversions.

In this month of Pax (12 May, 13 Kan) they celebrated a festival called Pacum-chac, for which the priests and chiefs of the smaller villages gathered at the larger towns, where they all watched for five nights in the temple of Cit-chac-coh, with prayers, offerings and incense, as has been related of the festival to Kukulcán in the month Xul, in November. Before these days were passed, they all went to the house of their war general, the Nacon (of whom we spoke on page 108), and with great pomp they conducted him to the temple, offering incense to him as to an idol, and then seating and incensing him as if he were a god; there he and they stayed through the five days, during which they ate and drank of the gifts that had been brought to the temple, and performed a great dance in the style of war manoeuvres, called in their language *Holcan-okot*, or the dance of the warriors. After these five days they went on to the fiesta which, since it was for matters of war and victory over their enemies, was very solemn.

First they went through the ceremony and sacrifices of the Fire, as I told under the month Mac; then in the usual manner they drove out the evil spirit with great solemnity. After this came prayers and the offering of gifts and incense, and while they were doing this the chiefs and those who had before assisted in this, again carried the Nacon on their shoulders around the temple, with incense. When they returned with him, the priests sacrificed a dog, drew out its heart and presented it between two platters to the demon, while the *chacs* each broke large jars full of liquor, and with this ended the festival. When it was over they ate and drank the gifts that had been brought, and then reconducted the Nacon to his home, with great ceremony, but without perfumes.

There they held a great fiesta in which the lords and the priests and leading men drank to intoxication, and the rest of the people went to their towns; but the Nacon did not join in the intoxication. On the next day, when the effects of the wine had worn off, all the lords and priests of the towns who had remained at the chief's house and taken part in this last act, received from him a great quantity of incense prepared for the purpose, which had been blessed by the holy priests. He then joined them and gave a long discourse in which with much emphasis he enjoined on them the festivals they should, in their own towns, celebrate for the gods, that the coming year might yield many things for their support. After the address, all departed with much expression of affection and noise, each going to his town and home.

There they busied themselves with the fiestas, which according to the circumstances, continued until the month Pop (21 June, 1 Kan), and which they called Sabacilthan, and performed as follows. They looked through the town for the richest men able to afford the costs of the fiesta, and set a day, to provide the most entertainment during the remaining three months before the new year. They gathered at the house of the feast maker, went through the ceremonies of driving away the evil spirit, burning copal, with offerings and dances, and making themselves such wine kegs, and such was the excess in these fiestas for these three months that it was painful to see them; for they went about scratched and bruised and red-eyed with the drink, all for this love of the wine for which they had destroyed themselves.

It has been told in the preceding chapters how the natives began their year following these 'nameless days', preparing there as with vigils for the celebration of the New Year festival; in the same interval they celebrated the festival of the Uvayeyab demon, for which they left their houses, which otherwise they left as little as possible; they offered besides gifts for the general festival, and counters for their gods and those of the temples. These counters they thus offered they never took for their own use, nor anything that was given to the god, but with them bought incense for burning. During these days they neither combed nor washed, nor otherwise cared for themselves, neither men nor women; neither did they perform any servile or heavy work, fearing lest evil fall on them.

CYCLE OF THE MAYA AND THEIR WRITINGS

Not only did the natives have a count for the year and months, as has been before set out, but they also had a certain method of counting time and their matters by ages, which they counted by twenty-year periods, counting thirteen twenties, with one of the twenty signs in their months, which they call Ahau, not in order, but going backwards as appears in the following circular design. In their language they call these periods *katuns*, with these making a calculation of ages that is marvellous; thus it was easy for the old man of whom I spoke in the first chapter to recall events which he said had taken place 300 years before. Had I not known of this calculation I should not have believed it possible to recall after such a period.

As to who it was that arranged this count of *katuns*, if it was the evil one it was so done as to serve in his honour; if it was a man, he must have been a great idolater, for to these *katuns* he added all the deceptions, auguries and impostures by which these people walked in their misery, completely blinded in error. Thus this was the science to which they gave most credit, held in highest regard, and of which not even all the priests knew the whole. The way they had for counting their affairs by this count, was that they had in the temple two idols dedicated to two of these characters. To the first, beginning the count with the cross above the circular design, they offered worship, with services and sacrifices to secure freedom from ills during the twenty years;

but after ten years of the first twenty had passed, they did no more than burn incense and do it reverence. When the twenty years of the first had passed, they began to follow the fates of the second, making their sacrifices; and then having taken away that first idol, they set up another for veneration during the next ten years.

Verbi gratia: the natives say that the Spaniards finally reached the city of Merida in the year of Our Lord's birth 1541, which was exactly at the first year of the era of Buluc (11) Ahau, which is in that block where the cross stands; also that they arrived in the month Pop, which is the first month of their year. If the Spaniards had not arrived, they would have worshipped the image of Buluc Ahau until the year '51, that is for ten years, and then would have set up another idol for Bolon (9) Ahau up to the year '61, when they would remove it from the temple and replace it with the idol for Vuc Ahau, then following the predictions of Bolon Ahau for another ten years, thus doing with all in their turn. Thus they venerated each *katun* for twenty years, and during ten years they governed themselves by their superstitions and deceits, all of which were so many and such as to hold in error these simple people, that one would have to marvel over it who did not know the things of Nature and the experience the devil possesses in dealing with them.

SIGNIFICANT MAYA BUILDINGS

If the number, grandeur and beauty of its buildings were to count toward the attainment of renown and reputation in the same way as gold, silver and riches have done for other parts of the Indies, Yucatan would have become as famous as Peru and New Spain have become, so many, in so many places, and so well built of stone are they, it is a marvel; the buildings themselves, and their number, are the most outstanding thing that has been discovered in the Indies.

Because this country, a good land as it is, is not today as it seems to have been in the time of prosperity when so many great edifices were erected with no native supply of metals for the work, I shall put here the reasons I have heard given by those who have seen these works. These are that they must have been the subjects of princes who wished to keep them occupied and therefore set them to these tasks; or else that they were so devoted to their idols that these temples were built by community work; or else that since the settlements were changed and thus new temples and sanctuaries were needed, as well as houses for the use of their lords, these being always constructed of wood and thatch; or again, the reason lay in the ample supply in the land of stone, lime and a certain white earth excellent for building use, so that it would seem an imaginary tale, save to those who have seen them.

It may be that this country holds a secret that up to the present has not been revealed, or which the natives of today cannot tell. To say that other nations compelled these people to such building, is not the answer, because of the evidences that they were built by the natives themselves; this is bared to view in one out of the many and great buildings that exist, where on the walls of the bastions there still remain figures of men naked save for the long girdles over the loins called in their language *ex*, together with other apparel the natives of today still wear, worked in very hard cement.

While I was living there, in a building we were demolishing there was found a large jar with three handles, adorned with figures applied on the outside; within, among the ashes of a cremated body, we found three counters of fine stone, such as the natives today use as money, all showing the people were natives. It is clear that if such they were, they were of higher grade than those of today, and greater in bodies and strength. This shows more clearly here in Izamal than elsewhere, there being here, as I say, today on the bastions figures in semi-relief, made of cement, and of men of great height. The same is true of the extremities of the arms and legs of the man whose ashes we found in the jar I have referred to; these also were very thick, and their burning a marvel. We see the same thing on the steps of the buildings, here only in Izamal and Mérida, of a good two palms in height.

Here in Izamal is a building, among the others, of a startling height and beauty. It has twenty steps, each more than two palms in height and in breadth, and being over 100 feet in length. These steps are of very large carved stones, although now much worn and damaged by time and water. Around them, as is shown by the curved line, is very strong dressed stone wall; at one and a half times the height of a man there is a cornice of beautiful stone going all the way around, from which the work continues to the height of the first stairway and a plaza.

From this plaza there rises another stairway like the first, but not so long nor with so many steps, again with an encircling wall. Above these steps there is another fine small platform, on which, close to the surrounding wall, is a very high mound with steps facing the south like the other great stairs, and on top of this a beautiful finely worked chapel of stone. I went to the top of this chapel, and Yucatan being a flat country I could see as far as the eye could reach, an amazing distance, as far as the sea. There were eleven or twelve of these buildings at Izamal, this being the largest, and all near together. There is no memory of the builders, who seem to have been the first inhabitants. It is eight leagues from the sea, in a beautiful site, good country and district, and so in 1549, with some importunity, we had the natives build a house for St Anthony on one of these structures. There and all around great benefit has come in its Christianity; so that two good communities have been established in this place, distinct from each other.

The second of the chief ancient structures, such that there is no record of their builders, are those at Tiho, thirteen leagues from those at Izamal, and like them eight leagues from the sea; and there are traces of there having been a fine paved road from one to the other. The Spaniards established a city here, and called it Mérida, from the strangeness and grandeur of the buildings; the chief one of which I shall [describe]. It must be noted that it is a squared site of great size, more than two runs of a horse. On the east front the stairway begins at the ground level, with seven steps as high as those at Izamal; on the other three sides, the south, west and north, there runs a very broad strong wall. On top of this first mass, all squared and of dry stone, and flat, there starts again on the east side another stairway, 28 to 30 feet further in than the other stairway, as I judge, and with steps equally large. On the north and south, but not on the west, it is again set back the same distance, with two strong walls reaching the height of the stairway, and continuing until they meet those of the west face, forming a great mass of dry stone in the center, built by hand, of an amazing height and greatness.

On the level top are buildings in the following manner: six feet back of the stairway is a long range not reaching to the ends, of very fine stonework, made up of cells on each side, 12 feet long by eight wide; the doors of these have no sign of facings or hinges for closing, but are flat and of stone elaborately worked, the whole marvellously built, and the tops of the doorways formed of single large stones. In the middle is a passageway like the arch of a bridge; above the doors of the cells there projected a relief of worked stone the whole length of the structure. Above this was a line of small pillars, half inset in the wall with the outer part rounded, and reaching to the level of the cell roofs. Above these there was another relief extending the whole length of the range; and then came the terrace, finished with a very hard stucco made with the water from the bark of a certain tree.

On the north was another range with cells, the same as the above, but the whole only half the length. On the west was another line of the cells, pierced at the fourth or fifth by an arcade going clear through the whole, like the one in the east front; then a round, rather tall building; then another arcade, and the rest cells like the others. This range crosses the whole court not quite in the centre, thus making two courts, one to the back on the west, the other on the east, surrounded by four ranges as described. The last of these ranges however, to the south, is quite different. This consists of two sections, arched along the front like the rest, the front being a corridor of very thick pillars topped by very beautifully worked single stones. In the middle is a wall against which comes the arch of the two rooms, with two passageways from one to the other; the whole is thus enclosed above and serves as a retreat.

About two good stone throws distant from this edifice is another very high and beautiful court, containing three finely ornamented pyramids, on top of them chapels, arched in the fashion they were used to employ. Quite a distance away was a pyramid, so large and beautiful that even after it had been used to build a large part of the city they founded around it, I cannot say that it shows any signs of coming to an end.

The buildings at Tikoch are not so many nor so sumptuous as many of these others, although they were good and noteworthy; I only mention them here on account of the great population there must have been, as I have before had to relate; thus I leave this here. These buildings are three leagues from Izamal toward the east, and seven leagues from Chichen Itza.

Chichen Itza, then, is a fine site, ten leagues from Izamal and eleven from Valladolid. Here as the old men of the natives say, there reigned three lords, brothers who (as they recall to have been told them by their ancestors) came from the land to the west, and gathered in these places a great settlement or communities and people whom they ruled for some years in great peace, and with justice. They greatly honoured their god, and thus erected many magnificent buildings; especially one, the greatest.

They say that these lords lived as celibates and with great propriety, being highly esteemed and obeyed by all while they so lived. In the course of time one of them failed, so that he died; although the natives say that he went away by the port of Bacalar, out of the country. However that was, his absence resulted in such a lowering among those who ruled after him that partisan dissensions entered the realm; they lived dissolutely and without restraint, to such a degree that the people came to hate them so greatly that they killed them, overthrew the regime and abandoned the site. The buildings and the sites, both beautiful, and only ten leagues from the sea, with fertile fields and districts all about, were deserted.

The principal edifice has four stairways looking to the four directions of the world, and 33 feet wide, with 91 steps to each that are killing to climb. The steps have the same rise and width as we give to ours. Each stairway has two low ramps level with the steps, two feet broad and of fine stonework, like all the rest of the structure. The structure is without corners, because starting from the base it narrows in, as shown, away from the ramps of the stairs, with round blocks rising by stages in a very graceful manner.

When I saw it there was at the foot of each side of the stairways the fierce mouth of a serpent, curiously worked from a single stone. When the stairways thus reach the summit, there is a small flat top, on which was a building with four rooms, each having a door in the middle, and arched above. The one at the north is by itself, with a corridor of thick pillars. In the centre is a sort of interior room, following the lines of the outside of the building, with a door opening into the corridor at the north, closed in the top by wooden beams; this served for burning the incense. At the entrance of this doorway or of the corridor, there is a sort of arms sculptured on a stone, which I could not well understand.

Around this structure there were, and still today are, many others, well built and large; all the ground about them was paved, traces being still visible, so strong was the cement of which they were made. In front of the north stairway, at some distance, there were two small theatres of masonry, with four staircases, and paved on top with stones, on which they presented plays and comedies to entertain the people.

From the court in front of these theatres there goes a beautiful broad paved way, leading to a well two stone throws across. Into this well they were and still are accustomed to throw men alive as a sacrifice to the gods in times of drought; they held that they did not die, even though they were not seen again. They also threw in many other offerings of precious stones and things they valued greatly; so if there were gold in this country, this well would have received most of it, so devout were the natives in this.

This well is seven long fathoms deep to the surface of the water, more than 100 feet wide, round, of natural rock marvellously smooth down to the water. The water looks green, caused as I think by the trees that surround it; it is very deep. At the top, near the mouth, is a small building where I found idols made in honour of all the principal buildings in the land, like the Pantheon at Rome. I found sculptured lions, vases and other things, so that I do not understand how anyone can say that these people had no tools. I also found two immense statues of men, carved of a single stone, nude save for the waist-covering the natives use. The heads were peculiar, with rings such as the natives use in their ears, and a collar that rested in a depression made in the chest to receive it, and wherewith the figure was complete.

MAYA SACRIFICES

The calendar festivals of this people that have been described above show us what and how many they were, and wherefor and how they were celebrated. But because their festivals were only to secure the goodwill or favour of their gods, or else holding them angry, they made neither more nor bloodier ones. They believed them angry whenever they were molested by pestilences, dissensions, or droughts or similar ills, and then they did not undertake to appease the demons by sacrificing animals, nor making offerings only of their food and drink, or their own blood and self-afflictions of vigils, fasts and continence; instead, forgetful of all natural piety and all law of reason they made sacrifices of human beings as easily as they did of birds, and as often as their accursed priests or the *chilánes* said it was necessary, or as it was the whim or will of their chiefs. And since there is not here the great population there is in Mexico, nor were they after the fall of Mayapan ruled by one head but by many, there were no such mass killings of men; nevertheless they still died miserably, since each town had the authority to sacrifice whomever the priests, or the chilán, or the chief saw fit; and to do this they had in their temples their public places as if it were the one thing of most importance in the world for the preservation of the State.

In addition to this slaughter in their towns, they had those accursed sanctuaries of Chichen Itza and Cozumel whither they sent an infinite number of poor creatures for sacrifice, one thrown from a height, another to have his heart torn out. From all such miseries may the merciful Lord see fit to free us for ever, He who saw fit to sacrifice himself to the Father, on the cross for all men.

THE TOLTECS

Désiré Charnay (1828–1915) was a French archaeologist, explorer and photographer. He is best known for his extensive work in the field of Mesoamerican archaeology. His book *Ancient Cities of the New World*, of which we present selected extracts here, published in 1883, is a chronicle of his journeys and an account of the archaeological sites he explored, including cities of the Aztec, Maya and other Mesoamerican civilizations.

Charnay was an early adopter of photography as a means of documentation, and his photographs of archaeological sites were a valuable contribution to the study of Mesoamerican cultures. His work helped to popularize the study of these ancient civilizations in Europe and provided essential visual records of the sites he visited.

As for Charnay's perspectives on Mesoamerica, it is important to keep in mind that he was a product of his time and his European background. This perspective led him to search for similarities or connections between the Toltecs and the ancient Mediterranean civilizations; not the approach taken today, of course: modern historians emphasize the importance of understanding the Toltecs within their own cultural context. And although Charnay's work was ground-breaking in its use of photography and documentation of archaeological sites, he gave little weight to indigenous sources, oral histories or local knowledge, instead relying on his own interpretations and the accounts of other European scholars. At times, Charnay's work on the Toltecs conflates them with other Mesoamerican cultures, resulting in overgeneralizations or misattributions. The Toltecs are often portrayed as the direct predecessors of the Maya and the Aztecs, with a strong emphasis on their influence in the region. While there is evidence of cultural continuity and influence, we now have a much more nuanced understanding of the complex relationships between different Mesoamerican cultures and the unique contributions and characteristics of each. As with any historical source, it is crucial to approach Charnay's work critically and in the context of more recent research and discoveries in the field of Mesoamerican archaeology.

Despite these limitations, Charnay's *Ancient Cities of the New World* remains an important historical document in the study of Mesoamerican archaeology. His extensive documentation of the sites he visited, along with his pioneering use of photography, has provided invaluable information for subsequent generations of scholars.

ANCIENT CITIES OF THE NEW WORLD

WHO WERE THE TOLTECS?

The Toltecs were one of the Nahuan tribes, which from the seventh to the fourteenth century spread over Mexico and Central America. Their existence has been denied by various modern historians, although all American writers agree that the numerous bands which followed them in the country received their civilization from them. It must be admitted, however, that our knowledge rests chiefly on traditionary legends full of anachronisms, transmitted to us by the nations that came after them; but it will be our care to fill up the enormous discrepancies to be met with at almost every page, by the monuments it has been our good fortune to bring to light. Two writers, Ixtlilxochitl and Mariano Veytia, have written about this people: the first in his *Historia chichimeca* and *Relación histórica de la nación tulteca*, the second in his *Historia antigua de México*; the latter being more explicit, it is from him that we will chiefly borrow, without neglecting, however, other chroniclers. Both made use of the same documents, drew from the same sources, the traditionary legends of their country; and Veytia, besides his own, had access to Botturini's valuable collection of Mexican manuscripts, so that he was well acquainted with American antiquities. Ixtlilxochitl, on the other hand, as might be expected, in writing the history of his ancestors, whose language he understood and whose hieroglyphs he could decipher, is inspired by patriotic zeal; and it will be found that these historians have just claims to our admiration for the compass of their inquiries, and the sagacity with which they conducted them.

A third writer, Ramirez [we assume Charnay is referring here to José Fernando Ramírez (1804–71)], by far the most illustrious of those who have treated the same subject, speaking of the two historians who preceded him, says: 'I am not claiming infallibility for our historians, yet it must surely be conceded that, if no credence is given to our own, the same measure must be meted out to all the traditions of other countries, for neither Diodorus, Josephus, Livy, Tacitus, nor other historians, are able to bring the array of documents with which our history abounds in support of their assertions [...]. Mexican history and biography, like those of other nations, are founded on tradition and historical documents; than which none are better authenticated or more trustworthy.'

Veytia, like all historians of that time, places the primitive home of the Toltecs in Asia, to make his account agree with Genesis, where it is said that after the destruction of the Babylonian Tower, 'The Lord scattered the sons of men upon the face of all the earth.' According to him, they crossed Tartary and entered America through the Behring Straits, by means of large flat canoes, and square rafts made of wood and reeds; the former are described, and called *acalli*, 'water houses', in their manuscripts. Directing their course southward, they built their first capital, Tlapallan, 'coloured', subsequently Huehue-Tlapallan, to distinguish it from a later Tlapallan. Huehue-Tlapallan was the cradle whence originated the various tribes which peopled America. Each tribe was called after the father or chief of the family, who was also its ruler; hence came the Olmecs, from Olmecatl; the Xicalancas, from Xicalantl, etc.; it is uncertain whether the Chichemecs derived their appellation from Cichen, the man, or Chichen, the town in Yucatan.

The Toltecs, by the common consent of historians, were the most cultured of all the Nahua tribes, and better acquainted with the mode of perpetuating the traditions of their origin and antiquities. To them is due the invention of hieroglyphs and characters, which, arranged after a certain method, reproduced their history on skins of animals, on aloe and palm leaves, or by knots of different colours, which they called *nepohualtzitzin*, 'historical events', and also by simple allegorical songs. This manner of writing history by maps, songs and knots, was handed down from father to son, and thus has come to us.

Tlacatzin was the next city they built; and here, after thirteen years of warfare, they separated from the main body of the nation and migrated some 70 miles to the south, where in 604 [CE] they founded Tlapallanco [or Tlapallanconco], 'small Tlapallan', in remembrance of their first capital. But the arrival of fresh immigrants caused them to remove further south, and, under the command of their wise man, Hueman, 'the Strong Hand', who is endowed with power, wisdom and intelligence, the Toltecs set out in 607, and marked their progress by building Jalisco, where they remained eight years; then Atenco, where they were five years; and twenty years at Iztachuexuca. In after times other Nahuan tribes followed them by different routes, as the ruins in New Mexico and the Mexican Valley everywhere attest.

Las Casas Grandes, the settlements in the Sierra Madre, the ruins of Zape, of Quemada, recalling the monuments at Mitla, others in Queretaro, together with certain features in the building of temples and altars, which remind one of the Mexican manuscripts from which the Toltec, Aztec and Yucatec temple was built, make it clear that the civilizing races came from the north-west; and Guillemin Tarayre, like ourselves, sees in the *calli* the embryo of the *teocalli*, which developed into the vast proportions of the pyramidal mounds found at Teotihuacan, Cholula, in Huasteca, Misteca, Tabasco and Yucatan.

The next city built by the Toltecs was Tollatzinco, where they remained sixteen years; and finally settled at Tollan or Tula, which became their capital. The date of its foundation is variously given; Ixtlilxochitl sets it down at 556, [historian Francisco Javier] Clavigero 667 and Veytia assigns 713 BCE as the probable date. In our estimation, this divergence of opinion confirms rather than invalidates the existence of this people.

When the Aztecs reached Anahuac, Atzacapotzalco, Colhuacan and Texcuco were small flourishing states. They had inherited from the Toltecs many useful arts, their code of morals, philosophy and religion, which in their turn they taught the Aztecs, so that the institutions and customs of these different tribes were common to all; and in default of documents which have been lost, we ascribe nearly all the historians of the Conquest relate of the Aztecs, whom they found the dominant race, as applicable to the Toltecs, the fountain of all progress both on the plateaus and in Central America, where we shall follow them. As for the Aztecs, who settled for the first time on the Mexican lake at the beginning of the fourteenth century, they were at that period nothing but a rude, barbarous tribe, and to the last day of their political existence they remained a military caste.

INTRODUCING TOLTEC CULTURE AND MYTHOLOGY

All the Toltecs did was excellent, graceful and delicate; exquisite remains of their buildings covered with ornamentation, together with pottery, toys, jewels and many other objects are found throughout New Spain, for, says Sahagun, 'they had spread everywhere'. Both Veytia and Ixtlilxochitl ascribe a common origin to the Nahua, Toltec, Acolhuan and Mexican tribes. 'The Toltecs were good architects and skilled in mechanic arts; they built great cities like Tula, the ruins of which are still visible; whilst at Totonac they erected palaces of cut stone, ornamented with designs and human figures, recalling their chequered history.'

'At Cuernavaca' (probably Xochicalco), he adds, 'were palaces entirely built of cut stone, without mortar, beams, girders, or wood of any kind.' [Historian Fray Juan de] Torquemada speaks of the Toltecs in the same terms, observing that 'they were supposed to have come from the west, and to have brought with them maize, cotton, seeds and the vegetables to be found in this country; that they were cunning artists in working gold, precious stones and other curiosities.' On the other hand, Clavigero thinks 'they were the first nation mentioned in American traditions, and justly celebrated among the Nahuas, for their culture and mechanic skill; and that the name Toltec came to be synonymous for architect and artificer.' Quotations might be multiplied *ad infinitum*, but the foregoing will suffice to prove the existence of this people and their peculiar genius.

Their law of succession was somewhat curious: each king was to rule one of their centuries [calendar cycles] of fifty-two years; if he lived beyond it he was required to give up the crown to his son, and, in case of death, a joint regency took the reins of government for the remaining years. Their sacred book, *Teomoxtli*, contained both their annals and their moral code. It is conjectured, with what evidence is uncertain, that they worshipped an 'unknown god', perhaps the origin of the 'unknown god' to whom the King of Texcuco raised an altar. Their principal deities, however, were Tonacatecuhtli, the 'Sun' and the 'Moon', to whom temples were first erected; to these they added Tlaloc, god of rain, and Quetzalcoatl, god of air and wisdom.

Tlaloc, according to Torquemada, was the oldest deity known, for when the Acolhuans, who followed the Chichemecs, arrived in the country, he was found on the highest summit of the Texcucan mountain. His paradise, called Tlalocan, was a place of delight, an Eden full of flowers and verdure; whilst the surrounding hills were called 'Tlaloc mounts'. He was emphatically the god of many places, of many names, and numerous personifications; as Popocatepetl he presided over the formation of clouds and rain, he was the 'world-fertilizer', the 'source of favourable weather', sometimes represented dark in colour, his face running with water to signify a rich yielding soil; he carried a thunderbolt in his right hand, a sign of thunder and lightning; whilst his left held a tuft of variegated feathers, emblem of the different hues of our globe; his tunic was blue hemmed with gold, like the heavens after rain. His wife, Chalchiuhtlicue, goddess of waters, was represented wearing a blue petticoat, the colour of the mountain Iztaccihuatl when seen at a distance, which was sacred to her.

Most historians mention Quetzalcoatl, at first a generic name, whom posterity endowed with every virtue and deified. His great temple was at Tula, but he was also worshipped in

Yucatan under the name of Cukulcan [Kukulkan], having the same meaning with Quetzalcoatl. He had travelled thither with a branch of the Toltecs, which, advancing from west to east, had taken Tabasco on their way, and occupied the peninsula earlier than a second branch, which entered the country by a southern route, under the command of their chief Tutulxiu, and became the rival and enemy of the first, whose reigning family were the Cocomes, or 'auditors.' The worship of Quetzalcoatl extended on the plateaus and in the peninsula, where the chiefs claimed to be descended from him. The symbol by which he is best known is 'feathered serpent'; but he was severally called Huemac, the 'Strong Hand', the 'white-bearded man', whose mantle was studded with crosses, or dressed in a tiger's skin; 'god of air', when he was the companion of Tlaloc, whose path he swept, causing a strong wind to prevail before the rainy season; and also a youthful, beardless man, etc. The various attributes of Quetzalcoatl and Tlaloc developed according to the people, the country and epoch. Such transformations have been observed among all nations: in India the great Agni was at first but the spark produced by rubbing two pieces of wood together, which became cloud, dawn, the sun, the flash, Indra, etc. With the Greeks, Apollo was the god of light, poetry, music, medicine, etc. The Christian religion presents the same phenomenon; for we have the Ancient of Days, the Dove, the Lamb, the Vine.

Thus Tlaloc, god of rain, is sometimes seen on ancient vases, his eyes circled with paper, his face running with water; or as an embryo cross, a perfect cross; and again in the form of a man lying on his back, supporting a vase to collect rain. The latter representation is found in Mexico, Tlaxcala and Yucatan. Several writers mention that crosses were found throughout Mexico, Yucatan and Tabasco, being another and later personification of Tlaloc. The *cultus* of the cross is of great antiquity and almost universal, for we find it in Greece, in India, on pottery of the Bronze Period.

QUETZALCOATL

The same may almost be said of the serpent. It was reverenced in Egypt, in America, and is found at the beginning of Genesis; whilst in the north-west of India, the Nagas were serpent worshippers, whose great ancestor Naga was supposed to have been present at the Creation as Genius of the Ocean. He was the god of wisdom, the titular deity of mankind; and we find him at Boeroe-Boedor, in Java, beautifully sculptured on a bas-relief, where Buddha is seen crossing the seas on a lotus wreath, whilst close to him two immense serpents (Nagas) are raising their heads towards him in token of reverence. He is also worshipped in Cambodia, and his image is reproduced on the magnificent monuments of Angcor-Tom.

The festival which was celebrated in honour of Quetzalcoatl during the *teoxihuitl*, 'sacred year', was preceded by a severe fasting of eighty days, during which the priests devoted to his service were subjected to horrible penances. He reigned successively at Izamal, in Yucatan, Chichen Itza and Mayapan, under the name of Cukulcan. To this god were ascribed the rites of confession and penance.

TOLTEC RELIGION AND CALENDAR

The religion of the Toltecs was mild, like their disposition; no human blood ever stained their altars, their offerings consisting of fruits, flowers and birds; nevertheless, their laws, which were the same for all classes, were stringent and severe.

Polygamy was forbidden, and kings themselves were not allowed concubines, whilst their priests were deserving of the respect which was shown them from prince and peasant alike. They had sculptors, mosaists, painters and smelters of gold and silver; and by means of moulds knew how to give metals every variety of shape; their jewellers and lapidaries could imitate all manner of animals, plants, flowers, birds, etc. Cotton was spun by the women, and given a brilliant colouring both from animal and mineral substances; it was manufactured of every degree of fineness, so that some looked like muslin, some like cloth, and some like velvet. They had also the art of interweaving with these the delicate hair of animals and birds' feathers, which made a cloth of great beauty.

Their calendar was adopted by all the tribes of Anahuac and Central America; it divided the year into eighteen months of twenty days each, adding five intercalary days to make up the full number of 365 days; these belonged to no month, and were regarded as unlucky. Both months and days were expressed by peculiar signs; and as the year has nearly six hours in excess of 365 days, they provided for this by intercalating six days at the end of four years, which formed leap year. *Tlapilli*, 'knots', were cycles of thirteen years; four of these cycles was a century, which they called *xiuhmolpilli*, 'binding up of knots', represented by a quantity of reeds bound together.

Besides the 'bundle' of fifty-two years, the Toltecs had a larger cycle of 104 years, called 'a great age', but not much used. The whole system rested on the repetition of the signs denoting the years, enabling one by means of dots to determine accurately to what cycle or what century each year belonged. And as these signs stood differently in each cycle, confusion was impossible; for the century being indicated by a number showing its place in the cycle, the dots would make it easy to determine to what age any given year belonged, according to its place at knot first, second, third, or fourth.

Thus for instance, the year *tecpatl* 'flint', *calli* 'house', *tochtli* 'rabbit' and *acatl* 'reed', beginning the great cycle, would have one, five, nine, thirteen dots in the first series; four, eight, twelve, in the second; three, seven, fourteen, in the third; and two, six, ten, in the fourth series, which would come first in the new cycle, and the latter having its appropriate sign would enable one to see at once that 'Flint' 12 was the twelfth year in the second series of the first cycle or century; that 'Flint' 2 was the second year in the fourth series of the first cycle, etc.

It will be seen later that the hieroglyph *calli* is the outline of the Toltec palace and temple, the foundation of his architecture, which never varies, and which we shall find in all monuments, whether we travel north or south, on the plateaus or in the lowlands; so that had everything else been destroyed, we might nevertheless pronounce with safety that all the monuments in North America were of Toltec origin. The genius of a nation, like that of an individual, has generally one dominant note, traceable through the various expressions of her art. India has topes and pagodas, Egypt sphinxes and hypostyle chambers, Greece three orders of columns. North America has only a plain wall ending with two projecting cornices having an upright or slanting frieze, more or less ornamented but of no appreciable difference.

TOLTEC CEREMONIES

A description of the ceremonies which took place at the end of every great cycle will find here a natural place, and enable us to understand subsequent events.

The Aztecs celebrated their great festival of the new fire at the end of each century [cycle] of fifty-two years, called by Sahagun *toxiuilpilli*, and by others *xiuhmolpilli*. As the end of the century drew near they were filled with apprehension, for if the fire failed to be rekindled, a universal dissolution was expected to follow. In their despair at such a contingency they threw away their idols, destroyed their furniture and domestic utensils, and suffered all fires to go out. A lofty mountain near Iztapalapan, some two leagues from Mexico, was the place chosen for kindling the new fire, which was affected by the friction of two sticks placed on the breast of [a] victim. The fire was soon communicated to a funeral pile, on which the body of the victim was placed and consumed. This ceremony always took place at midnight, and as the light mounted up towards heaven shouts of joy burst forth from the multitudes who covered the hills, the housetops and terraces of the temples, their eyes directed towards the mountain of sacrifice. Couriers, with torches lighted at the blazing fire, rapidly bore them to the inhabitants of the surrounding districts, whilst every part of the city was lighted with bonfires. The following days were given up to festivity, the houses were cleansed and whitewashed, the broken vessels were replaced by new ones, and the people dressed in their gayest apparel. If we except human sacrifice, this must have been a Toltec ceremony.

TULA AND THE PYRAMID OF THE SUN

Tula **extended over a plain** intersected by a muddy river winding round the foot of Mount Coatepetl, which commanded the city. [...]

First in order are three fragments of caryatides: one, a gigantic statue which we reproduce, is about 7 feet high; the head and upper part of the body below the hips are wanting, the legs are 1 foot 3 inches in diameter, and the feet 4 feet long. The two embroidered bits below the waist were no doubt the ends of the royal *maxtli*, the exact copy of which we shall see later on bas-reliefs in Chiapas, Palenque and Lorillard City. The greaves, of leather bands, are passed between the toes and fastened on the instep and above it by large knots, recalling the Roman *cacles*. This statue is of black basalt, like all the other fragments; and although exceedingly rude and archaic in character, is not wanting in beauty in some of its details. Next comes a column in two pieces, lying on the ground, having a round tenon which fitted closely into the mortise and ensured solidity; it is the only specimen we have found where such care had been bestowed.

The carving on the outward portion of the column consists of feathers or palms, whilst the reverse is covered with scales of serpents arranged in parallel sections. This fragment answers Sahagun's description of the columns of a temple dedicated to Quetzalcoatl, already mentioned, where rattlesnakes formed the ornamentation. It is also interesting from the fact that we shall see a similar column at Chichen Itza in a temple of the same god. Here also among other fragments I noticed a Greek column with a Doric capital, but on which I dare not pronounce definitely. All we can say is that it shows the marvellous building instinct of the Toltecs, and that we found some remains of a like description in the Yucatan peninsula. By far the most interesting object seen here, on account of the study and the archaeological issues it entails, is a large carved stone ring about 6 feet 5 inches in diameter, having a hole in the centre some 10 inches in circumference, evidently a tennis ring.

HISTORY OF TENNIS

Tennis, *tlacheo, tlachtli,* was first known in Anahuac and transmitted to the Chichemecs, Acolhuans and Aztecs by the Toltecs, who carried it with them to Tabasco, Yucatan, Uxmal and Chichen; and in the latter place we found a perfect tennis court with one ring still in place.

We must turn to Torquemada for full particulars respecting this national game, which was played in buildings of so typical a character as to be easily recognized. It consists of two thick parallel walls 32 feet high, at a distance of 98 feet from each other, having a ring fixed in the walls 22 feet hight; whilst at each extremity of the court stood a small temple in which preliminary ceremonies were performed before opening the game. It was played with a large India rubber ball; the rules required the player to receive it behind, not to let it touch the ground, and to wear a tight-fitting leather suit to make the ball rebound. But the greatest feat was to send the ball through the ring, when a scramble, a rush and much confusion followed, the winner having the right to plunder the spectators of their valuables. Sending the ball through the ring required so much dexterity, that he who succeeded was credited with a bad conscience or supposed to be doomed to an early death. Tennis seems to have been in such high repute with the natives that it was not confined to individuals, but also played between one city and another, and accompanied, says Veytia, by much betting, when they staked everything they possessed, even their liberty. But this writer errs in ascribing the game to the Aztecs in honour of their god Huitzilopochtli, as we shall show.

SIGNIFICANT FINDINGS AT TULA

Among other objects which we found at Tula is a large curiously carved shell of mother-of-pearl; the carving recalls Tizoc's stone, and notably the bas-reliefs at Palenque and Ocosinco in Chiapas; also two bas-reliefs, one in a rock outside the town, the other, by far the most valuable, in the wall of a private house, but very old and much injured, representing a full-face figure and another in profile; their nose, beard and dress are similar to those described by Veytia in the following passage: 'The Toltecs were above middle height, and owing to this they could be distinguished in later times from the other aborigines. Their complexion was clear, their hair thicker than the nations who followed them, although less so than the Spaniards. This is still observable among the few who remain claiming Toltec descent.'

These remains are priceless in every respect because of their analogy and intimate connection with all those we shall subsequently discover, forming the first links in the chain of evidence respecting our theory of the unity of American civilization, which it is our object to prove in the course of this work.

On beholding these caryatides, the question naturally arises as to what monument they were intended for; and in turning to Veytia, we read that under the Emperor Mitl (979–1035 CE) the Toltecs reached the zenith of their power; that their empire extended over 1,000 miles, bordering on the Atlantic and Pacific Oceans; and that the population was so dense as to cause the soil to be cultivated on the highest mountains, whilst an influential priesthood performed the sacred rites within innumerable sanctuaries.

The great cities of the high plateaus were Teotihuacan and Cholula, as later Palenque, Izamal and Cozumel were those of the warm region. This emperor, jealous of the flourishing state and religious superiority of Teotihuacan, 'the habitation of the gods', wished to set up a new and rival deity for the veneration of his people; to this end he chose the songstress of the marsh, the 'Frog', whom he presented as the goddess of waters. And that the new deity should be ushered in with due pomp and solemnity, he had a magnificent temple built in her honour, and her gold statue placed within the temple, covered with emeralds, the size of a palm, and cunningly worked so as to imitate nature. Up to that time, temples had been large mounds erected on the summits of mountains, like that of Tlaloc, or on artificial pyramids like that of Teotihuacan, where the idols were exposed to the elements; that of the Frog was the first which was built with stones and given a rectangular shape, having a kind of solid vault (*boveda*), also of stone, which by a skilful arrangement covered the whole edifice.

Here, then, we have a very plain description of the Indian vault, the Yucatec vault, seen by Guillemin Tarayre in the tombs at Las Casas Grandes, mentioned by Ixtlilxochitl as the distinguishing feature in the monuments of Toluca and Cuernavaca, and by Humboldt at Cholula in the following passage: 'On visiting the interior of the pyramid, I recognized a mortuary chamber, having the bricks of the ceiling so arranged as to diminish the pression of the roof. As the aborigines were unacquainted with the vault, they provided for it by placing horizontally and in gradual succession very large bricks, the upper slightly overlapping the lower, and in this way replaced the Gothic vault.' This remarkable writer further says, that 'Yucatan and Guatemala are countries where the people had come from Atylan and reached a certain degree of civilization.'

PALPAN AND THE TOLTECS

The plateau on the Palpan hill was occupied by a royal park, and maybe those of a few notables. Its direction is south-west, north-west, about a mile in length and half a mile in breadth, growing to a point towards the south-west, and fenced on two sides by a natural wall of perpendicular rocks overhanging the river. The plateau is covered with mounds, pyramids and esplanades, showing that here were the royal villas, temples and public edifices, but no trace of building, wall or ruin, is visible, for the whole area is shrouded with immense cactuses, nopals, gorambullos, gum trees and mesquites, amongst which towers the *biznaga*, a cactus which grows here to nearly 10 feet high by 6 feet wide. I was shown a plant of this kind near Pachuca, in which an Indian couple have established themselves.

The summits of pyramids, called *mogotes* by the natives, were always occupied by temples and palaces; the largest ... must have served as basements for the temples of the Sun and Moon.

I began my excavations by sounding the small mound ... to the north-east, where the side of a wall was visible; and I found everywhere the ground connecting houses, palaces and gardens, thickly coated with cement: but in the inner rooms the flooring was of red cement. The rubbish was cleared away, and in a few days a complete house was unearthed, consisting of several apartments of various size, nearly all on different levels; having frescoed walls, columns, pilasters, benches and cisterns, recalling a Roman *impluvium*, whilst flights of steps and narrow passages connected the various apartments. We had brought to light a Toltec house!

HOW THE TOLTECS LIVED

picked out of the rubbish many curious things: huge baked bricks, from one foot to nine inches by two and a two and a half in thickness; filters, straight and curved water pipes, vases and fragments of vases, enamelled terracotta cups, bringing to mind those at Tenenepanco; seals, one of which (an eagle's head) I had engraved for my personal use; bits which were curiously like old Japanese china; moulds, one having a head with a huge plait and hair smoothed on both sides of her face, like an old maid; besides innumerable arrowheads and knives of obsidian strewing the ground. In fact, a whole civilization.

This house was built on a somewhat modified natural elevation; the various apartments follow the direction of the ground and are ranged on different levels, numbering from zero elevation for the lowest to 8 feet for the highest. The walls are perpendicular, the roofs flat; and a thick coating of cement, the same everywhere, was used, whether for roofs, ceilings, floors, pavements, or roads.

On examining the monuments at Tula, we are filled with admiration for the marvellous building capacity of the people who erected them; for, unlike most primitive nations, they used every material at once. They coated their inner walls with mud and mortar, faced their outer walls with baked bricks and cut stone, had wooden roofs and brick and stone staircases. They were acquainted with pilasters (we found them in their houses), with caryatides, with square and round columns; indeed, they seem to have been familiar with every architectural device. That they were painters and decorators we have ample indications in the house we unearthed, where the walls are covered with rosettes, palms, red, white and grey geometrical figures on a black ground.

ROYAL BUILDINGS

My next soundings were towards the centre of the hill, which I took at first for a tomb; but finding nothing, I directed my men south-east, at the extremity of the hill. Here we attacked a pyramid of considerable size, thickly covered with vegetation, having a hole and a thick plaster coating, which, to my extreme delight, revealed an old palace, extending over an area of nearly 62 feet on one side, with an inner courtyard, a garden and numerous apartments on different levels, ranged from the ground floor to 8 feet high, exactly like the first house; the whole covering a surface of 2,500 square yards. We will give a description of it, together with the probable use of the various apartments. First is the inner courtyard, which we take as our level; to the right, paved with large pebbles, is the main entrance.

Facing this to the left is a small room about 4 feet high, which was entered by a flight of seven low steps; it is a Belvedere, from which a view of the whole valley could be obtained. Next comes perhaps a reception room, 32 feet long, having two openings towards the court. On the other side, to the north, is a smaller, narrower Belvedere, from which an anteroom, on a slightly lower level, furnished with benches, was reached. The main body of the palace consists of ten apartments of different size, with stuccoed walls and floors. The façade, 8 feet high, opens on the courtyard;

whilst two winding stone staircases to the right, and an equal number to the left, led to the apartments on the first storey. Brick steps, covered with a deep layer of cement, connected the various chambers. The cells on both sides of the main apartments may have been the servants' quarters.

Next is a kind of yard, without any trace of roof, and if we are to judge from Aztec dwellings, was probably an enclosure for domestic and wild animals. The Americans, says Clavigero, had no flocks; nevertheless, their table was well supplied by innumerable animals to be found about their dwellings, and unknown to Europe; whilst the poor people had an edible dog, *techichi*, the breed of which was lost by the abuse the Spaniards made of it in the early times of the Conquest.

Royal palaces had extensive spaces reserved for turkeys, ducks and every species of volatile [winged creature], a menagerie for wild animals, chambers for reptiles and birds of prey, and tanks for fish; so that the purpose we ascribe to these enclosures becomes highly probable. Here and there closed-up passages, walls rebuilt with materials other than those employed in the older construction, seem to indicate that the palace was occupied at two different periods; this would agree with Veytia when he says, 'that on the Chichemecs invading the country under the command of Xolotl, they found Tula (*c.* 1117) deserted, and grass growing in the streets; but that the King was so pleased with the site that he ordered the monuments to be repaired and the town inhabited. He followed the same policy at Teotihuacan and other places, ordering his people to preserve old names, and only authorizing them to give new appellations to those they should build themselves.'

The building we unearthed is entire, its outer wall intact; presenting a valuable specimen of the houses dating long before the Conquest. Here we found the same kind of objects as in our first excavations: plates, dishes, three-footed cups having striated bottoms and used for grinding chili pepper; fragments of pottery, enamels, terracotta whorls of different size covered with sunk designs having a hole in the centre. These whorls are called *malacates* by the natives, and used by indigenous women to this day. A round piece of wood or spindle stick is introduced in the hole of the whorl, projecting about five inches from the lower plane, and about nine inches from the upper. The spinner, who is sitting, rests the point of her spindle on a varnished plate, and impels it round with her thumb and forefinger, twisting the cotton or wool attached thereto. In Mexico, rich ladies used a golden plate.

The edifice [at the right wing of the palace] is undoubtedly a tennis court, for it answers exactly the description given by historians of such structures; moreover, I found one of the rings still in place. Veytia is wrong, therefore, in crediting the Mexicans with the invention of the game; were it so we should not have found a tennis court at Chichen Itza. [Pedro Aplicano] Mendieta relates how Tezacatlipoca came down from his celestial abode on a spider's ladder, and how in his long peregrinations on earth he visited Tula, brought thither by his jealousy of Quetzalcoatl, whom he challenged to play tennis; but the latter turning into a tiger discomfited him utterly. The spectators were so terrified that they fled, and in the tumult which ensued many were drowned in the river flowing close by.

This tradition shows plainly that tennis existed in the remote period of Quetzalcoatl's rule at Tula; that the game was of Toltec origin, that the court was on the hill, since the spectators in their precipitancy to run away were drowned, that Quetzalcoatl was a good tennis player, and that the expression, 'he was turned into a tiger', is merely honorific, applied to him on the spot for having sent his ball through the ring. This passage also explains the tiger frieze over the tennis court at Chichen Itza.

ORGANIZATION OF SOCIETY

The Toltecs had public granaries which were opened to the people in time of famine. A passage in *Cuauhtitlan's Annals* seems to indicate that the resistance they opposed to a grasping and bloodthirsty priesthood, was one of the chief causes of their downfall: 'Under the mild rule of Quetzalcoatl, demons tried in vain to persuade him to allow men born at Tula to be sacrificed. As for himself, his offerings were birds, serpents and butterflies he had captured in the valley.'

The Toltecs were peaceful, their organization was feudal and aristocratic, indicative of conquest, yet their government was paternal. Besides the great feudatory lords, they had military orders and titles, which were bestowed on distinguished soldiers for services in the field or the council, and finally the celebrated order of the *tecuhtlis*, which was divided in sub-orders of the 'tiger', the 'lion', the 'eagle' and other animals, each having its peculiar privileges. The initiatory ceremonies resembled somewhat those attending our knights of the Middle Ages, and may interest the reader.

INITIATION CEREMONIES

At the nomination of a candidate, all the *tecuhtlis* assembled in the house of the new knight, whence they set out in a body for the temple, where the high priest, at the request of the neophyte, perforated his nose and ears with a pointed tiger's bone, or an eagle's claw, inserting in the holes thus made twigs, which were changed every day for larger ones, until the healing of the wound; pronouncing the while invocations to the gods that they would give the novice the courage of the lion, the swiftness of the deer, etc.; followed by a speech in which he was reminded that he who aspires to the dignity of a tecuhtli must be ready to perform the duties of his new office. He was henceforth to be distinguished by greater meekness, patience, forbearance and moderation in all things, together with submission to the laws. After this speech, he was deprived of his rich garments, and dressed in a coarse tunic; the only articles of furniture allowed him were a common mat and a low stool. He was besmeared with a black preparation, and only broke his fast once in twenty-four hours with a tortilla and a small quantity of water.

Meanwhile the priests and *tecuhtlis* came in turns to feast before the novice, and make his fast more intolerable, heaping insults and injurious epithets upon the man who stood meekly before them; jostling and pointing their fingers jeeringly at him. At night he was only allowed to sleep a few minutes at a time; and if overcome by sleep, his guardians pricked him with the thorn of the maguey.

'At the expiration of sixty days the new knight, accompanied by friends and relatives, repaired to some temple of his own district, where he was received by the whole order of *tecuhtlis*, ranged in two rows on each side of the temple, from the main altar down to the entrance. He advanced alone, bowing right and left to each tecuhtli, until he reached the idol, where the mean garments he had worn so long were taken off by the oldest tecuhtli, his hair bound up in a knot on the top of his head with a red string; whilst a wreath, having a medallion with his motto graven on it, circled his brow. He was next clad in rich and fine apparel, ornamented and delicately embroidered; in his hands he received arrows and a bow; balls of gold were inserted in his ears and nostrils, and a precious stone, the distinctive badge of his order, hung from his lower lip. The ceremony ended with another discourse to the effect that the neophyte should aim at being liberal, just, free from arrogance and willing to devote his life to the service of his country and his gods.'

EDUCATION

The Toltecs paid great attention to the instruction of youth. Texcuco possessed schools of art, in which the broad principles laid down by their forefathers were doubtless remembered, differing from those of the Aztecs, whose exaggerated religiosity caused them to leave the education of children entirely in the hands of the priests. That the latter were less influential with the Toltecs seems indicated in the following passage: 'Among the various sumptuous edifices at Utatlan was the college, having a staff of seventy teachers, and 5,000 or 6,000 pupils, who were educated at the public expense.' The truth of this account is borne out by the fact that the city was only destroyed in 1524 by Alvarado, so that the early missionaries had ample opportunity given them to collect materials for a trustworthy history.

MARRIAGE AND FAMILY CUSTOMS/RELIGION

Marriage among the Toltecs was celebrated with ceremonies it may interest the reader to know something about. On this occasion friends and relations were invited, the walls of the best apartment were adorned with pretty devices, made with flowers and evergreens, whilst every table and bracket was covered with them. The bridegroom occupied a seat to the right, the bride sat on the floor to the left of the hearth, which stood in the middle of the room, where a bright fire was burning. Then the 'marriage-maker', as he was called, stood up and addressed the young people, reminding them of their mutual duties in the life they were about to enter, and, at the termination of his speech, they were given new cloaks, and received the good wishes and congratulations of their friends, who as they came up threw each in turn some perfume on the hearth. Now the bride and bridegroom were crowned with chaplets of flowers, and the day was wound up with dance, music and refreshments. There was also a religious ceremony similar to this in all respects, in which a priest officiated; when instead of cloaks they put on costly dresses with a skeleton head embroidered on them, and thus attired, the new married couple were accompanied to their home and left to themselves.

In order to have a complete idea of this extraordinary people, a few words upon their philosophy and ethics may find an appropriate place here. A Toltec maiden, about to enter into life, was admonished with great tenderness by her father to preserve simplicity in her manners and conversation, to have great neatness in attire and attention to personal cleanliness. He inculcated modesty, faithfulness and obedience to her husband, reminding her that this world is a place of sorrow and disappointment, but that God had given as a compensation domestic joys and material enjoyments; softening his advice by such endearing words as: 'daughter mine, my beloved daughter, my precious', etc.

Nor was the advice of a mother less touching – breathing throughout a parent's love: 'My beloved daughter, my little dove, you have heard the words which your father has told you. They are precious words, such as are rarely spoken, and which have proceeded from his heart. Speak calmly and deliberately; do not raise your voice very high, nor speak very low, but in a moderate tone. Neither mince, when you speak, nor when you salute, nor speak through your nose; but let your words be proper, and your voice gentle. In walking, see that you behave becomingly, neither going with haste, nor too slowly; yet, when it is necessary to go with haste, do so. When you are obliged to jump over a pool of water, do it with decency. Walk through the streets quietly; do not look hither and thither, nor turn your head to look at this and that; walk neither looking at the skies nor at the ground. See likewise that you neither paint your face nor your lips, in order to look well, since this is a mark of vile and immodest women. But that your husband may take pleasure in you, adorn yourself, wash yourself and wear nothing but clean clothes, but let this be done with moderation, since if you are over nice – too delicate – they will call you *tapetzeton*, *tinemaxoch*. This was the course and the manner of your ancestors. In this world it is necessary to live with prudence and circumspection. See that you guard yourself carefully and free from stain, for should you give your favour to another who is not your husband, you would be ruined past all recall; since for such a crime they will kill you, throw you into the street for an example to all the people, where your head will be crushed and dragged upon the ground,' etc.

We will end these quotations by the advice to a son: 'My beloved son, lay to heart the words I am going to utter, for they are from our forefathers, who admonished us to keep them locked up like precious gold leaf, and taught us that boys and girls are beloved of the Lord. For this reason the men of old, who were devoted to His service, held children in great reverence. They roused them out of their sleep, undressed them, bathed them in cold water, made them sweep the temples and offer copal to the gods. They washed their mouths, saying that God heard their prayers and accepted their exercises, their tears and their sorrow, because they were of a pure heart, perfect and without blemish, like *chalchihuitl* (precious stones). They added that this world was preserved for their sake, and that they were our intercessors before Him. Satraps, wise men and those killed by lightning were supposed to be particularly agreeable to the Sun, who called them to himself that they might live for ever in his presence in a perpetual round of delight,' etc.

And what can be more beautiful than the prayer addressed to Tlaloc: 'O Lord, liberal giver of all things, Lord of freshness and verdure, Lord of sweet-smelling paradise, Lord of incense and copal. Alas! Your vassals, the gods of water, have disappeared, and lie concealed in their deep caverns, having stowed away all things indispensable to life, although they continue to receive the *ulli yauhtli* and copal offering. They have also carried away their sister, the goddess of substance. O Lord, have pity on us that live. Our food goes to destruction, is lost and dried up for lack of water; it is as if turned to dust and mixed with spiders' webs. Wilt thou have no pity on the *macehuetes* and the common people, who are wasted with hunger, and go about unrecognizable and disfigured? They are blue under the eyes as with death; their mouths are dry as sedge; all the bones of their bodies show as in a skeleton. The children are disfigured and yellow as earth; not only those that begin to walk, but even those in the cradle. This torment of hunger comes to everyone; the very animals and birds suffer from dire want. It is pitiful to see the birds, some dragging themselves along with drooping wings, others falling down unable to walk, and others with their mouth still open through hunger and thirst. O Lord, Thou wert wont to give us abundantly of those things which are the life and joy of all the world, and precious as emeralds and sapphires; all these things have departed from us. O Lord God of nourishment, most kind and compassionate, what hast Thou determined to do with us? Hast Thou utterly forsaken us? Shall not Thy wrath and indignation be appeased? Wilt Thou destroy these Thy servants, and leave this city and kingdom desolate and uninhabited? Is it so decreed in heaven and hades? O Lord, grant, at least, that these innocent children, who cannot so much as walk, and those still in the cradle, may have something to eat, so that they may live and die not in this terrible famine. What have they done that they should be so tried, and should die of hunger? They have committed no iniquity, neither do they know what thing it is to sin; they neither offended the gods of heaven nor the gods of hell. We, if we have offended in many things, if our sins have reached heaven and hades and the uttermost parts of the world, it is but just that we should be destroyed. O Lord, invigorate the corn and other substances, much wished for and much needed, now sown and planted; for the ridges of the earth suffer sore need and anguish from lack of water. Grant, O Lord, that the people receive this favour and mercy at Thine hand; let them see and enjoy the verdure and coolness which are as precious stones. See good that the fruit and the substance of the Tlalocs be given, which are the clouds that these gods carry with them and that give us rain. May it please Thee, O Lord, that the animals and herbs be made glad, and that the fowls and birds of precious feather, such as the *quechotl* and the *çaquan*, fly and sing and feast upon the herbs and flowers. And let not this come about with thunder and lightning, symbols of Thy wrath; for if our lords the Tlalocs come in this way, the people, being lean and very weak with hunger, would be terrified.'

The degree of culture of a nation can be gauged from its religion, and notably its ideas of a future life. The beauty and eloquence-loving Greek discoursed upon philosophy walking under noble porticoes; the thoughts of the barbarous worshipper of Woden were of bloody fights, and of wassail in which he drank hydromel out of his enemies' skulls; the Arab goes to sleep cradled on the lap of houris; the Red Indian dreams of endless hunting fields, whilst the starving Bushman hopes for a heaven of plenty. The Toltec is the only one whose aspirations beyond the grave are free from grossness and cruelty; his heaven is a resting place for the weary, a perpetual spring, amidst flowers, fields of yellow maize, verdure and flowers.

PULQUE, ITS HISTORY AND CONSEQUENCES

From these graver matters we will pass to the legend, told by Veytia, which makes Papantzin the inventor of pulque; and although, in our opinion, he places this event too late, it is none the less instructive as showing another side of Toltec history. In the year 1049, or, according to Clavigero, 1024–30, Tecpancaltzin was one day taking his siesta in the palace, when Papantzin, one of his great nobles, presented himself together with his daughter, the beautiful Xochitl ('flower'), bearing, with other gifts to the king, a kind of liqueur, made from the maguey juice by a process of which Papantzin was the inventor.

The new drink pleased the royal palate, and the lovely form and face of the young maiden were still more pleasing to the royal taste. The king expressed his desire to have more of the new beverage at the hands of the fair Xochitl, adding that she might bring it unattended save by her nurse. Proud of the honour shown him, Papantzin a few days later sent Xochitl, accompanied by a dueña, with some pulque. Xochitl was introduced alone to the presence of Tecpancaltzin. Bravely the maiden resisted the monarch's protestations of ardent love, but alone and unprotected she was unable to resist the threats and violence used against her.

She was then sent to the strongly guarded palace of Palpan near the capital; and there, cut off from all communication with parents or friends, she lived as the king's mistress. Her father meanwhile was told that his daughter had been entrusted by the king to the care of some matrons, who would perfect her education and fit her for a high position among the court ladies.

Meanwhile the king visited Xochitl, and in 1051 a child was born, who received the name of Meconetzin ('child of the maguey'), and later that of Topiltzin (the 'Justicer'), by which he is known in history. But at last Papantzin, suspecting that all was not right with his daughter, visited the palace of Palpan in the disguise of a labourer; he found her and listened to the tale of her shame.

His wrath knew no bounds, but he was quieted with the king's promise that the child should be proclaimed heir to the throne, and that, should the queen die, Xochitl would succeed her as his legitimate consort. It should be mentioned that polygamy and concubinage were strictly forbidden among the Toltecs of that period; that the laws were binding on king and peasant alike; and this explains why Tecpancaltzin was obliged to keep his love for Xochitl secret, until he was free to proclaim her publicly his queen; a step which was fraught with endless evils for his country, since after his death the Toltec princes, who were thus deprived of their hope of succession, broke out into open hostilities.

The most powerful of these and nearest to the throne was Huehuetzin; with him were banded the caciques of the northern provinces beyond Jalisco and those bordering on the Atlantic Ocean, when after years of warfare, followed by calamitous inundations, tempests, droughts, famine and pestilence (1097), the Toltecs, greatly reduced in numbers, dispersed; some directing their march south (the Toluca and Cuernavaca branch), others going north (the Tula and Teotihuacan branch) founded establishments at Tehuantepec, Guatemala, Goatzacoalco, Tabasco and Campeche; whilst a few remained at Cholula and Chapultepec.

Ixtlilxochitl places this event in 1008. Sixteen hundred are said to have settled at Colhuacan, intermarried with Chichemec caciques, and founded the family from which the kings of Texcuco were descended. Clavigero writes that the miserable remains of the nation found a remedy in flight (1031–50), some settling in Yucatan and Guatemala, whilst others, with the two sons of Topiltzin, remained in the Tula valley, and that their grandsons were subsequently closely connected with the royal families of Mexico, Texcuco and Colhuacan. Finally Torquemada writes 'that they were counselled by the devil to abandon their country to escape utter annihilation, and that the account of their migrations is to be found in Acolhuan histories, written in peculiar characters as is the custom of these aborigines.'

TOLTEC INFLUENCE

The Toltec soldiers wore a quilted cotton tunic that fitted closely to the body and protected also the shoulders and thighs; their offensive weapons consisted of spears, light javelins and clubs studded with steel, silver or gold nails. They used a copper currency, which a short while ago was still found among the Tutupecans.

These quotations, which might be multiplied, clearly prove that the Toltecs migrated south, following the coasts of both oceans; that they ceased to exist as a nation after the disruption of their empire; but that their scattered remnants carried on the work of civilization in Central America, on the high plateaus, and in Anahuac; evidenced in the strong resemblance that the civilizations of these various regions bear to one another.

We will close this chapter with a few words about the Chichemecs, who occupied the valley after the Toltecs. Their emperor Xolotl made Tenayuca, to the west of Lake Texcuco, his capital, and despatched four chiefs, with a strong escort, to explore the country in every direction. They were absent four years, and in their report (1124) they stated that they had met with some Toltecs in the region formerly held by them; but that the greater proportion had founded important colonies in the far-off provinces of Tehuantepec, Guatemala, Tecocotlan and Tabasco. Nopaltzin, the son of this emperor, sent likewise emissaries from Teotihuacan, whose report was to the effect that they had found a few Toltecs scattered in five different places, who told them of their hardships, adding that most of their fellow citizens had gone farther west and south.

From these quotations it is clearly seen that the date of the oldest edifices in Tabasco cannot be anterior to the beginning of the twelfth century; that Toltec influence was felt simultaneously on the high plateaus and in Central America, shown by the flourishing small Toltec state of Colhuacan, where King Architometl (1231) had revived those arts and sciences his ancestors had initiated, and which, since their extermination, had fallen into utter decay. This king succeeded so well in his enlightened policy that his country became an intelligent centre, which proved so beneficial to the barbarous Chichemecs.

Nopaltzin, following the example of Xolotl, compelled those of his subjects who still lived in caverns to build houses, live in communities, cultivate the land and feed on prepared viands. He invited jewellers and lapidaries from Colhuacan to teach his people, instituting prizes for those who became proficient in mechanical arts, and also for those who made astrology, historical paintings and the deciphering of ancient manuscripts their particular study. And, lastly, in the closing words of Veytia's account, he says: 'Among the documents I possess for the completion of my work are several bearing on the Mexicans. I found no difficulty in reading the paintings and maps; but although they are systematically classified as regards events posterior to their arrival in the valley, it is very different with their antiquities, their origin, and their wanderings; their documents relating to this period being more rare and obscure than those of the Toltecs.'

TEOTIHUACAN AND THE TOLTECS

Teotihuacan was a flourishing city at the time of the Toltecs, and the rival of Tula; and like her was destroyed and subsequently rebuilt by the Chichemec emperor Xolotl, preserving under the new regime her former supremacy. In the opinion of Veytia, Torquemada and other historians, Teotihuacan was a Toltec city; and my excavations in bringing to light palaces having nearly the same arrangement as those at Tula, will confirm their opinion. The orientation of this city is indicated by Clavigero in the following passage:

'The famous edifices at Teotihuacan, 3 miles north of this village and 25 from Mexico, are still in existence.'

The two principal pyramids were dedicated to the Sun and Moon, and were taken as models for building later temples in this region. That of the Sun is the most considerable, measuring 680 feet at the base by 180 feet high. Like all great pyramids, they were divided into four storeys, three of which are still visible, but the intermediate gradations are almost effaced. A temple stood on the summit of the larger mound, having a colossal statue of the Sun, made of one single block of stone.

Its breast had a hollow, in which was placed a planet of fine gold. This statue was destroyed by Zumarraga, first Bishop of Mexico, and the gold seized by the insatiable Spaniards. The interior of the pyramid is composed of clay and volcanic pebbles, incrusted on the surface with the light porous stone, *tetzontli*; over this was a thick coating of white stucco, such as was used for dwellings. Where the pyramid is much defaced, its incline is from 31 to 36 degrees, and where the coatings of cement still adhere, 47 degrees. The ascent was arduous, especially with a burning sun beating down upon us; but when we reached the top, we were amply repaid by the glorious view which unfolded before our enraptured gaze. To the north the Pyramid of the Moon, and the great 'Path of Death' (Micoatl), with its tombs and tumuli, covering a space of 9 square miles; to the south and south-west the hills of Tlascala, the villages of S. Martin and S. Juan, the snowy top of Iztaccihuatl towering above the Matlacinga range; and in the west the Valley of Mexico with its lakes, whilst far, far away the faint outline of the Cordilleras was perceptible in this clear atmosphere.

The outline of the pyramids is everywhere visible, and serves as a beacon to guide the traveller to the ruins of Teotihuacan, about 37 miles north of Mexico. Besides these, there are some smaller mounds to the south, indicating that the ancient city extended as far as Matlacinga hill, which bounds the valley on this side, whilst it stretched 6 miles to the north.

There is an immense mound known as the Citadel, measuring over 1,950 feet at the sides. It is a quadrangular enclosure, consisting of four embankments some 19 feet high and 260 feet thick, on which are ranged fifteen pyramids; whilst, towards the centre, a narrower embankment is occupied by a higher pyramid, which connects the north and south walls. The shape of the citadel bears a strong resemblance to a vast tennis court, and if not the latter, it was in all probability used for public ceremonies, but never as a citadel.

A little further is a dry watercourse, which becomes a torrent in the rainy season. The bed is full of obsidian pebbles, some transparent, some opaque green, but most of a greyish tint. On the opposite bank of the torrent we observed in some places three layers of cement, laid down in the same way, and consisting of the same materials, as I can certify, notwithstanding all that has been said to the contrary.

This cement is identical with that of Tula, except that there it was probably done for the sake of solidity, since it is only to be met with on the declivity of the hill; whereas here, where the city was demolished several times, it was due to the fact that the new occupant did not care to clear the ground of all the rubbish, but contented himself with smoothing down the old coating and laying a new one on the top of it. This supposition becomes almost a certainty when we add that numerous fragments of pottery have been found between the layers. This is, besides, amply exemplified in Rome and other cities, where ancient monuments are divided from later ones by thick layers of detritus; nor is it necessary for a long interval to have occurred between the two. On the other hand, if we suppose the soil between the coatings to have accumulated there by the work of time, an antiquity must be ascribed to these first constructions which would simply be ridiculous; and we think that if Mendoza had visited the ground, his conclusions would have been much modified.

Traces of edifices and walls occupy the base of the torrent, showing that the bed was narrower formerly than it is now, and that it was presumably embanked and spanned by several bridges. As we advance towards the Pyramid of the Sun, fragments of all kinds meet our eyes in every direction; the fields are strewn with pottery, masks, small figures, Lares, ex-votos, small idols, broken cups, stone axes, etc. I select for myself some masks which portray the various Indian types with marvellous truth, and at times not without some artistic skill. Among them are types which do not seem to belong to America: a negro, whose thick lips, flat nose, and woollen hair proclaim his African origin; below this a Chinese head, Caucasian and Japanese specimens; heads with retreating foreheads, like those displayed at Palenque, and not a few with Greek profiles. The lower jaw is straight or projecting, the faces smooth or bearded; in short, it is a wonderful medley, indicative of the numerous races who succeeded each other, and amalgamated on this continent, which, until lately, was supposed to be so new, and is in truth so old.

MOUNDS

Some writers, on viewing the configuration of these massive mounds, have erroneously concluded that they were built for the same purpose as the Egyptian pyramids; but we cannot sufficiently impress on the reader that in America the pyramid was synonymous with temple, or used as basement for temples and palaces. People may have been buried in the former, as they were buried in the latter; but that is no evidence of any analogy subsisting between them.

In Egypt the pyramid was a sepulchre and nothing more, which received additions each successive year, and assumed smaller or greater dimensions, according to the longevity of the sovereign who erected it. The gigantic pyramids of Cheops, Chephren, and Mycerinus, correspond to reigns of sixty years each; the smaller correspond to short reigns in which kings were not given time for constructing great monuments. Now, the American mounds belong to one epoch, were built on one plan without any intermission. Architecture, whether civil or religious, entirely differs in the two countries. In Egypt palaces were built of wood; in America they were built of stone. Among Egyptians temples were colossal; among Americans, on the contrary, they were small, primitive, hardly more than altars. The temple was all-important with the former, the palace with the latter. In fact, the two polities were diametrically opposed, save on such points of contact as are common to all races in the early stage of their civilization.

Some writers, arguing from the existence of a civilization anterior to the Incas, concluded, with some show of reason, that there existed a pre-Toltec civilization also; but a moment's reflection will show that no parallel exists between the two; for the former, in a climate eminently favourable to the preservation of monuments, has hardly left any trace, whilst the latter, in a climate peculiarly destructive, has left whole cities and monuments in almost perfect preservation. In Peru, the people who followed the earlier races used extant remains for the foundations of their monuments, as, for instance, at Cuzco; whereas in Mexico and Central America monuments were repaired and restored on the same plan as that on which they had been erected. It follows that in Peru edifices are totally different in character from the foundations and cyclopean walls which support them, unless the ruins of Las Casas Grandes be considered pre-Toltec; but even so they would be the remains of edifices constructed by the first Nahua tribes in their progress towards the south.

RUINS OF A TEOTIHUACAN PALACE

After a brief survey I discovered traces of cement, which made it evident that part of the village [S. Juan] is built on the site of the ancient city; so I made up my mind to try my luck here before venturing into the very heart of the ruins, which I wished to take time to study. I began by opening four trenches in a small square used for bullfighting, not far from Plaza Mayor. The first two yielded nothing particular, the next gave more satisfactory results; for here we came upon some dozen children's tombs, and five or six adults', if we are to judge from vases and other objects we found, for nothing could be made of the bones, which crumbled into dust. The few vases we unearthed are made of black clay, with hollow lines, not unlike those at Tula. They have flat bottoms from six to seven inches wide, with open brims, and from two to three inches high. Close to them were found traces of skeletons, which we know to have been those of poor people, for the bodies of the rich were burnt and their ashes placed in tombs. The vases were often found in couples; they are unfortunately so old, the ground is so hard as to form one mass with the vase, and so notwithstanding all our precautions, all our care in digging the ground and taking it up with daggers, they were broken to pieces, and I was only able to save a few.

As to the bodies, they were so far gone, that it was impossible to ascertain their position; they were generally found from 1 foot 3 inches to 1 foot 9 inches, and 3 feet 3 inches deep. The children were buried in a kind of circular vases, with upright brims; two of the skeletons were almost perfect, but the skulls, as thin as a sheet of paper, fell to pieces at my touch. On the same day I unearthed a goodly number of terracotta figures, a fine moulded mask, an axe, a few pots, one of which is ribbed and beautifully moulded, a number of small round pebbles, evidently marbles buried with the children; besides a large quantity of obsidian knives, by far the finest and lightest I have seen; round pieces of slate, presumably used as currency, *bezotes*, rings worn on the lower lip, arrowheads, whilst numerous sheets of mica were found in every tomb. Among human remains we also noticed those of the *techichi*, edible dog, parts of birds and victuals, to sustain the dead on his long journey beyond the grave.

In the nearby Pachucha are the cuevas or pits of old quarries, which were subsequently used as catacombs; they are 2 miles and a half west of the Pyramid of the Moon. The first we visit has a circular aperture of considerable size, with three narrow low galleries branching off in different directions at an angle of 40 to 45 degrees. The first explorers of these caves found human remains side by side with those of ruminants. The next cavern, of far greater dimensions, is 350 feet further off. We enter one of the galleries, and walk for ten minutes before we can see the end; my guide assures me that this gallery extends as far as the Pyramid of the Sun, 3 miles beyond; that the whole country around is undermined by these cuevas, the soil of which is conglomerate.

We now come to large halls, supported by incredibly small pillars; the population round about use them as ballrooms twice a year, and nothing can give an idea of the almost magic effect they then present. In this cueva the conglomerate is split up into gigantic isolated blocks of the most fantastic, weird shapes, in juxtaposition with a perpendicular calcareous formation. The next cavern we visit has a well and a rotunda in the centre; ghastly stories are told of the brigands who formerly used this cueva as a burial place for their victims after having plundered them; wild suppositions which derive a colouring from the numerous human remains to be found everywhere, which are, however, undoubtedly the bones of the earlier natives, as the thickness of the skulls sufficiently indicates.

I return to the 'Path of Death', composed of a great number of small mounds, Tlateles, the tombs of great men. They are arranged symmetrically in avenues terminating at the sides of the great pyramids, on a plain of some 620 feet to 975 feet in length; fronting them are cemented steps, which must have been used as seats by the spectators during funeral ceremonies or public festivities. On the left, amidst a mass of ruins, are broken pillars, said to have belonged to a temple; the huge capitals have some traces of sculpture. Next comes a quadrangular block, of which a cast is to be found in the main gallery of the Trocadéro.

In the course of my excavations I had found now and again numerous pieces of worked obsidian, precious stones, beads, etc., within the circuit of ants' nests, which these busy insects had extracted from the ground in digging their galleries; and now on the summit of the lesser pyramid I again came upon my friends, and among the things I picked out of their nests was a perfect earring of obsidian, very small and as thin as a sheet of paper. It is not so curious as it seems at first, for we are disturbing a ground formed by fifty generations.

Glass does not seem to have been known to the natives, for although Tezcatlipoca was often figured with a pair of spectacles, they may only have been figurative ones like those of the manuscripts, terracotta, or bas-reliefs, for there is nothing to show that they had any idea of optics.

I now went back to my men, when to my great delight I found they had unearthed two large slabs showing the entrance of two sepulchres; they were the first I had yet found, and considering them very important, I immediately telegraphed to Messrs. Chavero and Berra, both of whom are particularly interested in American archaeology. I expected to see them come by the very next train, to view not only the tombstones, but also the palace, which attracted a great number of visitors; but to my surprise one sent word that he had a headache, whilst the other pleaded a less poetic ailment. *Ab uno disce omnes*; most American writers speak of ancient monuments from hearsay – from foreign travellers who have visited them – they never having taken the trouble to travel any distance to see them.

BURIAL RITUALS

One of the slabs closed a vault, and the other a cave with perpendicular walls; we went down the former by a flight of steps in fairly good condition, yet it was a long and rather dangerous affair, for we were first obliged to demolish a wall facing us, in which we found a skull, before we could get to the room which contained the tombs. The vases within them are exactly like those we found in the plaza, except that one is filled with a fatty substance – like burnt flesh – mixed with some kind of stuff [woollen cloth or fabric], the woof [woven fabric] of which is still discernible, besides beads of serpentine, bones of dogs and squirrels, knives of obsidian twisted by the action of fire.

We know from Sahagun that the dead were buried with their clothes and their dogs to guide and defend them on their long journey: 'When the dead were ushered into the presence of the king of the nether world, Mictlantecutli, they offered him papers, bundles of sticks, pine wood and perfumed reeds, together with loosely twisted threads of white and red cotton, a manta, a maxtli, tunics and shirts. When a woman died her whole wardrobe was carefully put aside, and a portion burnt eighty days after; this operation was repeated on that day [every?] twelve months for four years, when everything that had belonged to the deceased was finally consumed. The dead then came out of the first circle to go successively through nine others encompassed by a large river. On its banks were a number of dogs which helped their owners to cross the river; whenever a ghost neared the bank, his dog immediately jumped into the river and swam by his side or carried him to the opposite bank.' It was on this account that natives had always several small dogs about them.

The speech which was addressed to the dead when laid out previous to being buried is so remarkable as to make one suspect that the author unconsciously added something of his own: 'Son, your earthly hardships and sufferings are over. We are but mortal, and it has pleased the Lord to call you to himself. We had the privilege of being intimately acquainted with you; but now you share the abode of the gods, whither we shall all follow, for such is the destiny of man. The place is large enough to receive everyone; but although all are bound for the gloomy bourn, none ever return.' Then followed the speech addressed to the nearest kinsman of the dead: 'O son, cheer up; eat, drink and let not your mind be cast down. Against the divine fiat who can contend? This is not of man's doing; it is the Lord's. Take comfort to bear up against the evils of daily life; for who is able to add a day, an hour, to his existence? Cheer up, therefore, as becomes a man.'

ANCIENT TOMBS

But to return to our tombstones. They are both alike, being about 5 feet high, 3 feet five inches broad, and 6 inches and a half thick. The upper side is smooth, the lower has some carving in the shape of a cross, four big tears or drops of water, and a pointed tongue in the centre, which, starting from the bottom of the slab, runs up in a line parallel to the drops.

Knowing how general was the worship of Tlaloc among the natives, I conjectured this had been a monument to the god of rain, to render him propitious to the dead; a view shared and enlarged upon by Dr. [Ernest-Theodore] Hamy [French anthropologist and ethnologist] in a paper read before the Académie des Sciences in November, 1882; and that I should be in accord with the eminent specialist on American antiquities is a circumstance to make me proud. I may add that the carving of this slab is similar to that of the cross on the famous bas-relief at Palenque; so that the probability of the two monuments having been erected to the god of rain is much strengthened thereby.

As our slabs are far more archaic than those at Palenque, we think we are justified in calling them earlier in time – the parent samples of the later ones. Nor is our assumption unsupported, for we shall subsequently find that the cult of Tlaloc and Quetzalcoatl was carried by the Toltecs in their distant peregrinations. These slabs, therefore, and the pillars we found in the village, acquire a paramount importance in establishing the affiliation of Toltec settlements in Tabasco, Yucatan and other places, furnishing us with further data in regard to certain monuments at Palenque, the steles of Tikal and the massive monolith idols of Copan.

TENENEPANCO AND NAHUALAC CEMETERIES

The examination of burial sites at Tenenpanco laid bare trenches branching off in every direction so as to embrace the whole plateau were at once made and brought to light wholly undisturbed tombs. The first was that of a woman whose head I was able to preserve intact: the bones of all the rest were unfortunately reduced to a gelatinous paste. The dead were buried at a depth varying from some two feet to four feet eight inches; the bodies doubled up, both chin and arms resting on their knees; hands and feet were gone. Within the tomb, over the head, was a *sebile*, or hollow terracotta plate, two small black earthen horns, besides several vases. The whole was damp and moist, the vases filled with earth and water, and the utmost care was required in taking up such fragile objects. They soon, however, hardened by exposure, when they could be easily and safely cleaned and packed.

As far as could be judged from the bones and pottery, one of the tombs contained the bodies of a man and a woman. Another, probably that of a chief, had no human remains left, but I found a great variety of precious objects, made of *chalchihuitl*, a hard green stone, which takes a fine polish, a kind of jade or serpentine, much valued by the natives; besides these were numerous arrows of obsidian, beads for necklaces, some of hard stone, some of terracotta and a few small figures. A singular circumstance marked this tomb; not a single bead, not a single ornament but was broken, presumably at the time of the burial, as a token of grief. It is at least the only plausible solution which can be given for so many hard and resisting objects having been systematically destroyed.

Moreover, by far the largest proportion of these granite or porphyry beads, whether owing to their great antiquity or their having lain in a very destructive soil, crumbled away at our touch. Broadly speaking, the tombs which had not been disturbed were two to one; the dead had been buried without any regard to their position.

FINDINGS OF THE TOLTEC CIVILIZATION

Our **excavations yielded stupendous results**: kitchen utensils, every variety of vases representing the Toltec god Tlaloc, fruit cups, jewel cups, with feet shaped like a duck's bill or a boar's head; chocolate cups with porpoise-like handles; beads, jewels, a whole civilization emerges from these tombs, and carries us back to the life of this long-forgotten people. Here we have caricatures of ancient warriors; further on a water carrier bearing his jars like the modern '*aguadores*'; next are toys and tiny terracotta chariots, some are broken, some still preserve their four wheels; they were, presumably, a fond mother's memento who, ages gone by, buried them with her beloved child. These chariots are shaped like a flattened coyote (a kind of long-bodied fox) with its straight ears and pointed face, and the wheels fit into four terracotta stumps; on my renewing the wood axletree, which had been destroyed long since, the chariots began to move.

Many more objects were brought to light from these tombs – richly ornamented 'fusaïoles', marbles, necklaces, baby tables, which, like the toy chariots, represented some quadruped – resembling Greek toys. This coincidence between people so different and so far removed from each other is not surprising, for elementary ideas generally find a common expression. It should also be observed that these toys, however rude, do not necessarily mark a very ancient epoch. Early manifestations live on through ages and are found side by side with the highest civilizations, and are still to be met among the people long after the well-to-do possess objects of art.

The 9th of July was one of our best days. Out of ten tombs five were found intact and yielded sixty remarkable pieces, one of which is unique and of peculiar interest. It is a three-footed terracotta cup some six inches by three by one and a half at the bottom inside; wonderful to relate, it emerged without a blot from its gloomy abode. Both the inside and outside are covered with pretty devices painted white, yellow, blue, green and red, fused into a harmonious whole. The colours are in relief and like enamels. Next, one almost as beautiful but smaller, and covered with dirt, was found. These two lovely cups were put out to dry in the sun, when, to my horror, I saw that one was fast scaling off, whilst the brilliant colours of the other were fading visibly. To remove them into the shade was the work of an instant, but, alas! it did not arrest the work of destruction, which continued at an alarming pace. A photograph of the finest cup, as well as the colours of the paintings, was immediately obtained, but it only gives a faint idea of the beauty of this charming work of art.

From these tombs were likewise unearthed a number of diminutive brass bells, which were used both as ornaments and currency; besides large fat vases with a hand painted red over a black ground. This was a Toltec memento, either symbolic of Hueman or of Quetzalcoatl, so often seen on the walls of Yucatec palaces, and likewise on the monuments of some North American tribes. But our most curious 'find' was a perfectly well-preserved human brain, the skull of which was gone. This cerebral mass had been protected from the pressure of its surroundings by a stout cup into which it was wedged. No doubt was possible: the two lobes, the circumvolution of the brain to the minute red lines of the blood vessels, all was there.

The fact that a human brain could have been found in good preservation when the skull had disappeared, was received with Homeric laughter; all I can say is that it is so, that the finding of it was witnessed by my associates; that in every tomb where the skull should have been, was invariably observed a whitish substance, which at first was mistaken for lime, but which subsequently whenever it was met with, the men instantly cried out: 'Aqui està uno – here is one' (body), and near it vases and fragments clearly indicating the presence of a tomb. These brains, however, not having been protected like the first, were all flattened into a white cake of some five inches by two in thickness. The only explanation I can offer is that at an elevation of 13,000 feet, close to the volcanic cone of Popocatepetl, in a soil saturated with sulphureous vapours (a film of sulphide always extended over my nitrate of silver washes), the same chemical combinations which destroyed the bones, may have acted as a preservative on cerebral matter. But it will be asked, why not have borne away that wonderful brain? I ought to have done so, no doubt, but without alcohol the thing was impossible; besides, had I done so, should I have a better chance of convincing people at a distance?

The toy chariots found no better favour with the public. Our illustrations [not included here], however, will settle once for all this vexed question. As must appear to the most inexperienced eye, the character of these toys is exceedingly archaic, nor am I aware that any museum or private collection has anything to show at all approaching them. This was conceded, but it was denied that they were chariots at all – the wheels were only 'malacates', i.e. 'fusaïoles'! Numerous spindles were indeed found by us in the cemetery. Profuse collections may be seen and compared in every museum, when the most ignorant must see that these wheels are quite different to 'fusaïoles' or whorls. It will be said that this toy was but the copy of a chariot brought in by the Spaniards; but a glance at the drawing will show how absurd is the assumption, and carry conviction to the most incredulous.

Granted that is so, what inference do you draw from it? That the Mexicans had chariots? Hardly, since all authorities are silent on the subject, and when we know that the only means of transportation was afforded by carriers. But if such chariots were not available in distant expeditions across rivers, over mountain paths, through immense forests, it was not so within the radius of a city having good roads; and what is there against the possibility of a handcart corresponding with ours having been in use?

I am far from affirming that it was so, although certain expressions and quotations might be adduced which would show the supposition to be not so far-fetched as it looks on the face of it. We read in the Ramirez manuscript, for instance, that Montezuma [Moctezuma] II set out for his Huaxateca expedition with a numerous army and *carruages*. Why should the Indian writer have used an ambiguous word meaning both 'chariot' and 'transport', when the former must already have been extant when he wrote – that is, after the Conquest? Farther, Padre Duran relates how this same Moctezuma, wishing to erect a temalacatl, had a huge block quarried at Aculco, near Amecameca; and [existing drawings] shows this block raised by means of a rude chariot having clog wheels, drawn by a multitude of natives. The text, it is true, does not specify a chariot; but if they were unknown, how do they come in his drawing? It is unaccountable, too, that no mention is made of the stone having been brought on rollers or wheels, seeing that it could not have come so great a distance by any other means. It is altogether a mystery.

Lastly, Juarros, in describing the battle at Pinar, fought against Alvarado, mentions war engines, or what would now be called ammunition carts, moving on *rodadillos*, which were drawn by armed men wherever they were required. These carts were loaded with arrows, spears, shields, stones, slings, etc., and men, chosen for the service, distributed them as they were wanted. Does 'rodadillo' mean here a clog wheel or a roller? If these carts carried arms to combatants in different parts of the field of battle, does it not follow that they moved on wheels, since rollers would have made the diminutive 'forts' immovable, contrary to the end proposed?

Should, however, both quotations and arguments seem valueless, it might be added that the toy chariots were perhaps of primeval Toltec invention, the use of which had been lost after their expulsion from the plateaus.

THE DOMAIN OF TLALOC

But to return to the cemetery. Whether it be considered Toltec or otherwise, whether ancient or comparatively modern, we hold to its antiquity, to its being essentially Nahua, dedicated to Tlaloc, the god of rain and plenty, the fertilizer of the earth, the Lord of Paradise, the protector of green harvests. We are in his dominions, for he was believed to reside where the clouds gather, on the highest mountain tops.

Vases [were] unearthed at Tenenepanco, five of which portray this god, with his prominent eyes, the drops of water streaming down his face, making up his teeth, his beard or moustachios; he holds in his right hand a writhing serpent, thereby representing the flash and the thunderbolt – his voice as heard in storms. In the Nahualac Plate four vases also figure the same god.

The nations who succeeded the Toltecs on the plateaus adopted this eminently Toltec deity, who was one of the most popular gods down to the Conquest. The later tribes, however, discarding the mild practices of the Toltecs, stained his cult with human sacrifices. We will add a few quotations showing how great was the analogy between the places consecrated to Tlaloc and the Tenenepanco cemetery.

Torquemada calls him the god of paradise and great delights; that his statue on the highest mountain of Texcuco represented a man seated on a square slab, having at the back a huge stone jar, into which *ulli*, maize, beans and other vegetables were placed by the devotees, and that this offering was renewed every year. Ixtlilxochitl mentions, *inter alia*, that five or six young children were yearly sacrificed to this deity, their hearts torn out, and their bodies buried; and we read in Father Duran that Moctezuma and the allied princes repaired on the hill on which a child seven or eight years old was sacrificed. This festival was celebrated in the month of April, when the maize was above the ground. The next quotation from Torquemada is by far the most interesting, for it mentions Popocatepetl and the surrounding hills where we are carrying on our explorations:

Indians entertained a great respect for this mountain, whose climate was mild, and the abundance of whose waters made the land around unusually fertile, and here children and slaves were slain in honour of Tlaloc. To the south is another mighty hill, Teocuinani, 'the Divine Singer', so called by the natives because whenever the clouds shroud its summit the volcano bursts forth in flashes of lightning and claps of thunder, spreading terror among the whole population, who hasten to the hill to offer men, incense, paper crowns, feathers, plates, urns, goblets, cups, toys and vases' (exactly what we have found). 'Close by was a well-constructed house, Ayauchcalli, 'house of rest', in which stood an idol of green stone, chalchihuitl, about the size of a child eight years old. On the arrival of the Spaniards this idol was carried away and buried in the mountains by the Indians, together with numerous objects of gold, silver and precious stones.

We have often seen clouds collected around the top of Teocuinani (El Fraile), and many a time have we heard the dread voice of the Divine Singer; if our Tenenepanco cemetery is not the one spoken of by Father Duran, it is assuredly its nearest neighbour, and we are convinced that this site was once sacred to Tlaloc, consequently ancient, and that besides the victims sacrificed, both men and women were buried here as in consecrated ground, with their utensils, arms and ornaments.

PALENQUE TEMPLES

Some writers have called Palenque a capital, and the great edifice known as the palace a royal mansion, but they have erred, for if there was a royal palace it was not the one we have described. Like Teotihuacan, Izamal and Cozumel, Palenque was a holy place, an important religious centre, a city which was resorted to as a place of pilgrimage, teeming with shrines and temples, a vast and much-sought burial place. In this and in no other way can be explained the silence surrounding this great city, which was probably peopled by a floating population dispersed at the first alarm of the Conquest.

This important city is apparently without civic architecture; no public buildings are found, there seems to have been nothing but temples and tombs. Consequently, the great edifice was not a royal palace, but rather a priestly habitation, a magnificent convent occupied by the higher clergy of this holy centre, as the reliefs everywhere attest.

Had Palenque been the capital of an empire, the palace a kingly mansion, the history of her people, fragments of domestic life, pageants, recitals of battles and conquests, would be found among the reliefs which everywhere cover her edifices, as in Mexico, at Chichen Itza and other cities in Yucatan; whereas the reliefs in Palenque show nothing of the kind. On them we behold peaceful, stately subjects, usually a personage standing with a sceptre, sometimes a calm, majestic figure whose mouth emits a flame, emblem of speech and oratory. They are surrounded by prostrated acolytes, whose bearing is neither that of slaves nor of captives; for the expression of their countenance, if submissive, is open and serene, and their peaceful attitude indicates worshippers and believers; no arms are found among these multitudes, nor spear, nor shield, nor bow, nor arrow, nothing but preachers and devotees.

THE TEMPLE OF INSCRIPTIONS

The Temple of Inscriptions is the largest known at Palenque, standing on a pyramid of some 48 feet high, to the southwest angle of the palace; its façade, 74 feet by nearly 25 deep, is composed of a vast gallery occupying the whole front, and of three compartments of different sizes, a large central chamber and two small ones at the sides. The front gallery is pierced with five apertures, supported by six pillars of 6 feet 9 inches by 3 feet 7 inches thick. The two corner pillars were covered with *katunes*, and the other four with bas-reliefs. No sanctuary is found in the building known as the Temple of Inscriptions, but both the gallery and the central room have flagstones covered with inscriptions. Two panels enclosed in the wall of the gallery measure 13 feet wide by 7 feet 8 inches high, one in the central chamber is over 7 feet by 6 feet. Amidst the *katunes* of this panel Waldeck has seen fit to place three or four elephants. What end did he propose to himself in giving this fictitious representation? Presumably to give a prehistoric origin to these ruins, since it is an ascertained fact that elephants in a fossil state only have been found on the American continent. It is needless to add that neither Catherwood, who drew these inscriptions most minutely, nor myself who brought impressions of them away, nor living man, ever saw these elephants and their fine trunks.

But such is the mischief engendered by preconceived opinions. With some writers it would seem that to give a recent date to these monuments would deprive them of all interest. It would have been fortunate had explorers been imbued with fewer prejudices and gifted with a little more common sense, for then we should have known the truth with regard to these ruins long since. Of all the buildings the temple was the best preserved, as seen in every detail. The floor, which in the palace is but a layer of plaster, is laid down here with beautiful slabs 9 feet 9 inches on one side by 5 feet by 7 inches thick.

The roof is unfortunately in a very ruinous state, and the dense vegetation which covers it prevents seeing anything of the large figures which presumably occupied its surface; even a photograph is difficult to get, for want of sufficient space.

TEMPLES OF THE SUN AND THE CROSS

Three other temples are found on a plateau, some 200 yards south-east of the palace at the foot of Cerro Alto. First in order is a small temple of the Sun, in a perfect state of preservation; the front measures 38 feet by 27 feet deep. The pilasters, the roof and superstructure were all covered with sculptures and complicated decorations. Anyone who is acquainted with sacred Japanese architecture would be struck with the resemblance of this temple to a Japanese sanctuary. How is this to be explained? A theory might be started with respect to the probable Asiatic origin of the Toltec tribes; of the influence of a Japanese civilization, through the steady traffic they formerly carried on, on the coast north-west of America, as also by fortuitous immigrations resulting from shipwrecks. In the present day, the average of Japanese vessels shipwrecked on the Californian coast is only two a year. However it may be, we will for the present leave to others the task of elucidating the question of origin.

The interior of the temple is a large room, receiving its light through three apertures in the façade; the end is occupied by a sanctuary, and each side by a small dark room. The sanctuary is a kind of oblong tabernacle, crowned with a richly decorated frieze and stuccoed mouldings. Two pilasters supported the roof, and formerly were covered with inscriptions or sculptured slabs representing various subjects; these flags have been broken or taken away, and not one remains *in loco*.

The end of the sanctuary is occupied by three slabs in juxtaposition, with sculptures of a religious character; in the central portion or tablet is a hideous face, with protruding tongue, identical with that found on the Aztec calendar in Mexico, known as the Tablet of the Sun. This symbolical figure is found also at Tikal carved in wood.

Three distinct subjects are present inside: in the central slab is a cross, branching out with palms supporting two figures; the body of the cross, which rests on a hideous head, is sculptured in the centre, and at the upper end are two human figures, crowned by a symbolic bird having a long tail and eagle claws. The left slab represents a man richly habited, with collar, medallion, girdle and greaves; the right slab a woman, to judge from her size, long plait of hair and peculiar clothing. This female is borne on palms having the very well-preserved outline of human heads. Both the male and female seem to stand before the symbolic bird offering presents, the nature of which it is not easy to specify. To the rear of each device is an inscription of sixty-eight characters, doubtless explanatory of the ceremony the whole sculpture represents, but which no one has yet been able to read.

We are of opinion that the Temple of the Cross was a sanctuary consecrated to Tlaloc and Quetzalcoatl, and that the altar in the same Temple was dedicated to Tlaloc; our only ground for this belief, however, is the cross, which we know was a later symbolic personification of the god of rain; but we will leave this question until we come to Lorillard, where monuments of the same kind, and the authority of ancient writers, will furnish data to strengthen our theory. It may not be irrelevant to add that neither temples nor palaces were provided with doors, and that stuff or matting curtains were used for all apertures, indicated by the large and small rings fixed on the pilasters on each side of the entrances, and the whole length of the inner cornice. We know that neither the Toltecs nor Aztecs had doors to their houses, which seems to show great respect for property, or as Clavigero puts it, 'the severity of the laws was a powerful preservative.' What he says of Mexico is equally applicable to Palenque: 'Houses had no doors, for they deemed that dwellings were sufficiently guarded by the stringency of the laws; and the people, not to be overlooked by their neighbours, had curtains to all the openings, while resounding pottery, or some other rattling object, was suspended over the entrance to warn the inmates whenever a stranger raised the curtain to pass into the house. No one was allowed admittance who had not the owner's full permission to do so, unless the degree of relationship or necessity justified the liberty.'

REMAINS OF THE CITY

Our labours in the palace did not prevent our making explorations on the hill or mountain. We had spied to the north of the palace, some 812 feet distant, a group of four houses, or small palaces, the ruins of which appeared sufficiently interesting to be reproduced, which I did, after having had the southern portion cleared of its luxuriant vegetation, when I found that the whole length of the northern side was occupied by a dead wall, without apertures or fronts of any kind, facing the palace and overlooking a deep precipice. These structures, like those we discovered subsequently, were all built on the same plan, but in various sizes and dimensions. The inner vault of the left building, however, is ornamented with round lines forming pretty devices, unlike the others, which are quite plain. The pyramids on which these structures were reared had three storeys supported by perpendicular walls. To this group of buildings belonged a small sanctuary or chapel; notwithstanding its dilapidated condition it deserves mention because of some decorative remains, which give a good idea of what must have been its profuse ornamentation.

After our visit to the Lion's Temple, now in a deplorable state of dilapidation, we crossed the high-banked river and reached a high level at the base of Cerro Alto, where we came upon a cluster of buildings composed of diminutive compartments which were used as tombs; two more were found by us in some other buildings to the north of the palace. These small monuments were constructed with uncemented stones, and were in good preservation. The tombs measured 6 feet 7 inches by 1 foot 8 inches to 1 foot 9 inches wide; they occupied the centre of the rooms and were built with flagstones; the bodies were found with two large flat-bottomed vases, ornamented with a little sunk flower, identical with those found at Teotihuacan.

Among the innumerable ruins we discovered were five temples; one, to judge from the height of the pyramid, which was divided into four storeys, and its noble remains must have been important. As we descend the river to the north-west, pyramids, ruined buildings, groups of low houses, temples and palaces, are found occupying the slopes of the Cordilleras, from the crest of the lesser chain to their base. The buildings are found on the high level and temples on eminences, followed by a vast space apparently unoccupied, perhaps the site of ancient gardens. To form an accurate idea of the plan of the city would necessitate the felling of forest over several square miles, an undertaking not to be thought of in our case. Bridges and roads connected the various edifices; some of these roads or streets measure several hundred yards, and I found one bridge of 32 feet square with one single opening, 3 feet 6 inches by 9 feet 9 inches deep. All were built with uncemented stones. Now most bridges have crumbled away, the torrents they spanned are blocked up, and the waters are drained through beds they have hewn for themselves, running over the structures and depositing on their façades stalactites which give them a strange appearance.

The explorer who sees the complete desolation of this ancient city must bear in mind, that in a tropical region excessively hot and damp a long time is not necessary to destroy even structures of solid stone, in order to avoid attributing great antiquity to these ruins. Now the ornamentation, both in the palaces of Palenque, on the upper part of friezes, or the dress of figures, consists of small rolls or round lines of plaster, studded with diminutive spheres or dots, which, as we explained before, were added at the very last, and is clearly seen in our restoration. That ornamentation at once so fragile could not last many hundred years in such surroundings, is proved by the fact that on the least touch round lines and dots come down, and that the ground is strewn with them. If we examine the stairways, which on both sides of the courtyard of the palace connected the two edifices, we shall find the steps unworn, the stairs new; yet communication must have been incessant, and if for long ages thousands of people descended and ascended these stairs, would not the wear and tear be traceable?

The stairs of our public buildings are worn away in no time; if we find them entire at Palenque, it is a proof that they were not long trodden. Nor is this all. The roofs, the walls and courts of the palaces are so well hidden under the thick vegetation which covers them, that a stranger might pass a few yards distant and never suspect their presence. The size of the trees growing between and over these structures has been adduced as a conclusive proof of the age of these monuments. Waldeck calculated their age at 2,000 years and more; [engineer Felipe] Lorainzar computed that these monuments must be 1,700 years old, because he found a mahogany table made of one single piece from a tree in these ruins. His reasoning was based on the erroneous notion that a concentric circle represents one year, whereas I ascertained that in a tropical country nature never rests; for chancing to cut a twig some eighteen months old, I counted no less than eighteen concentric circles. To assure myself that this was not an isolated fact, I cut branches and trees of every size and description, when the same phenomenon occurred in exactly the same proportions. More than this: in my first expedition to Palenque in 1859, I had the eastern side of the palace cleared of its dense vegetation to secure a good photograph. Consequently, the trees that have grown since cannot be more than twenty-two years old; now one of the cuttings measuring some 2 feet in diameter, had upwards of 230 concentric circles; that is at the rate of one in a month, or even less; it follows that the seventeen centuries of Mr. Lorainzar must be reduced to 150 or at most 200 years.

IZAMAL EN ROUTE FOR CHICHEN

Izamal, like many other places in the peninsula, was built on the site of an indigenous city; here, as elsewhere, the chief care of the Spaniards was to destroy alike palaces, temples and written documents, bidding the natives forget their ancient traditions. [Spanish Franciscan Bishop Diego de] Landa, who wrote forty-five years after the Conquest (1566), speaks of the edifices at Izamal as twelve in number, adding that the founders were unknown; whilst [Franciscan chronicler Bernardo] Lizana, sixty years later (1626), with fewer opportunities for collecting legends, gives their history in full, together with the Indian names and their signification; but unfortunately in his time the monuments had dwindled down to five.

Landa says these monuments are of unknown origin, yet in another place he affirms they are the work of the existing race, since he writes: 'Among the remains of monuments which were destroyed are found fragments of human figures and other decorations, such as the natives make even now with very hard cement.' He further mentions having found in a tomb 'stone ornaments artistically wrought, similar to the currency in present use among the natives.'

The great mound to the north is called Kinich-Kakmó, 'The Sun's face with fiery rays', from an idol which stood in the temple crowning its summit. The monument consists of two parts: the basement, nearly 650 feet, surmounted by an immense platform, and the small pyramid to the north. 'Great veneration was felt for the idol or deity of Kinich-Kakmó, and in times of public calamity, the entire population flocked to this shrine with peace offerings, when at midday a fire descended and consumed the sacrifice, in the presence of the assembled multitude. Then the officiating priest notified the will of the deity whether for good or for evil, and prophesied more or less the secret longings of their hearts: but as they could not always guess aright, it not unfrequently happened that their expectations were not fulfilled.'

Facing this to the south was another great mound, known as Ppapp-Hol-Chac, 'the House of Heads and Lightning', the priest's house, presumably similar to those still standing in various towns of Yucatan. The upper portion of this pyramid was levelled down, and on its lower platform was erected the Franciscan church and convent.

The third pyramid to the east supported a temple dedicated to Izamat-Ul, Izamna, or Zamna, the great founder of the ancient Maya empire. 'To him were brought', says Lizana, 'the sick, the halt, and the dead, and he healed and restored them all to life by the touch of his hand'; hence the appellation Kab-Ul, the Miraculous Hand, applied to him. He is often represented by a hand only, which recalled him to the memory of his worshippers. His other names are the Strong, the Mighty Hand, the Long-handed Chief, who wrote the code of the Toltecs, and as such has been identified with Quetzalcoatl, with whom he shared the government; he conducting the civil power, whilst Quetzalcoatl, the virgin-born deity, looked after the spiritual.

'The temple in which these miracles were performed, was much frequented; for this reason four good roads had been constructed, leading to Guatemala, Chiapas and Tabasco. Traces of them can even now be seen in various places.' We also have found marks of a cemented road, from Izamal to the sea facing the island of Cozumel.

TOLTEC COLOSSAL HEADS

Lastly the fourth pyramid to the west, had on its summit the palace of Hunpictok, 'the commander-in-chief of eight thousand flints.' On its side near the basement, consisting of stones laid without mortar, and rounded off at the corners like those of the Aké pyramid, stood the gigantic face reproduced by Stephens, but which has since disappeared. This head is so interesting that I cannot deprive the reader of the description given by the American traveller: 'It is 7 feet 8 inches high. The features were first rudely formed by small rough stones, fixed in the side of the mound by means of mortar, and afterwards perfected with stucco so hard that it has successfully resisted the action of air and water for centuries.' The stone forming the chin alone measures 1 foot 6 inches; the figure has enormous moustachios, and a resemblance may be traced to the gigantic faces in stone at Copan, where the plaster has crumbled away and left the stone bare. The resemblance to the Aké pyramids is remarkable and leads us to conclude that the latter were decorated in the same manner. Here also on the east side is found a figure, from which may be traced the builder's mode of working.

This colossal head is 13 feet high; the eyes, nose and under lip were first formed by rough stones coated over with mortar; the ornaments to the right and left were obtained by the same means; the latter are the best preserved, while double spirals, symbols of wind or speech, may be seen, similar to those in Mexico, at Palenque and Chichen Itza. On the western side of this pyramid, which has been cleared towards the basement, we discovered one of the finest bas-reliefs it has been our fortune to see in Yucatan. Its principal subject is a crouching tiger with a human head and retreating forehead, less exaggerated than those at Palenque, beautifully moulded, and reminding us of the orders of knighthood in which the tiger had the pre-eminence; nor could a better device be imagined for the house of the commander-in-chief at Izamal. To conclude, these documents, which would be a dead letter to one who had not followed the various migrations from north to south, enable us to reconstruct here also a Toltec centre. It may be noted that if numerous monuments are still found in Yucatan, their existence is due to the small number of Spaniards settled in these regions at the time of the Conquest, and more especially to their being at a distance from the centres occupied by the conquerors.

THE RUINS OF CHICHEN ITZA

The ruins of Chichen are 2 miles east of Pisté, and were used as pasture for the cattle of the inhabitants, who at stated periods had the woods cut down, when the monuments were easily distinguished.

This was not my first visit to Chichen, nevertheless my emotion was profound on beholding again the gigantic outline of El Castillo, which we had decided beforehand should be our headquarters, as from its elevated position it offered many strategical advantages, which would secure us against surprise. El Castillo occupies nearly the centre of the ruins; below it to the east was the marketplace, and two small palaces which belonged to it; to the north, a stately but ruinous building, the cenoté and the temple attached; to the north-west, the famous tennis court; to the west and south-west, the Chichan-Chob, the Caracol and the other cenoté, the Nuns' Palace, the Akab-Sib; and farther south, the hacienda, which has long been abandoned.

Here it may be remarked that Yucatan had centres rather than cities; for the groups of dwellings and palaces we find resemble in no way our cities of the present day, although they are continually compared to Spanish places, notably Sevilla, by the conquerors. They consist everywhere of temples and palaces, either of the reigning prince or caciques, of public edifices scattered about, apparently at random, covering a vast area, with cemented roads and gardens intervening, while the avenues were occupied by the dwellings of dependents and slaves. This is borne out by Landa, who says: 'Before the arrival of the Spaniards the aborigines lived in common, were ruled by severe laws, and the lands were cultivated and planted with useful trees. The centre of their towns was occupied by the temples and squares, round which were grouped the palaces of the lords and the priests, and so on in successive order to the outskirts, which were allotted to the lower classes. The wells, necessarily few, were found close to the dwellings of the nobles, who lived in close community for fear of their enemies, and not until the time of the Spaniards did they take to the woods.'

These last words plainly indicate the sudden desertion of Indian cities at the coming of the Spaniards.

The word used by Landa is *pueblo*, 'hamlet', meaning, perhaps, town; at all events, it shows that even after the breaking up of the Maya empire (from great provinces) into small independent principalities, the people had preserved their ancient customs. Chichen Itza, 'the mouth of the wells', from the two cenotés around which the town was built, is more recent than Izamal or Aké, but older than Uxmal, although it belongs, like the latter, to the 'cut stone period.'

Our information respecting it is of the vaguest, and Aguilar and Montejo are equally silent on the subject, while E. Ancona is of opinion that the greater portion of the writings and documents treating of the conquest of Yucatan have been lost, or at any rate have escaped our investigations. Nevertheless, we find in a letter of Montejo to the King of Spain, April 13th, 1529, published by Brinton, of Philadelphia, from the unpublished documents and archives of the Indies, this remarkable passage: 'This region is covered with great and beautiful cities and a dense population' ('ciudades muy frescas', recent, new). Could he have expressed more clearly that the cities he had visited were lately built? Can these places have disappeared and left no trace? Who were the builders of the noble ruins that have filled with admiration everyone who has visited them?

Unfortunately, whether we consult the traditions collected too late, or the Perez manuscript with its doubtful dates, we find no certain data to go upon; in the latter we read that the Toltecs travelled in 360 from Bacalar (Ziyancan) to Chichen;

left it in 452 to return in 888, when they remained until 936; that a governor of Chichen was defeated in 1258 by a prince of Mayapan, etc.; in fact, a mere roll of obscure names without any meaning. If we would find an ascertained historical fact, we must turn to [Spanish Franciscan historian Diego Lopez de] Cogolludo and Landa, who wrote from 1420 to 1460, where the Chichemec exodus is recorded, corresponding to the capture and destruction of Mayapan.

The cause of this emigration (or elopement, since there was a lady in the case) is thus told by Cogolludo: 'A king of Chichen, called Canek (a generic name of the sovereigns of the Iztaes), fell desperately in love with a young princess, who, whether she did not return his affection, or whether she was obliged to obey a parent's mandate, married a more powerful Yucatec cacique. The discarded lover, unable to bear his loss, moved by love and despair, armed his dependents and suddenly fell upon his successful rival; when the gaiety of the feast was exchanged for the din of war, and amidst the confusion the Chichen prince disappeared, carrying off the beautiful bride. But conscious that his power was less than his rival's, and fearing his vengeance, he fled the country with most of his vassals.'

Thus runs the legend; the historical fact is that the inhabitants of Chichen did emigrate, and did establish in the Peten lagoons, 100 leagues to the south, a little principality with Tayasal for its capital, seen by Cortez in his journey to Honduras, and brought under the Spanish sway as late as 1696. That a whole population should abandon their native city, is an example of the facility with which these peoples moved from one place to another at a moment's notice; nevertheless, we cannot accept the reasons given by Cogolludo for this migration, so little in accordance with the deep-seated love of the Maya for their country. It is more likely that one or a series of calamities incident to a primitive race, such as war, pestilence, famine, more or less periodical among the aborigines, was the true cause of their migration.

One thing is clear, that Chichen was inhabited scarcely sixty years before the Conquest, when her monuments were entire; and it is equally clear that a city possessed of two considerable cenotés, so important in a country without water, was not left uninhabited, and that the vacuum left by the exodus was soon filled up, the city preserving its normal existence down to the time of the Spaniards. I am well aware that this kind of evidence will not suit people fond of the marvellous, yet the paucity of documents allows us only a tentative theory, but it will be our care to collect probabilities in such vast numbers, knitting them into a cumulative whole by a patient comparison of monuments, sculptures, bas-reliefs, customs, arms and public ceremonies, so as to make the evidence absolute.

Had Aguilar, who was wrecked and made prisoner on this coast, and lived for nearly eight years as factotum of a powerful cacique, been more observant, we might have a graphic and thorough description of the public and private life among the Maya; but like the rest of his countrymen, his ideas were turned into quite a different channel, so much so that he has not even recorded the name of the place where later Cortez found him. Ancona tells us that the conquest of Yucatan was hastened by Aguilar, who, when in Mexico with Cortez, persuaded Montejo that 'the region was fertile and covered with magnificent monuments' – words of paramount importance, since Aguilar could not have mentioned them in such terms, had they been in ruins or hid away in the woods. It may also be inferred from the incessant mutual warfare of the caciques, that the country had lost its unity and was split up into several provinces, which Herrera says were 'eighteen in number covered with stately edifices.' According to the same authority Montejo had a return of the whole population taken, that he might apportion them among his followers, when everyone received no less than 2,000 or 3,000. This, however, is obviously a gross exaggeration, for supposing the 400 soldiers of Montejo to have dwindled down to 300, the mean population of the district would have amounted to 750,000, which is quite impossible. At all events, the Spaniards occupied Chichen Itza for two years, but nothing is known of their doings, for Montejo was no writer, nor did he, like Cortez, have chroniclers to record his deeds.

THE NUNNERY

To return to our excavations, 'El Palacio de las Monjas', or Nuns' Palace, is one of the most important monuments at Chichen Itza, and possesses a greater number of apartments than any other. Whether the name is due to this circumstance, or from its traditionary appellation, is uncertain; but we know from Mexican writers that it was the custom among the Aztecs to dedicate girls of noble birth to the service of the gods, on their attaining the age of twelve or thirteen. Some remained there until they were about to be married; some few took perpetual vows; others, on account of some vow they had made during sickness, or that the gods might send them a good husband, entered the Nunnery for one, two, three or four years.

They were called deaconesses or sisters; they lived under the superintendence of staid matrons of good character, and upon entering the convent, each girl had her hair cut short.

They all slept in one dormitory, and were not allowed to undress before retiring to rest, that they might always be ready when the signal was given to rise. They occupied their time with weaving and embroidering the tapestry and ornamental work of the temple. They rose in the night to renew the incense in the braziers, a matron leading the procession; the maidens with eyes modestly cast down filed up to the altar, and returned in the same manner; they fasted often, and were required to sweep the temples and keep a constant supply of fresh flowers on the altars. They did penance for the slightest infringement of their religious rules by pricking their tongues and ears with the spines of the maguey plant. Death was the punishment of the Mexican maiden who violated her vow of chastity.

It has been supposed, from the latter custom, that an order of Vestals, similar to those in Rome, existed in America, but the analogy is more apparent than real. According to Clavigero, priesthood was not binding for life among the Maya. Of the different male and female religious orders, those dedicated to Quetzalcoatl deserve particular mention; their members had to submit to the strictest observances, but in compensation the people paid them almost divine honours, whilst their power and influence were boundless. Their chief or superior bore the name of Quetzalcoatl, and never walked abroad except to visit some royal personage. Thus the Nunnery may very well have been both a convent and a priestly abode.

It is not a considerable pile, the façade measuring only some 29 feet by 19 feet 6 inches high, while its grotesque, heavy ornamentation reminds us in its details of a Chinese carving. The base up to the first cornice is occupied by eight large superimposed idols, and four of these figures are enclosed within two very salient cornices. The door is crowned with a medallion representing a cacique or priest with the usual headdress of feathers, the inscription of the palace and stone spires, some of which have entirely disappeared, while the outline of the rest is much defaced. The whole length of the frieze of the north façade has a row of similar gigantic heads, bearing the general characteristics of the ornamentation observable throughout this structure. The Nunnery is typical of the Toltec calli, of which we gave a drawing in our chapter on Tula. The left wing is but 26 feet wide by 13 feet deep and about 32 feet high; it consists of three cornices, with two friezes intervening in which the same designs are repeated; the first two high-reliefs represent stooping figures, one having his body locked in a tortoise shell, while the centre and the sides of the frieze are decorated with grotesque figures like those of the main façade, which, with small variations, are the same throughout the peninsula. These monstrous masks have been called elephants by [French antiquarian, cartographer, artist and explorer Jean-Frédéric Maximilien de] Waldeck and others, who wished to claim a fabulous antiquity for these monuments, but the types they most resemble are the Japanese or Chinese. Here, as at Palenque, the upper portion of the wall is ornamented so as to enhance the effect of height.

The main body of the Nunnery rests on a perpendicular pyramid, the platform of which is occupied by a solidly constructed building, intersected with small apartments having two niches facing each other, traversed by a corridor running from east to west of the pyramid. Over this is a smaller structure or third storey. The first platform is reached by a steep, broad stairway 50 feet wide, which continues with additional steps to the second platform, where the apartments of the ruined building were but cells. The ornamentation of the first story differs from that of other buildings at Chichen; it consists of small sunk panels, having in the centre a large rose-like device, framed with exquisitely moulded stones. The lintels, likewise of stone, were covered with sculptures and inscriptions now fallen into decay; we could only collect three, and even these are much defaced. In this building are curious traces of masonry out of character with the general structure, showing the place to have been occupied at two different epochs.

This second construction, or rather restoration, was affected with the materials of the ancient building, as is seen in the fragments of sculptured stones which in the later construction are identical with those of the first, save that they were put up haphazard, so that the systematic ornamentation of the older structure is no longer reproduced, but in places a thick plaster coating was laid over the whole. The rebuilding may have been the work of the aborigines, since we know that Chichen was abandoned and reoccupied towards the middle of the fifteenth century; or, more likely still, the clumsy restoration may have been the work of the Spaniards during their sojourn in the city, when the Nunnery, from its elevated position, constituted a valuable fortress. Traces of their passage are observable in various other buildings, notably in the Castillo, where their natural fanaticism, coupled with their ignorance, caused them to see in the portraiture of the national and religious life of the Maya, representations of the devil. This could not be suffered to remain, and as they were unable to demolish the temples and palaces in which they lived, they whitewashed the ornamentation, in order that their eyes might not be constantly offended by the subjects therein represented.

We try with small success to undo their savage work by means of daggers, brushes and repeated washes, taking up much time, but in most cases the relief is lost to science, being much too defaced to allow us to take squeezes. The idea that the chiefs who erected these monuments were the authors of their defacement is too absurd for serious consideration.

THE FORTRESS

The Castillo, or rather temple, is reared on a pyramid, facing north and south, and is the most interesting monument at Chichen; its four sides are occupied with staircases, facing the cardinal points. Our drawing shows the western façade. The base of the pyramid measures 175 feet; it consists of nine small esplanades, narrowing towards the top, supported by perpendicular walls, and terminates in a structure about 39 feet on one side by 21 feet high. The upper platform is 68 feet above the level of the plain, having a flight of ninety steps, 39 feet wide, leading up to it.

The name of El Castillo (the fortress), given to this building is appropriate enough; since throughout Central America, temples, in times of war, became real strongholds, on whose gigantic terraces the last desperate conflict was waged against an invading and victorious foe. The struggle might last some time, but was always attended with heavy loss, for each terrace had to be carried against men resolved to die. In the assault on the great temple in Mexico, the Spaniards were several times repulsed before they could get possession of the four esplanades of the pyramid; and when these were taken a fierce encounter followed on the upper platform, which only ended with the utter annihilation of the Aztecs, who were either slaughtered on the spot or hurled down the sides of the pyramid.

The only decoration of the western and southern sides consists in two beautiful cornices, while the interior of the long corridor shows no trace of ornamentation, save over the doors, where gigantic warriors are sculptured. The principal or northern façade must have been very striking when Landa saw it in 1560. Our photograph shows its dilapidated condition, but it can easily be reconstructed. It consists of a portico supported by two massive columns connected by wooden lintels, resembling that in the Nunnery; this portico gives access to a gallery which occupies the whole width of the building. A large room, which must have been the sanctuary, is entered by the only opening out of the gallery, while two pillars with square capitals supported a double corbel vault. Here the stairway was wider, and on each side, forming a balustrade, is a gigantic plumed serpent, whose head and protruding tongue run down the balustrade. All these columns, pillars and wooden lintels, are covered with sculptures and bas-reliefs, the impressions of which kept us closely at work for several days.

As in Mexico, Palenque and Tula, there were no doors properly so called at Chichen, and no traces of hinges are found; but a bamboo or wickerwork screen was suspended across the entrance, and secured at night with a bar. The inner rooms were divided off by hangings, which probably also served to cover the windows. We notice everywhere the small holes in the pillars into which the bars fitted.

Landa mentions the two serpents of the grand staircase, and that the corridor was probably used for burning perfumes: 'Over the door is a kind of coat of arms sculptured in stone, which I could not read. Extending round this edifice is a series of solid constructions; the intervening distances are coated with cement in perfect condition, which looks quite new, so hard was the mortar in which it was laid.' These stucco layers are facsimiles of those at Tula and Teotihuacan, and characteristic of the Toltecs.

It was in this temple that the striking analogy between the sculptures and the bas-reliefs of the plateaus with those at Chichen was first revealed to us; and since the dates of the Toltec emigrations are known, we can fix approximately the age of these monuments. We know, on the other hand, that the Aztec civilization was but a reflex directly derived from the Toltecs, so that in some of their manifestations the two civilizations must resemble each other; from all which it may be seen that these monuments are both Toltec and recent.

The balustrade on the grand staircase consists of a plumed serpent like those forming the outer wall of the temple in Mexico; an emblem of Quetzalcoatl, a deity common to the Toltecs, the Aztecs and the Maya. He is often found on Yucatec buildings. In Mexico, a serpent biting his tail was a favourite design with the Aztecs as a frieze to their houses, or over their entrances, and this we shall also observe at Uxmal. Further, the two columns of the temple façade furnish a still more striking example: the bases represent two serpents' heads, whilst the shafts were ornamented with feathers, proving that the temple was dedicated to Cukulcan (Quetzalcoatl). These shafts are almost an exact reproduction of a Toltec column we unearthed at Tula, as seen in our cuts. The two columns are found 300 leagues from each other, separated by an interval of several centuries; but if, as we firmly believe, the Tula column is Toltec, the other must be so too, for it could not be the result of mere accident. I have only compared the shafts, for the simple reason that the Tula column has no capital.

The bas-relief on the capital of the other consists of a standing figure with upraised arms supporting the entablature; he wears large bracelets, huge feathers form his headdress, his feet are covered with shoes fastened on the instep by a leather knot, a collar of precious stones is around his neck, a richly embroidered maxtli falls to the ground and he wears the long flowing beard characteristic of Quetzalcoatl.

Bas-reliefs [...] from pillars in the sanctuary [...] represent figures in gala costumes, one of which is distinguished by a long beard, and all have the aquiline nose ascribed to the Toltecs. These pillars are occupied by three bas-reliefs, a large one in the centre and two smaller at each side of it. The central relief is a life-size figure of a priest, to judge from the total absence of arms about all the figures on these pillars. The caryatides on the smaller reliefs, notably the lower one, have double spirals over the mouth, presumably a symbol of wind and speech. This spiral about Quetzalcoatl on the outer relief of the altar [is also seen] in the Temple of the Cross at Palenque. All these caryatides represent long-bearded men, whose type is identical with those on the Tula relief, as may be seen by the most superficial comparison of the two.

But is the spiral an emblem of speech? That it is so may be assumed from the upper caryatid, which only supporting the entablature has no spiral about the mouth, while the lower one not only bears aloft the central figure and the edifice, but it seems to carry, to create and breathe life into the whole, as the emblem of civilization. At least so it struck us when we looked at these bearded figures which support the pillars, and saw the symbolical sign of quickening speech around the mouth of each, and considered that the Toltecs were the builders of these monuments, which they reared by their mighty word, in accordance with their pacific and civilizing character, as described by Herrera and Landa. I am well aware that this assumption rests on no scientific basis, nevertheless I hope to bring so many data in its favour as to make it highly probable.

The most remarkable feature about the relief on the capital is its striking resemblance to the caryatides in high relief found on the terrace and façade of Angcor-Thom's palace, given by [French explorer] Francis Garnier; in both the same attitude and dress are observable; the latter consists of the *patoi* with the Cambodians, and the maxtli with the Toltecs; while the sculpture is primitive in both, the only difference being in the relief [...]. Akab-Sib, 'writing in the dark', is a modern appellation, due to a bas-relief found on the lintel of an inner door at the extremity of the building. We can give no explanation respecting this relief. The figure it represents is sitting before a vase full of indistinct objects, with outstretched arm and forefinger pointed, whether in question or command is uncertain – not much for the imagination to go upon. We will restrict ourselves to pointing out the analogy of the characters in the inscriptions with those at Palenque. The structure consists of eighteen rooms, reared on a plain pyramid, with a stairway to the east, without any ornamentation.

The Caracol is a round building, 22 feet in diameter, with a double inner corridor and a central pillar; it is a kind of tower, used probably for civil or religious ceremonies, for we have found this kind of structure at Cozumel and in all the great centres.

The Chichan-Chob, 'Red House', is a small building about 100 yards north of the Caracol; it stands on a rectangular platform, reached by a flight of twelve or fifteen steps. It is the best-preserved monument at Chichen, and might be even now a pleasant residence; for time seems to have respected and to have left untouched its plain, smooth walls, and from its general appearance it cannot date further back than towards the last years of the city in the fifteenth century. Three doorways to the north lead into a corridor extending over the whole length of the building, whence three more openings give access to as many apartments in a perfect state of preservation. Over these doorways, and running the whole length of the corridor, is a narrow stone tablet, on which is graven a row of hieroglyphics very much damaged, of which Stephens gave a faithful reproduction.

RUINED TEMPLES

The situation of Chichen is due probably to the great cenotés which supplied the city with abundant water, and which differ from the complicated underground passages noted in other parts of the state, being immense natural pits of great depth, with perpendicular sides. Of these cenotés, that for general use occupied the centre of the place; picturesque must have been the throng of white-robed women who peopled its steps at all hours of the day to fetch water for household purposes, carrying double-handled urns on their shoulders or on their hips just as they do at the present day. The other, or sacred cenoté, lies in a tangle of wood on the confines of the city, to which a path had to be opened. We find midway a large broken statue of Tlaloc, similar to the two we reproduce further on; the upper portion of the body and the head are wanting. Near it are ruinous heaps, remains of two temples, their base occupied by immense heads of Quetzalcoatl, who seems to have been the tutelary deity of Chichen. On fragments of walls still standing, I notice bas-reliefs in excellent preservation, one representing a large fish with a human head, and the other a figure of a man after death.

Landa's description of these temples would lead us to infer that they were entire in his time, for he says: 'Some distance north of the Castillo were two small theatres built with square blocks; four flights of steps led to the top, paved with fine slabs, and on which low comedies were performed.' Notwithstanding Landa and Cogolludo's testimony, we think they were temples on whose summits the Christianized natives performed their religious ceremonies, which from fear of anathemas they represented to the good bishop as comedies.

The sacred cenoté lies 150 yards beyond; it is oblong in shape, and the two diameters measure from 130 to 165 feet. The surface of the water cannot be reached, for the wall, some 65 feet high, is entire and perpendicular throughout. The desolation of this *aguado*, its walls shrouded with brambles, shrubs and lianas, the sombre forest beyond, but above all the lugubrious associations attaching to it, fill the imagination with indescribable melancholy.

Hither pilgrims repaired, and here offerings were made; for Chichen was a holy city, and among her shrines the cenoté held a conspicuous place, as the following passage from Landa will show: 'From the courtyard of the theatre, a good wide road led to a well some little distance beyond (the road was therefore in perfectly good condition), into which in times of drought the natives used to throw men, as indeed they still do (1560), as an offering to their deities, fully believing that they would not die, even though they disappeared. Precious stones and other valuable objects were also offered; and had the country been rich in gold, this well would contain a vast quantity, because of the great veneration of the natives for it. The *aguado* is round, of great depth, measuring over 100 feet in width and cunningly hewn out of the rock.

'The green colour of the water is due to the foliage; on its banks rises a small building filled with idols in honour of all the principal edifices in the country, exactly like the Pantheon in Rome. I cannot say whether this is an ancient practice or an innovation of the aborigines, who find here their idols to which they can bring their offerings. I also found sculptured lions, vases and other objects, which, from the manner they were fashioned, must have been wrought with metal instruments; besides two statues of considerable size of one single block, with peculiar heads, earrings and the maxtli round their loins.' This passage is very remarkable, but the Abbé Brasseur, who translated it, does not seem to have grasped its true meaning. What, there was a plastered road in good preservation, a temple filled with idols brought thither by the existing natives, more than forty years after the Conquest, there were numerous offerings in honour of the various poliote deities, statues representing the Maya in their national costume, and yet it is urged that these temples were constructed before the Christian era! Landa's account ought to convince the most prejudiced; proving the town to have been, if not quite recent, comparatively so, and inhabited when Montejo occupied it for the first time, in 1527, since thirty-three years later (1560) devotees were still visiting its shrines. This is also the conclusion arrived at by [John Lloyd] Stephens, who had fewer data in support of it.

These pages had already been written when I received [the] *Chicxulub Chronicles*, written at the time of the Conquest, by the Cacique [native chief] Nakuk-Peck; translated and published by [Dr. Daniel] Brinton, [titled *The Maya Chronicles*], Philadelphia, 1882, containing most valuable information whereby my theory is strengthened with all the weight of an official document.

In section four of the *Chronicles*, Nakuk-Peck, writing of Montejo's expedition to Chichen Itza, 1527, says: 'He set out to reconnoitre the place called Chichen Itza, whence he invited the chief of the town to come and see him; and the people said unto him: "There is a King, my Lord, there is a King, even Cocom aun Peck, King Peck, King Chel of Chicantum"; and Captain Cupul said to him: "Stranger warrior, take your rest in these palaces." So spoke Captain Cupul.' After this, can it be further doubted that Chichen was inhabited at the Conquest? Of Izamal he says (in section eighteen): 'When the Spaniards established themselves at Merida in 1542, the chief orator, the high-priest Kinich-Kakmó and the King of the Tutulxius from Mani, made their submission.' Obviously Kinich-Kakmó was the generic name for the high-priests at Izamal who were in full possession of their religious prerogatives at the coming of the Spaniards; consequently the temples and palaces of both Izamal and Chichen were then inhabited. These passages tell us, moreover, what we did not yet know – that after the fall of Mayapan the head of the Cocomes took possession of the principality of Chichen (the fall of Mayapan and the migration of the Chichemecs were probably contemporaneous events), that Kinich-Kakmó was the ally of Tutulxiu, King of Mani, since, jointly with him, he offered his alliance to Montejo, and that the latter and Cocom, both of Toltec descent, were enemies struggling for supremacy over the province.

We read in Torquemada and other writers that the first to arrive in the country were the Cocomes, penetrating the peninsula from Tabasco towards the end of the twelfth century, under the command of their chief Quetzalcoatl, after they had already subdued and civilized most of the northern portion of Yucatan. They were succeeded a century later by the Tutulxius, who marked their passage through the Usumacinta Valley by the erection of Lorillard and Tikal.

Herrera and Landa tell us that 'several tribes came from Chiapas, having entered Yucatan by the south, although this is not generally known to the natives themselves, but he (Landa) conjectures it from the great number of names and verbal constructions common to Chiapas and Yucatan, as from considerable vestiges of deserted localities (Palenque, Ocosingo and Lorillard, etc.). These tribes dwelt in the wilderness south of the peninsula, journeying hence to the hilly region of Kabah, Uxmal, etc., where they settled down under their chief Tutulxiu, spreading everywhere the worship of the Sun, the Moon, Tlaloc and Quetzalcoatl, their chief deities. They lived in great peace with the former inhabitants, and with one another. They had no arms, snaring animals with nets or taking them with lazos.' Yet these kindred tribes, the Cocomes and Tutulxius, so mild in disposition, became fierce and quarrelsome soon after the settlement of the latter in the district, both struggling for supremacy. In this conflict, Mayapan was successively occupied by the victorious party, while both succumbed to the caciques, who, taking advantage of these inter-tribal contentions, consolidated their power, when the peninsula was divided into eighteen independent provinces, continually at war with each other, which finally worked the destruction of the Maya-Toltec civilization.

TENNIS COURTS

The tennis court is at once the largest and the best preserved of any structure of this description; it consists of two perpendicular parallel walls from north to south, 34 by 325 feet, 32 feet high, and 113 feet apart. Both ends are occupied by two small temples always seen in structures of this kind. The southern edifice has no ornamentation of any interest; the northern, which is shown in our cut, contains a single apartment, with a portico to the south supported by columns, forming a balcony whence the grandees witnessed the game sheltered from the fierce rays of the sun.

The ruinous condition of this building will not allow us to judge of its external decoration; but the columns and the walls in the interior are covered with rows of human figures in bas-relief, so damaged, however, that the subjects represented cannot be recognized. The inner walls facing each other, have in the centre of each, some 15 feet from the ground, two stone rings with a hole through the centre, similar to the one we dug up at Tula. The vast proportions of this tlachtli indicate that the national Nahua game was as eagerly played in Yucatan as on the tableland.

OTHER SIGNIFICANT FINDINGS

From the remaining sculptured fragments, whether bases, shafts of columns, or reliefs, representing Quetzalcoatl, we are induced to believe that this stately building was dedicated to this god; all the more that the south end of the eastern wall is occupied by a monument where his symbolical image is everywhere seen. It consists of two apartments of different size, richly decorated; a portico gave access to the main chamber (our cut shows its dimensions), where the bases of the columns are covered with finely sculptured serpents' heads with protruding tongues, over 9 feet long, bearing the characteristics of those on the great temple at Mexico which date 1484–86.

The southern façade of this monument has a beautiful, interlaced frieze, with a procession of tigers, divided by richly fringed shields, bearing a strong resemblance to those of the various tribes, published by [Francesco Antonio] Lorenzana with [Hernan] Cortez's letters, and similar to those generally seen in the Mexican manuscripts. We think we recognize in this a monument of Quetzalcoatl commemorating his victory over

MESOAMERICA ANCIENT ORIGINS

Tezcatlipoca in his football match which took place at Tula, and that this is so seems highly probable.

In the chamber which stood over the ruined portico there was, twenty years ago, a series of paintings descriptive of domestic and public life among the Maya, now entirely destroyed by barbarous explorers, or by the inhabitants of Pisté. Stephens, who saw them, says that they were painted in bright colours of blue, red, yellow and green. Fortunately for us, three sides of the pillars at the entrance are still covered with sculptures, as also the lintels, and all are in better preservation than any at Chichen Itza. Here also we find numerous analogies with Mexican monuments, which, it should be recollected, were the result of Toltec teaching.

All the human figures seen on these monuments have the usual type of the Toltecs of the high plateaus. Their gala dress is identical to the dress of the figures on Tizoc's stone. It is always a headdress of feathers, a heavy collar of precious stones, a bundle of arrows in the left hand, while the right carries a knife similar to that carried by the figures of the Cuauhxicalli, so that we might almost fancy we are following in the train of a Nahua pageant so vividly portrayed by Sahagun, when he says: 'In the feast of the God of Fire, which was held in the month Izcalli' (the eighteenth month), 'the nobles wore a high-fronted paper coronet, with no back to it, a kind of false nose of blue paper, a collar and medallions around their necks, while in their hands was carried a wooden knife, the lower half of which was painted red and the upper white.' Figures wear the mitre just described with the piece of paper about the nose, while the collar and the wooden knife may be seen in both, just like those we see on Tizoc's stone. The analogy is as curious as it is striking.

Besides the huge feather headdress, they carry in their hands spears barbed with feathers, like the figures to the extreme left on Tizoc's stone. These warriors are distributed in groups of two, the conqueror to the left, the vanquished to the right; the latter in the act of presenting the sacred knife he holds in his hand, as a sign of submission. Some of the warriors, instead of the knife, have a two-handed sword, *macana*, furnished with blades of obsidian of Toltec manufacture; a few have their noses pierced, and wear a golden ball, or the obsidian *bezoté*, on their underlip, as a badge of knighthood, which they had adopted from the Nahuas of the Uplands. Further, each figure, whether in the Mexican or Maya bas-relief, wears a kind of casque, fashioned in the shape of a crocodile, a bird, a serpent, or a duck's head, etc., with his name on it. Slight differences of style may occur here and there; for these monuments belong to remote epochs, while Tizoc's stone only dates back to 1485; but the fact that they are found at a distance of more than 900 miles from each other does not make their resemblance less marvellous.

We will end our comparisons with a description of the following statues. One was discovered at Chichen Itza five or six years ago, by Leplongeon, an American explorer; the other in the neighbourhood of Tlascala, close to Mexico, at a considerable distance from the former. The two statues represent the Toltec god Tlaloc, according to Mr. Hamy, whose view I take. This view receives additional probability from the existence of a third statue, which was found I know not where, and which is the property of Mr. Baron of Mexico, who bought it among several other Aztec antiquities, and had it placed in his beautiful garden at Tacubaya, whence it has, I suppose, been removed to Spain. 'This statue,' says Jesus Sanchez, 'is smaller than the other two, measuring but 3 feet by 1 foot 7 inches by 2 feet high. It also represents a man lying on his back, his legs drawn up, his feet on the ground, and holding with both hands a vase which rests against his body.'

There is no doubt that the same deity is figured in these three statues, whatever the ornamentation, which varies according to the epoch, the locality, or the imagination of the artist. But Sanchez adds, 'recollecting that a number of Mexican statues were sculptured also beneath their base, I turned this, when I discovered several devices in relief. The sculptor had carved on the surface of the stone a sheet of water, aquatic plants, two frogs and a fish; while the bank was occupied by beans and grains of maize, which are among the attributes of Tlaloc.'

KABAH AND UXMAL

Ancient historians have made no mention of Kabah, Sachey, Labphak, or Iturbide, cities lying thirty or forty leagues south of Merida. Nevertheless, their rulers are incidentally mentioned under the general appellation of 'people of the Sierra.'

Kabah was an important city, to judge from its monuments, which extend over a large space, consisting of high pyramids, immense terraces, triumphal arches and stately palaces. The village, left to itself since the rebellion, has become an impenetrable forest, making a thorough exploration almost impossible. We were only able to visit half a dozen structures, of which only two are still standing. But these, coupled with those at Uxmal and Chichen, will suffice to give an idea of Yucatec architecture and civilization.

The front of the first palace is richly decorated, consisting of large figures like those at Chichen, and recalling to mind the gigantic superimposed wooden idols met in the islands of the Pacific. The ornamentation of this monument is so elaborate that the architecture entirely disappears under it. Two salient cornices form a frame to immense friezes which, in their details, would compare favourably with our proudest monuments. The advanced state of ruin in which the structure is found, makes it difficult to judge of its original plan; but enough remains to show how unlike other monuments were the decorations which extended over the whole façade, some 162 feet.

This palace, like all Yucatec monuments, rises on a two-storey pyramid; fronting it is a vast esplanade, which had a cistern on each side, while the centre was occupied by a 'picoté'. Over the front, narrowing towards the top, was a decorative wall, usually found in Indian structures. Another peculiarity of these monuments is their facing south and west, and north and east, instead of the four cardinal points. The interior of this edifice has a double range of apartments, the finest we have as yet seen, measuring 29 feet long by 9 feet wide, and 19 feet high, supported by half arches of overlapping stones. One of the inner chambers is entered from the front apartment by three steps cut from a single block of stone, the lower step taking the form of a scroll. The walls at the sides, although half-demolished, still show traces of rich decoration, which consisted of the usual device, whilst the projecting great figures of the façade are also noticeable on the steps, on each side of which are large round eyes. The mouth was below.

All the apartments, and probably all the monuments, had their walls painted with figures and inscriptions, as shown in the few fragments which still remain. 'Among the Maya,' says Viollet-le-Duc, 'painting went hand-in-hand with architecture, supplementing each other.' A picture as understood among us held a very secondary place, while outer decorations were all-important in the monuments at Kabah, which were of brilliant colours, and must have greatly enhanced the striking effect produced by these semi-barbarous, yet withal magnificent edifices.

The second palace, 160 yards north-east of the first, is likewise reared on a pyramid, fronted by an esplanade with two cisterns and a picoté; it has besides a second plateau, consisting of a range of ruined apartments. A flight of steps to the centre, supported by a half-triangular arch, leads to the edifice. This palace is only 16 feet high, and in strong contrast with the rich, elaborate ornamentation of the first. Its outer walls are plain, except groups of three short pilasters each surrounding the edifice above the cornice, forming a sloping rather than perpendicular frieze, like those at Palenque, and in most Yucatec monuments. The front, 162 feet, is almost entire and pierced by seven openings; two have columns and primitive rude capitals, corresponding to the same number of narrow low apartments. As usual the ornamental wall is narrowing towards the top, and is distinctly seen through the vegetation covering the roof.

The rear is a complete ruin. Traces of painting, of which tracings were made, are still visible in the central chamber. It was here that I thought I recognized the rude drawing of a horse and his rider, which was hailed with Homeric laughter; but, although I was mistaken in my supposition, I was very near the truth, since the fact I erroneously heralded at Kabah was found in the north. The discovery is due to [Stephen] Salisbury, who, in 1861, whilst exploring a group of mounds and structures, near the hacienda of Xuyum, 15 miles north of Merida, unearthed the remains of two horses' heads, made of very hard chalk, with bristling hair like a zebra. The work shows considerable artistic skill, and the explorer thinks that it formed part of some bas-reliefs which had belonged to the demolished monuments. Indeed, it is highly probable that these heads were placed on the edifices built by the natives between Montejo's departure in 1530 and his return in 1541; proving that the aborigines had skilfully copied the Spanish horses, and that there was at Xuyum one monument at least similar to those we know. To comment on this would be sheer loss of time.

To the left of this building is a rectangular pyramid, with several storeys, 162 feet at the base by 113 feet. Four outer staircases led up from storey to storey to edifices in an advanced state of ruin, having apartments extending all round, and doorways, some supported by columns, while others are mere openings, as shown in our drawing, which reproduces the north-west side. In this monument and in the second palace are found for the first time lintels of stone, nearly all in very good preservation. Historians have told us nothing regarding Kabah; nevertheless, we have some guiding landmarks from which to reconstruct its history and that of Uxmal, of which in all probability it was a close ally, since the two cities lie at a distance of 5 leagues from each other, and were connected by a plastered road, traces of which are still visible. Consequently the same fate must have been common to both. We know that a century before the Conquest the lord of Mayapan ruled over the whole peninsula, having razed to the ground the capitals of his vanquished rivals, amongst whom were the caciques of Uxmal, Kabah, Labna, etc. This king of Mayapan introduced into the country a force of Mexican soldiers for the maintenance of his authority; and to ensure the good behaviour of the caciques he obliged them to reside at his court, where their state of vassalage was made up to them by a life of great pomp, at the expense of the sovereign.

PYRAMID OF KABAH

Now as the Aztec independence only dates from the reign of Itzcoatl (1426), their conquests and subsequent power cannot be earlier than the reign of Moctezuma I (1440); it is obvious, therefore, that they were not in a position to send reinforcements before 1440 to the ruler of Mayapan. This autocracy lasted but a few years; a coalition of the people of the Sierra was formed, war broke out, the king of Mayapan was vanquished, the city captured and sacked, when the hostage caciques returned to their native provinces. Landa places this event in 1420, whilst Herrera gives 1460 as the probable date. We think the latter justifies his chronology, since he writes 'that seventy years elapsed between the fall of Mayapan and the coming of the Spaniards, varied by years of plenty, storms, pestilence, intestine wars, followed by twenty years of peace and prosperity down to the arrival of the Europeans.'

He further states that each cacique took away from Mayapan all the scientific books they could conveniently carry, and that on their return home they erected temples and palaces, which is the reason why so many buildings are seen in Yucatan; that following on the division of the territory into independent provinces, the people multiplied exceedingly, so that the whole region seemed but one single city.' Landa says 'the monuments were built by the natives in possession of the country at the time of the Conquest, since the bas-reliefs represent them with their types, their arms and their dress'; and 'that on going through the woods and forests, groups of houses and palaces of marvellous construction were found.' This is sufficiently clear, and whether these monuments were inhabited or not at the coming of the Spaniards, is beside the question. On the other hand, the prosperity mentioned by Herrera and Landa found expression in the peculiar monument, which in its original plan represented the florid style, always observable at the end or the brilliant beginning of a new art, being the reproduction of an older style, varied by elaborate ornamentation of questionable taste.

It is usual for a nation to commemorate a return to independence by the erection of triumphal arches, statues and monuments. That this was the case at Kabah is shown in the two remarkable bas-reliefs in our drawings, which were probably part of a monument raised in honour of the victory obtained by the allied caciques. Like the Tizoc stone, these bas-reliefs represent a conqueror, in the rich Yucatec costume, receiving the sword of a captive Aztec; the latter is easily recognized from his plainer headdress and the maxtli girding his loins. His headdress is identical to those described by Lorenzana in his letters to Cortez and Charles V, and not unlike those which the Mexican conquerors sometimes exacted from their vanquished foes. The other bas-relief has the same characteristics, but the headdress is even more significant, for it is fashioned out of the head of an animal like those of the Mexican manuscripts. In this relief the conqueror spares the life of the vanquished, bidding him depart in peace. It is obvious, nay, we affirm, that this is a representation of a battle between Yucatecs and Mexicans dating somewhere between 1460 and 1470; since we know that Mayapan was the only city which implored the aid of the Aztecs, and that after its destruction the inhabitants obtained permission to establish themselves in the province of Maxcanu, east of Merida, where their descendants are found to this very day. These repetitions were necessary to convince a class of archaeologists who claim for these monuments a hoary antiquity.

THE AZTECS

*H**istory of the Conquest of Mexico* is a four-volume work written by American historian William Hickling Prescott (1796—1859), published in 1843. The book provides a comprehensive account of the Spanish conquest of the Aztec Empire, led by Hernán Cortés, and the subsequent fall of the Aztec ruler Moctezuma II. Here we present selected extracts covering up to the reigns of Nezahualpilli and Moctezuma – before the discovery by the Spanish.

Prescott's work is based on extensive research, including primary sources such as the writings of early Spanish chroniclers like Bernal Díaz del Castillo and Bartolomé de las Casas, as well as later historians and scholars. Put another way, Prescott's account is largely based on primary sources written by Spanish conquistadors and their enablers. These sources often present a one-sided and biased view of the events, favouring the Spanish perspective and downplaying or justifying the atrocities committed against the Aztecs – a colonizer's perspective. Modern historians would argue that Prescott did not sufficiently question or contextualize these biased accounts.

As a nineteenth-century American historian, Prescott was undoubtedly influenced by his own cultural biases and the Eurocentric worldview prevalent in his time, introducing a second layer of bias to that introduced by his source materials. His work perpetuates stereotypes or misconceptions about the Aztec civilization and its people, portraying them as 'barbaric' or 'savage' in comparison to the Spanish. Modern historians are more cautious about making value judgments and emphasize understanding the Aztecs within their cultural context, appreciating their achievements and complexities without imposing a Eurocentric perspective.

Prescott's account of the conquest often focuses on the actions and decisions of the Spanish conquistadors, particularly Hernán Cortés, at the expense of recognizing the agency of the indigenous peoples. Today, historians emphasize the importance of understanding the complex political and social dynamics among different indigenous groups in the region (many of whom had themselves been victims of Aztec aggression), as well as their roles in shaping the outcome of the conquest. This includes acknowledging the alliances formed between indigenous groups and the Spanish, which were crucial in the eventual defeat of the Aztec Empire.

While useful as a historical document, therefore, Prescott's work should be approached with a critical mindset and checked against the interpretations of more recent work.

HISTORY OF THE CONQUEST OF MEXICO

POLITICAL AND SOCIAL INSTITUTIONS OF THE AZTECS

Of all that extensive empire which once acknowledged the authority of Spain in the New World, no portion, for interest and importance, can be compared with Mexico – and this equally, whether we consider the variety of its soil and climate; the inexhaustible stores of its mineral wealth; its scenery, grand and picturesque beyond example; the character of its ancient inhabitants, not only far surpassing in intelligence that of the other North American races, but reminding us, by their monuments, of the primitive civilization of Egypt and Hindustan; or, lastly, the peculiar circumstances of its Conquest, adventurous and romantic as any legend devised by Norman or Italian bard of chivalry.

But in order that the reader may have a better understanding of the subject, it will be well, before entering on it, to take a general survey of the political and social institutions of the races who occupied the land at the time of its discovery.

The country of the ancient Mexicans, or Aztecs as they were called, formed but a very small part of the extensive territories comprehended in the modern republic of Mexico. Its boundaries cannot be defined with certainty. They were much enlarged in the latter days of the empire, when they may be considered as reaching from about the eighteenth degree north to the twenty-first, on the Atlantic; and from the fourteenth to the nineteenth, including a very narrow strip, on the Pacific. In its greatest breadth, it could not exceed five degrees and a half, dwindling, as it approached its south-eastern limits, to less than two. It covered, probably, less than 16,000 square leagues. Yet such is the remarkable formation of this country, that, though not more than twice as large as New England, it presented every variety of climate, and was capable of yielding nearly every fruit, found between the equator and the Arctic Circle.

All along the Atlantic, the country is bordered by a broad tract, called the *tierra caliente*, or hot region, which has the usual high temperature of equinoctial lands. Parched and sandy plains are intermingled with others, of exuberant fertility, almost impervious from thickets of aromatic shrubs and wildflowers, in the midst of which tower up trees of that magnificent growth which is found only within the tropics. In this wilderness of sweets lurks the fatal malaria, engendered, probably, by the decomposition of rank vegetable substances in a hot and humid soil. The season of the bilious fever – *vómito*, as it is called – which scourges these coasts, continues from the spring to the autumnal equinox, when it is checked by the cold winds that descend from Hudson's Bay. These winds in the winter season frequently freshen into tempests, and sweeping down the Atlantic coast and the winding Gulf of Mexico, burst with the fury of a hurricane on its unprotected shores, and on the neighbouring West India islands. Such are the mighty spells with which Nature has surrounded this land of enchantment, as if to guard the golden treasures locked up within its bosom. The genius and enterprise of man have proved more potent than her spells.

After passing some 20 leagues across this burning region, the traveller finds himself rising into a purer atmosphere. His limbs recover their elasticity. He breathes more freely, for his senses are not now oppressed by the sultry heats and intoxicating perfumes of the valley. The aspect of nature, too, has changed, and his eye no longer revels among the gay variety of colours with which the landscape was painted there. The vanilla, the indigo and the flowering cacao groves disappear as he advances. The sugar cane and the glossy leaved banana still accompany him; and, when he has ascended about 4,000 feet, he sees in the unchanging verdure, and the rich foliage of the liquid-amber tree, that he has reached the height where clouds and mists settle, in their passage from the Mexican Gulf. This is the region of perpetual humidity; but he welcomes it with pleasure, as announcing his escape from the influence of the deadly *vómito*. He has entered the *tierra templada*, or temperate region, whose character resembles that of the temperate zone of the globe. The features of the scenery become grand, and even terrible. His road sweeps along the base of mighty mountains, once gleaming with volcanic fires, and still resplendent in their mantles of snow, which serve as beacons to the mariner, for many a league at sea. All around he beholds traces of their ancient combustion, as his road passes along vast tracts of lava, bristling in the innumerable fantastic forms into which the fiery torrent has been thrown by the obstacles in its career. Perhaps, at the same moment, as he casts his eye down some steep slope, or almost unfathomable ravine, on the margin of the road, he sees their depths glowing with the rich blooms and enamelled vegetation of the tropics.

Such are the singular contrasts presented, at the same time, to the senses, in this picturesque region!

Still pressing upwards, the traveller mounts into other climates, favourable to other kinds of cultivation. The yellow maize, or Indian corn, as we usually call it, has continued to follow him up from the lowest level; but he now first sees fields of wheat, and the other European grains brought into the country by the conquerors. Mingled with them, he views the plantations of the aloe or maguey (*agave Americana*), applied to such various and important uses by the Aztecs. The oaks now acquire a sturdier growth, and the dark forests of pine announce that he has entered the *tierra fria*, or cold region – the third and last of the great natural terraces into which the country is divided. When he has climbed to the height of between 7,000 and 8,000 feet, the weary traveller sets his foot on the summit of the Cordillera of the Andes – the colossal range that, after traversing South America and the Isthmus of Darien, spreads out, as it enters Mexico, into that vast sheet of tableland which maintains an elevation of more than 6,000 feet, for the distance of nearly 200 leagues, until it gradually declines in the higher latitudes of the north.

Across this mountain rampart a chain of volcanic hills stretches, in a westerly direction, of still more stupendous dimensions, forming, indeed, some of the highest land on the globe. Their peaks, entering the limits of perpetual snow, diffuse a grateful coolness over the elevated plateaus below; for these last, though termed 'cold', enjoy a climate the mean temperature of which is not lower than that of the central parts of Italy. The air is exceedingly dry; the soil, though naturally good, is rarely clothed with the luxuriant vegetation of the lower regions. It frequently, indeed, has a parched and barren aspect, owing partly to the greater evaporation which takes place on these lofty plains, through the diminished pressure of the atmosphere, and partly, no doubt, to the want of trees to shelter the soil from the fierce influence of the summer sun. In the time of the Aztecs, the tableland was thickly covered with larch, oak, cypress and other forest trees, the extraordinary dimensions of some of which, remaining to the present day, show that the curse of barrenness in later times is chargeable more on man than on nature. Indeed, the early Spaniards made as indiscriminate war on the forest as did our Puritan ancestors, though with much less reason. After once conquering the country, they had no lurking ambush to fear from the submissive, semi-civilized native, and were not, like our forefathers, obliged to keep watch and ward for a century. This spoliation of the ground, however, is said to have been pleasing to their imaginations, as it reminded them of the plains of their own Castile – the tableland of Europe; where the nakedness of the landscape forms the burden of every traveller's lament who visits that country.

Midway across the continent, somewhat nearer the Pacific than the Atlantic Ocean, at an elevation of nearly 7,500 feet, is the celebrated Valley of Mexico. It is of an oval form, about 67 leagues in circumference, and is encompassed by a towering rampart of porphyritic rock, which nature seems to have provided, though ineffectually, to protect it from invasion.

The soil, once carpeted with a beautiful verdure and thickly sprinkled with stately trees, is often bare, and, in many places, white with the incrustation of salts caused by the draining of the waters. Five lakes are spread over the Valley, occupying one-tenth of its surface. On the opposite borders of the largest of these basins, much shrunk in its dimensions since the days of the Aztecs, stood the cities of Mexico and Tezcuco, the capitals of the two most potent and flourishing states of Anahuac, whose history, with that of the mysterious races that preceded them in the country, exhibits some of the nearest approaches to civilization to be met with anciently on the North American continent.

Of these races the most conspicuous were the Toltecs. Advancing from a northerly direction, but from what region is uncertain, they entered the territory of Anahuac, probably before the close of the seventh century. Of course, little can be gleaned with certainty respecting a people whose written records have perished, and who are known to us only through the traditionary legends of the nations that succeeded them. By the general agreement of these, however, the Toltecs were well instructed in agriculture and many of the most useful mechanic arts; were nice workers of metals; invented the complex arrangement of time adopted by the Aztecs; and, in short, were the true fountains of the civilization which distinguished this part of the continent in later times. They established their capital at Tula, north of the Mexican Valley, and the remains of extensive buildings were to be discerned there at the time of the Conquest. The noble ruins of religious and other edifices, still to be seen in various parts of New Spain, are referred to this people, whose name, 'Toltec', has passed into a synonym for 'architect'. Their shadowy history reminds us of those primitive races who preceded the ancient Egyptians in the march of civilization; fragments of whose monuments, as they are seen to this day, incorporated with the buildings of the Egyptians themselves, give to these latter the appearance of almost modern constructions.

After a period of four centuries, the Toltecs, who had extended their sway over the remotest borders of Anahuac, having been greatly reduced, it is said, by famine, pestilence and unsuccessful wars, disappeared from the land as silently and mysteriously as they had entered it. A few of them still lingered behind, but much the greater number, probably, spread over the region of Central America and the neighbouring isles; and the traveller now speculates on the majestic ruins of Mitla and Palenque, as possibly the work of this extraordinary people.

After the lapse of another 100 years, a numerous and rude tribe, called the Chichimecs, entered the deserted country from the regions of the far North-west. They were speedily followed by other races, of higher civilization, perhaps of the same family with the Toltecs, whose language they appear to have spoken. The most noted of these were the Aztecs or Mexicans, and the Acolhuans. The latter, better known in later times by the name of Tezcucans, from their capital, Tezcuco, on the eastern border of the Mexican lake, were peculiarly fitted, by their comparatively mild religion and manners, for receiving the tincture of civilization which could be derived from the few Toltecs that still remained in the country. This, in their turn, they communicated to the barbarous Chichimecs, a large portion of whom became amalgamated with the new settlers as one nation.

Availing themselves of the strength derived, not only from this increase of numbers, but from their own superior refinement, the Acolhuans gradually stretched their empire over the ruder tribes in the north; while their capital was filled with a numerous population, busily employed in many of the more useful and even elegant arts of a civilized community. In this palmy state, they were suddenly assaulted by a warlike neighbour, the Tepanecs, their own kindred, and inhabitants of the same valley as themselves. Their provinces were overrun, their armies beaten, their king assassinated and the flourishing city of Tezcuco became the prize of the victor. From this abject condition the uncommon abilities of the young prince, Nezahualcoyotl, the rightful heir to the crown, backed by the efficient aid of his Mexican allies, at length redeemed the state, and opened to it a new career of prosperity, even more brilliant than the former.

The Mexicans, with whom our history is principally concerned, came also, as we have seen, from the remote regions of the North – the populous hive of nations in the New World, as it has been in the Old. They arrived on the borders of Anahuac towards the beginning of the thirteenth century, sometime after the occupation of the land by the kindred races. For a long time they did not establish themselves in any permanent residence, but continued shifting their quarters to different parts of the Mexican Valley, enduring all the casualties and hardships of a migratory life. On one occasion they were enslaved by a more powerful tribe; but their ferocity soon made them formidable to their masters. After a series of wanderings and adventures which need not shrink from comparison with the most extravagant legends of the heroic ages of antiquity, they at length halted on the south-western borders of the principal lake, in the year 1325. They there beheld, perched on the stem of a prickly pear, which shot out from the crevice of a rock that was washed by the waves, a royal eagle of extraordinary size and beauty, with a serpent in his talons, and his broad wings opened to the rising sun. They hailed the auspicious omen, announced by an oracle as indicating the site of their future city, and laid its foundations by sinking piles into the shallows; for the low marshes were half buried underwater. On these they erected their light fabrics of reeds and rushes, and sought a precarious subsistence from fishing, and from the wild fowl which frequented the waters, as well as from the cultivation of such simple vegetables as they could raise on their floating gardens. The place was called Tenochtitlan, in token of its miraculous origin, though only known to Europeans by its other name of Mexico, derived from their war god, Mexitli. The legend of its foundation is still further commemorated by the device of the eagle and the cactus, which form the arms of the modern Mexican republic. Such were the humble beginnings of the Venice of the Western World.

FORMING THE AZTEC EMPIRE

The forlorn condition of the new settlers was made still worse by domestic feuds. A part of the citizens seceded from the main body, and formed a separate community on the neighbouring marshes. Thus divided, it was long before they could aspire to the acquisition of territory on the mainland. They gradually increased, however, in numbers, and strengthened themselves yet more by various improvements in their polity and military discipline, while they established a reputation for courage as well as cruelty in war which made their name terrible throughout the Valley. In the early part of the fifteenth century, nearly 100 years from the foundation of the city, an event took place which created an entire revolution in the circumstances and, to some extent, in the character of the Aztecs. This was the subversion of the Tezcucan monarchy by the Tepanecs, already noticed. When the oppressive conduct of the victors had at length aroused a spirit of resistance, its prince, Nezahualcoyotl, succeeded, after incredible perils and escapes, in mustering such a force as, with the aid of the Mexicans, placed him on a level with his enemies. In two successive battles, these were defeated with great slaughter, their chief slain and their territory, by one of those sudden reverses which characterize the wars of petty states, passed into the hands of the conquerors. It was awarded to Mexico, in return for its important services.

Then was formed that remarkable league, which, indeed, has no parallel in history. It was agreed between the states of Mexico, Tezcuco and the neighbouring little kingdom of Tlacopan, that they should mutually support each other in their wars, offensive and defensive, and that in the distribution of the spoil one-fifth should be assigned to Tlacopan, and the remainder be divided, in what proportions is uncertain, between the other powers.

The Tezcucan writers claim an equal share for their nation with the Aztecs. But this does not seem to be warranted by the immense increase of territory subsequently appropriated by the latter. And we may account for any advantage conceded to them by the treaty, on the supposition that, however inferior they may have been originally, they were, at the time of making it, in a more prosperous condition than their allies, broken and dispirited by long oppression. What is more extraordinary than the treaty itself, however, is the fidelity with which it was maintained. During a century of uninterrupted warfare that ensued, no instance occurred where the parties quarrelled over the division of the spoil, which so often makes shipwreck of similar confederacies among civilized states.

The allies for some time found sufficient occupation for their arms in their own valley; but they soon overleaped its rocky ramparts, and by the middle of the fifteenth century, under the first Moctezuma, had spread down the sides of the tableland to the borders of the Gulf of Mexico. Tenochtitlan, the Aztec capital, gave evidence of the public prosperity. Its frail tenements were supplanted by solid structures of stone and lime. Its population rapidly increased. Its old feuds were healed. The citizens who had seceded were again brought under a common government with the main body, and the quarter they occupied was permanently connected with the parent city; the dimensions of which, covering the same ground, were much larger than those of the modern capital of Mexico.

Fortunately, the throne was filled by a succession of able princes, who knew how to profit by their enlarged resources and by the martial enthusiasm of the nation. Year after year saw them return, loaded with the spoils of conquered cities, and with throngs of devoted captives, to their capital. No state was able long to resist the accumulated strength of the confederates. At the beginning of the sixteenth century, just before the arrival of the Spaniards, the Aztec dominion reached across the continent, from the Atlantic to the Pacific, and, under the bold and bloody Ahuitzotl, its arms had been carried far over the limits already noticed as defining its permanent territory, into the farthest corners of Guatemala and Nicaragua. This extent of empire, however limited in comparison with that of many other states, is truly wonderful, considering it as the acquisition of a people whose whole population and resources had so recently been comprised within the walls of their own petty city, and considering, moreover, that the conquered territory was thickly settled by various races, bred to arms like the Mexicans, and little inferior to them in social organization. The history of the Aztecs suggests some strong points of resemblance to that of the ancient Romans, not only in their military successes, but in the policy which led to them.

AZTEC NOBILITY

The form of government differed in the different states of Anahuac. With the Aztecs and Tezcucans it was monarchical and nearly absolute. The two nations resembled each other so much in their political institutions that one of their historians has remarked, in too unqualified a manner indeed, that what is told of one may be always understood as applying to the other. I shall direct my inquiries to the Mexican polity, borrowing an illustration occasionally from that of the rival kingdom.

The government was an elective monarchy. Four of the principal nobles, who had been chosen by their own body in the preceding reign, filled the office of electors, to whom were added, with merely an honorary rank, however, the two royal allies of Tezcuco and Tlacopan. The sovereign was selected from the brothers of the deceased prince, or, in default of them, from his nephews. Thus the election was always restricted to the same family. The candidate preferred must have distinguished himself in war, though, as in the case of the last Moctezuma, he were a member of the priesthood. This singular mode of supplying the throne had some advantages. The candidates received an education which fitted them for the royal dignity, while the age at which they were chosen not only secured the nation against the evils of minority, but afforded ample means for estimating their qualifications for the office. The result, at all events, was favourable; since the throne, as already noticed, was filled by a succession of able princes, well qualified to rule over a warlike and ambitious people. The scheme of election, however defective, argues a more refined and calculating policy than was to have been expected from a barbarous nation.

The new monarch was installed in his regal dignity with much parade of religious ceremony, but not until, by a victorious campaign, he had obtained a sufficient number of captives to grace his triumphal entry into the capital and to furnish victims for the dark and bloody rites which stained the Aztec superstition. Amidst this pomp of human sacrifice he was crowned. The crown, resembling a mitre in its form, and curiously ornamented with gold, gems and feathers, was placed on his head by the lord of Tezcuco, the most powerful of his royal allies. The title of 'King', by which the earlier Aztec princes are distinguished by Spanish writers, is supplanted by that of 'Emperor' in the later reigns, intimating, perhaps, his superiority over the confederated monarchies of Tlacopan and Tezcuco.

The Aztec princes, especially towards the close of the dynasty, lived in a barbaric pomp, truly Oriental. Their spacious palaces were provided with halls for the different councils who aided the monarch in the transaction of business. The chief of these was a sort of privy council, composed in part, probably, of the four electors chosen by the nobles after the accession, whose places, when made vacant by death, were immediately supplied as before. It was the business of this body, so far as can be gathered from the very loose accounts given of it, to advise the king, in respect to the government of the provinces, the administration of the revenues, and, indeed, on all great matters of public interest.

In the royal buildings were accommodations, also, for a numerous bodyguard of the sovereign, made up of the chief nobility. It is not easy to determine with precision, in these barbarian governments, the limits of the several orders. It is certain there was a distinct class of nobles, with large, landed possessions, who held the most important offices near the person of the prince, and engrossed the administration of the provinces and cities. Many of these could trace their descent from the founders of the Aztec monarchy. According to some writers of authority, there were thirty great *caciques*, who had their residence, at least a part of the year, in the capital, and who could muster 100,000 vassals each on their estates. Without relying on such wild statements, it is clear, from the testimony of the conquerors, that the country was occupied by numerous powerful chieftains, who lived like independent princes on their domains. If it be true that the kings encouraged, or, indeed, exacted, the residence of these nobles in the capital, and required hostages in their absence, it is evident that their power must have been very formidable.

Their estates appear to have been held by various tenures, and to have been subject to different restrictions. Some of them, earned by their own good swords or received as the recompense of public services, were held without any limitation, except that the possessors could not dispose of them to a plebeian. Others were entailed on the eldest male issue, and, in default of such, reverted to the crown. Most of them seem to have been burdened with the obligation of military service. The principal chiefs of Tezcuco, according to its chronicler, were expressly obliged to support their prince with their armed vassals, to attend his court, and aid him in the council. Some, instead of these services, were to provide for the repairs of his buildings, and to keep the royal demesnes in order, with an annual offering, by way of homage, of fruits and flowers. It was usual, if we are to believe historians, for a new king, on his accession, to confirm the investiture of estates derived from the crown.

AZTEC JUDICIAL SYSTEM

It **cannot be denied** that we recognize, in all this, several features of the feudal system, which, no doubt, lose nothing of their effect under the hands of the Spanish writers, who are fond of tracing analogies to European institutions. But such analogies lead sometimes to very erroneous conclusions. The obligation of military service, for instance, the most essential principle of a fief, seems to be naturally demanded by every government from its subjects. As to minor points of resemblance, they fall far short of that harmonious system of reciprocal service and protection which embraced, in nice gradation, every order of a feudal monarchy. The kingdoms of Anahuac were in their nature despotic, attended, indeed, with many mitigating circumstances unknown to the despotisms of the East; but it is chimerical to look for much in common – beyond a few accidental forms and ceremonies – with those aristocratic institutions of the Middle Ages which made the court of every petty baron the precise image in miniature of that of his sovereign.

The legislative power, both in Mexico and Tezcuco, resided wholly with the monarch. This feature of despotism, however, was in some measure counteracted by the constitution of the judicial tribunals – of more importance, among a rude people, than the legislative, since it is easier to make good laws for such a community than to enforce them, and the best laws, badly administered, are but a mockery. Over each of the principal cities, with its dependent territories, was placed a supreme judge, appointed by the crown, with original and final jurisdiction in both civil and criminal cases. There was no appeal from his sentence to any other tribunal, nor even to the king. He held his office during life; and anyone who usurped his ensigns was punished with death.

Below this magistrate was a court, established in each province, and consisting of three members. It held concurrent jurisdiction with the supreme judge in civil suits, but in criminal an appeal lay to his tribunal. Besides these courts, there was a body of inferior magistrates, distributed through the country, chosen by the people themselves in their several districts. Their authority was limited to smaller causes, while the more important were carried up to the higher courts. There was still another class of subordinate officers, appointed also by the people, each of whom was to watch over the conduct of a certain number of families and report any disorder or breach of the laws to the higher authorities.

In Tezcuco the judicial arrangements were of a more refined character; and a gradation of tribunals finally terminated in a general meeting or parliament, consisting of all the judges, great and petty, throughout the kingdom, held every eighty days in the capital, over which the king presided in person. This body determined all suits which, from their importance or difficulty, had been reserved for its consideration by the lower tribunals. It served, moreover, as a council of state, to assist the monarch in the transaction of public business.

Such are the vague and imperfect notices that can be gleaned, respecting the Aztec tribunals, from the hieroglyphical paintings still preserved, and from the most accredited Spanish writers. These, being usually ecclesiastics, have taken much less interest in this subject than in matters connected with religion. They find some apology, certainly, in the early destruction of most of the Indian paintings, from which their information was, in part, to be gathered.

On the whole, however, it must be inferred that the Aztecs were sufficiently civilized to evince a solicitude for the rights both of property and of persons. The law, authorizing an appeal to the highest judicature in criminal matters only, shows an attention to personal security, rendered the more obligatory by the extreme severity of their penal code, which would naturally have made them more cautious of a wrong conviction. The existence of a number of coordinate tribunals, without a central one of supreme authority to control the whole, must have given rise to very discordant interpretations of the law in different districts. But this is an evil which they shared in common with most of the nations of Europe.

The provision for making the superior judges wholly independent of the crown was worthy of an enlightened people. It presented the strongest barrier that a mere constitution could afford against tyranny. It is not, indeed, to be supposed that, in

a government otherwise so despotic, means could not be found
for influencing the magistrate. But it was a great step to fence
round his authority with the sanction of the law; and no one of
the Aztec monarchs, so far as I know, is accused of an attempt
to violate it.

To receive presents or a bribe, to be guilty of collusion in
any way with a suitor, was punished, [by] a judge, with death.
Who, or what tribunal, decided as to his guilt, does not appear.
In Tezcuco this was done by the rest of the court. But the king
presided over that body. The Tezcucan prince Nezahualpilli,
who rarely tempered justice with mercy, put one judge to death
for taking a bribe, and another for determining suits in his own
house – a capital offence, also, by law.

The judges of the higher tribunals were maintained
from the produce of a part of the crown lands, reserved
for this purpose. They, as well as the supreme judge, held
their offices for life. The proceedings in the courts were
conducted with decency and order. The judges wore an
appropriate dress, and attended to business both parts of
the day, dining always, for the sake of [efficiency], in an
apartment of the same building where they held their
session; a method of proceeding much commended by the
Spanish chroniclers, to whom [efficiency] was not very
familiar in their own tribunals. Officers attended to preserve
order, and others summoned the parties and produced them
in court. No counsel was employed; the parties stated their
own case and supported it by their witnesses. The oath of
the accused was also admitted in evidence. The statement
of the case, the testimony, and the proceedings of the trial
were all set forth by a clerk, in hieroglyphical paintings, and

handed over to the court. The paintings were executed with so much accuracy that in all suits respecting real property they were allowed to be produced as good authority in the Spanish tribunals, very long after the Conquest; and a chair for their study and interpretation was established at Mexico in 1553, which has long since shared the fate of most other provisions for learning in that unfortunate country.

A capital sentence was indicated by a line traced with an arrow across the portrait of the accused. In Tezcuco, where the king presided in the court, this, according to the national chronicler, was done with extraordinary parade. His description, which is of rather a poetical cast, I give in his own words. 'In the royal palace of Tezcuco was a courtyard, on the opposite sides of which were two halls of justice. In the principal one, called the "tribunal of God", was a throne of pure gold, inlaid with turquoises and other precious stones. On a stool in front was placed a human skull, crowned with an immense emerald of a pyramidal form, and surmounted by an aigrette of brilliant plumes and precious stones. The skull was laid on a heap of military weapons, shields, quivers, bows and arrows. The walls were hung with tapestry, made of the hair of different wild animals, of rich and various colours, festooned by gold rings and embroidered with figures of birds and flowers. Above the throne was a canopy of variegated plumage, from the centre of which shot forth resplendent rays of gold and jewels. The other tribunal, called "the King's", was also surmounted by a gorgeous canopy of feathers, on which were emblazoned the royal arms. Here the sovereign gave public audience and communicated his despatches. But when he decided important causes, or confirmed a capital sentence, he passed to the "tribunal of God", attended by the fourteen great lords of the realm, marshalled according to their rank. Then, putting on his mitred crown, incrusted with precious stones, and holding a golden arrow, by way of sceptre, in his left hand, he laid his right upon the skull, and pronounced judgment.' All this looks rather fine for a court of justice, it must be owned. But it is certain that the Tezcucans, as we shall see hereafter, possessed both the materials and the skill requisite to work them up in this manner. Had they been a little further advanced in refinement, one might well doubt their having the bad taste to do so.

LAWS AND REVENUES

The laws of the Aztecs were registered, and exhibited to the people, in their hieroglyphical paintings. Much the larger part of them, as in every nation imperfectly civilized, relates rather to the security of persons than of property. The great crimes against society were all made capital. Even the murder of a slave was punished with death. Adulterers were stoned to death. Thieving, according to the degree of the offence, was punished by slavery or death. Yet the Mexicans could have been under no great apprehension of this crime, since the entrances to their dwellings were not secured by bolts or fastenings of any kind. It was a capital offence to remove the boundaries of another's lands; to alter the established measures; and for a guardian not to be able to give a good account of his ward's property. These regulations evince a regard for equity in dealings, and for private rights, which argues a considerable progress in civilization.

Prodigals, who squandered their patrimony, were punished in like manner; a severe sentence, since the crime brought its adequate punishment along with it. Intemperance, which was the burden, moreover, of their religious homilies, was visited with the severest penalties; as if they had foreseen in it the consuming canker of their own as well as of the other Indian races in later times. It was punished in the young with death, and in older persons with loss of rank and confiscation of property. Yet a decent conviviality was not meant to be proscribed at their festivals, and they possessed the means of indulging it, in a mild fermented liquor, called *pulque*, which is still popular, not only with the Indian, but the European population of the country.

The rites of marriage were celebrated with as much formality as in any Christian country; and the institution was held in such reverence that a tribunal was instituted for the sole purpose of determining questions relating to it. Divorces could not be obtained until authorized by a sentence of this court, after a patient hearing of the parties.

But the most remarkable part of the Aztec code was that relating to slavery. There were several descriptions of slaves: prisoners taken in war, who were almost always reserved for the dreadful doom of sacrifice; criminals, public debtors, persons who, from extreme poverty, voluntarily resigned their freedom, and children who were sold by their own parents. In the last instance, usually occasioned also by poverty, it was common for the parents, with the master's consent, to substitute others of their children successively, as they grew up; thus distributing the burden as equally as possible among the different members of the family. The willingness of freemen to incur the penalties of this condition is explained by the mild form in which it existed.

The contract of sale was executed in the presence of at least four witnesses. The services to be exacted were limited with great precision. The slave was allowed to have his own family, to hold property and even other slaves. His children were free. No one could be born to slavery in Mexico; an honourable distinction, not known, I believe, in any civilized community where slavery has been sanctioned. Slaves were not sold by their masters, unless when these were driven to it by poverty. They were often liberated by them at their death, and sometimes, as there was no natural repugnance founded on difference of blood and race, were married to them. Yet a refractory or vicious slave might be led into the market, with a collar round his neck, which intimated his bad character, and there be publicly sold, and, on a second sale, reserved for sacrifice.

Such are some of the most striking features of the Aztec code, to which the Tezcucan bore great resemblance. With some exceptions, it is stamped with the severity, the ferocity indeed, of a rude people, hardened by familiarity with scenes of blood, and relying on physical instead of moral means for the correction of evil. Still, it evinces a profound respect for the great principles of morality, and as clear a perception of these principles as is to be found in the most cultivated nations.

The royal revenues were derived from various sources. The crown lands, which appear to have been extensive, made their returns in kind. The places in the neighbourhood of the capital were bound to supply workmen and materials for building the king's palaces and keeping them in repair. They were also to furnish fuel, provisions and whatever was necessary for his ordinary domestic expenditure, which was certainly on no stinted scale. The principal cities, which had numerous villages and a large territory dependent on them, were distributed into districts, with each a share of the lands allotted to it, for its support. The inhabitants paid a stipulated part of the produce to the crown. The vassals of the great chiefs, also, paid a portion of their earnings into the public treasury; an arrangement not at all in the spirit of the feudal institutions.

In addition to this tax on all the agricultural produce of the kingdom, there was another on its manufactures. The nature and the variety of the tributes will be best shown by an enumeration of some of the principal articles. These were cotton dresses, and mantles of feather work exquisitely made; ornamented armour; vases and plates of gold; gold dust, bands and bracelets; crystal, gilt and varnished jars and goblets; bells, arms and utensils of copper; reams of paper; grain, fruits, copal, amber, cochineal, cacao, wild animals and birds, timber, lime, mats, etc. In this curious medley of the most homely commodities and the elegant superfluities of luxury, it is singular that no mention should be made of silver, the great staple of the country in later times, and the use of which was certainly known to the Aztecs.

MILITARY INSTITUTIONS

Garrisons were established in the larger cities – probably those at a distance and recently conquered – to keep down revolt, and to enforce the payment of the tribute. Tax-gatherers were also distributed throughout the kingdom, who were recognized by their official badges, and dreaded from the merciless rigour of their exactions. By a stern law, every defaulter was liable to be taken and sold as a slave. In the capital were spacious granaries and warehouses for the reception of the tributes. A receiver-general was quartered in the palace, who rendered in an exact account of the various contributions, and watched over the conduct of the inferior agents, in whom the least malversation was summarily punished. This functionary was furnished with a map of the whole empire, with a minute specification of the imposts assessed on every part of it. These imposts, moderate under the reigns of the early princes, became so burdensome under those at the close of the dynasty, being rendered still more oppressive by the manner of collection, that they bred disaffection throughout the land, and prepared the way for its conquest by the Spaniards.

Communication was maintained with the remotest parts of the country by means of couriers. Post-houses were established on the great roads, about 2 leagues distant from each other. The courier, bearing his dispatches in the form of a hieroglyphical painting, ran with them to the first station, where they were taken by another messenger and carried forward to the next, and so on till they reached the capital. These couriers, trained from childhood, travelled with incredible swiftness – not 4 or 5 leagues an hour, as an old chronicler would make us believe, but with such speed that dispatches were carried from 100 to 200 miles a day. Fresh fish was frequently served at Moctezuma's table in twenty-four hours from the time it had been taken in the Gulf of Mexico, 200 miles from the capital. In this way intelligence of the movements of the royal armies was rapidly brought to court; and the dress of the courier, denoting by its colour the nature of his tidings, spread joy or consternation in the towns through which he passed.

But the great aim of the Aztec institutions, to which private discipline and public honours were alike directed, was the profession of arms. In Mexico, as in Egypt, the soldier shared with the priest the highest consideration. The king, as we have seen, must be an experienced warrior. The tutelary deity of the Aztecs was the god of war. A great object of their military expeditions was to gather hecatombs of captives for his altars. The soldier who fell in battle was transported at once to the region of ineffable bliss in the bright mansions of the Sun. Every war, therefore, became a crusade; and the warrior, animated by a religious enthusiasm like that of the early Saracen or the Christian crusader, was not only raised to a contempt of danger, but courted it, for the imperishable crown of martyrdom. Thus we find the same impulse acting in the most opposite quarters of the globe, and the Asiatic, the European and the American, each earnestly invoking the holy name of religion in the perpetration of human butchery.

The question of war was discussed in a council of the king and his chief nobles. Ambassadors were sent, previously to its declaration, to require the hostile state to receive the Mexican gods and to pay the customary tribute. The persons of ambassadors were held sacred throughout Anahuac. They were lodged and entertained in the great towns at the public charge, and were everywhere received with courtesy, so long as they did not deviate from the high roads on their route. When they did, they forfeited their privileges. If the embassy proved unsuccessful, a defiance, or open declaration of war, was sent; quotas were drawn from the conquered provinces, which were always subjected to military service, as well as the payment of taxes; and the royal army, usually with the monarch at its head, began its march.

The Aztec princes made use of the incentives employed by European monarchs to excite the ambition of their followers. They established various military orders, each having its privileges and peculiar insignia. There seems, also, to have existed a sort of knighthood of inferior degree. It was the cheapest reward of martial prowess, and whoever had not reached it was excluded from using ornaments on his arms or his person, and obliged to wear a coarse white stuff, made from the threads of the aloe, called *nequen*. Even the members of the royal family were not excepted from this law, which reminds one of the occasional practice of Christian knights, to wear plain armour, or shields without device, till they had achieved some doughty feat of chivalry. Although the military orders were thrown open to all, it is probable that they were chiefly filled with persons of rank, who, by their previous training and connections, were able to come into the field under peculiar advantages.

The dress of the higher warriors was picturesque and often magnificent. Their bodies were covered with a close vest of quilted cotton, so thick as to be impenetrable to the light missiles of Indian warfare. This garment was so light and serviceable that it was adopted by the Spaniards. The wealthier chiefs sometimes wore, instead of this cotton mail, a cuirass made of thin plates of gold or silver. Over it was thrown a surcoat of the gorgeous featherwork in which they excelled. Their helmets were sometimes of wood, fashioned like the heads of wild animals, and sometimes of silver, on the top of which waved a panache of variegated plumes, sprinkled with precious stones and ornaments of gold. They wore also collars, bracelets and earrings of the same rich materials.

Their armies were divided into bodies of 8,000 men; and these, again, into companies of 300 or 400, each with its own commander. The national standard, which has been compared to the ancient Roman, displayed, in its embroidery of gold and featherwork, the armorial ensigns of the state. These were significant of its name, which, as the names of both persons and places were borrowed from some material object, was easily expressed by hieroglyphical symbols. The companies and the great chiefs had also their appropriate banners and devices, and the gaudy hues of their many coloured plumes gave a dazzling splendour to the spectacle.

Their tactics were such as belong to a nation with whom war, though a trade, is not elevated to the rank of a science. They advanced singing, and shouting their war cries, briskly charging the enemy, as rapidly retreating, and making use of ambuscades, sudden surprises and the light skirmish of guerrilla warfare. Yet their discipline was such as to draw forth the encomiums of the Spanish conquerors. 'A beautiful sight it was,' says one of them, 'to see them set out on their march, all moving forward so gayly, and in so admirable order!' In battle they did not seek to kill their enemies, so much as to take them prisoners; and they never scalped, like other North American tribes. The valour of a warrior was estimated by the number of his prisoners; and no ransom was large enough to save the devoted captive.

Their military code bore the same stern features as their other laws. Disobedience of orders was punished with death. It was death, also, for a soldier to leave his colours, to attack the enemy before the signal was given, or to plunder another's booty or prisoners. One of the last Tezcucan princes, in the spirit of an ancient Roman, put two sons to death – after having cured their wounds – for violating the last-mentioned law.

I must not omit to notice here an institution the introduction of which in the Old World is ranked among the beneficent fruits of Christianity. Hospitals were established in the principal cities, for the cure of the sick and the permanent refuge of the disabled soldier; and surgeons were placed over them, 'who were so far better than those in Europe,' says an old chronicler, 'that they did not protract the cure in order to increase the pay.'

Such is the brief outline of the civil and military polity of the ancient Mexicans; less perfect than could be desired in regard to the former, from the imperfection of the sources whence it is drawn. Whoever has had occasion to explore the early history of modern Europe has found how vague and unsatisfactory is the political information which can be gleaned from the gossip of monkish annalists. How much is the difficulty increased in the present instance, where this information, first recorded in the dubious language of hieroglyphics, was interpreted in another language, with which the Spanish chroniclers were imperfectly acquainted, while it related to institutions of which their past experience enabled them to form no adequate conception! Amidst such uncertain lights, it is in vain to expect nice accuracy of detail. All that can be done is to attempt an outline of the more prominent features, that a correct impression, so far as it goes, may be produced on the mind of the reader.

Enough has been said, however, to show that the Aztec and Tezcucan races were advanced in civilization very far beyond the wandering tribes of North America. The degree of civilization which they had reached, as inferred by their political institutions, may be considered, perhaps, not much short of that enjoyed by our Saxon ancestors under Alfred. In respect to the nature of it, they may be better compared with the Egyptians; and the examination of their social relations and culture may suggest still stronger points of resemblance to that ancient people. [...]

AZTEC MYTHOLOGY

The civil polity of the Aztecs is so closely blended with their religion that without understanding the latter it is impossible to form correct ideas of their government or their social institutions. I shall endeavour to give a brief sketch of their mythology and their careful provisions for maintaining a national worship.

Mythology may be regarded as the poetry of religion, or rather as the poetic development of the religious principle in a primitive age. It is the effort of untutored man to explain the mysteries of existence, and the secret agencies by which the operations of nature are conducted. Although the growth of similar conditions of society, its character must vary with that of the rude tribes in which it originates; and the ferocious Goth, quaffing mead from the skulls of his slaughtered enemies, must have a very different mythology from that of the effeminate native of Hispaniola, loitering away his hours in idle pastimes, under the shadow of his bananas.

At a later and more refined period, we sometimes find these primitive legends combined into a regular system under the hands of the poet, and the rude outline moulded into forms of ideal beauty, which are the objects of adoration in a credulous age, and the delight of all succeeding ones. Such were the beautiful inventions of Hesiod and Homer, 'who,' says the Father of History, 'created the theogony of the Greeks'; an assertion not to be taken too literally, since it is hardly possible that any man should create a religious system for his nation. They only filled up the shadowy outlines of tradition with the bright touches of their own imaginations, until they had clothed them in beauty which kindled the imaginations of others. The power of the poet, indeed, may be felt in a similar way in a much riper period of society. To say nothing of the *Divina Commedia*, who is there that rises from the perusal of *Paradise Lost* without feeling his own conceptions of the angelic hierarchy quickened by those of the inspired artist, and a new and sensible form, as it were, given to images which had before floated dim and undefined before him?

The last-mentioned period is succeeded by that of philosophy; which, disclaiming alike the legends of the primitive age and the poetical embellishments of the succeeding one, seeks to shelter itself from the charge of impiety by giving an allegorical interpretation to the popular mythology, and thus to reconcile the latter with the genuine deductions of science.

The Mexican religion had emerged from the first of the schools we have been considering, and, although little affected by poetical influences, had received a peculiar complexion from the priests, who had digested as thorough and burdensome a ceremonial as ever existed in any nation. They had, moreover, thrown the veil of allegory over early tradition, and invested their deities with attributes savouring much more of the grotesque conceptions of the Eastern nations in the Old World, than of the lighter fictions of Greek mythology, in which the features of humanity, however exaggerated, were never wholly abandoned.

In contemplating the religious system of the Aztecs, one is struck with its apparent incongruity, as if some portion of it had emanated from a comparatively refined people, open to gentle influences, while the rest breathes a spirit of unmitigated ferocity. It naturally suggests the idea of two distinct sources, and authorizes the belief that the Aztecs had inherited from their predecessors a milder faith, on which was afterwards engrafted their own mythology. The latter soon became dominant, and gave its dark colouring to the creeds of the conquered nations – which the Mexicans, like the ancient Romans, seem willingly to have incorporated into their own – until the same funereal superstition settled over the farthest borders of Anahuac.

The Aztecs recognized the existence of a supreme Creator and Lord the universe. They addressed him, in their prayers, as 'the God by whom we live', 'omnipresent, that knoweth all thoughts, and giveth all gifts', 'without whom man is as nothing', 'invisible, incorporeal, one God, of perfect perfection and purity', 'under whose wings we find repose and a sure defence.' These sublime attributes infer no inadequate conception of the true God. But the idea of unity – of a being with whom volition is action, who has no need of inferior ministers to execute his purposes – was too simple, or too vast, for their understandings; and they sought relief, as usual, in a plurality of deities, who presided over the elements, the changes of the seasons, and the various occupations of man. Of these, there were thirteen principal deities, and more than 200 inferior; to each of whom some special day or appropriate festival was consecrated.

At the head of all stood the terrible Huitzilopochtli, the Mexican Mars; although it is doing injustice to the heroic war god of antiquity to identify him with this sanguinary monster. This was the patron deity of the nation. His fantastic image was loaded with costly ornaments. His temples were the most stately and august of the public edifices; and his altars reeked with the blood of human hecatombs in every city of the empire. Disastrous indeed must have been the influence of such a superstition on the character of the people.

A far more interesting personage in their mythology was Quetzalcoatl, god of the air, a divinity who, during his residence on earth, instructed the natives in the use of metals, in agriculture, and in the arts of government. He was one of those benefactors of their species, doubtless, who have been deified by the gratitude of posterity. Under him, the earth teemed with fruits and flowers, without the pains of culture. An ear of Indian corn was as much as a single man could carry. The cotton, as it grew, took, of its own accord, the rich dyes of human art. The air was filled with intoxicating perfumes and the sweet melody of birds. In short, these were the halcyon days, which find a place in the mythic systems of so many nations in the Old World. It was the golden age of Anahuac.

From some cause, not explained, Quetzalcoatl incurred the wrath of one of the principal gods, and was compelled to abandon the country. On his way he stopped at the city of Cholula, where a temple was dedicated to his worship, the massy ruins of which still form one of the interesting relics of antiquity in Mexico. When he reached the shores of the Mexican Gulf, he took leave of his followers, promising that he and his descendants would revisit them hereafter, and then, entering his wizard skiff, made of serpents' skins, embarked on the great ocean for the fabled land of Tlapallan. He was said to have been tall in stature, with white skin, long, dark hair and a flowing beard. The Mexicans looked confidently to the return of the benevolent deity; and this remarkable tradition, deeply cherished in their hearts, prepared the way, as we shall see hereafter, for the future success of the Spaniards.

We have not space for further details respecting the Mexican divinities, the attributes of many of whom were carefully defined, as they descended, in regular gradation, to the *penates* or household gods, whose little images were to be found in the humblest dwelling.

RELIGIOUS BELIEFS AND CEREMONIES

The Aztecs felt the curiosity, common to man in almost every stage of civilization, to lift the veil which covers the mysterious past and the more awful future. They sought relief, like the nations of the Old Continent, from the oppressive idea of eternity, by breaking it up into distinct cycles, or periods of time, each of several thousand years' duration. There were four of these cycles, and at the end of each, by the agency of one of the elements, the human family was swept from the earth, and the sun blotted out from the heavens, to be again rekindled.

They imagined three separate states of existence in the future life. The wicked, comprehending the greater part of mankind, were to expiate their sins in a place of everlasting darkness. Another class, with no other merit than that of having died of certain diseases, capriciously selected, were to enjoy a negative existence of indolent contentment. The highest place was reserved, as in most warlike nations, for the heroes who fell in battle, or in sacrifice. They passed at once into the presence of the Sun, whom they accompanied with songs and choral dances in his bright progress through the heavens; and, after some years, their spirits went to animate the clouds and singing birds of beautiful plumage, and to revel amidst the rich blossoms and odours of the gardens of paradise. Such was the heaven of the Aztecs; more refined in its character than that of the more polished pagan, whose Elysium reflected only the martial sports or sensual gratifications of this life. In the destiny they assigned to the wicked, we discern similar traces of refinement; since the absence of all physical torture forms a striking contrast to the schemes of suffering so ingeniously devised by the fancies of the most enlightened nations. In all this, so contrary to the natural suggestions of the ferocious Aztec, we see the evidences of a higher civilization, inherited from their predecessors in the land.

Our limits will allow only a brief allusion to one or two of their most interesting ceremonies. On the death of a person, his corpse was dressed in the peculiar habiliments of his tutelar deity. It was strewed with pieces of paper, which operated as charms against the dangers of the dark road he was to travel. A throng of slaves, if he were rich, was sacrificed at his obsequies. His body was burned, and the ashes, collected in a vase, were preserved in one of the apartments of his house. Here we have successively the usages of the Roman Catholic, the Mussulman, the Tartar, and the ancient Greek and Roman; curious coincidences, which may show how cautious we should be in adopting conclusions founded on analogy.

A more extraordinary coincidence may be traced with Christian rites, in the ceremony of naming their children. The lips and bosom of the infant were sprinkled with water, and 'the Lord was implored to permit the holy drops to wash away the sin that was given to it before the foundation of the world; so that the child might be born anew.' We are reminded of Christian morals, in more than one of their prayers, in which they used regular forms. 'Wilt thou blot us out, O Lord, for ever? Is this punishment intended, not for our reformation, but for our destruction?' Again, 'Impart to us, out of thy great mercy, thy gifts, which we are not worthy to receive through our own merits.' 'Keep peace with all,' says another petition; 'bear injuries with humility; God, who sees, will avenge you.' But the most striking parallel with Scripture is in the remarkable declaration that 'he who looks too curiously on a woman commits adultery with his eyes.' These pure and elevated maxims, it is true, are mixed up with others of a puerile, and even brutal, character, arguing that confusion of the moral perceptions which is natural in the twilight of civilization. One would not expect, however, to meet, in such a state of society, with doctrines as sublime as any inculcated by the enlightened codes of ancient philosophy.

THE SACERDOTAL ORDER

But although the Aztec mythology gathered nothing from the beautiful inventions of the poet or from the refinements of philosophy, it was much indebted, as I have noticed, to the priests, who endeavoured to dazzle the imagination of the people by the most formal and pompous ceremonial. The influence of the priesthood must be greatest in an imperfect state of civilization, where it engrosses all the scanty science of the time in its own body. This is particularly the case when the science is of that spurious kind which is less occupied with the real phenomena of nature than with the fanciful chimeras of human superstition. Such are the sciences of astrology and divination, in which the Aztec priests were well initiated; and, while they seemed to hold the keys of the future in their own hands, they impressed the ignorant people with sentiments of superstitious awe, beyond that which has probably existed in any other country – even in ancient Egypt.

The sacerdotal order was very numerous; as may be inferred from the statement that 5,000 priests were, in some way or other, attached to the principal temple in the capital. The various ranks and functions of this multitudinous body were discriminated with great exactness. Those best instructed in music took the management of the choirs. Others arranged the festivals conformably to the calendar. Some superintended the education of youth, and others had charge of the hieroglyphical paintings and oral traditions; while the dismal rites of sacrifice were reserved for the chief dignitaries of the order. At the head of the whole establishment were two high priests, elected from the order, as it would seem, by the king and principal nobles, without reference to birth, but solely for their qualifications, as shown by their previous conduct in a subordinate station. They were equal in dignity, and inferior only to the sovereign, who rarely acted without their advice in weighty matters of public concern.

The priests were each devoted to the service of some particular deity, and had quarters provided within the spacious precincts of their temple; at least, while engaged in immediate attendance there, – for they were allowed to marry, and have families of their own. In this monastic residence they lived in all the stern severity of conventual discipline. Thrice during the day, and once at night, they were called to prayers. They were frequent in their ablutions and vigils, and mortified the flesh by fasting and cruel penance – drawing blood from their bodies by flagellation, or by piercing them with the thorns of the aloe; in short, by practising all those austerities to which fanaticism (to borrow the strong language of the poet) has resorted, in every age of the world, 'In hopes to merit heaven by making earth a hell.'

The great cities were divided into districts, placed under the charge of a sort of parochial clergy, who regulated every act of religion within their precincts. It is remarkable that they administered the rites of confession and absolution. The secrets of the confessional were held inviolable, and penances were imposed of much the same kind as those enjoined in the Roman Catholic Church. There were two remarkable peculiarities in the Aztec ceremony. The first was, that, as the repetition of an offence once atoned for was deemed inexpiable, confession was made but once in a man's life, and was usually deferred to a late period of it, when the penitent unburdened his conscience and settled at once the long arrears of iniquity. Another peculiarity was, that priestly absolution was received in place of the legal punishment of offences, and authorized an acquittal in case of arrest. Long after the Conquest, the simple natives, when they came under the arm of the law, sought to escape by producing the certificate of their confession.

One of the most important duties of the priesthood was that of education, to which certain buildings were appropriated within the enclosure of the principal temple. Here the youth of both sexes, of the higher and middling orders, were placed at a very tender age. The girls were entrusted to the care of priestesses; for women were allowed to exercise sacerdotal functions, except those of sacrifice. In these institutions the boys were drilled in the routine of monastic discipline; they decorated the shrines of the gods with flowers, fed the sacred fires, and took part in the religious chants and festivals. Those in the higher school – the Calmecac, as it was called – were initiated in their traditionary lore, the mysteries of hieroglyphics, the principles of government, and such branches of astronomical and natural science as were within the compass of the priesthood. The girls learned various feminine employments, especially to weave and embroider rich coverings for the altars of the gods. Great attention was paid to the moral discipline of both sexes. The most perfect decorum prevailed; and offences were punished with extreme rigour, in some instances with death itself. Terror, not love, was the spring of education with the Aztecs.

At a suitable age for marrying, or for entering into the world, the pupils were dismissed, with much ceremony, from the convent, and the recommendation of the principal often introduced those most competent to responsible situations in public life. Such was the crafty policy of the Mexican priests, who, by reserving to themselves the business of instruction, were enabled to mould the young and plastic mind according to their own wills, and to train it early to implicit reverence for religion and its ministers; a reverence which still maintained its hold on the iron nature of the warrior, long after every other vestige of education had been effaced by the rough trade to which he was devoted.

To each of the principal temples, lands were annexed for the maintenance of the priests. These estates were augmented by the policy or devotion of successive princes, until, under the last Moctezuma, they had swollen to an enormous extent, and covered every district of the empire. The priests took the management of their property into their own hands; and they seem to have treated their tenants with the liberality and indulgence characteristic of monastic corporations. Besides the large supplies drawn from this source, the religious order was enriched with the first fruits, and such other offerings as piety or superstition dictated. The surplus beyond what was required for the support of the national worship was distributed in alms among the poor; a duty strenuously prescribed by their moral code. Thus we find the same religion inculcating lessons of pure philanthropy, on the one hand, and of merciless extermination, as we shall soon see, on the other. The inconsistency will not appear incredible to those who are familiar with the history of the Roman Catholic Church, in the early ages of the Inquisition.

TEMPLES AND FESTIVALS

The Mexican temples – *teocallis*, 'houses of God', as they were called – were very numerous. There were several hundreds in each of the principal cities, many of them, doubtless, very humble edifices. They were solid masses of earth, cased with brick or stone, and in their form somewhat resembled the pyramidal structures of ancient Egypt. The bases of many of them were more than 100 feet square, and they towered to a still greater height. They were distributed into four or five storeys, each of smaller dimensions than that below. The ascent was by a flight of steps, at an angle of the pyramid, on the outside. This led to a sort of terrace, or gallery, at the base of the second storey, which passed quite round the building to another flight of stairs, commencing also at the same angle as the preceding and directly over it, and leading to a similar terrace; so that one had to make the circuit of the temple several times before reaching the summit.

In some instances the stairway led directly up the centre of the western face of the building. The top was a broad area, on which were erected one or two towers, 40 or 50 feet high, the sanctuaries in which stood the sacred images of the presiding deities. Before these towers stood the dreadful stone of sacrifice, and two lofty altars, on which fires were kept, as inextinguishable as those in the temple of Vesta. There were said to be 600 of these altars, on smaller buildings within the enclosure of the great temple of Mexico, which, with those on the sacred edifices in other parts of the city, shed a brilliant illumination over its streets, through the darkest night.

From the construction of their temples, all religious services were public. The long processions of priests, winding round their massive sides, as they rose higher and higher towards the summit, and the dismal rites of sacrifice performed there, were all visible from the remotest corners of the capital, impressing on the spectator's mind a superstitious veneration for the mysteries of his religion, and for the dread ministers by whom they were interpreted.

This impression was kept in full force by their numerous festivals. Every month was consecrated to some protecting deity; and every week, nay, almost every day, was set down in their calendar for some appropriate celebration; so that it is difficult to understand how the ordinary business of life could have been compatible with the exactions of religion. Many of their ceremonies were of a light and cheerful complexion, consisting of the national songs and dances, in which both sexes joined. Processions were made of women and children crowned with garlands and bearing offerings of fruits, the ripened maize, or the sweet incense of copal and other odoriferous gums, while the altars of the deity were stained with no blood save that of animals. These were the peaceful rites derived from their Toltec predecessors, on which the fierce Aztecs engrafted a superstition too loathsome to be exhibited in all its nakedness, and one over which I would gladly draw a veil altogether, but that it would leave the reader in ignorance of their most striking institution, and one that had the greatest influence in forming the national character.

HUMAN SACRIFICES

Human sacrifices were adopted by the Aztecs early in the fourteenth century, about 200 years before the Conquest. Rare at first, they became more frequent with the wider extent of their empire; till, at length, almost every festival was closed with this cruel abomination. These religious ceremonials were generally arranged in such a manner as to afford a type of the most prominent circumstances in the character or history of the deity who was the object of them. A single example will suffice.

One of their most important festivals was that in honour of the god Tezcatlipoca, whose rank was inferior only to that of the Supreme Being. He was called 'the soul of the world', and supposed to have been its creator. He was depicted as a handsome man, endowed with perpetual youth. A year before the intended sacrifice, a captive, distinguished for his personal beauty, and without a blemish on his body, was selected to represent this deity. Certain tutors took charge of him, and instructed him how to perform his new part with becoming grace and dignity. He was arrayed in a splendid dress, regaled with incense and with a profusion of sweet-scented flowers, of which the ancient Mexicans were as fond as their descendants at the present day. When he went abroad, he was attended by a train of the royal pages, and, as he halted in the streets to play some favourite melody, the crowd prostrated themselves before him, and did him homage as the representative of their good deity. In this way he led an easy, luxurious life, till within a month of his sacrifice. Four beautiful girls, bearing the names of the principal goddesses, were then selected to share the honours of his bed; and with them he continued to live in idle dalliance, feasted at the banquets of the principal nobles, who paid him all the honours of a divinity.

At length the fatal day of sacrifice arrived. The term of his short-lived glories was at an end. He was stripped of his gaudy apparel, and bade adieu to the fair partners of his revelries. One of the royal barges transported him across the lake to a temple which rose on its margin, about a league from the city. Hither the inhabitants of the capital flocked, to witness the consummation of the ceremony. As the sad procession wound up the sides of the pyramid, the unhappy victim threw away his gay chaplets of flowers, and broke in pieces the musical instruments with which he had solaced the hours of captivity. On the summit he was received by six priests, whose long and matted locks flowed disorderly over their sable robes, covered with hieroglyphic scrolls of mystic import. They led him to the sacrificial stone, a huge block of jasper, with its upper surface somewhat convex. On this the prisoner was stretched. Five priests secured his head and his limbs; while the sixth, clad in a scarlet mantle, emblematic of his bloody office, dexterously opened the breast of the wretched victim with a sharp razor of *itztli* – a volcanic substance, hard as flint – and, inserting his hand in the wound, tore out the palpitating heart. The minister of death, first holding this up towards the sun, an object of worship throughout Anahuac, cast it at the feet of the deity to whom the temple was devoted, while the multitudes below prostrated themselves in humble adoration. The tragic story of this prisoner was expounded by the priests as the type of human destiny, which, brilliant in its commencement, too often closes in sorrow and disaster.

Such was the form of human sacrifice usually practised by the Aztecs. It was the same that often met the indignant eyes of the Europeans in their progress through the country, and from the dreadful doom of which they themselves were not exempted. There were, indeed, some occasions when preliminary tortures, of the most exquisite kind – with which it is unnecessary to shock the reader – were inflicted, but they always terminated with the bloody ceremony above described. It should be remarked, however, that such tortures were not the spontaneous suggestions of cruelty, as with the North American indigenous peoples, but were all rigorously prescribed in the Aztec ritual, and doubtless were often inflicted with the same compunctious visitings which a devout familiar of the Holy Office might at times experience in executing its stern decrees. Women, as well as the other sex, were sometimes reserved for sacrifice. On some occasions, particularly in seasons of drought, at the festival of the insatiable Tlaloc, the god of rain, children, for the most part infants, were offered up. As they were borne along in open litters, dressed in their festal robes, and decked with the fresh blossoms of spring, they moved the hardest heart to pity, though their cries were drowned in the wild chant of the priests, who read in their tears a favourable augury for their petition. These innocent victims were generally bought by the priests of parents who were poor, but who stifled the voice of nature, probably less at the suggestions of poverty than of a wretched superstition.

The most loathsome part of the story – the manner in which the body of the sacrificed captive was disposed of – remains yet to be told. It was delivered to the warrior who had taken him in battle, and by him, after being dressed, was served up in an entertainment to his friends. This was not the coarse repast of famished cannibals, but a banquet teeming with delicious beverages and delicate viands, prepared with art, and attended by both sexes, who, as we shall see hereafter, conducted themselves with all the decorum of civilized life. Surely, never were refinement and the extreme of barbarism brought so closely in contact with each other.

Human sacrifices have been practised by many nations, not excepting the most polished nations of antiquity; but never by any, on a scale to be compared with those in Anahuac. The amount of victims immolated on its accursed altars would stagger the faith of the least scrupulous believer. Scarcely any author pretends to estimate the yearly sacrifices throughout the empire at less than 20,000, and some carry the number as high as 50,000!

On great occasions, as the coronation of a king or the consecration of a temple, the number becomes still more appalling. At the dedication of the great temple of Huitzilopochtli, in 1486, the prisoners, who for some years had been reserved for the purpose, were drawn from all quarters to the capital. They were ranged in files, forming a procession nearly 2 miles long. The ceremony consumed several days, and 70,000 captives are said to have perished at the shrine of this terrible deity! But who can believe that so numerous a body would have suffered themselves to be led unresistingly like sheep to the slaughter? Or how could their remains, too great for consumption in the ordinary way, be disposed of, without breeding a pestilence in the capital? Yet the event was of recent date, and is unequivocally attested by the best-informed historians. One fact may be considered certain. It was customary to preserve the skulls of the sacrificed, in buildings appropriated to the purpose. The companions of Cortés counted 136,000 in one of these edifices! Without attempting a precise calculation, therefore, it is safe to conclude that thousands were yearly offered up, in the different cities of Anahuac, on the bloody altars of the Mexican divinities.

Indeed, the great object of war, with the Aztecs, was quite as much to gather victims for their sacrifices as to extend their empire. Hence it was that an enemy was never slain in battle, if there were a chance of taking him alive. To this circumstance the Spaniards repeatedly owed their preservation.

When Moctezuma was asked why he had suffered the republic of Tlascala to maintain her independence on his borders, he replied, 'that she might furnish him with victims for his gods'! As the supply began to fail, the priests, the Dominicans of the New World, bellowed aloud for more, and urged on their superstitious sovereign by the denunciations of celestial wrath. Like the militant churchmen of Christendom in the Middle Ages, they mingled themselves in the ranks, and were conspicuous in the thickest of the fight, by their hideous aspect and frantic gestures. Strange, that, in every country, the most fiendish passions of the human heart have been those kindled in the name of religion!

The influence of these practices on the Aztec character was as disastrous as might have been expected. Familiarity with the bloody rites of sacrifice steeled the heart against human sympathy, and begat a thirst for carnage, like that excited in the Romans by the exhibitions of the circus. The perpetual recurrence of ceremonies, in which the people took part, associated religion with their most intimate concerns, and spread the gloom of superstition over the domestic hearth, until the character of the nation wore a grave and even melancholy aspect, which belongs to their descendants at the present day. The influence of the priesthood, of course, became unbounded. The sovereign thought himself honoured by being permitted to assist in the services of the temple. Far from limiting the authority of the priests to spiritual matters, he often surrendered his opinion to theirs, where they were least competent to give it. It was their opposition that prevented the final capitulation which would have saved the capital. The whole nation, from the peasant to the prince, bowed their necks to the worst kind of tyranny, that of a blind fanaticism.

In reflecting on the revolting usages recorded in the preceding pages, one finds it difficult to reconcile their existence with anything like a regular form of government, or an advance in civilization. Yet the Mexicans had many claims to the character of a civilized community. One may, perhaps, better understand the anomaly, by reflecting on the condition of some of the most polished countries in Europe in the sixteenth century, after the establishment of the modern Inquisition – an institution which yearly destroyed its thousands, by a death more painful than the Aztec sacrifices; which armed the hand of brother against brother, and, setting its burning seal upon the lip, did more to stay the march of improvement than any other scheme ever devised by human cunning.

Human sacrifice, however cruel, has nothing in it degrading to its victim. It may be rather said to ennoble him by devoting him to the gods. Although so terrible with the Aztecs, it was sometimes voluntarily embraced by them, as the most glorious death and one that opened a sure passage into paradise. The Inquisition, on the other hand, branded its victims with infamy in this world, and consigned them to everlasting perdition in the next.

One detestable feature of the Aztec superstition, however, sank it far below the Christian. This was its cannibalism, though, in truth, the Mexicans were not cannibals in the coarsest acceptation of the term. They did not feed on human flesh merely to gratify a brutish appetite, but in obedience to their religion. Their repasts were made of the victims whose blood had been poured out on the altar of sacrifice. This is a distinction worthy of notice. Still, cannibalism, under any form or whatever sanction, cannot but have a fatal influence on the nation addicted to it. It suggests ideas so loathsome, so degrading to man, to his spiritual and immortal nature, that it is impossible the people who practise it should make any great progress in moral or intellectual culture. The Mexicans furnish no exception to this remark. The civilization which they possessed descended from the Toltecs, a race who never stained their altars, still less their banquets, with the blood of man. All that deserved the name of science in Mexico came from this source; and the crumbling ruins of edifices attributed to them, still extant in various parts of New Spain, show a decided superiority in their architecture over that of the later races of Anahuac. It is true, the Mexicans made great proficiency in many of the social and mechanic arts, in that material culture – if I may so call it – the natural growth of increasing opulence, which ministers to the gratification of the senses. In purely intellectual progress they were behind the Tezcucans, whose wise sovereigns came into the abominable rites of their neighbours with reluctance and practised them on a much more moderate scale.

In this state of things, it was beneficently ordered by Providence that the land should be delivered over to another race, who would rescue it from the brutish superstitions that daily extended wider and wider with extent of empire. The debasing institutions of the Aztecs furnish the best apology for their conquest. It is true, the conquerors brought along with them the Inquisition. But they also brought Christianity, whose benign radiance would still survive when the fierce flames of fanaticism should be extinguished; dispelling those dark forms of horror which had so long brooded over the fair region of Anahuac.

AZTEC HIEROGLYPHICS

It is a relief to turn from the gloomy pages of the preceding [section] to a brighter side of the picture, and to contemplate the same nation in its generous struggle to raise itself from a state of barbarism and to take a positive rank in the scale of civilization. It is not the less interesting that these efforts were made on an entirely new theatre of action, apart from those influences that operate in the Old World; the inhabitants of which, forming one great brotherhood of nations, are knit together by sympathies that make the faintest spark of knowledge, struck out in one quarter, spread gradually wider and wider, until it has diffused a cheering light over the remotest. It is curious to observe the human mind, in this new position, conforming to the same laws as on the ancient continent, and taking a similar direction in its first inquiries after truth – so similar, indeed, as, although not warranting, perhaps, the idea of imitation, to suggest at least that of a common origin.

In the Eastern hemisphere we find some nations, as the Greeks, for instance, early smitten with such a love of the beautiful as to be unwilling to dispense with it even in the graver productions of science; and other nations, again, proposing a severer end to themselves, to which even imagination and elegant art were made subservient. The productions of such a people must be criticized, not by the ordinary rules of taste, but by their adaptation to the peculiar end for which they were designed. Such were the Egyptians in the Old World, and the Mexicans in the New. We have already had occasion to notice the resemblance borne by the latter nation to the former in their religious economy. We shall be more struck with it in their scientific culture, especially their hieroglyphical writing and their astronomy.

To describe actions and events by delineating visible objects seems to be a natural suggestion, and is practised, after a certain fashion, by the rudest savages. The North American Indian carves an arrow on the bark of trees to show his followers the direction of his march, and some other sign to show the success of his expeditions. But to paint intelligibly a consecutive series of these actions – forming what Warburton has happily called 'picture writing' – requires a combination of ideas that amounts to a positively intellectual effort. Yet further, when the object of the painter, instead of being limited to the present, is to penetrate the past, and to gather from its dark recesses lessons of instruction for coming generations, we see the dawnings of a literary culture, and recognize the proof of a decided civilization in the attempt itself, however imperfectly it may be executed. The literal imitation of objects will not answer for this more complex and extended plan. It would occupy too much space, as well as time in the execution. It then becomes necessary to abridge the pictures, to confine the drawing to outlines, or to such prominent parts of the bodies delineated as may readily suggest the whole. This is the *representative* or *figurative* writing, which forms the lowest stage of hieroglyphics.

But there are things which have no type in the material world; abstract ideas, which can only be represented by visible objects supposed to have some quality analogous to the idea intended. This constitutes *symbolical* writing, the most difficult of all to the interpreter, since the analogy between the material and immaterial object is often purely fanciful, or local in its application. Who, for instance, could suspect the association which made a beetle represent the universe, as with the Egyptians, or a serpent typify time, as with the Aztecs?

The third and last division is the *phonetic*, in which signs are made to represent sounds, either entire words, or parts of them. This is the nearest approach of the hieroglyphical series to that beautiful invention, the alphabet, by which language is resolved into its elementary sounds, and an apparatus supplied for easily and accurately expressing the most delicate shades of thought.

The Egyptians were well skilled in all three kinds of hieroglyphics. But, although their public monuments display the first class, in their ordinary intercourse and written records it is now certain that they almost wholly relied on the phonetic character. Strange that, having thus broken down the thin partition which divided them from an alphabet, their latest monuments should exhibit no nearer approach to it than their earliest. The Aztecs, also, were acquainted with the several varieties of hieroglyphics. But they relied on the figurative infinitely more than on the others. The Egyptians were at the top of the scale, the Aztecs at the bottom.

In casting the eye over a Mexican manuscript, or map, as it is called, one is struck with the grotesque caricatures it exhibits of the human figure; monstrous, overgrown heads, on puny, misshapen bodies, which are themselves hard and angular in their outlines, and without the least skill in composition. On closer inspection, however, it is obvious that it is not so much a rude attempt to delineate nature, as a conventional symbol, to express the idea in the most clear and forcible manner; in the same way as the pieces of similar value on a chess board, while they correspond with one another in form, bear little resemblance, usually, to the objects they represent. Those parts of the figure are most distinctly traced which are the most important. So, also, the colouring, instead of the delicate gradations of nature, exhibits only gaudy and violent contrasts, such as may produce the most vivid impression. 'For even colours,' as Gama observes, 'speak in the Aztec hieroglyphics'.

But in the execution of all this the Mexicans were much inferior to the Egyptians. The drawings of the latter, indeed, are exceedingly defective, when criticized by the rules of art; for they were as ignorant of perspective as the Chinese, and only exhibited the head in profile, with the eye in the centre, and with total absence of expression. But they handled the pencil more gracefully than the Aztecs, were truer to the natural forms of objects, and, above all, showed great superiority in abridging the original figure by giving only the outline, or some characteristic or essential feature. This simplified the process and facilitated the communication of thought. An Egyptian text has almost the appearance of alphabetical writing in its regular lines of minute figures. A Mexican text looks usually like a collection of pictures, each one forming the subject of a separate study. This is particularly the case with the delineations of mythology; in which the story is told by a conglomeration of symbols, that may remind one more of the mysterious anaglyphs sculptured on the temples of the Egyptians, than of their written records.

The Aztecs had various emblems for expressing such things as, from their nature, could not be directly represented by the painter; as, for example, the years, months, days, the seasons, the elements, the heavens and the like. A 'tongue' denoted speaking; a 'footprint', travelling; a 'man sitting on the ground', an earthquake. These symbols were often very arbitrary, varying with the caprice of the writer; and it requires a nice discrimination to interpret them, as a slight change in the form or position of the figure intimated a very different meaning. An ingenious writer asserts that the priests devised secret symbolic characters for the record of their religious mysteries. It is possible. But the researches of [French philologist and Orientalist Jean-François] Champollion lead to the conclusion that the similar opinion formerly entertained respecting the Egyptian hieroglyphics is without foundation.

Lastly, they employed, as above stated, phonetic signs, though these were chiefly confined to the names of persons and places; which, being derived from some circumstance or characteristic quality, were accommodated to the hieroglyphical system. Thus, the town Cimatlan was compounded of *cimatl*, a 'root', which grew near it, and *tlan*, signifying 'near'; Tlaxcallan meant 'the place of bread', from its rich fields of corn; Huexotzinco, 'a place surrounded by willows'. The names of persons were often significant of their adventures and achievements. That of the great Tezcucan prince Nezahualcoyotl signified 'hungry fox', intimating his sagacity, and his distresses in early life. The emblems of such names were no sooner seen, than they suggested to every Mexican the person and place intended, and, when painted on their shields or embroidered on their banners, became the armorial bearings by which city and chieftain were distinguished, as in Europe in the age of chivalry.

But, although the Aztecs were instructed in all the varieties of hieroglyphical painting, they chiefly resorted to the clumsy method of direct representation. Had their empire lasted, like the Egyptian, several thousand years, instead of the brief space of 200, they would doubtless, like them, have advanced to the more frequent use of the phonetic writing. But, before they could be made acquainted with the capabilities of their own system, the Spanish Conquest, by introducing the European alphabet, supplied their scholars with a more perfect contrivance for expressing thought, which soon supplanted the ancient pictorial character.

Clumsy as it was, however, the Aztec picture writing seems to have been adequate to the demands of the nation, in their imperfect state of civilization. By means of it were recorded all their laws, and even their regulations for domestic economy; their tribute rolls, specifying the imposts of the various towns; their mythology, calendars and rituals; their political annals, carried back to a period long before the foundation of the city. They digested a complete system of chronology, and could specify with accuracy the dates of the most important events in their history; the year being inscribed on the margin, against the particular circumstance recorded. It is true, history, thus executed, must necessarily be vague and fragmentary. Only a few leading incidents could be presented. But in this it did not differ much from the monkish chronicles of the Dark Ages, which often dispose of years in a few brief sentences – quite long enough for the annals of barbarians.

In order to estimate correctly the picture writing of the Aztecs, one must regard it in connection with oral tradition, to which it was auxiliary. In the colleges of the priests the youth were instructed in astronomy, history, mythology, etc.; and those who were to follow the profession of hieroglyphical painting were taught the application of the characters appropriated to each of these branches. In an historical work, one had charge of the chronology, another of the events. Every part of the labour was thus mechanically distributed. The pupils, instructed in all that was before known in their several departments, were prepared to extend still further the boundaries of their imperfect science. The hieroglyphics served as a sort of stenography, a collection of notes, suggesting to the initiated much more than could be conveyed by a literal interpretation. This combination of the written and the oral comprehended what may be called the literature of the Aztecs.

MANUSCRIPTS

Their manuscripts were made of different materials – of cotton cloth, or skins nicely prepared; of a composition of silk and gum; but, for the most part, of a fine fabric from the leaves of the aloe, *agave Americana*, called by the natives *maguey*, which grows luxuriantly over the tablelands of Mexico. A sort of paper was made from it, resembling somewhat the Egyptian papyrus, which, when properly dressed and polished, is said to have been more soft and beautiful than parchment. Some of the specimens, still existing, exhibit their original freshness, and the paintings on them retain their brilliancy of colours. They were sometimes done up into rolls, but more frequently into volumes, of moderate size, in which the paper was shut up, like a folding screen, with a leaf or tablet of wood at each extremity, that gave the whole, when closed, the appearance of a book. The length of the strips was determined only by convenience. As the pages might be read and referred to separately, this form had obvious advantages over the rolls of the ancients.

At the time of the arrival of the Spaniards, great quantities of these manuscripts were treasured up in the country. Numerous persons were employed in painting, and the dexterity of their operations excited the astonishment of the conquerors. Unfortunately, this was mingled with other and unworthy feelings. The strange, unknown characters inscribed on them excited suspicion. They were looked on as magic scrolls, and were regarded in the same light with the idols and temples, as the symbols of a pestilent superstition, that must be extirpated. The first archbishop of Mexico, Don Juan de Zumárraga – a name that should be as immortal as that of Omar – collected these paintings from every quarter, especially from Tezcuco, the most cultivated capital in Anahuac, and the great depository of the national archives. He then caused them to be piled up in a 'mountain-heap' – as it is called by the Spanish writers themselves – in the marketplace of Tlatelolco, and reduced them all to ashes! His greater countryman, Archbishop Ximenes, had celebrated a similar *auto-da-fé* of Arabic manuscripts, in Granada, some twenty years before. Never did fanaticism achieve two more signal triumphs than by the annihilation of so many curious monuments of human ingenuity and learning!

The unlettered soldiers were not slow in imitating the example of their prelate. Every chart and volume which fell into their hands was wantonly destroyed; so that, when the scholars of a later and more enlightened age anxiously sought to recover some of these memorials of civilization, nearly all had perished, and the few surviving were jealously hidden by the natives. Through the indefatigable labours of a private individual, however, a considerable collection was eventually deposited in the archives of Mexico, but was so little heeded there that some were plundered, others decayed piecemeal from the damps and mildews, and others, again, were used up as wastepaper! We contemplate with indignation the cruelties inflicted by the early conquerors. But indignation is qualified with contempt when we see them thus ruthlessly trampling out the spark of knowledge, the common boon and property of all mankind. We may well doubt which has the stronger claim to civilization, the victor or the vanquished.

A few of the Mexican manuscripts have found their way, from time to time, to Europe, and are carefully preserved in the public libraries of its capitals. They are brought together in the magnificent work of Lord Kingsborough; but not one is there from Spain. The most important of them, for the light it throws on the Aztec institutions, is the Mendoza Codex; which, after its mysterious disappearance for more than a century, has at length reappeared in the Bodleian Library at Oxford. It has been several times engraved. The most brilliant in colouring, probably, is the Borgian collection, in Rome. The most curious, however, is the Dresden Codex, which has excited less attention than it deserves. Although usually classed among Mexican manuscripts, it bears little resemblance to them in its execution; the figures of objects are more delicately drawn, and the characters, unlike the Mexican, appear to be purely arbitrary, and are possibly phonetic. Their regular arrangement is quite equal to the Egyptian. The whole infers a much higher civilization than the Aztec, and offers abundant food for curious speculation.

Some few of these maps have interpretations annexed to them, which were obtained from the natives after the Conquest. The greater part are without any, and cannot now be unriddled. Had the Mexicans made free use of a phonetic alphabet, it might have been originally easy, by mastering the comparatively few signs employed in this kind of communication, to have got a permanent key to the whole. A brief inscription has furnished a clue to the vast labyrinth of Egyptian hieroglyphics. But the Aztec characters, representing individuals, or, at most, species, require to be made out separately; a hopeless task, for which little aid is to be expected from the vague and general tenor of the few interpretations now existing. There was, as already mentioned, until late in the last century, a professor in the University of Mexico, especially devoted to the study of the national picture writing. But, as this was with a view to legal proceedings, his information, probably, was limited to deciphering titles. In less than 100 years after the Conquest, the knowledge of the hieroglyphics had so far declined that a diligent Tezcucan writer complains he could find in the country only two persons, both very aged, at all competent to interpret them.

It is not probable, therefore, that the art of reading these picture writings will ever be recovered; a circumstance certainly to be regretted. [...] they could scarcely fail to throw some additional light on the previous history of the nation, and that of the more polished people who before occupied the country. This would be still more probable, if any literary relics of their Toltec predecessors were preserved; and, if report be true, an important compilation from this source was extant at the time of the invasion, and may have perhaps contributed to swell the holocaust of Zumárraga. It is no great stretch of fancy to suppose that such records might reveal the successive links in the mighty chain of migration of the primitive races, and, by carrying us back to the seat of their possessions in the Old World, have solved the mystery which has so long perplexed the learned, in regard to the settlement and civilization of the New.

Besides the hieroglyphical maps, the traditions of the country were embodied in the songs and hymns, which, as already mentioned, were carefully taught in the public schools. These were various, embracing the mythic legends of a heroic age, the warlike achievements of their own, or the softer tales of love and pleasure. Many of them were composed by scholars and persons of rank and are cited as affording the most authentic record of events. The Mexican dialect was rich and expressive, though inferior to the Tezcucan, the most polished of the idioms of Anahuac. None of the Aztec compositions have survived, but we can form some estimate of the general state of poetic culture from the odes which have come down to us from the royal house of Tezcuco. Sahagun has furnished us with translations of their more elaborate prose, consisting of prayers and public discourses, which give a favourable idea of their eloquence, and show that they paid much attention to rhetorical effect. They are said to have had, also, something like theatrical exhibitions, of a pantomimic sort, in which the faces of the performers were covered with masks, and the figures of birds or animals were frequently represented; an imitation to which they may have been led by the familiar delineation of such objects in their hieroglyphics. In all this we see the dawning of a literary culture, surpassed, however, by their attainments in the severer walks of mathematical science.

ARITHMETIC

They devised a system of notation in their arithmetic that was sufficiently simple. The first twenty numbers were expressed by a corresponding number of dots. The first five had specific names; after which they were represented by combining the fifth with one of the four preceding; as five and one for six, five and two for seven, and so on. Ten and fifteen had each a separate name, which was also combined with the first four, to express a higher quantity. These four, therefore, were the radical characters of their oral arithmetic, in the same manner as they were of the written with the ancient Romans; a more simple arrangement, probably, than any existing among Europeans.

Twenty was expressed by a separate hieroglyphic – a flag. Larger sums were reckoned by twenties, and, in writing, by repeating the number of flags. The square of twenty, 400, had a separate sign, that of a plume, and so had the cube of twenty, or 8,000, which was denoted by a purse, or sack. This was the whole arithmetical apparatus of the Mexicans, by the combination of which they were enabled to indicate any quantity. For greater expedition, they used to denote fractions of the larger sums by drawing only a part of the object. Thus, half or three-quarters of a plume, or of a purse, represented that proportion of their respective sums, and so on. With all this, the machinery will appear very awkward to us, who perform our operations with so much ease by means of the Arabic or, rather, Indian ciphers. It is not much more awkward, however, than the system pursued by the great mathematicians of antiquity, unacquainted with the brilliant invention, which has given a new aspect to mathematical science, of determining the value, in a great measure, by the relative position of the figures.

CHRONOLOGY

In the measurement of time, the Aztecs adjusted their civil year by the solar. They divided it into eighteen months of twenty days each. Both months and days were expressed by peculiar hieroglyphics – those of the former often intimating the season of the year, like the French months at the period of the Revolution. Five complementary days, as in Egypt, were added, to make up the full number of 365. They belonged to no month, and were regarded as peculiarly unlucky. A month was divided into four weeks, of five days each, on the last of which was the public fair, or market day. This arrangement, differing from that of the nations of the Old Continent, whether of Europe or Asia, has the advantage of giving an equal number of days to each month, and of comprehending entire weeks, without a fraction, both in the months and in the year.

As the year is composed of nearly six hours more than 365 days, there still remained an excess, which, like other nations who have framed a calendar, they provided for by intercalation; not, indeed, every fourth year, as the Europeans, but at longer intervals, like some of the Asiatics. They waited till the expiration of fifty-two vague years, when they interposed thirteen days, or rather twelve and a half, this being the number which had fallen in arrear. Had they inserted thirteen, it would have been too much, since the annual excess over 365 is about eleven minutes less than six hours. But, as their calendar at the time of the Conquest was found to correspond with the European (making allowance for the subsequent Gregorian reform), they would seem to have adopted the shorter period of twelve days and a half, which brought them, within an almost inappreciable fraction, to the exact length of the tropical year, as established by the most accurate observations. Indeed, the intercalation of twenty-five days in every 104 years shows a nicer adjustment of civil to solar time than is presented by any European calendar; since more than five centuries must elapse before the loss of an entire day. Such was the astonishing precision displayed by the Aztecs, or, perhaps, by their more polished Toltec predecessors, in these computations, so difficult as to have baffled, till a comparatively recent period, the most enlightened nations of Christendom!

The chronological system of the Mexicans, by which they determined the date of any particular event, was also very remarkable. The epoch from which they reckoned corresponded with the year 1091 of the Christian era. It was the period of the reform of their calendar, soon after their migration from Aztlan. They threw the years, as already noticed, into great cycles, of fifty-two each, which they called 'sheafs', or 'bundles', and represented by a quantity of reeds bound together by a string. As often as this hieroglyphic occurs in their maps, it shows the number of half-centuries.

To enable them to specify any particular year, they divided the great cycle into four smaller cycles, or indictions, of thirteen years each. They then adopted two periodical series of signs, one consisting of their numerical dots, up to thirteen, the other, of four hieroglyphics of the years. These latter they repeated in regular succession, setting against each one a number of the corresponding series of dots, continued also in regular succession up to thirteen. The same system was pursued through the four indictions, which thus, it will be observed, began always with a different hieroglyphic of the year from the preceding; and in this way each of the hieroglyphics was made to combine successively with each of the numerical signs, but never twice with the same; since four, and thirteen, the factors of fifty-two – the number of years in the cycle – must admit of just as many combinations as are equal to their product.

Thus every year had its appropriate symbol, by which it was at once recognized. And this symbol, preceded by the proper number of 'bundles' indicating the half-centuries, showed the precise time which had elapsed since the national epoch of 1091. The ingenious contrivance of a periodical series, in place of the cumbrous system of hieroglyphical notation, is not peculiar to the Aztecs, and is to be found among various nations on the Asiatic continent – the same in principle, though varying materially in arrangement.

The solar calendar above described might have answered all the purposes of the people; but the priests chose to construct another for themselves. This was called a 'lunar reckoning', though nowise accommodated to the revolutions of the moon. It was formed, also, of two periodical series, one of them consisting of thirteen numerical signs, or dots, the other, of the twenty hieroglyphics of the days. But, as the product of these combinations would be only 260, and as some confusion might arise from the repetition of the same terms for the remaining 105 days of the year, they invented a third series, consisting of nine additional hieroglyphics, which, alternating with the two preceding series, rendered it impossible that the three should coincide twice in the same year, or indeed in less than 2340 days; since $20 \times 13 \times 9 = 2,340$. Thirteen was a mystic number, of frequent use in their tables. Why they resorted to that of nine, on this occasion, is not so clear.

This second calendar rouses a holy indignation in the early Spanish missionaries, and Father Sahagun loudly condemns it, as 'most unhallowed, since it is founded neither on natural reason, nor on the influence of the planets, nor on the true course of the year; but is plainly the work of necromancy, and the fruit of a compact with the Devil'! One may doubt whether the superstition of those who invented the scheme was greater than that of those who thus impugned it. At all events, we may, without having recourse to supernatural agency, find in the human heart a sufficient explanation of its origin; in that love of power, that has led the priesthood of many a faith to affect a mystery the key to which was in their own keeping.

ASTRONOMY

By means of this calendar, the Aztec priests kept their own records, regulated the festivals and seasons of sacrifice, and made all their astrological calculations. The false science of astrology is natural to a state of society partially civilized, where the mind, impatient of the slow and cautious examination by which alone it can arrive at truth, launches at once into the regions of speculation, and rashly attempts to lift the veil – the impenetrable veil – which is drawn around the mysteries of nature. It is the characteristic of true science to discern the impassable, but not very obvious, limits which divide the province of reason from that of speculation. Such knowledge comes tardily. How many ages have rolled away, in which powers that, rightly directed, might have revealed the great laws of nature, have been wasted in brilliant but barren reveries on alchemy and astrology!

The latter is more particularly the study of a primitive age; when the mind, incapable of arriving at the stupendous fact that the myriads of minute lights glowing in the firmament are the centres of systems as glorious as our own, is naturally led to speculate on their probable uses, and to connect them in some way or other with man, for whose convenience every other object in the universe seems to have been created. As the eye of the simple child of nature watches, through the long nights, the stately march of the heavenly bodies, and sees the bright hosts coming up, one after another, and changing with the changing seasons of the year, he naturally associates them with those seasons, as the periods over which they hold a mysterious influence. In the same manner, he connects their appearance with any interesting event of the time, and explores, in their flaming characters, the destinies of the newborn infant. Such is the origin of astrology, the false lights of which have continued from the earliest ages to dazzle and bewilder mankind, till they have faded away in the superior illumination of a comparatively recent period.

The astrological scheme of the Aztecs was founded less on the planetary influences than on those of the arbitrary signs they had adopted for the months and days. The character of the leading sign in each lunar cycle of thirteen days gave a complexion to the whole; though this was qualified in some degree by the signs of the succeeding days, as well as by those of the hours. It was in adjusting these conflicting forces that the great art of the diviner was shown. In no country, not even in ancient Egypt, were the dreams of the astrologer more implicitly deferred to. On the birth of a child, he was instantly summoned. The time of the event was accurately ascertained; and the family hung in trembling suspense, as the minister of Heaven cast the horoscope of the infant and unrolled the dark volume of destiny. The influence of the priest was confessed by the Mexican in the very first breath which he inhaled.

We know little further of the astronomical attainments of the Aztecs. That they were acquainted with the cause of eclipses is evident from the representation, on their maps, of the disc of the moon projected on that of the sun. Whether they had arranged a system of constellations is uncertain; though that they recognized some of the most obvious, as the Pleiades, for example, is evident from the fact that they regulated their festivals by them. We know of no astronomical instruments used by them, except the dial. An immense circular block of carved stone, disinterred in 1790, in the great square of Mexico, has supplied an acute and learned scholar with the means of establishing some interesting facts in regard to Mexican science. This colossal fragment, on which the calendar is engraved, shows that they had the means of settling the hours of the day with precision, the periods of the solstices and of the equinoxes, and that of the transit of the sun across the zenith of Mexico.

We cannot contemplate the astronomical science of the Mexicans, so disproportioned to their progress in other walks of civilization, without astonishment. An acquaintance with some of the more obvious principles of astronomy is within the reach of the rudest people. With a little care, they may learn to connect the regular changes of the seasons with those of the place of the sun at his rising and setting. They may follow the march of the great luminary through the heavens by watching the stars that first brighten on his evening track or fade in his morning beams. They may measure a revolution of the moon, by marking her phases, and may even form a general idea of the number of such revolutions in a solar year. But that they should be capable of accurately adjusting their festivals by the movements of the heavenly bodies, and should fix the true length of the tropical year, with a precision unknown to the great philosophers of antiquity, could be the result only of a long series of nice and patient observations, evincing no slight progress in civilization. But whence could the rude inhabitants of these mountain regions have derived this curious erudition? Not from the barbarous hordes who roamed over the higher latitudes of the North; nor from the more polished races on the Southern continent, with whom, it is apparent, they had no intercourse. If we are driven, in our embarrassment, like the greatest astronomer of our age, to seek the solution among the civilized communities of Asia, we shall still be perplexed by finding, amidst general resemblance of outline, sufficient discrepancy in the details to vindicate, in the judgments of many, the Aztec claim to originality.

I shall conclude the account of Mexican science with that of a remarkable festival, celebrated by the natives at the termination of the great cycle of fifty-two years. We have seen, in the preceding chapter, their tradition of the destruction of the world at four successive epochs. They looked forward confidently to another such catastrophe, to take place, like the preceding, at the close of a cycle, when the sun was to be effaced from the heavens, the human race from the earth, and when the darkness of chaos was to settle on the habitable globe. The cycle would end in the latter part of December, and as the dreary season of the winter solstice approached, and the diminished light of day gave melancholy presage of its speedy extinction, their apprehensions increased; and on the arrival of the five 'unlucky' days which closed the year they abandoned themselves to despair. They broke in pieces the little images of their household gods, in whom they no longer trusted. The holy fires were suffered to go out in the temples, and none were lighted in their own dwellings. Their furniture and domestic utensils were destroyed; their garments torn in pieces; and everything was thrown into disorder, for the coming of the evil genii who were to descend on the desolate earth.

On the evening of the last day, a procession of priests, assuming the dress and ornaments of their gods, moved from the capital towards a lofty mountain, about 2 leagues distant. They carried with them a noble victim, the flower of their captives, and an apparatus for kindling the *new fire*, the success of which was an augury of the renewal of the cycle. On reaching the summit of the mountain, the procession paused till midnight; when, as the constellation of the Pleiades approached the zenith, the *new fire* was kindled by the friction of the sticks placed on the wounded breast of the victim. The flame was soon communicated to a funeral pile, on which the body of the slaughtered captive was thrown. As the light streamed up towards heaven, shouts of joy and triumph burst forth from the countless multitudes who covered the hills, the terraces of the temples, and the housetops, with eyes anxiously bent on the mount of sacrifice. Couriers, with torches lighted at the blazing beacon, rapidly bore them over every part of the country; and the cheering element was seen brightening on altar and hearthstone, for the circuit of many a league, long before the sun, rising on his accustomed track, gave assurance that a new cycle had commenced its march, and that the laws of nature were not to be reversed for the Aztecs.

The following thirteen days were given up to festivity. The houses were cleansed and whitened. The broken vessels were replaced by new ones. The people, dressed in their gayest apparel, and crowned with garlands and chaplets of flowers, thronged in joyous procession to offer up their oblations and thanksgivings in the temples. Dances and games were instituted, emblematical of the regeneration of the world. It was the carnival of the Aztecs; or rather the national jubilee, the great secular festival, like that of the Romans, or ancient Etruscans, which few alive had witnessed before, or could expect to see again.

AZTEC AGRICULTURE

It is hardly possible that a nation so far advanced as the Aztecs in mathematical science should not have made considerable progress in the mechanical arts, which are so nearly connected with it. Indeed, intellectual progress of any kind implies a degree of refinement that requires a certain cultivation of both useful and elegant art. The savage wandering through the wide forest, without shelter for his head or raiment for his back, knows no other wants than those of animal appetites, and, when they are satisfied, seems to himself to have answered the only ends of existence. But man, in society, feels numerous desires, and artificial tastes spring up, accommodated to the various relations in which he is placed, and perpetually stimulating his invention to devise new expedients to gratify them. [...]

Husbandry, to a very limited extent, was practised by most of the rude tribes of North America. Wherever a natural opening in the forest, or a rich strip of *interval*, met their eyes, or a green slope was found along the rivers, they planted it with beans and Indian corn. [...] That they tilled the soil at all was a peculiarity which honourably distinguished them from other tribes of hunters, and raised them one degree higher in the scale of civilization.

Agriculture in Mexico was in the same advanced state as the other arts of social life. In few countries, indeed, has it been more respected. It was closely interwoven with the civil and religious institutions of the nation. There were peculiar deities to preside over it; the names of the months and of the religious festivals had more or less reference to it. The public taxes, as we have seen, were often paid in agricultural produce. All except the soldiers and great nobles, even the inhabitants of the cities, cultivated the soil. The work was chiefly done by the men; the women scattering the seed, husking the corn and taking part only in the lighter labours of the field. In this they presented an honourable contrast to the other tribes of the continent, who imposed the burden of agriculture, severe as it is in the North, on their women. Indeed, the sex was as tenderly regarded by the Aztecs in this matter, as it is, in most parts of Europe, at the present day.

There was no want of judgment in the management of their ground. When somewhat exhausted, it was permitted to recover by lying fallow. Its extreme dryness was relieved by canals, with which the land was partially irrigated; and the same end was promoted by severe penalties against the destruction of the woods, with which the country, as already noticed, was well covered before the Conquest. Lastly, they provided for their harvests ample granaries, which were admitted by the conquerors to be of admirable construction. In this provision we see the forecast of civilized man.

Among the most important articles of husbandry, we may notice the banana, whose facility of cultivation and exuberant returns are so fatal to habits of systematic and hardy industry. Another celebrated plant was the cacao, the fruit of which furnished the chocolate – from the Mexican *chocolatl* – now so common a beverage throughout Europe. The vanilla, confined to a small district of the seacoast, was used for the same purposes, of flavouring their food and drink, as with us.

The great staple of the country, as, indeed, of the American continent, was maize, or Indian corn, which grew freely along the valleys, and up the steep sides of the Cordilleras to the high level of the tableland. Its gigantic stalks, in these equinoctial regions, afford a saccharine matter, not found to the same extent in northern latitudes, and supplied the natives with sugar little inferior to that of the cane itself, which was not introduced among them till after the Conquest. But the miracle of nature was the great Mexican aloe, or *maguey*, whose clustering pyramids of flowers, towering above their dark coronals of leaves, were seen sprinkled over many a broad acre of the tableland. As we have already noticed, its bruised leaves afforded a paste from which paper was manufactured; its juice was fermented into an intoxicating beverage, *pulque*, of which the natives, to this day, are excessively fond; its leaves further supplied an impenetrable thatch for the more humble dwellings; thread, of which coarse stuffs were made, and strong cords, were drawn from its tough and twisted fibres; pins and needles were made of the thorns at the extremity of its leaves; and the root, when properly cooked, was converted into a palatable and nutritious food. The *agave*, in short, was meat, drink, clothing and writing materials, for the Aztec! Surely, never did Nature enclose in so compact a form so many of the elements of human comfort and civilization!

It would be obviously out of place to enumerate in these pages all the varieties of plants, many of them of medicinal virtue, which have been introduced from Mexico into Europe. Still less can I attempt a catalogue of its flowers, which, with their variegated and gaudy colours, form the greatest attraction of our greenhouses. The opposite climates embraced within the narrow latitudes of New Spain have given to it, probably, the richest and most diversified flora to be found in any country on the globe. These different products were systematically arranged by the Aztecs, who understood their properties, and collected them into nurseries, more extensive than any then existing in the Old World. It is not improbable that they suggested the idea of those 'gardens of plants' which were introduced into Europe not many years after the Conquest.

MECHANICAL ARTS

The Mexicans were as well acquainted with the mineral as with the vegetable treasures of their kingdom. Silver, lead and tin they drew from the mines of Tasco; copper from the mountains of Zacotollan. These were taken not only from the crude masses on the surface, but from veins wrought in the solid rock, into which they opened extensive galleries. In fact, the traces of their labours furnished the best indications for the early Spanish miners. Gold, found on the surface, or gleaned from the beds of rivers, was cast into bars, or, in the form of dust, made part of the regular tribute of the southern provinces of the empire. The use of iron, with which the soil was impregnated, was unknown to them. Notwithstanding its abundance, it demands so many processes to prepare it for use that it has commonly been one of the last metals pressed into the service of man. The age of iron has followed that of brass, in fact as well as in fiction.

They found a substitute in an alloy of tin and copper, and, with tools made of this bronze, could cut not only metals, but, with the aid of a silicious dust, the hardest substances, as basalt, porphyry, amethysts and emeralds. They fashioned these last, which were found very large, into many curious and fantastic forms. They cast, also, vessels of gold and silver, carving them with their metallic chisels in a very delicate manner. Some of the silver vases were so large that a man could not encircle them with his arms. They imitated very nicely the figures of animals, and, what was extraordinary, could mix the metals in such a manner that the feathers of a bird, or the scales of a fish, should be alternately of gold and silver.

They employed another tool, made of *itztli*, or obsidian, a dark transparent mineral, exceedingly hard, found in abundance in their hills. They made it into knives, razors and their serrated swords. It took a keen edge, though soon blunted. With this they wrought the various stones and alabasters employed in the construction of their public works and principal dwellings. I shall defer a more particular account of these to the body of the narrative, and will only add here that the entrances and angles of the buildings were profusely ornamented with images, sometimes of their fantastic deities, and frequently of animals. The latter were executed with great accuracy. 'The former,' according to Torquemada, 'were the hideous reflection of their own souls. And it was not till after they had been converted to Christianity that they could model the true figure of a man.' The old chronicler's facts are well founded, whatever we may think of his reasons. The allegorical phantasms of his religion, no doubt, gave a direction to the Aztec artist, in his delineation of the human figure; supplying him with an imaginary beauty in the personification of divinity itself. As these superstitions lost their hold on his mind, it opened to the influences of a purer taste; and, after the Conquest, the Mexicans furnished many examples of correct, and some of beautiful, portraiture.

Sculptured images were so numerous that the foundations of the cathedral in the *plaza mayor*, the great square of Mexico, are said to be entirely composed of them. This spot may, indeed, be regarded as the Aztec forum – the great depository of the treasures of ancient sculpture, which now lie hidden in its bosom. Such monuments are spread all over the capital, however, and a new cellar can hardly be dug, or foundation laid, without turning up some of the mouldering relics of barbaric art. But they are little heeded, and, if not wantonly broken in pieces at once, are usually worked into the rising wall or supports of the new edifice. Two celebrated bas-reliefs of the last Moctezuma and his father, cut in the solid rock, in the beautiful groves of Chapoltepec, were deliberately destroyed, as late as the eighteenth century, by order of the government! The monuments of the barbarian meet with as little respect from civilized man as those of the civilized man from the barbarian.

The most remarkable piece of sculpture yet disinterred is the great calendar stone, noticed in the preceding chapter. It consists of dark porphyry, and in its original dimensions, as taken from the quarry, is computed to have weighed nearly fifty tons. It was transported from the mountains beyond Lake Chalco, a distance of many leagues, over a broken country intersected by watercourses and canals. In crossing a bridge which traversed one of these latter, in the capital, the supports gave way, and the huge mass was precipitated into the water, whence it was with difficulty recovered. The fact that so enormous a fragment of porphyry could be thus safely carried for leagues, in the face of such obstacles, and without the aid of cattle – for the Aztecs, as already mentioned, had no animals of draught – suggests to us no mean ideas of their mechanical skill, and of their machinery, and implies a degree of cultivation little inferior to that demanded for the geometrical and astronomical science displayed in the inscriptions on this very stone.

The ancient Mexicans made utensils of earthenware for the ordinary purposes of domestic life, numerous specimens of which still exist. They made cups and vases of a lacquered or painted wood, impervious to wet and gaudily coloured. Their dyes were obtained from both mineral and vegetable substances. Among them was the rich crimson of the cochineal, the modern rival of the famed Tyrian purple. It was introduced into Europe from Mexico, where the curious little insect was nourished with great care on plantations of cactus, since fallen into neglect. The natives were thus enabled to give a brilliant colouring to the webs which were manufactured, of every degree of fineness, from the cotton raised in abundance throughout the warmer regions of the country. They had the art, also, of interweaving with these the delicate hair of rabbits and other animals, which made a cloth of great warmth as well as beauty, of a kind altogether original; and on this they often laid a rich embroidery, of birds, flowers, or some other fanciful device.

But the art in which they most delighted was their *plumaje*, or featherwork. With this they could produce all the effects of a beautiful mosaic. The gorgeous plumage of the tropical birds, especially of the parrot tribe, afforded every variety of colour; and the fine down of the hummingbird, which revelled in swarms among the honeysuckle bowers of Mexico, supplied them with soft aerial tints that gave an exquisite finish to the picture. The feathers, pasted on a fine cotton web, were wrought into dresses for the wealthy, hangings for apartments and ornaments for the temples. No one of the American fabrics excited such admiration in Europe, whither numerous specimens were sent by the conquerors. It is to be regretted that so graceful an art should have been suffered to fall into decay.

MERCHANTS AND TRADE

There were no shops in Mexico, but the various manufactures and agricultural products were brought together for sale in the great marketplaces of the principal cities. Fairs were held there every fifth day, and were thronged by a numerous concourse of persons, who came to buy or sell from all the neighbouring country. A particular quarter was allotted to each kind of article. The numerous transactions were conducted without confusion, and with entire regard to justice, under the inspection of magistrates appointed for the purpose. The traffic was carried on partly by barter, and partly by means of a regulated currency, of different values. This consisted of transparent quills of gold dust; of bits of tin, cut in the form of a T; and of bags of cacao, containing a specified number of grains. 'Blessed money,' exclaims Peter Martyr, 'which exempts its possessors from avarice, since it cannot be long hoarded, nor hidden under ground!'

There did not exist in Mexico that distinction of castes found among the Egyptian and Asiatic nations. It was usual, however, for the son to follow the occupation of his father.

The different trades were arranged into something like guilds; each having a particular district of the city appropriated to it, with its own chief, its own tutelar deity, its peculiar festivals and the like. Trade was held in avowed estimation by the Aztecs. 'Apply thyself, my son,' was the advice of an aged chief, 'to agriculture, or to featherwork, or some other honourable calling. Thus did your ancestors before you. Else how would they have provided for themselves and their families? Never was it heard that nobility alone was able to maintain its possessor.'

But the occupation peculiarly respected was that of the merchant. It formed so important and singular a feature of their social economy as to merit a much more particular notice than it has received from historians. The Aztec merchant was a sort of itinerant trader, who made his journeys to the remotest borders of Anahuac, and to the countries beyond, carrying with him merchandise of rich stuffs, jewellery, slaves and other valuable commodities. The slaves were obtained at the great market of Azcapozalco, not many leagues from the capital, where fairs were regularly held for the sale of these unfortunate beings. They were brought thither by their masters, dressed in their gayest apparel, and instructed to sing, dance and display their little stock of personal accomplishments, so as to recommend themselves to the purchaser. Slave-dealing was an honourable calling among the Aztecs.

With this rich freight, the merchant visited the different provinces, always bearing some present of value from his own sovereign to their chiefs, and usually receiving others in return, with a permission to trade. Should this be denied him, or should he meet with indignity or violence, he had the means of resistance in his power. He performed his journeys with a number of companions of his own rank, and a large body of inferior attendants who were employed to transport the goods. Fifty or sixty pounds were the usual load for a man. The whole caravan went armed, and so well provided against sudden hostilities that they could make good their defence, if necessary, till reinforced from home. In one instance, a body of these militant traders stood a siege of four years in the town of Ayotlan, which they finally took from the enemy. Their own government, however, was always prompt to embark in a war on this ground, finding it a very convenient pretext for extending the Mexican empire. It was not unusual to allow the merchants to raise levies themselves, which were placed under their command. It was, moreover, very common for the prince to employ the merchants as a sort of spies, to furnish him information of the state of the countries through which they passed, and the dispositions of the inhabitants towards himself.

Thus their sphere of action was much enlarged beyond that of a humble trader, and they acquired a high consideration in the body politic. They were allowed to assume insignia and devices of their own. Some of their number composed what is called by the Spanish writers a council of finance; at least, this was the case in Tezcuco. They were much consulted by the monarch, who had some of them constantly near his person, addressing them by the title of 'uncle', which may remind one of that of *primo*, or 'cousin', by which a grandee of Spain is saluted by his sovereign. They were allowed to have their own courts, in which civil and criminal cases, not excepting capital, were determined; so that they formed an independent community, as it were, of themselves. And, as their various traffic supplied them with abundant stores of wealth, they enjoyed many of the most essential advantages of an hereditary aristocracy.

That trade should prove the path to eminent political preferment in a nation but partially civilized, where the names of soldier and priest are usually the only titles to respect, is certainly an anomaly in history. It forms some contrast to the standard of the more polished monarchies of the Old World, in which rank is supposed to be less dishonoured by a life of idle ease or frivolous pleasure than by those active pursuits which promote equally the prosperity of the state and of the individual. If civilization corrects many prejudices, it must be allowed that it creates others.

DOMESTIC MANNERS

We shall be able to form a better idea of the actual refinement of the natives by penetrating into their domestic life and observing the intercourse between the sexes. We have, fortunately, the means of doing this. We shall there find the ferocious Aztec frequently displaying all the sensibility of a cultivated nature; consoling his friends under affliction, or congratulating them on their good fortune, as on occasion of a marriage, or of the birth or the baptism of a child, when he was punctilious in his visits, bringing presents of costly dresses and ornaments, or the more simple offering of flowers, equally indicative of his sympathy. The visits at these times, though regulated with all the precision of Oriental courtesy, were accompanied by expressions of the most cordial and affectionate regard.

The discipline of children, especially at the public schools, as stated in a previous chapter, was exceedingly severe. But after she had come to a mature age the Aztec maiden was treated by her parents with a tenderness from which all reserve seemed banished. In the counsels to a daughter about to enter into life, they conjured her to preserve simplicity in her manners and conversation, uniform neatness in her attire, with strict attention to personal cleanliness. They inculcated modesty, as the great ornament of a woman, and implicit reverence for her husband; softening their admonitions by such endearing epithets as showed the fulness of a parent's love.

Polygamy was permitted among the Mexicans, though chiefly confined, probably, to the wealthiest classes. And the obligations of the marriage vow, which was made with all the formality of a religious ceremony, were fully recognized, and impressed on both parties. [...] Their long black hair, covered, in some parts of the country, by a veil made of the fine web of the *pita* [maguey], might generally be seen wreathed with flowers, or, among the richer people, with strings of precious stones, and pearls from the Gulf of California. They appear to have been treated with much consideration by their husbands, and passed their time in indolent tranquillity, or in such feminine occupations as spinning, embroidery and the like, while their maidens beguiled the hours by the rehearsal of traditionary tales and ballads.

The women partook equally with the men of social festivities and entertainments. These were often conducted on a large scale, both as regards the number of guests and the costliness of the preparations. Numerous attendants, of both sexes, waited at the banquet. The halls were scented with perfumes, and the courts strewed with odoriferous herbs and flowers, which were distributed in profusion among the guests, as they arrived. Cotton napkins and ewers of water were placed before them, as they took their seats at the board; for the venerable ceremony of ablution before and after eating was punctiliously observed by the Aztecs. Tobacco was then offered to the company, in pipes, mixed up with aromatic substances, or in the form of cigars, inserted in tubes of tortoiseshell or silver. They compressed the nostrils with the fingers, while they inhaled the smoke, which they frequently swallowed. Whether the women, who sat apart from the men at table, were allowed the indulgence of the fragrant weed, as in the most polished circles of modern Mexico, is not told us. It is a curious fact that the Aztecs also took the dried leaf in the pulverized form of snuff.

The table was well provided with substantial meats, especially game; among which the most conspicuous was the turkey, erroneously supposed, as its name imports, to have come originally from the East. These more solid dishes were flanked by others of vegetables and fruits, of every delicious variety found on the North American continent. The different viands were prepared in various ways, with delicate sauces and seasoning, of which the Mexicans were very fond. Their palate was still further regaled by confections and pastry, for which their maize-flour and sugar supplied ample materials. One other dish, of a disgusting nature, was sometimes added to the feast, especially when the celebration partook of a religious character. On such occasions a slave was sacrificed, and his flesh, elaborately dressed, formed one of the chief ornaments of the banquet. Cannibalism, in the guise of an Epicurean science, becomes even the more revolting.

The meats were kept warm by chafing dishes. The table was ornamented with vases of silver, and sometimes gold, of delicate workmanship. The drinking cups and spoons were of the same costly materials, and likewise of tortoiseshell. The favourite beverage was the *chocolatl*, flavoured with vanilla and different spices. They had a way of preparing the froth of it, so as to make it almost solid enough to be eaten, and took it cold. The fermented juice of the maguey, with a mixture of sweets and acids, supplied, also, various agreeable drinks, of different degrees of strength, and formed the chief beverage of the elder part of the company.

As soon as they had finished their repast, the young people rose from the table, to close the festivities of the day with dancing. They danced gracefully, to the sound of various instruments, accompanying their movements with chants of a pleasing though somewhat plaintive character. The older guests continued at table, sipping *pulque*, and gossiping about other times, till the virtues of the exhilarating beverage put them in good humour with their own. Intoxication was not rare in this part of the company, and, what is singular, was excused in them, though severely punished in the younger. The entertainment was concluded by a liberal distribution of rich dresses and ornaments among the guests, when they withdrew, after midnight, 'some commending the feast, and others condemning the bad taste or extravagance of their host; in the same manner,' says an old

Spanish writer, 'as with us.' Human nature is, indeed, much the same all the world over.

In this remarkable picture of manners, which I have copied faithfully from the records of earliest date after the Conquest, we find no resemblance to the other races of North American natives. Some resemblance we may trace to the general style of Asiatic pomp and luxury. But in Asia, woman, far from being admitted to unreserved intercourse with the other sex, is too often jealously immured within the walls of the harem. European civilization, which accords to this loveliest portion of creation her proper rank in the social scale, is still more removed from some of the brutish usages of the Aztecs. That such usages should have existed with the degree of refinement they showed in other things is almost inconceivable. It can only be explained as the result of religious superstition; superstition which clouds the moral perception, and perverts even the natural senses, till man, civilized man, is reconciled to the very things which are most revolting to humanity. Habits and opinions founded on religion must not be taken as conclusive evidence of the actual refinement of a people.

The Aztec character was perfectly original and unique. It was made up of incongruities apparently irreconcilable. It blended into one the marked peculiarities of different nations, not only of the same phase of civilization, but as far removed from each other as the extremes of barbarism and refinement. It may find a fitting parallel in their own wonderful climate, capable of producing, on a few square leagues of surface, the boundless variety of vegetable forms which belong to the frozen regions of the North, the temperate zone of Europe, and the burning skies of Arabia and Hindustan.

THE TEZCUCANS

The reader would gather but an imperfect notion of the civilization of Anahuac, without some account of the Acolhuans, or Tezcucans, as they are usually called; a nation of the same great family with the Aztecs, whom they rivalled in power and surpassed in intellectual culture and the arts of social refinement. Fortunately, we have ample materials for this in the records left by Ixtlilxochitl, a lineal descendant of the royal line of Tezcuco, who flourished in the century of the Conquest. With every opportunity for information he combined much industry and talent, and, if his narrative bears the high colouring of one who would revive the faded glories of an ancient but dilapidated house, he has been uniformly commended for his fairness and integrity. I shall confine myself to the prominent features of the two reigns which may be said to embrace the golden age of Tezcuco, without attempting to weigh the probability of the details, which I will leave to be settled by the reader, according to the measure of his faith.

The Acolhuans came into the Valley, as we have seen, about the close of the twelfth century, and built their capital of Tezcuco on the eastern borders of the lake, opposite to Mexico. From this point they gradually spread themselves over the northern portion of Anahuac, when their career was checked by an invasion of a kindred race, the Tepanecs, who, after a desperate struggle, succeeded in taking their city, slaying their monarch and entirely subjugating his kingdom. This event took place about 1418; and the young prince, Nezahualcoyotl, the heir to the crown, then fifteen years old, saw his father butchered before his eyes, while he himself lay concealed among the friendly branches of a tree which overshadowed the spot.

Not long after his flight from the field of his father's blood, the Tezcucan prince fell into the hands of his enemy, was borne off in triumph to his city, and was thrown into a dungeon. He effected his escape, however, through the connivance of the governor of the fortress, an old servant of his family, who took the place of the royal fugitive, and paid for his loyalty with his life. He was at length permitted, through the intercession of the reigning family in Mexico, which was allied to him, to retire to that capital, and subsequently to his own, where he found a shelter in his ancestral palace. Here he remained unmolested for eight years, pursuing his studies under an old preceptor, who had had the care of his early youth, and who instructed him in the various duties befitting his princely station.

At the end of this period the Tepanec usurper died, bequeathing his empire to his son, Maxtla, a man of fierce and suspicious temper. Nezahualcoyotl hastened to pay his obeisance to him, on his accession. But the tyrant refused to receive the little present of flowers which he laid at his feet, and turned his back on him in presence of his chieftains. One of his attendants, friendly to the young prince, admonished him to provide for his own safety, by withdrawing, as speedily as possible, from the palace, where his life was in danger. He lost no time, consequently, in retreating from the inhospitable court, and returned to Tezcuco. Maxtla, however, was bent on his destruction. He saw with jealous eye the opening talents and popular manners of his rival, and the favour he was daily winning from his ancient subjects.

He accordingly laid a plan for making away with him at an evening entertainment. It was defeated by the vigilance of the prince's tutor, who contrived to mislead the assassins and to substitute another victim in the place of his pupil. The baffled tyrant now threw off all disguise, and sent a strong party of soldiers to Tezcuco, with orders to enter the palace, seize the person of Nezahualcoyotl and slay him on the spot. The prince, who became acquainted with the plot through the watchfulness of his preceptor, instead of flying, as he was counselled, resolved to await his enemies. They found him playing at ball, when they arrived, in the court of his palace. He received them courteously, and invited them in, to take some refreshments after their journey. While they were occupied in this way, he passed into an adjoining saloon, which excited no suspicion, as he was still visible through the open doors by which the apartments communicated with each other. A burning censer stood in the passage, and, as it was fed by the attendants, threw up such clouds of incense as obscured his movements from the soldiers. Under this friendly veil he succeeded in making his escape by a secret passage, which communicated with a large earthen pipe formerly used to bring water to the palace. Here he remained till nightfall, when, taking advantage of the obscurity, he found his way into the suburbs, and sought a shelter in the cottage of one of his father's vassals.

The Tepanec monarch, enraged at this repeated disappointment, ordered instant pursuit. A price was set on the head of the royal fugitive. Whoever should take him, dead or alive, was promised, however humble his degree, the hand of a noble lady, and an ample domain along with it. Troops of armed men were ordered to scour the country in every direction. In the course of the search, the cottage in which the prince had taken refuge was entered. But he fortunately escaped detection by being hid under a heap of maguey fibres used for manufacturing cloth. As this was no longer a proper place of concealment, he sought a retreat in the mountainous and woody district lying between the borders of his own state and Tlascala.

Here he led a wretched, wandering life, exposed to all the inclemencies of the weather, hiding himself in deep thickets and caverns, and stealing out, at night, to satisfy the cravings of appetite; while he was kept in constant alarm by the activity of his pursuers, always hovering on his track. On one occasion he sought refuge from them among a small party of soldiers, who proved friendly to him and concealed him in a large drum around which they were dancing. At another time he was just able to turn the crest of a hill as his enemies were climbing it on the other side, when he fell in with a girl who was reaping *chia* – a Mexican plant, the seed of which was much used in the drinks of the country. He persuaded her to cover him up with the stalks she had been cutting. When his pursuers came up, and inquired if she had seen the fugitive, the girl coolly answered that she had, and pointed out a path as the one he had taken. Notwithstanding the high rewards offered, Nezahualcoyotl seems to have incurred no danger from treachery, such was the general attachment felt to himself and his house. 'Would you not deliver up the prince, if he came in your way?' he inquired of a young peasant who was unacquainted with his person. 'Not I,' replied the other. 'What, not for a fair lady's hand, and a rich dowry beside?' rejoined the prince. At which the other only shook his head and laughed. On more than one occasion his faithful people submitted to torture, and even to lose their lives, rather than disclose the place of his retreat.

However gratifying such proofs of loyalty might be to his feelings, the situation of the prince in these mountain solitudes became every day more distressing. It gave a still keener edge to his own sufferings to witness those of the faithful followers who chose to accompany him in his wanderings. 'Leave me,' he would say to them, 'to my fate! Why should you throw away your own lives for one whom fortune is never weary of persecuting?' Most of the great Tezcucan chiefs had consulted their interests by a timely adhesion to the usurper. But some still clung to their prince, preferring proscription, and death itself, rather than desert him in his extremity.

In the meantime, his friends at a distance were active in measures for his relief. The oppressions of Maxtla, and his growing empire, had caused general alarm in the surrounding states, who recalled the mild rule of the Tezcucan princes. A coalition was formed, a plan of operations concerted, and, on the day appointed for a general rising, Nezahualcoyotl found himself at the head of a force sufficiently strong to face his Tepanec adversaries. An engagement came on, in which the latter were totally discomfited; and the victorious prince, receiving everywhere on his route the homage of his joyful subjects, entered his capital, not like a proscribed outcast, but as the rightful heir, and saw himself once more enthroned in the halls of his fathers.

Soon after, he united his forces with the Mexicans, long disgusted with the arbitrary conduct of Maxtla. The allied powers, after a series of bloody engagements with the usurper, routed him under the walls of his own capital. He fled to the baths, whence he was dragged out, and sacrificed with the usual cruel ceremonies of the Aztecs; the royal city of

Azcapozalco was razed to the ground, and the wasted territory was henceforth reserved as the great slave market for the nations of Anahuac.

These events were succeeded by the remarkable league among the three powers of Tezcuco, Mexico and Tlacopan, of which some account has been given in a previous chapter. Historians are not agreed as to the precise terms of it; the writers of the two former nations each insisting on the paramount authority of his own in the coalition. All agree in the subordinate position of Tlacopan, a state, like the others, bordering on the lake. It is certain that in their subsequent operations, whether of peace or war, the three states shared in each other's councils, embarked in each other's enterprises, and moved in perfect concert together, till just before the coming of the Spaniards.

AMNESTY AND REFORM

The first measure of Nezahualcoyotl, on returning to his dominions, was a general amnesty. It was his maxim 'that a monarch might punish, but revenge was unworthy of him'. In the present instance he was averse even to punish, and not only freely pardoned his rebel nobles, but conferred on some, who had most deeply offended, posts of honour and confidence. Such conduct was doubtless politic, especially as their alienation was owing, probably, much more to fear of the usurper than to any disaffection towards himself. But there are some acts of policy which a magnanimous spirit only can execute.

The restored monarch next set about repairing the damages sustained under the late misrule, and reviving, or rather remodelling, the various departments of government. He framed a concise, but comprehensive, code of laws, so well suited, it was thought, to the exigencies of the times, that it was adopted as their own by the two other members of the triple alliance. It was written in blood, and entitled the author to be called the Draco rather than 'the Solon of Anahuac', as he is fondly styled by his admirers. Humanity is one of the best fruits of refinement. It is only with increasing civilization that the legislator studies to economize human suffering, even for the guilty; to devise penalties not so much by way of punishment for the past as of reformation for the future.

He divided the burden of government among a number of departments, as the council of war, the council of finance, the council of justice. This last was a court of supreme authority, both in civil and criminal matters, receiving appeals from the lower tribunals of the provinces, which were obliged to make a full report, every four months, or eighty days, of their own proceedings to this higher judicature. In all these bodies, a certain number of citizens were allowed to have seats with the nobles and professional dignitaries. There was, however, another body, a council of state, for aiding the king in the despatch of business, and advising him in matters of importance, which was drawn altogether from the highest order of chiefs. It consisted of fourteen members; and they had seats provided for them at the royal table.

Lastly, there was an extraordinary tribunal, called the council of music, but which, differing from the import of its name, was devoted to the encouragement of science and art. Works on astronomy, chronology, history, or any other science, were required to be submitted to its judgment, before they could be made public. This censorial power was of some moment, at least with regard to the historical department, where the wilful perversion of truth was made a capital offence by the bloody code of Nezahualcoyotl. Yet a Tezcucan author must have been a bungler, who could not elude a conviction under the cloudy veil of hieroglyphics. This body, which was drawn from the best-instructed persons in the kingdom, with little regard to rank, had supervision of all the productions of art, and of the nicer fabrics. It decided on the qualifications of the professors in the various branches of science, on the fidelity of their instructions to their pupils, the deficiency of which was severely punished, and it instituted examinations of these latter. In short, it was a general board of education for the country. On stated days, historical compositions, and poems treating of moral or traditional topics, were recited before it by their authors. Seats were provided for the three crowned heads of the empire, who deliberated with the other members on the respective merits of the pieces, and distributed prizes of value to the successful competitors.

Such are the marvellous accounts transmitted to us of this institution; an institution certainly not to have been expected among the aborigines of America. It is calculated to give us a higher idea of the refinement of the people than even the noble architectural remains which still cover some parts of the continent. Architecture is, to a certain extent, a sensual gratification. It addresses itself to the eye, and affords the best scope for the parade of barbaric pomp and splendour. It is the form in which the revenues of a semi-civilized people are most likely to be lavished. The most gaudy and ostentatious specimens of it, and sometimes the most stupendous, have been reared by such hands. It is one of the first steps in the great march of civilization. But the institution in question was evidence of still higher refinement. It was a literary luxury, and argued the existence of a taste in the nation which relied for its gratification on pleasures of a purely intellectual character.

The influence of this academy must have been most propitious to the capital, which became the nursery not only of such sciences as could be compassed by the scholarship of the period, but of various useful and ornamental arts. Its historians, orators, and poets were celebrated throughout the country. Its archives, for which accommodations were provided in the royal palace, were stored with the records of primitive ages. Its idiom, more polished than the Mexican, was, indeed, the purest of all the Nahuatlac dialects, and continued, long after the Conquest, to be that in which the best productions of the native races were composed. Tezcuco claimed the glory of being the Athens of the Western world.

Among the most illustrious of her bards was the emperor himself – for the Tezcucan writers claim this title for their chief, as head of the imperial alliance. He doubtless appeared as a competitor before that very academy where he so often sat as a critic. Many of his odes descended to a late generation, and are still preserved, perhaps, in some of the dusty repositories of Mexico or Spain. The historian Ixtlilxochitl has left a translation, in Castilian, of one of the poems of his royal ancestor. It is not easy to render his version into corresponding English rhyme, without the perfume of the original escaping in this double filtration. They remind one of the rich breathings of Spanish-Arab poetry, in which an ardent imagination is tempered by a not unpleasing and moral melancholy. But, though sufficiently florid in diction, they are generally free from the meretricious ornaments and hyperbole with which the minstrelsy of the East is usually tainted. They turn on the vanities and mutability of human life – a topic very natural for a monarch who had himself experienced the strangest mutations of fortune. There is mingled in the lament of the Tezcucan bard, however, an Epicurean philosophy, which seeks relief from the fears of the future in the joys of the present. 'Banish care,' he says: 'if there are bounds to pleasure, the saddest life must also have an end. Then weave the chaplet of flowers, and sing thy songs in praise of the all-powerful God, for the glory of this world soon fadeth away. Rejoice in the green freshness of thy spring; for the day will come when thou shalt sigh for these joys in vain; when the sceptre shall pass from thy hands, thy servants shall wander desolate in thy courts, thy sons and the sons of thy nobles, shall drink the dregs of distress, and all the pomp of thy victories and triumphs shall live only in their recollection. Yet the remembrance of the just shall not pass away from the nations, and the good thou hast done shall ever be held in honour. The goods of this life, its glories and its riches, are but lent to us, its substance is but an illusory shadow, and the things of today shall change on the coming of the morrow. Then gather the fairest flowers from thy gardens, to bind round thy brow, and seize the joys of the present ere they perish.'

THE DEVELOPMENT OF TEZCUCO

At about the year 1470, Nezahualcoyotl, full of years and honours, felt himself drawing near his end. Almost half a century had elapsed since he mounted the throne of Tezcuco. He had found his kingdom dismembered by faction and bowed to the dust beneath the yoke of a foreign tyrant. He had broken that yoke; had breathed new life into the nation, renewed its ancient institutions, extended wide its domain; had seen it flourishing in all the activity of trade and agriculture, gathering strength from its enlarged resources, and daily advancing higher and higher in the great march of civilization. All this he had seen, and might fairly attribute no small portion of it to his own wise and beneficent rule. His long and glorious day was now drawing to its close; and he contemplated the event with the same serenity which he had shown under the clouds of its morning and in its meridian splendour.

A short time before his death, he gathered around him those of his children in whom he most confided, his chief counsellors, the ambassadors of Mexico and Tlacopan, and his little son, the heir to the crown, his only offspring by the queen. He was then not eight years old, but had already given, as far as so tender a blossom might, the rich promise of future excellence.

After tenderly embracing the child, the dying monarch threw over him the robes of sovereignty. He then gave audience to the ambassadors, and, when they had retired, made the boy repeat the substance of the conversation. He followed this by such counsels as were suited to his comprehension, and which, when remembered through the long vista of afteryears, would serve as lights to guide him in his government of the kingdom. He besought him not to neglect the worship of 'the unknown God', regretting that he himself had been unworthy to know him, and intimating his conviction that the time would come when he should be known and worshipped throughout the land.

He next addressed himself to that one of his sons in whom he placed the greatest trust, and whom he had selected as the guardian of the realm. 'From this hour,' said he to him, 'you will fill the place that I have filled, of father to this child; you will teach him to live as he ought; and by your counsels he will rule over the empire. Stand in his place, and be his guide, till he shall be of age to govern for himself.' Then, turning to his other children, he admonished them to live united with one another, and to show all loyalty to their prince, who, though a child, already manifested a discretion far above his years. 'Be true to him,' he added, 'and he will maintain you in your rights and dignities.'

Feeling his end approaching, he exclaimed, 'Do not bewail me with idle lamentations. But sing the song of gladness, and show a courageous spirit, that the nations I have subdued may not believe you disheartened, but may feel that each one of you is strong enough to keep them in obedience!' The undaunted spirit of the monarch shone forth even in the agonies of death. That stout heart, however, melted, as he took leave of his children and friends, weeping tenderly over them, while he bade each a last adieu. When they had withdrawn, he ordered the officers of the palace to allow no one to enter it again. Soon after, he expired, in the seventy-second year of his age, and the forty-third of his reign.

Thus died the greatest monarch, and perhaps the best, who ever sat upon an Indian throne. His character is delineated with tolerable impartiality by his kinsman, the Tezcucan chronicler: 'He was wise, valiant, liberal; and, when we consider the magnanimity of his soul, the grandeur and success of his enterprises, his deep policy, as well as daring, we must admit him to have far surpassed every other prince and captain of this New World. He had few failings himself, and rigorously punished those of others. He preferred the public to his private interest; was most charitable in his nature, often buying articles, at double their worth, of poor and honest persons, and giving them away again to the sick and infirm. In seasons of scarcity he was particularly bountiful, remitting the taxes of his vassals, and supplying their wants from the royal granaries. He put no faith in the idolatrous worship of the country. He was well instructed in moral science, and sought, above all things, to obtain light for knowing the true God. He believed in one God only, the Creator of heaven and earth, by whom we have our being, who never revealed himself to us in human form, nor in any other; with whom the souls of the virtuous are to dwell after death, while the wicked will suffer pains unspeakable. He invoked the Most High, as 'He by whom we live', and 'Who has all things in himself'. He recognized the Sun for his father, and the Earth for his mother. He taught his children not to confide in idols, and only to conform to the outward worship of them from deference to public opinion. If he could not entirely abolish human sacrifices, derived from the Aztecs, he at least restricted them to slaves and captives.

I have occupied so much space with this illustrious prince that but little remains for his son and successor, Nezahualpilli. I have thought it better, in our narrow limits, to present a complete view of a single epoch, the most interesting in the Tezcucan annals, than to spread the inquiries over a broader but comparatively barren field. Yet Nezahualpilli, the heir to the crown, was a remarkable person, and his reign contains many incidents which I regret to be obliged to pass over in silence.

He had, in many respects, a taste similar to his father's, and, like him, displayed a profuse magnificence in his way of living and in his public edifices. He was more severe in his morals, and, in the execution of justice, stern even to the sacrifice of natural affection. Several remarkable instances of this are told; one, among others, in relation to his eldest son, the heir to the crown, a prince of great promise. The young man entered into a poetical correspondence with one of his father's concubines, the lady of Tula, as she was called, a woman of humble origin, but of uncommon endowments. She wrote verses with ease, and could discuss graver matters with the king and his ministers. She maintained a separate establishment, where she lived in state, and acquired, by her beauty and accomplishments, great ascendency over her royal lover. With this favourite the prince carried on a correspondence in verse – whether of an amorous nature does not appear. At all events, the offence was capital. It was submitted to the regular tribunal, who pronounced sentence of death on the unfortunate youth; and the king, steeling his heart against all entreaties and the voice of nature, suffered the cruel judgment to be carried into execution. We might, in this case, suspect the influence of baser passions on his mind, but it was not a solitary instance of his inexorable justice towards those most near to him. He had the stern virtue of an ancient Roman, destitute of the softer graces which make virtue attractive. When the sentence was carried into effect, he shut himself up in his palace for many weeks, and commanded the doors and windows of his son's residence to be walled up, that it might never again be occupied.

Nezahualpilli resembled his father in his passion for astronomical studies, and is said to have had an observatory on one of his palaces. He was devoted to war in his youth, but, as he advanced in years, resigned himself to a more indolent way of life, and sought his chief amusement in the pursuit of his favourite science, or in the soft pleasures of the sequestered gardens of Tezcotzinco. This quiet life was ill suited to the turbulent temper of the times, and of his Mexican rival, Moctezuma. The distant provinces fell off from their allegiance; the army relaxed its discipline; disaffection crept into its ranks; and the wily Moctezuma, partly by violence, and partly by stratagems unworthy of a king, succeeded in plundering his brother monarch of some of his most valuable domains. Then it was that he arrogated to himself the title and supremacy of emperor, hitherto borne by the Tezcucan princes as head of the alliance. Such is the account given by the historians of that nation, who in this way explain the acknowledged superiority of the Aztec sovereign, both in territory and consideration, on the landing of the Spaniards.

These misfortunes pressed heavily on the spirits of Nezahualpilli. Their effect was increased by certain gloomy prognostics of a near calamity which was to overwhelm the country. He withdrew to his retreat, to brood in secret over his sorrows. His health rapidly declined; and in the year 1515, at the age of fifty-two, he sank into the grave; happy, at least, that by this timely death he escaped witnessing the fulfilment of his own predictions, in the ruin of his country, and the extinction of the Indian dynasties for ever.

In reviewing the brief sketch here presented of the Tezcucan monarchy, we are strongly impressed with the conviction of its superiority, in all the great features of civilization, over the rest of Anahuac. The Mexicans showed a similar proficiency, no doubt, in the mechanic arts, and even in mathematical science. But in the science of government, in legislation, in speculative doctrines of a religious nature, in the more elegant pursuits of poetry, eloquence and whatever depended on refinement of taste and a polished idiom, they confessed themselves inferior, by resorting to their rivals for instruction and citing their works as the masterpieces of their tongue. The best histories, the best poems, the best code of laws, the purest dialect, were all allowed to be Tezcucan. The Aztecs rivalled their neighbours in splendour of living, and even in the magnificence of their structures. They displayed a pomp and ostentatious pageantry truly Asiatic. But this was the development of the material rather than the intellectual principle. They wanted the refinement of manners essential to a continued advance in civilization. An insurmountable limit was put to theirs by that bloody mythology which threw its withering taint over the very air that they breathed.

The superiority of the Tezcucans was owing, doubtless, in a great measure to that of the two sovereigns whose reigns we have been depicting. There is no position which affords such scope for ameliorating the condition of man as that occupied by an absolute ruler over a nation imperfectly civilized. From his elevated place, commanding all the resources of his age, it is in his power to diffuse them far and wide among his people. He may be the copious reservoir on the mountain top, drinking in the dews of heaven, to send them in fertilizing streams along the lower slopes and valleys, clothing even the wilderness in beauty. Such were Nezahualcoyotl and his illustrious successor, whose enlightened policy, extending through nearly a century, wrought a most salutary revolution in the condition of their country. It is remarkable that we, the inhabitants of the same continent, should be more familiar with the history of many a barbarian chief, both in the Old and New World, than with that of these truly great men, whose names are identified with the most glorious period in the annals of the Indian races.

What was the actual amount of the Tezcucan civilization it is not easy to determine, with the imperfect light afforded us. It was certainly far below anything which the word conveys, measured by a European standard. In some of the arts, and in any walk of science, they could only have made, as it were, a beginning. But they had begun in the right way, and already showed a refinement in sentiment and manners, a capacity for receiving instruction, which, under good auspices, might have led them on to indefinite improvement. Unhappily, they were fast falling under the dominion of the warlike Aztecs. And that people repaid the benefits received from their more polished neighbours by imparting to them their own ferocious superstition, which, falling like a mildew on the land, would soon have blighted its rich blossoms of promise and turned even its fruits to dust and ashes.

ANCIENT KINGS & LEADERS

Ancient cultures often traded with and influenced
each other, while others grew independently.
This section provides the key leaders from a
number of regions, to offer comparative insights
into developments across the ancient world.

MESOAMERICAN LEADERS

There is **dispute** about the dates and position of some Mesoamerican rulers due to a lack of cohesion within different cultures, especially in the earlier periods, partly because of migration. This list aims to provide an overview of the major Mesoamerican peoples of the Olmecs, Maya, Toltecs and Aztecs. It is not exhaustive and dates are approximate. There may also be differences in name spellings between different sources.

OLMEC LEADERS

Although it is clear from archaeological findings of the Olmecs that their society was organized and was likely hierarchical, little is known of its rulers, either legendary or historical, although some believe the many sculptures or colossal heads found were created to glorify their rulers. There is, however, no record such as the Maya *Popol Vuh* which lists specific rulers or the dates of their rule.

The Olmecs seemed to have worshipped a god similar to Quetzalcoatl, a figure seen in many other Mesoamerican cultures. Archaeological studies indicate they also worshipped deities which symbolized rain, maize and the earth; however, there is no confirmation whether these deities were thought to be legendary Olmec leaders.

MAYA LEADERS

There are numerous gods related to the Maya culture, as well as various interpretations of creation myths. Many of the Maya rulers took names associated with gods, such as K'awiil (God K, associated with fertility, maize and lightning), K'inich Ajaw (God G, associated with the sun), Chaak (associated with thunder and rain) and Kukulkan (serpent deity, sometimes considered a Maya ruler).

The following lists focus on several significant Maya cities. Cities are listed alphabetically. Where names are unknown, rulers are identified by numbers.

Caracol

Te' K'ab Chaak	c. 331–349 CE
K'ahk' Ujol K'inich I	c. 470 CE
Yajaw Te' K'inich I	484–514/531 CE
K'an I	531–c. 534 CE
Yajaw Te' K'inich II	553–c. 595/99 CE
Knot Ajaw	599–613/8 CE
K'an II	618–658 CE
K'ahk' Ujol K'inich II	658–c. 680/5 CE
Ruler VII	c. 700/2 CE
Tom Yohl K'inich	c. 744–793 CE
K'inich Joy K'awiil	c. 798/9
K'inich Tobil Yopaat	c. 810–830/5 CE

K'an III	c. 835–849 CE
Ruler XIII	c. 859 CE

Calakmul

Yuknoom Ch'een I	c. 484–520 CE
K'altuun Hix	c. 520/537–546 CE
Ut Chanal	c. 561–572 CE
Yax Yopaat	c. 572/3–579 CE
Uneh Chan	579–611 CE
Yuknoom Ti' Chan	c. 619 CE
Tajoom Uk'ab K'ahk'	622–630 BE
Yuknoom Head	630/1–636 CE
Yuknoom Ch'een II the Great	636–686 CE
Yuknoom Yich'aak K'ank'	686–c. 695/8
Split Earth (co-ruler?)	c. 695 CE
Yuknoom Tok'	702–731/6 CE
Wamaw K'awiil	c. 736–741 CE
Bolon K'awiil	c. 751–771 CE
Great Serpent	c. 751 CE
Bolon K'awiil II	c. 771–789 CE
Kan Pet	c. 849 CE
Aj Tok'	c. 909 CE

Copan

K'inich Yax K'uk' Mo'	c. 426–435/7 CE
Ruler 2	c. 437–470 CE
Ruler 3	c. 455–465 CE
Ruler 4	c. 465/470–476 CE
Ruler 5	c. 475/480 CE
Ruler 6	c. 490 CE

Bahlam Nehn	c. 504–544 CE
Ruler 8	c. 532–551 CE
Ruler 9	551–553 CE
Tzi-Bahlam	553–578 CE
K'ak Chan Yopaat	578–628 CE
Chan Imix K'awiil	628–695 CE
Waxaklahun Ubah K'awiil	695–738 CE
K'ahk' Joplaj Chan K'awiil	738–749 CE
K'ahk' Yipyaj Chan K'awiil	749–761/3 CE
Yax Pasaj Chan Yopaat	763–c. 810/20 CE
Ukit Tok'	c. 822–830 CE

Naranjo

Tzik'in Bahlam	? CE
Naatz Chan Ahk	? CE
Tahjal Chaak	? CE
Aj Wosaaj Chan K'inich	546–615 CE
K'uxaj	615–631 CE
K'ahk' Xiiw Chan Chaahk	c. 644–680 CE
Wak Chanil of Dos Pilas	682–741 CE
K'ak' Tiliw Chan Chaak	c. 693–728 CE
Yax Mayuy Chan Chaak	c. 741–744 CE
K'ak' Yipiy Chann Chaak	746–? CE
K'ahk' Ukalaw Chan Chaak	755–780/4 CE
Itzamnaaj K'awiil	784–810 CE
Waxaklajuun Ub'aah K'awiil	c. 814–? CE

Palenque

K'uk' Bahlam I	431–435 CE
Casper	435–487 CE

B'utz Aj Sak Chilik	487–501 CE
Ahkal Mo'Nahb I	501–524 CE
K'an Joy Chitam I	529–565 CE
Ahkal Mo' Nahb II	565–570 CE
Kan Bahlam I	572–583 CE
Yohl Ik'nal	583–604 CE
Ajen Yohl Mat	605–612 CE
Sak K'uk'	612–615 CE
K'inich Janaab' Pakal I the Great	615–683 CE
K'inich Kan Bahlam II	684–702 CE
K'inich K'an Joy Chitam II	c. 702–721 CE
K'inich Ahkal Mo' Nahb III	c. 721–736/40 CE
K'inich Janaab Pakal II	c. 742–? CE
K'inich Kan Bahlam III	c. 751/761 CE
K'inich K'uk' Bahlam II	c. 764–783 CE
Janaab Pakal III	799–? CE

Tikal

Yax Ehb' Xook (founded Tikal lineage)	c. 90 CE
? Bahlam	c. 292
Sihyaj Chan K'awiil I	c. 300/7
Unen Bahlam	c. 317 CE
K'inich Muwaan Jol	?–369 CE
Chak Tok Ich'aak I	359/60–378 CE
Yax Nuun Ayiin I	379–404 CE
Sihyaj Chan K'awiil II	411–456/7 CE
K'an Chitam	458–486/8 CE
Chak Tok Ich'aak II	486–508 CE
Yo K'in (co-ruler)	511–527 CE
Kaloomte Bahlam (co ruler)	c. 511–527 CE

Bird Claw	c. 593 CE
Wak Chan K'awiil	537–562 CE
K'inich Waaw	562/593–628 CE
K'inich Wayaan	c. 635 CE
K'inich Muwaan Jol II	c. 645 CE
Nun Ujol Chaak	657–679 CE
Jasaw Chan K'awiil I	682–734 CE
Yik'in Chan K'awiil	734–760/6 CE
28th Ruler	c. 766 CE
Yax Nuun Ayiin II	768–790/4 CE
Nuun Ujol K'inich	c. 800 CE
Dark Sun	c. 810 or 849 CE
Jewel K'awiil	c. 849 CE
Jasaw Chan K'awiil II	c. 869 CE

Yaxchilan

Yopaat Bahlam I	c. 359 CE
Itzamnaaj Bahlam I	? CE
Yaxun Bahlam I	378–389 CE
Yax Deer-Antler Skull	389–402 CE
Ruler 5	402 BC
K'inich Tatb'u Jol I	? CE
Moon Skull	c. 454–467 CE
Yaxun Bahlam II	467–? CE
Joy Bahlam I	c. 508–518 CE
K'inich Tatb'u Jol II	526/37–550 CE
Joy Bahlam II	c. 560/4–570 CE
Itzamnaaj Bahlam II	c. 599–611 CE
K'inich Tatb'u Jol III	? CE
Yaxun Bahlam III	631–681 CE

Itzamnaaj Bahlam III	681–742 CE
Yopaat Bahlam II	c. 749 CE
Yaxun Bahlam IV	752–768 CE
Itzamnaaj Bahlam IV	769–800 CE
K'inich Tatb'u Jol IV	c. 808 CE

TOLTEC LEADERS

There is much dispute over the rulers of the Toltecs, both over who ruled and when. A sample of the records follow, which show the scale of discrepancies. As in other Mesoamerican cultures, the god Quetzalcoatl was worshipped and is sometimes considered as either the founder and first Toltec ruler, or its last ruler.

This list is from Fernando de Alva Ixtlilxochitl (1568/80–1648 CE), a nobleman of Aztec descent who chronicled indigenous Mesoamerican history.

Chalchiuhtlanetzin	510–562 CE
Ixtlilcuechahauac	562–614 CE
Huetzin	614–666 CE
Totepeuh	666–718 CE
Nacaxoc	718–770 CE
Tlacomihua	770–826 CE
Xihuiqueniitzin	826–830 CE
Tecpancaltzin Iztaccaltzin	830–875 CE
Meconetzin	875–927 CE
Mitl	927–979 CE
Xiuhtlaltzin	979–983 CE

Tecpancaltzin	983–1031 CE
Topiltzin	1031–1063 CE

This list is from the Anales de Cuauhtilan, part of the Codex Chimalpopoca, a record of pre-Hispanic Mesoamerican history and mythology which was written after the Spanish conquest. It is now thought to be lost.

Mixcoamazatzin	701–767 CE
Huetzin	767–782 CE
Ilhuitimal	783–821 CE
Ce Acatl Topiltzin Quetzalcoatl (mythological figure)	822–844 CE
Matlacxochitl	844–880 CE
Nauhyotzin	880–895 CE
Matlaccoatzin	896–924 CE
Tlilcoatzin	925–947 CE
Huemac (Atecpanecatl)	948–1023 CE

Most sources agree that Toltec society largely fell apart in the late eleventh and early twelfth centuries after a large-scale migration from Tollan, the capital city of the Toltec Empire. This was thought to be because of war and famine.

AZTEC LEADERS

Aztec creation myths say that people had lived through four great ages or iterations and that theirs was the fifth. Each previous age had ended in destruction when the gods decided the people were not worthy. In this age, known as the Fifth Sun, the gods Quetzalcoatl and Texcatlipoca came to earth to destroy the earth monster, Tlatecuhtli, whom they ripped in two to create the sky and the earth. Quetzalcoatl then restored humanity to the earth.

The following lists give the rulers of three major Aztec cities, Tenochtitlan, Texcoco and Tlacopan.

Tenochtitlan

Leaders of the Pre-Aztec Empire

Tenoch (legendary founder of the city of Tenochtitlan; preceded by the sun god Huitzilopochtli)	1325–1375 CE
Acamapichtli, first ruler of Tenochtitlan	c. 1367/76–1387 CE
Huitzilihuitl	1391–1415 CE
Chīmalpopōca	1415–1426/7 CE
Xihuitl Temoc	1427 (ruled for only 60 days)

Leaders of the Aztec Empire up to the Spanish Invasion

Itzcōātl (founding member of Aztec Empire)	1427–1440 CE
Motēuczōma I Ilhuicamīna	1440–1466/8 CE
Atotoztli	1466–1472 CE
Axayacatl	1469/72–1481 CE
Tizocic	1481–1486 CE
Āhuizotl	1486–1502 CE
Motēuczōma II Xocoyotzin	1502–1520 CE
Cuitlāhuac	1520 (80 days)
Cuāuhtemōc (partly under Spanish rule)	1520–1524

Texcoco
Leaders of the Pre-Aztec Empire

Quinatzin Tlaltecatzin (first known ruler)	1298–1357 CE
Techotlalatzin	1357 or 1377–1409 CE
Ixtlilxochitl Ome Tochtli	1409–1418 CE
Yancuiltzin (co-ruled)	1418–1431 CE
Tochpili (co-ruled)	1418–1431 CE

Leaders of the Aztec Empire up to the Spanish Invasion

Nezahualcoyōtl (founding member of Aztec Empire)	1431–1472 CE
Nezahualpilli	1472/3–1515 CE
Cacamatzin	1516–1519/20 CE
Cuicuizcatl (not officially recognized)	1519–1520 CE
Coanacoch	1520–1521 CE

Tlacopan
Leaders of the pre-Aztec Empire

Aculnahuacatl Tzaqualcatl (first known ruler)	c. 1400–1430 CE

Leaders of the Aztec Empire up to the Spanish Invasion

Totoquihuaztli I (founding member of Aztec Empire)	c. 1430–1469 CE
Chimalopopoca	c. 1469–1489 CE
Totoquihuaztli II	1489–1519 CE
Tetlepanquetzaltzin	1519–1524 CE

SUMERIAN KING LIST

This list is **based on** the *Sumerian King List* or *Chronicle of the One Monarchy*. The lists were often originally carved into clay tablets and several versions have been found, mainly in southern Mesopotamia. Some of these are incomplete and others contradict one another. Dates are based on archaeological evidence as far as possible but are thus approximate. There may also be differences in name spellings between different sources. Nevertheless, the lists remain an invaluable source of information.

As with many civilizations, lists of leaders often begin with mythological and legendary figures before they merge into the more solidly historical, hence why you will see some reigns of seemingly impossible length.

After the kingship descended from heaven, the kingship was in Eridug.

Alulim	28,800 years (8 *sars**)
Alalngar	36,000 years (10 *sars*)

Then Eridug fell and the kingship was taken to Bad-tibira.

En-men-lu-ana	43,200 years (12 *sars*)
En-mel-gal-ana	28,800 years (8 *sars*)
Dumuzid the Shepherd (or Tammuz)	36,000 years (10 *sars*)

Then Bad-tibira fell and the kingship was taken to Larag.

En-sipad-zid-ana   28,800 years (8 *sars*)

Then Larag fell and the kingship was taken to Zimbir.

En-men-dur-ana   21,000 years (5 *sars* and 5 *ners*)

Then Zimbir fell and the kingship was taken to Shuruppag.

Ubara-Tutu   18,600 years (5 *sars* and 1 *ner**)

Then the flood swept over.

*A *sar* is a numerical unit of 3,600; a *ner* is a numerical unit of 600.

FIRST DYNASTY OF KISH

After the flood had swept over, and the kingship had descended from heaven, the kingship was in Kish.

Jushur	1,200 years	Zuqaqip	900 years
Kullassina-bel	960 years	Atab (or A-ba)	600 years
Nangishlisma	1,200 years	Mashda (son of	
En-tarah-ana	420 years	Atab)	840 years
Babum	300 years	Arwium (son of	
Puannum	840 years	Mashda)	720 years
Kalibum	960 years	Etana the Shepherd	1,500 years
Kalumum	840 years	Balih (son of Etana)	400 years

En-me-nuna 660 years

Melem-Kish (son of
    Enme-nuna) 900 years

Barsal-nuna (son of
    Enme-nuna) 1,200 years

Zamug (son of
    Barsal-nuna) 140 years

Tizqar (son of Zamug)
    305 years

Ilku 900 years

Iltasadum 1,200 years

Enmebaragesi 900 years
    (earliest proven ruler
    based on archaeological
    sources; Early Dynastic
    Period, 2900–2350 BCE)

Aga of Kish (son of
    Enmebaragesi) 625 years
    (Early Dynastic Period,
    2900–2350 BCE)

Then Kish was defeated and the kingship was taken to E-anna.

FIRST RULERS OF URUK

Mesh-ki-ang-gasher (son of Utu)   324 years (Late Uruk Period,
                                                4000–3100 BCE)

Enmerkar (son of Mesh-ki-ang-gasher)   420 years (Late Uruk
                                                Period, 4000–3100 BCE)

Lugal-banda the shepherd   1200 years (Late Uruk
                                                Period, 4000–3100 BCE)

Dumuzid the fisherman   100 years (Jemdet Nasr Period,
                                                3100–2900 BCE)

Gilgamesh   126 years (Early Dynastic Period,
                                                2900–2350 BCE)

Ur-Nungal (son of Gilgamesh)   30 years

Udul-kalama (son of Ur-Nungal)   15 years

La-ba'shum   9 years

En-nun-tarah-ana   8 years

Mesh-he	36 years
Melem-ana	6 years
Lugal-kitun	36 years

Then Unug was defeated and the kingship was taken to Urim (Ur).

FIRST DYNASTY OF UR

Mesh-Ane-pada	80 years
Mesh-ki-ang-Nuna (son of Mesh-Ane-pada)	36 years
Elulu	25 years
Balulu	36 years

Then Urim was defeated and the kingship was taken to Awan.

DYNASTY OF AWAN

Three kings of Awan	356 years

Then Awan was defeated and the kingship was taken to Kish.

SECOND DYNASTY OF KISH

Susuda the fuller	201 years
Dadasig	81 years
Mamagal the boatman	360 years
Kalbum (son of Mamagal)	195 years

Tuge	360 years
Men-nuna (son of Tuge)	180 years
Enbi-Ishtar	290 years
Lugalngu	360 years

Then Kish was defeated and the kingship was taken to Hamazi.

DYNASTY OF HAMAZI

Hadanish	360 years

Then Hamazi was defeated and the kingship was taken to Unug (Uruk).

SECOND DYNASTY OF URUK

En-shag-kush-ana	60 years (*c.* 25th century BCE)
Lugal-kinishe-dudu	120 years
Argandea	7 years

Then Unug was defeated and the kingship was taken to Urim (Ur).

SECOND DYNASTY OF UR

Nanni	120 years
Mesh-ki-ang-Nanna II (son of Nanni)	48 years

Then Urim was defeated and the kingship was taken to Adab.

DYNASTY OF ADAB

Lugal-Ane-mundu   90 years (*c.* 25th century BCE)

Then Adab was defeated and the kingship was taken to Mari.

DYNASTY OF MARI

Anbu	30 years	Zizi of Mari, the fuller	20 years
Anba (son of Anbu)	17 years	Limer the 'gudug'	
Bazi the		priest	30 years
leatherworker	30 years	Sharrum-iter	9 years

Then Mari was defeated and the kingship was taken to Kish.

THIRD DYNASTY OF KISH

Kug-Bau (Kubaba)   100 years (*c.* 25th century BCE)

Then Kish was defeated and the kingship was taken to Akshak.

DYNASTY OF AKSHAK

Unzi	30 years	Ishu-Il	24 years
Undalulu	6 years	Shu-Suen (son of	
Urur	6 years	Ishu-Il)	7 years
Puzur-Nirah	20 years		

Then Akshak was defeated and the kingship was taken to Kish.

FOURTH DYNASTY OF KISH

Puzur-Suen (son of Kug-bau)	25 years (*c.* 2350 BCE)
Ur-Zababa (son of Puzur-Suen)	400 years (*c.* 2300 BCE)
Zimudar	30 years
Usi-watar (son of Zimudar)	7 years
Eshtar-muti	11 years
Ishme-Shamash	11 years
Shu-ilishu	15 years
Nanniya the jeweller	7 years

Then Kish was defeated and the kingship was taken to Unug (Uruk).

THIRD DYNASTY OF URUK

Lugal-zage-si	25 years (*c.* 2296–2271 BCE)

Then Unug was defeated and the kingship was taken to Agade (Akkad).

DYNASTY OF AKKAD

Sargon of Akkad	56 years (*c.* 2270–2215 BCE)
Rimush of Akkad (son of Sargon)	9 years (*c.* 2214–2206 BCE)
Manishtushu (son of Sargon)	15 years (*c.* 2205–2191 BCE)

Naram-Sin of Akkad (son of
  Manishtushu)   56 years (*c.* 2190–2154 BCE)
Shar-kali-sharri (son of Naram-Sin) 24 years (*c.* 2153–2129 BCE)

Then who was king? Who was not the king?

Irgigi, Nanum, Imi and Ilulu   3 years (four rivals who fought
                                  to be king during a three-year
                                  period; *c.* 2128–2125 BCE)
Dudu of Akkad   21 years (*c.* 2125–2104 BCE)
Shu-Durul (son of Duu)   15 years (*c.* 2104–2083 BCE)

Then Agade was defeated and the kingship was taken to Unug (Uruk).

FOURTH DYNASTY OF URUK

Ur-ningin   7 years (*c.* 2091?–2061? BCE)
Ur-gigir (son of Ur-ningin)   6 years
Kuda   6 years
Puzur-ili   5 years
Ur-Utu (or Lugal-melem; son of Ur-gigir) 6 years

Unug was defeated and the kingship was taken to the army of Gutium.

GUTIAN RULE

Inkišuš   6 years (*c.* 2147–2050 BCE)
Sarlagab (or Zarlagab)   6 years

Shulme (or Yarlagash)	6 years
Elulmeš (or Silulumeš or Silulu)	6 years
Inimabakeš (or Duga)	5 years
Igešauš (or Ilu-An)	6 years
Yarlagab	3 years
Ibate of Gutium	3 years
Yarla (or Yarlangab)	3 years
Kurum	1 year
Apilkin	3 years
La-erabum	2 years
Irarum	2 years
Ibranum	1 year
Hablum	2 years
Puzur-Suen (son of Hablum)	7 years
Yarlaganda	7 years
Si'um (or Si-u)	7 years
Tirigan	40 days

Then the army of Gutium was defeated and the kingship taken to Unug (Uruk).

FIFTH DYNASTY OF URUK

Utu-hengal	427 years / 26 years / 7 years
	(conflicting dates; *c.* 2055–2048 BCE)

THIRD DYNASTY OF UR

Ur-Namma (or Ur-Nammu)	18 years (*c*. 2047–2030 BCE)
Shulgi (son of Ur-Namma)	48 years (*c*. 2029–1982 BCE)
Amar-Suena (son of Shulgi)	9 years (*c*. 1981–1973 BCE)
Shu-Suen (son of Amar-Suena)	9 years (*c*. 1972–1964 BCE)
Ibbi-Suen (son of Shu-Suen)	24 years (*c*. 1963–1940 BCE)

Then Urim was defeated. The very foundation of Sumer was torn out. The kingship was taken to Isin.

DYNASTY OF ISIN

Ishbi-Erra	33 years (*c*. 1953–1920 BCE)
Shu-Ilishu (son of Ishbi-Erra)	20 years
Iddin-Dagan (son of Shu-Ilishu)	20 years
Ishme-Dagan (son of Iddin-Dagan)	20 years
Lipit-Eshtar (son of Ishme-Dagan or Iddin Dagan)	11 years
Ur-Ninurta (son of Ishkur)	28 years
Bur-Suen (son of Ur-Ninurta)	21 years
Lipit-Enlil (son of Bur-Suen)	5 years
Erra-imitti	8 years
Enlil-bani	24 years
Zambiya	3 years
Iter-pisha	4 years
Ur-du-kuga	4 years
Suen-magir	11 years
Damiq-ilishu (son of Suen-magir)	23 years

ANCIENT EGYPTIAN PHARAOHS

There is dispute about the dates and position of pharaohs within dynasties due to several historical sources being incomplete or inconsistent. This list aims to provide an overview of the ancient Egyptian dynasties, but is not exhaustive and dates are approximate. There may also be differences in name spellings between different sources. Also please note that the throne name is given first, followed by the personal name – more commonly they are known by the latter.

ANCIENT EGYPTIAN DEITIES

Ancient Egyptian gods and goddesses were worshipped as deities. They were responsible for maat (divine order or stability), and different deities represented different natural forces, such as Ra the Sun God. After the Egyptian state was first founded in around 3100 BCE, pharaohs claimed to be divine representatives of these gods and were thought to be successors of the gods.

While there are many conflicting Egyptian myths, some of the significant gods and goddesses and their significant responsibilities are listed here.

Amun/Amen/Amen-Ra	Creation
Atem/Tem	Creation, the sun

Ra	The sun
Isis	The afterlife, fertility, magic
Osiris	Death and resurrection, agriculture
Hathor	The sky, the sun, motherhood
Horus	Kingship, the sky
Set	Storms, violence, deserts
Maat	Truth and justice, she personifies *maat*
Anubis	The dead, the underworld

PREDYNASTIC AND EARLY DYNASTIC PERIODS (*c.* 3000–2686 BCE)

First Dynasty (*c.* 3150–2890 BCE)

The first dynasty begins at the unification of Upper and Lower Egypt.

Narmer (Menes/M'na?)	*c.* 3150 BCE
Aha (Teti)	*c.* 3125 BCE
Djer (Itej)	54 years
Djet (Ita)	10 years
Merneith (possibly the first female Egyptian pharaoh)	*c.* 2950 BCE
Khasti (Den)	42 years
Merybiap (Adjib)	10 years
Semerkhet (Iry)	8.5 years
Qa'a (Qebeh)	34 years
Sneferka	*c.* 2900 BCE
Horus-Ba (Horus Bird)	*c.* 2900 BCE

Second Dynasty (*c.* 2890–2686 BCE)

Little is known about the second dynasty of Egypt.

Hetepsekhemwy (Nebtyhotep)	15 years
Nebra	14 years
Nynetjer (Banetjer)	43–45 years
Ba	unknown
Weneg-Nebty	c. 2740 BCE
Wadjenes (Wadj-sen)	c. 2740 BCE
Nubnefer	unknown
Senedj	c. 47 years
Peribsen (Seth-Peribsen)	unknown
Sekhemib (Sekhemib-Perenmaat)	c. 2720 BCE
Neferkara I	25 years
Neferkasokkar	8 years
Horus Sa	unknown
Hudejefa (real name missing)	11 years
Khasekhemwy (Bebty)	18 years

OLD KINGDOM (c. 2686–2181 BCE)

Third Dynasty (c. 2686–2613 BCE)

The third dynasty was the first dynasty of the Old Kingdom. Its capital was at Memphis.

Djoser (Netjerikhet)	c. 2650 BCE
Sekhemkhet (Djoser-Teti)	2649–2643 BCE
Nebka? (Sanakht)	c. 2650 BCE
Qahedjet (Huni?)	unknown
Khaba (Huni?)	2643–2637 BCE
Huni	2637–2613 BCE

Fourth Dynasty (*c.* 2613–2498 BCE)

The fourth dynasty is sometimes known as the 'golden age' of Egypt's Old Kingdom.

Snefru (Nebmaat)	2613–2589 BCE
Khufu, or Cheops (Medjedu)	2589–2566 BCE
Djedefre (Kheper)	2566–2558 BCE
Khafre (Userib)	2558–2532 BCE
Menkaure (Kakhet)	2532–2503 BCE
Shepseskaf (Shepeskhet)	2503–2498 BCE

Fifth Dynasty (*c.* 2498–2345 BCE)

There is some doubt over the succession of pharaohs in the fifth dynasty, especially Shepseskare.

Userkaf	2496/8–2491 BCE
Sahure	2490–2477 BCE
Neferirkare-Kakai	2477–2467 BCE
Neferefre (Izi)	2460–2458 BCE
Shepseskare (Netjeruser)	few months between 2458 and 2445 BCE
Niuserre (Ini)	2445–2422 BCE
Menkauhor (Kaiu)	2422–2414 BCE
Djedkare (Isesi)	2414–2375 BCE
Unis (Wenis)	2375–2345 BCE

Sixth Dynasty (*c.* 2345–2181 BCE)

Teti	2345–2333 BCE
Userkare	2333–2332 BCE
Meryre (Pepi I)	2332–2283 BCE

Merenre I (Nemtyemsaf I)	2283–2278 BCE
Neferkare (Pepi II)	2278–2183 BCE
Merenre II (Nemtyemsaf II)	2183 or 2184 BCE
Netjerkare (Siptah I) or Nitocris	2182–2179 BCE

FIRST INTERMEDIATE PERIOD (c. 2181–2040 BCE)

Seventh and Eighth Dynasties (c. 2181–2160 BCE)

There is little evidence on this period in ancient Egyptian history, which is why many of the periods of rule are unknown.

Menkare	c. 2181 BCE
Neferkare II	unknown
Neferkare III (Neby)	unknown
Djedkare (Shemai)	unknown
Neferkare IV (Khendu)	unknown
Merenhor	unknown
Sneferka (Neferkamin I)	unknown
Nikare	unknown
Neferkare V (Tereru)	unknown
Neferkahor	unknown
Neferkare VI (Peiseneb)	unknown to 2171 BCE
Neferkamin (Anu)	c. 2170 BCE
Qakare (Ibi)	2175–2171 BCE
Neferkaure	2167–2163 BCE
Neferkauhor (Khuwihapi)	2163–2161 BCE
Neferiirkkare (Pepi)	2161–2160 BCE

Ninth Dynasty (*c.* 2160–2130 BCE)

There is little evidence on this period in ancient Egyptian history which is why many of the periods of rule are unknown.

Maryibre (Khety I)	2160 BCE to unknown
Name unknown	unknown
Naferkare VII	unknown
Seneh (Setut)	unknown

The following pharaohs and their dates of rule are unknown or widely unconfirmed.

Tenth Dynasty (*c.* 2130–2040 BCE)

Rulers in the Tenth dynasty were based in Lower Egypt.

Meryhathor	2130 BCE to unknown
Neferkare VIII	2130–2040 BCE
Wahkare (Khety III)	unknown
Merykare	unknown to 2040 BCE
Name unknown	unknown

Eleventh Dynasty (*c.* 2134–1991 BCE)

Rulers in the eleventh dynasty were based in Upper Egypt.

Intef the Elder	unknown
Tepia (Mentuhotep I)	unknown to 2133 BCE
Sehertawy (Intef I)	2133–2117 BCE
Wahankh (Intef II)	2117–2068 BCE
Nakhtnebtepefer (Intef III)	2068–2060/40 BCE

MIDDLE KINGDOM (c. 2040–1802 BCE)

Eleventh Dynasty Continued (c. 2134–1991 BCE)

This period is usually known as the beginning of the Middle Kingdom.

Nebhepetre (Mentuhotep II)   2060–2040 BCE as king of Upper
            Egypt, 2040–2009 BCE as King of Upper and Lower Egypt
Sankhkare (Mentuhotep III)   2009–1997 BCE
Nebtawyre (Mentuhotep IV)   1997–1991 BCE

Twelfth Dynasty (c. 1991–1802 BCE)

The twelfth dynasty was one of the most stable prior to the New Kingdom, and is often thought to be the peak of the Middle Kingdom.

Sehetepibre (Amenemhat I)   1991–1962 BCE
Kheperkare (Senusret I / Sesostris I)   1971–1926 BCE
Nubkaure (Amenemhat II)   1929–1895 BCE
Khakheperre (Senusret II / Sesostris II)   1898–1878 BCE
Khakaure (Senusret III / Sesostris III)   1878–1839 BCE
Nimaatre (Amenemhat III)   1860–1815 BCE
Maakherure (Amenemhat IV)   1815–1807 BCE
Sobekkare (Sobekneferu/Nefrusobek)   1807–1802 BCE

SECOND INTERMEDIATE PERIOD (c. 1802–1550 BCE)

Thirteenth Dynasty (c. 1802–c. 1649 BCE)

There is some ambiguity on the periods of rule of the thirteenth dynasty, but it is marked by a period of several short rules. This dynasty is often combined with the eleventh, twelfth and fourteenth dynasties under the Middle Kingdom.

Sekhemre Khutawy (Sobekhotep I)	1802–1800 BCE
Mehibtawy Sekhemkare (Amenemhat Sonbef)	1800–1796 BCE
Nerikare (Sobek)	1796 BCE
Sekhemkare (Amenemhat V)	1796–1793 BCE
Ameny Qemau	1795–1792 BCE
Hotepibre (Qemau Siharnedjheritef)	1792–1790 BCE
Lufni	1790–1788 BCE
Seankhibre (Amenemhat VI)	1788–1785 BCE
Semenkare (Nebnuni)	1785–1783 BCE
Sehetepibre (Sewesekhtawy)	1783–1781 BCE
Sewadijkare I	1781 BCE
Nedjemibre (Amenemhat V)	1780 BCE
Khaankhre (Sobekhotep)	1780–1777 BCE
Renseneb	1777 BCE
Awybre (Hor)	1777–1775 BCE
Sekhemrekhutawy Khabaw	1775–1772 BCE
Djedkheperew	1772–1770 BCE
Sebkay	unknown
Sedjefakare (Kay Amenemhat)	1769–1766 BCE
Khutawyre (Wegaf)	c. 1767 BCE
Userkare (Khendjer)	c. 1765 BCE
Smenkhkare (Imyremeshaw)	started in 1759 BCE
Sehetepkare (Intef IV)	c. 10 years
Meribre (Seth)	ended in 1749 BCE
Sekhemresewadjtawy (Sobekhotep III)	1755–1751 BCE
Khasekhemre (Neferhotep I)	1751–1740 BCE

Menwadjre (Sihathor)	1739 BCE
Khaneferre (Sobekhotep IV)	1740–1730 BCE
Merhotepre (Sobekhotep V)	1730 BCE
Knahotepre (Sobekhotep VI)	c. 1725 BCE
Wahibre (Ibiau)	1725–1714 BCE
Merneferre (Ay I)	1714–1691 BCE
Merhotepre (Ini)	1691–1689 BCE
Sankhenre (Sewadjtu)	1675–1672 BCE
Mersekhemre (Ined)	1672–1669 BCE
Sewadjkare II (Hori)	c. 5 years
Merkawre (Sobekhotep VII)	1664–1663 BCE
Seven kings (names unknown)	1663–? BCE

Note: the remaining pharaohs of the thirteenth dynasty are not listed here as they are either unknown or there is a lot of ambiguity about when they ruled.

Fourteenth Dynasty (c. 1805/1710–1650 BCE)

Rulers in the fourteenth dynasty were based at Avaris, the capital of this dynasty.

Sekhaenre (Yakbim)	1805–1780 BCE
Nubwoserre (Ya'ammu)	1780–1770 BCE
Khawoserre (Qareh)	1770–1745 BCE
Aahotepre ('Ammu)	1760–1745 BCE
Maaibre (Sheshi)	1745–1705 BCE
Aasehre (Nehesy)	c. 1705 BCE
Khakherewre	unknown
Nebefawre	c. 1704 BCE
Sehebre	1704–1699 BCE

Merdjefare   c. 1699 BCE

Note: the remaining pharaohs of the fourteenth dynasty are not listed here as they are either unknown or there is a lot of ambiguity about when they ruled.

Fifteenth Dynasty (*c.* 1650–1544 BCE)

The fifteenth dynasty was founded by Salitas and covered a large part of the Nile region.

Salitas	c. 1650 BCE
Semqen	1649 BCE to unknown
'Aper-'Anat	unknown
Sakir-Har	unknown
Seuserenre (Khyan)	c. 30 to 35 years
Nebkhepeshre (Apepi)	1590 BCE?
Nakhtyre (Khamudi)	1555–1544 BCE

Sixteenth Dynasty (*c.* 1650–1580 BCE)

Rulers in the sixteenth dynasty were based at Thebes, the capital of this dynasty. The name and date of rule of the first pharaoh is unknown.

Sekhemresementawy (Djehuti)	3 years
Sekhemresemeusertawy (Sobekhotep VIII)	16 years
Sekhemresankhtawy (Neferhotep III)	1 year
Seankhenre (Mentuhotepi)	less than a year
Sewadjenre (Nebiryraw)	26 years
Neferkare (?) (Nebiryraw II)	c. 1600 BCE
Semenre	c. 1600 BCE

Seuserenre (Bebiankh)	12 years
Djedhotepre (Dedumose I)	c. 1588–1582 BCE
Djedneferre (Dedumose II)	c. 1588–1582 BCE
Djedankhre (Montensaf)	c. 1590 BCE
Merankhre (Mentuhotep VI)	c. 1585 BCE
Seneferibre (Senusret IV)	unknown
Sekhemre (Shedwast)	unknown

Seventeenth Dynasty (c. 1650–1550 BCE)

Rulers in the seventeenth dynasty ruled Upper Egypt.

Sekhemrewahkhaw (Rahotep)	c. 1620 BCE
Sekhemre Wadjkhaw (Sobekemsaf I)	c. 7 years
Sekhemre Shedtawy (Sobekemsaf II)	unknown to c. 1573 BCE
Sekhemre-Wepmaat (Intef V)	c. 1573–1571 BCE
Nubkheperre (Intef VI)	c. 1571–1565 BCE
Sekhemre-Heruhirmaat (Intef VII)	late 1560s BCE
Senakhtenre (Ahmose)	c. 1558 BCE
Seqenenre (Tao I)	1558–1554 BCE
Wadkheperre (Kamose)	1554–1549 BCE

NEW KINGDOM (c. 1550–1077 BCE)

Eighteenth Dynasty (c. 1550–1292 BCE)

The first dynasty of Egypt's New Kingdom marked the beginning of Ancient Egypt's highest power and expansion.

Nebpehtire (Ahmose I)	c. 1550–1525 BCE
Djeserkare (Amenhotep I)	1541–1520 BCE

Aakheperkare (Thutmose I)	1520–1492 BCE
Aakheperenre (Thutmose II)	1492–1479 BCE
Maatkare (Hatshepsut)	1479–1458 BCE
Menkheperre (Thutmose III)	1458–1425 BCE
Aakheperrure (Amenhotep II)	1425–1400 BCE
Menkheperure (Thutmose IV)	1400–1390 BCE
Nebmaatre 'the Magnificent' (Amehotep III)	1390–1352 BCE
Neferkheperure Waenre (Amenhotep IV)	1352–1336 BCE
Ankhkheperure (Smenkhkare)	1335–1334 BCE
Ankhkheperure mery Neferkheperure (Neferneferuaten III)	1334–1332 BCE
Nebkheperure (Tutankhamun)	1332–1324 BCE
Kheperkheperure (Aya II)	1324–1320 BCE
Djeserkheperure Setpenre (Haremheb)	1320–1292 BCE

Nineteenth Dynasty (c. 1550–1292 BCE)

The nineteenth dynasty is also known as the Ramessid dynasty as it includes Ramesses II, one of the most famous and influential Egyptian pharaohs.

Menpehtire (Ramesses I)	1292–1290 BCE
Menmaatre (Seti I)	1290–1279 BCE
Usermaatre Setpenre 'the Great', 'Ozymandias' (Ramesses II)	1279–1213 BCE
Banenre (Merneptah)	1213–1203 BCE
Menmire Setpenre (Amenmesse)	1203–1200 BCE
Userkheperure (Seti II)	1203–1197 BCE
Sekhaenre (Merenptah Siptah)	1197–1191 BCE
Satre Merenamun (Tawosret)	1191–1190 BCE

Twentieth Dynasty (c. 1190–1077 BCE)

This, the third dynasty of the New Kingdom, is generally thought to mark the start of the decline of Ancient Egypt.

Userkhaure (Setnakht)	1190–1186 BCE
Usermaatre Meryamun (Ramesses III)	1186–1155 BCE
Heqamaatre Setpenamun (Ramesses IV)	1155–1149 BCE
Heqamaatre Setpenamun (Ramesses IV)	1155–1149 BCE
Usermaatre Sekheperenre (Ramesses V)	1149–1145 BCE
Nebmaatre Meryamun (Ramesses VI)	1145–1137 BCE
Usermaatre Setpenre Meryamun (Ramesses VII)	1137–1130 BCE
Usermaatre Akhenamun (Ramesses VIII)	1130–1129 BCE
Neferkare Setpenre (Ramesses IX)	1128–1111 BCE
Khepermaatre Setpenptah (Ramesses X)	1111–1107 BCE
Menmaatre Setpenptah (Ramesses XI)	1107–1077 BCE

Twenty-first Dynasty (c. 1077–943 BCE)

Rulers in the twenty-first dynasty were based at Tanis and mainly governed Lower Egypt.

Hedjkheperre-Setpenre (Nesbanadjed I)	1077–1051 BCE
Neferkare (Amenemnisu)	1051–1047 BCE
Aakkheperre (Pasebakhenniut I)	1047–1001 BCE
Usermaatre (Amenemope)	1001–992 BCE
Aakheperre Setepenre (Osorkon the Elder)	992–986 BCE
Netjerikheperre-Setpenamun (Siamun)	986–967 BCE
Titkheperure (Pasebakhenniut II)	967–943 BCE

Twenty-second Dynasty (c. 943–728 BCE)

Sometimes called the Bubastite dynasty. Its pharaohs came from Libya.

Hedjkheneperre Setpenre (Sheshonq I)	943–922 BCE
Sekhemkheperre Setepenre (Osorkon I)	922–887 BCE
Heqakheperre Setepenre (Sheshonq II)	887–885 BCE
Tutkheperre (Sheshonq Llb)	c. the 880s BCE
Hedjkheperre Setepenre (Takelot I Meriamun)	885–872 BCE
Usermaatre Setpenre (Sheshonq III)	837–798 BCE
Hedjkheperre Setepenre (Sheshonq IV)	798–785 BCE
Usermaatre Setpenre (Pami Meriamun)	785–778 BCE
Aakheperre (Sheshonq V)	778–740 BCE
Usermaatre (Osorkon IV)	740–720 BCE

Twenty-third and Twenty-fourth Dynasties
(c. 837–720 BCE)

These dynasties were led mainly by Libyans and mainly ruled Upper Egypt.

Hedjkheperre Setpenre (Takelot II)	837–813 BCE
Usermaatre Setpenamun (Meriamun Pedubaste I)	826–801 BCE
Usermaatre Meryamun (Sheshonq VI)	801–795 BCE
Usermaatre Setpenamun (Osorkon III)	795–767 BCE
Usermaatre-Setpenamun (Takelot III)	773–765 BCE
Usermaatre-Setpenamun (Meriamun Rudamun)	765–762 BCE
Shepsesre (Tefnakhte)	732–725 BCE
Wahkare (Bakenrenef)	725–720 BCE

Twenty-fifth Dynasty (c. 744–656 BCE)

Also known as the Kushite period, the twenty-fifth dynasty follows the Nubian invasions.

Piankhy (Piye)	744–714 BCE
Djedkaure (Shebitkku)	714–705 BCE
Neferkare (Shabaka)	705–690 BCE
Khuinefertemre (Taharqa)	690–664 BCE

LATE PERIOD (c. 664–332 BCE)

Twenty-sixth Dynasty (c. 664 – 525 BCE)

Also known as the Saite period, the twenty-sixth dynasty was the last native period before the Persian invasion in 525 BCE.

Wahibre (Psamtik I)	664–610 BCE
Wehemibre (Necho II)	610–595 BCE
Neferibre (Psamtik II)	595–589 BCE
Haaibre (Apreis)	589–570 BCE
Khemibre (Amasis II)	570–526 BCE
Ankhkaenre (Psamtik III)	526–525 BCE

Twenty-seventh Dynasty (c. 525–404 BCE)

The twenty-seventh dynasty is also known as the First Egyptian Satrapy and was ruled by the Persian Achaemenids.

Mesutre (Cambyses II)	525–1 July 522 BCE
Seteture (Darius I)	522–November 486 BCE
Kheshayarusha (Xerxes I)	November 486–December 465 BCE
Artabanus of Persia	465–464 BCE
Arutakhshashas (Artaxerxes I)	464–424 BCE
Ochus (Darius II)	July 423–March 404 BCE

Twenty-eighth Dynasty (*c.* 404–398 BCE)

The twenty-eighth dynasty consisted of a single pharaoh.

Amunirdisu (Amyrtaeus)	404–398 BCE

Twenty-ninth Dynasty (*c.* 398–380 BCE)

The twenty-ninth dynasty was founded following the overthrow of Amyrtaeus.

Baenre Merynatjeru (Nepherites I)	398–393 BCE
Khnemmaatre Setepenkhnemu (Hakor)	*c.* 392–391 BCE
Userre Setepenptah (Psammuthis)	*c.* 391 BCE
Khnemmaatre Setepenkhnemu (Hakor)	*c.* 390–379 BCE
Nepherites II	*c.* 379 BCE

Thirtieth Dynasty (*c.* 379–340 BCE)

The thirtieth dynasty is thought to be the final native dynasty of Ancient Egypt.

Kheperkare (Nectanebo I)	*c.* 379–361 BCE
Irimaatenre (Teos)	*c.* 361–359 BCE
Snedjemibre Setepenanhur (Nectanebo II)	*c.* 359–340 BCE

Thirty-first Dynasty (*c.* 340–332 BCE)

The thirty-first dynasty is also known as the Second Egyptian Satrapy and was ruled by the Persian Achaemenids.

Ochus (Artaxerxes III)	*c.* 340–338 BCE
Arses (Artaxerxes IV)	338–336 BCE
Darius III	336–332 BCE

MACEDONIAN/ARGEAD DYNASTY (c. 332–309 BCE)

Alexander the Great conquered Persia and Egypt in 332 BCE.

Setpenre Meryamun (Alexander III of Macedon 'the Great')	332–323 BCE
Setpenre Meryamun (Philip Arrhidaeus)	323–317 BCE
Khaibre Setepenamun (Alexander IV)	317–309 BCE

PTOLEMAIC DYNASTY (c. 305–30 BCE)

The Ptolemaic dynasty in Egypt was the last dynasty of Ancient Egypt before it became a province of Rome.

Ptolemy I Soter	305–282 BCE
Ptolemy II Philadelphos	284–246 BCE
Arsinoe II	c. 277–270 BCE
Ptolemy III Euergetes	246–222 BCE
Berenice II	244/243–222 BCE
Ptolemy IV Philopater	222–204 BCE
Arsinoe III	220–204 BCE
Ptolemy V Epiphanes	204–180 BCE
Cleopatra I	193–176 BCE
Ptolemy VI Philometor	180–164, 163–145 BCE
Cleopatra II	175–164 BCE, 163–127 BCE and 124–116 BCE
Ptolemy VIII Physcon	171–163 BCE, 144–131 BCE and 127–116 BCE
Ptolemy VII Neos Philopator	145–144 BCE

Cleopatra III	142–131 BCE, 127–107 BCE
Ptolemy Memphites	113 BCE
Ptolemy IX Soter	116–110 BCE
Cleopatra IV	116–115 BCE
Ptolemy X Alexander	110–109 BCE
Berenice III	81–80 BCE
Ptolemy XI Alexander	80 BCE
Ptolemy XII Auletes	80–58 BCE, 55–51 BCE
Cleopatra V Tryphaena	79–68 BCE
Cleopatra VI	58–57 BCE
Berenice IV	58–55 BCE
Cleopatra VII	52–30 BCE
Ptolemy XIII Theos Philopator	51–47 BCE
Arsinoe IV	48–47 BCE
Ptolemy XIV Philopator	47–44 BCE
Ptolemy XV Caesar	44–30 BCE

In 30 BCE, Egypt became a province of the Roman Empire.

ANCIENT GREEK MONARCHS

This list is not exhaustive and dates are approximate. Where dates of rule overlap, emperors either ruled jointly or ruled in opposition to one another. There may also be differences in name spellings between different sources.

Because of the fragmented nature of Greece prior to its unification by Philip II of Macedon, this list includes mythological and existing rulers of Thebes, Athens and Sparta as some of the leading ancient Greek city-states. These different city-states had some common belief in the mythological gods and goddesses of ancient Greece, although their accounts may differ.

KINGS OF THEBES (c. 753–509 bce)

These rulers are mythological. There is much diversity over who the kings actually were, and the dates they ruled.

Calydnus (son of Uranus)
Ogyges (son of Poseidon, thought to be king of Boeotia or Attica)
Cadmus (Greek mythological hero known as the founder of Thebes, known as Cadmeia until the reign of Amphion and Zethus)
Pentheus (son of Echion, one of the mythological Spartoi, and Agave, daughter of Cadmus)

Polydorus (son of Cadmus and Harmonia, goddess of harmony)

Nycteus (like his brother Lycus, thought to be the son of a Spartoi and a nymph, or a son of Poseidon)

Lycus (brother of Nyceteus)

Labdacus (grandson of Cadmus)

Lycus (second reign as regent for Laius)

Amphion and Zethus (joint rulers and twin sons of Zeus, constructed the city walls of Thebes)

Laius (son of Labdacus, married to Jocasta)

Oedipus (son of Laius, killed his father and married his mother, Jocasta)

Creon (regent after the death of Laius)

Eteocles and Polynices (brothers/sons of Oedipus; killed each other in battle)

Creon (regent for Laodamas)

Laodamas (son of Eteocles)

Thersander (son of Polynices)

Peneleos (regent for Tisamenus)

Tisamenus (son of Thersander)

Autesion (son of Tisamenes)

Damasichthon (son of Peneleos)

Ptolemy (son of Damasichton, 12 century BCE)

Xanthos (son of Ptolemy)

KINGS OF ATHENS

Early legendary kings who ruled before the mythological flood caused by Zeus, which only Deucalion (son of Prometheus) and a few others survived (date unknown).

Periphas (king of Attica, turned into an eagle by Zeus)

Ogyges (son of Poseidon, thought to be king of either Boeotia or Attica)

Actaeus (king of Attica, father-in-law to Cecrops I)

Erechtheid Dynasty (1556–1127 BCE)

Cecrops I (founder and first king of Athens; half-man, half-serpent who married Actaeus' daughter)	1556–1506 BCE
Cranaus	1506–1497 BCE
Amphictyon (son of Deucalion)	1497–1487 BCE
Erichthonius (adopted by Athena)	1487–1437 BCE
Pandion I (son of Erichthonius)	1437–1397 BCE
Erechtheus (son of Pandion I)	1397–1347 BCE
Cecrops II (son of Erechtheus)	1347–1307 BCE
Pandion II (son of Cecrops II)	1307–1282 BCE
Aegeus (adopted by Pandion II, gave his name to the Aegean Sea)	1282–1234 BCE
Theseus (son of Aegeus, killed the minotaur)	1234–1205 BCE
Menestheus (made king by Castor and Pollux when Theseus was in the underworld)	1205–1183 BCE
Demophon (son of Theseus)	1183–1150 BCE
Oxyntes (son of Demophon)	1150–1136 BCE
Apheidas (son of Oxyntes)	1136–1135 BCE
Thymoetes (son of Oxyntes)	1135–1127 BCE

Melanthid Dynasty (1126–1068 BCE)

Melanthus (king of Messenia, fled to Athens when expelled)	1126–1089 BCE
Codrus (last of the semi-mythological Athenian kings)	1089–1068 BCE

LIFE ARCHONS OF ATHENS (1068–753 BCE)

These rulers held public office up until their deaths.

Medon	1068–1048 BCE	Pherecles	864–845 BCE
Acastus	1048–1012 BCE	Ariphon	845–825 BCE
Archippus	1012–993 BCE	Thespieus	824–797 BCE
Thersippus	993–952 BCE	Agamestor	796–778 BCE
Phorbas	952–922 BCE	Aeschylus	778–755 BCE
Megacles	922–892 BCE	Alcmaeon	755–753 BCE
Diognetus	892–864 BCE		

From this point, archons led for a period of ten years up to 683 BCE, then a period of one year up to 485 CE. Selected important leaders – including archons and tyrants – in this later period are as follows:

SELECTED LATER LEADERS OF ATHENS

Peisistratos 'the Tyrant of Athens'	561, 559–556, 546–527 BCE
Cleisthenes (archon)	525–524 BCE
Themistocles (archon)	493–492 BCE
Pericles	c. 461–429 BCE

KINGS OF SPARTA

These rulers are mythological and are thought to be descendants of the ancient tribe of Leleges. There is much diversity over who the kings actually were, and the dates they ruled.

Lelex (son of Poseidon or Helios, ruled Laconia)	*c.* 1600 BCE
Myles (son of Lelex, ruled Laconia)	*c.* 1575 BCE
Eurotas (son of Myles, father of Sparta)	*c.* 1550 BCE

From the Lelegids, rule passed to the Lacedaemonids when Lacedaemon married Sparta.

Lacedaemon (son of Zeus, husband of Sparta)
Amyklas (son of Lacedaemon)
Argalus (son of Amyklas)
Kynortas (son of Amyklas)
Perieres (son of Kynortas)
Oibalos (son of Kynortas)
Tyndareos (first reign; son of Oibalos, father of Helen of Troy)
Hippocoon (son of Oibalos)
Tyndareos (second reign; son of Oibaos, father of Helen of Troy)

From the Lacedaemons, rule passed to the Atreids when Menelaus married Helen of Troy.

Menelaus (son of Atreus, king of Mycenae, and husband of Helen)	*c.* 1250 BCE
Orestes (son of Agamemnon, Menelaus' brother)	*c.* 1150 BCE
Tisamenos (son of Orestes)	
Dion	*c.* 1100 BCE

From the Atreids, rule passed to the Heraclids following war.

Aristodemos (son of Aristomachus, great-great-grandson of Heracles)

Theras (served as regent for Aristodemes' sons, Eurysthenes and Procles)

Eurysthenes   c. 930 BCE

From the Heraclids, rule passed to the Agiads, founded by Agis I. Only major kings during this period are listed here.

Agis I (conceivably the first historical Spartan king) c. 930–900 BCE

Alcamenes   c. 740–700 BCE,
                                        during First Messenian War

Cleomenes I (important leader in the
    Greek resistance against the Persians)   524 – 490 BCE

Leonidas I (died while leading the
    Greeks – the 300 Spartans – against
    the Persians in the Battle of
    Thermopylae, 480 BCE)   490–480 BCE

Cleomenes III (exiled following the
    Battle of Sellasia)   c. 235–222 BCE

KINGS OF MACEDON

Argead Dynasty (808–309 BCE)

Karanos	c. 808–778 BCE	Alcetas I	c. 576–547 BCE
Koinos	c. 778–750 BCE	Amyntas I	c. 547–498 BCE
Tyrimmas	c. 750–700 BCE	Alexander I	c. 498–454 BCE
Perdiccas I	c. 700–678 BCE	Alcetas II	c. 454–448 BCE
Argaeus I	c. 678–640 BCE	Perdiccas II	c. 448–413 BCE
Philip I	c. 640–602 BCE	Archelaus I	c. 413–339 BCE
Aeropus I	c. 602–576 BCE	Craterus	c. 399 BCE

Orestes	c. 399–396 BCE	Perdiccas III	c. 368–359 BCE
Aeropus II	c. 399–394/93 BCE	Amyntas IV	c. 359 BCE
Archelaus II	c. 394–393 BCE	Philip II	c. 359–336 BCE
Amyntas II	c. 393 BCE	Alexander III 'the Great'	
Pausanias	c. 393 BCE	(also King of Persia and	
Amyntas III	c. 393 BCE; first reign	Pharaoh of Egypt by end of reign)	c. 336–323 BCE
Argeus II	c. 393–392 BCE	Philip III	c. 323–317 BCE
Amyntas III	c. 392–370 BCE	Alexander IV	c. 323/ 317–309 BCE
Alexander II	c. 370–368 BCE		

Note: the Corinthian League or Hellenic League was created by Philip II and was the first time that the divided Greek city-states were unified under a single government.

Post-Argead Dynasty (309–168 BCE, 149–148 BCE)

Cassander	c. 305–297 BCE
Philip IV	c. 297 BCE
Antipater II	c. 297–294 BCE
Alexpander V	c. 297–294 BCE

Antigonid, Alkimachid and Aeacid Dynasties (294–281 BCE)

Demetrius	c. 294–288 BCE
Lysimachus	c. 288–281 BCE
Pyrrhus	c. 288–285 BCE; first reign

Ptolemaic Dynasty (281–279 BCE)

Ptolemy Ceraunus (son of Ptolemy I of Egypt)	c. 281–279 BCE
Meleager	279 BCE

Antipatrid, Antigonid, Aeacid Dynasties, Restored
(279–167 BCE)

Antipater	c. 279 BCE
Sosthenes	c. 279–277 BCE
Antigonus II	c. 277–274 BCE; first reign
Pyrrhus	c. 274–272 BCE; second reign
Antigonus II	c. 272–239 BCE; second reign
Demetrius II	c. 239–229 BCE
Antigonus III	c. 229–221 BCE
Philip V	c. 221–179 BCE
Perseus (deposed by Romans)	c. 179–168 BCE
Revolt by Philip VI (Andriskos)	c. 149–148 BCE

SELEUCID DYNASTY (c. 320 BCE–63 CE)

Seleucus I Nicator	c. 320–315, 312–305, 305–281 BCE
Antiochus I Soter	c. 291, 281–261 BCE
Antiochus II Theos	c. 261–246 BCE
Seleucus II Callinicus	c. 246–225 BCE
Seleucus III Ceraunus	c. 225–223 BCE
Antiochus III 'the Great'	c. 223–187 BCE
Seleucus IV Philopator	c. 187–175 BCE
Antiochus (son of Seleucus IV)	c. 175–170 BCE
Antiochus IV Epiphanes	c. 175–163 BCE
Antiochus V Eupater	c. 163–161 BCE
Demetrius I Soter	c. 161–150 BCE
Alexander I Balas	c. 150–145 BCE
Demetrius II Nicator	c. 145–138 BCE; first reign
Antiochus VI Dionysus	c. 145–140 BCE

Diodotus Tryphon	c. 140–138 BCE
Antiochus VII Sidetes	c. 138–129 BCE
Demetrius II Nicator	c. 129–126 BCE; second reign
Alexander II Zabinas	c. 129–123 BCE
Cleopatra Thea	c. 126–121 BCE
Seleucus V Philometor	c. 126/125 BCE
Antiochus VIII Grypus	c. 125–96 BCE
Antiochus IX Cyzicenus	c. 114–96 BCE
Seleucus VI Epiphanes	c. 96–95 BCE
Antiochus X Eusebes	c. 95–92/83 BCE
Demetrius III Eucaerus	c. 95–87 BCE
Antiochus XI Epiphanes	c. 95–92 BCE
Philip I Philadelphus	c. 95–84/83 BCE
Antiochus XII Dionysus	c. 87–84 BCE
Seleucus VII	c. 83–69 BCE
Antiochus XIII Asiaticus	c. 69–64 BCE
Philip II Philoromaeus	c. 65–63 BCE

Ptolemaic Dynasty (305–30 BCE)

The Ptolemaic dynasty in Greece was the last dynasty of Ancient Egypt before it became a province of Rome.

Ptolemy I Soter	305–282 BCE
Ptolemy II Philadelphos	284–246 BCE
Arsinoe II	c. 277–270 BCE
Ptolemy III Euergetes	246–222 BCE
Berenice II	244/243–222 BCE
Ptolemy IV Philopater	222–204 BCE
Arsinoe III	220–204 BCE
Ptolemy V Epiphanes	204–180 BCE

Cleopatra I	193–176 BCE
Ptolemy VI Philometor	180–164, 163–145 BCE
Cleopatra II	175–164 BCE, 163–127 BCE and 124–116 BCE
Ptolemy VIII Physcon	171–163 BCE, 144–131 BCE and 127–116 BCE
Ptolemy VII Neos Philopator	145–144 BCE
Cleopatra III	142–131 BCE, 127–107 BCE
Ptolemy Memphites	113 BCE
Ptolemy IX Soter	116–110 BCE
Cleopatra IV	116–115 BCE
Ptolemy X Alexander	110–109 BCE
Berenice III	81–80 BCE
Ptolemy XI Alexander	80 BCE
Ptolemy XII Auletes	80–58 BCE, 55–51 BCE
Cleopatra V Tryphaena	79–68 BCE
Cleopatra VI	58–57 BCE
Berenice IV	58–55 BCE

In 27 BCE, Caesar Augustus annexed Greece and it became integrated into the Roman Empire.

ANCIENT ROMAN LEADERS

This list is not exhaustive and some dates are approximate. The legitimacy of some rulers is also open to interpretation. Where dates of rule overlap, emperors either ruled jointly or ruled in opposition to one another. There may also be differences in name spellings between different sources.

KINGS OF ROME (753–509 BCE)

Romulus (mythological founder and first ruler of Rome)	753–716 BCE
Numa Pompilius (mythological)	715–672 BCE
Tullus Hostilius (mythological)	672–640 BCE
Ancus Marcius (mythological)	640–616 BCE
Lucius Tarquinius Priscus (mythological)	616–578 BCE
Servius Tullius (mythological)	578–534 BCE
Lucius Tarquinius Superbus (Tarquin the Proud; mythological)	534–509 BCE

ROMAN REPUBLIC (509-27 BCE)

During this period, two consuls were elected to serve a joint one-year term. Therefore, only a selection of significant consuls are included here.

Lucius Junius Brutus (semi-mythological)	509 BCE
Marcus Porcius Cato (Cato the Elder)	195 BCE
Scipio Africanus	194 BCE
Cnaeus Pompeius Magnus (Pompey the Great)	70, 55 and 52 BCE
Marcus Linius Crassus	70 and 55 BCE
Marcus Tullius Cicero	63 BCE
Caius Julius Caesar	59 BCE
Marcus Aemilius Lepidus	46 and 42 BCE
Marcus Antonius (Mark Anthony)	44 and 34 BCE
Marcus Agrippa	37 and 28 BCE

PRINCIPATE (27 BCE-284 CE)

Julio-Claudian Dynasty (27 BCE–68 CE)

Augustus (Caius Octavius Thurinus, Caius Julius Caesar, Imperator Caesar Divi filius)	27 BCE–14 CE
Tiberius (Tiberius Julius Caesar Augustus)	14–37 CE
Caligula (Caius Caesar Augustus Germanicus)	37–41 CE
Claudius (Tiberius Claudius Caesar Augustus Germanicus)	41–54 CE
Nero (Nero Claudius Caesar Augustus Germanicus)	54–68 CE

Year of the Four Emperors (68–69 CE)

Galba (Servius Sulpicius Galba Caesar Augustus)	68–69 CE
Otho (Marcus Salvio Otho Caesar Augustus)	Jan–Apr 69 CE
Vitellius (Aulus Vitellius Germanicus Augustus)	Apr–Dec 69 CE

Note: the fourth emperor, Vespasian, is listed below.

Flavian Dynasty (66–96 CE)

Vespasian (Caesar Vespasianus Augustus)	69–79 CE
Titus (Titus Caesar Vespasianus Augustus)	79–81 CE
Domitian (Caesar Domitianus Augustus)	81–96 CE

Nerva-Antonine Dynasty (69–192 CE)

Nerva (Nerva Caesar Augustus)	96–98 CE
Trajan (Caesar Nerva Traianus Augustus)	98–117 CE
Hadrian (Caesar Traianus Hadrianus Augustus)	138–161 CE
Antonius Pius (Caesar Titus Aelius Hadrianus Antoninus Augustus Pius)	138–161 CE
Marcus Aurelius (Caesar Marcus Aurelius Antoninus Augustus)	161–180 CE
Lucius Verus (Lucius Aurelius Verus Augustus)	161–169 CE
Commodus (Caesar Marcus Aurelius Commodus Antoninus Augustus)	180–192 CE

Year of the Five Emperors (193 CE)

Pertinax (Publius Helvius Pertinax)	Jan–Mar 193 CE
Didius Julianus (Marcus Didius Severus Julianus)	Mar–Jun 193 CE

Note: Pescennius Niger and Clodius Albinus are generally regarded as usurpers, while the fifth, Septimius Severus, is listed below

Severan Dynasty (193–235 CE)

Septimius Severus (Lucius Septimius Severus Pertinax)	193–211 CE
Caracalla (Marcus Aurelius Antonius)	211–217 CE
Geta (Publius Septimius Geta)	Feb–Dec 211 CE
Macrinus (Caesar Marcus Opellius Severus Macrinus Augustus)	217–218 CE
Diadumenian (Marcus Opellius Antonius Diadumenianus)	May–Jun 218 CE
Elagabalus (Caesar Marcus Aurelius Antoninus Augustus)	218–222 CE
Severus Alexander (Marcus Aurelius Severus Alexander)	222–235 CE

Crisis of the Third Century (235–285 CE)

Maximinus 'Thrax' (Caius Julius Verus Maximus)	235–238 CE
Gordian I (Marcus Antonius Gordianus Sempronianus Romanus)	Apr–May 238 CE
Gordian II (Marcus Antonius Gordianus Sempronianus Romanus)	Apr–May 238 CE
Pupienus Maximus (Marcus Clodius Pupienus Maximus)	May–Aug 238 CE
Balbinus (Decimus Caelius Calvinus Balbinus)	May–Aug 238 CE
Gordian III (Marcus Antonius Gordianus)	Aug 238–Feb 244 CE
Philip I 'the Arab' (Marcus Julius Philippus)	244–249 CE
Philip II 'the Younger' (Marcus Julius Severus Philippus)	247–249 CE
Decius (Caius Messius Quintus Traianus Decius)	249–251 CE
Herennius Etruscus (Quintus Herennius Etruscus Messius Decius)	May/Jun 251 CE

Trebonianus Gallus (Caius Vibius Trebonianus Gallus)   251–253 CE
Hostilian (Caius Valens Hostilianus Messius
   Quintus)   Jun–Jul 251 CE
Volusianus (Caius Vibius Afinius Gallus
   Veldumnianus Volusianus)   251–253 CE
Aemilian (Marcus Aemilius Aemilianus)   Jul–Sep 253 CE
Silbannacus (Marcus Silbannacus)   Sep/Oct 253 CE
Valerian (Publius Licinius Valerianus)   253–260 CE
Gallienus (Publius Licinius Egnatius Gallienus)   253–268 CE
Saloninus (Publius Licinius Cornelius
   Saloninus Valerianus)   Autumn 260 CE
Claudius II Gothicus (Marcus Aurelius Claudius)   268–270 CE
Quintilus (Marcus Aurelius Claudias
   Quintillus)   Apr–May/Jun 270 CE
Aurelian (Luciua Domitius Aurelianus)   270–275 CE
Tacitus (Marcus Claudius Tacitus)   275–276 CE
Florianus (Marcus Annius Florianus)   276–282 CE
Probus (Marcus Aurelius Probus Romanus;
   in opposition to Florianus)   276–282 CE
Carus (Marcus Aurelias Carus)   282–283 CE
Carinus (Marcus Aurelius Carinus)   283–285 CE
Numerian (Marcus Aurelius Numerianus)   283–284 CE

DOMINATE (284–610)

Tetrarchy (284–324)

Diocletian 'Lovius' (Caius Aurelius Valerius Diocletianus)   284–305
Maximian 'Herculius' (Marcus Aurelius Valerius
   Maximianus; ruled the western provinces)   286–305/late 306–308

Galerius (Caius Galerius Valerius Maximianus; ruled the eastern provinces)	305–311
Constantius I 'Chlorus' (Marcus Flavius Valerius Constantius; ruled the western provinces)	305–306
Severus II (Flavius Valerius Severus; ruled the western provinces)	306–307
Maxentius (Marcus Aurelius Valerius Maxentius)	306–312
Licinius (Valerius Licinanus Licinius; ruled the western, then the eastern provinces)	308–324
Maximinus II 'Daza' (Aurelius Valerius Valens; ruled the western provinces)	316–317
Martinian (Marcus Martinianus; ruled the western provinces)	Jul–Sep 324

Constantinian Dynasty (306–363)

Constantine I 'the Great' (Flavius Valerius Constantinus; ruled the western provinces then whole)	306–337
Constantine II (Flavius Claudius Constantinus)	337–340
Constans I (Flavius Julius Constans)	337–350
Constantius II (Flavius Julius Constantius)	337–361
Magnentius (Magnus Magnentius)	360–353
Nepotianus (Julius Nepotianus)	Jun 350
Vetranio	Mar–Dec 350
Julian 'the Apostate' (Flavius Claudius Julianus)	361–363
Jovian (Jovianus)	363–364

Valentinianic Dynasty (364–392)

Valentinian I 'the Great' (Valentinianus)	364–375
Valens (ruled the eastern provinces)	364–378

Procopius (revolted against Valens)	365–366
Gratian (Flavius Gratianus Augustus; ruled the western provinces then whole)	375–383
Magnus Maximus	383–388
Valentinian II (Flavius Valentinianus)	388–392
Eugenius	392–394

Theodosian Dynasty (379–457)

Theodosius I 'the Great' (Flavius Theodosius)	Jan 395
Arcadius	383–408
Honorius (Flavius Honorius)	395–432
Constantine III	407–411
Theodosius II	408–450
Priscus Attalus; usurper	409–410
Constantius III	Feb–Sep 421
Johannes	423–425
Valentinian III	425–455
Marcian	450–457

Last Emperors in the West (455–476)

Petronius Maximus	Mar–May 455
Avitus	455–456
Majorian	457–461
Libius Severus (Severus III)	461–465
Anthemius	467–472
Olybrius	Apr–Nov 472
Glycerius	473–474
Julius Nepos	474–475
Romulus Augustulus (Flavius Momyllus Romulus Augustulus)	475–476

Leonid Dynasty (East, 457–518)

Leo I (Leo Thrax Magnus)	457–474
Leo II	Jan–Nov 474
Zeno	474–475
Basiliscus	475–476
Zeno (second reign)	476–491
Anastasius I 'Dicorus'	491–518

Justinian Dynasty (East, 518–602)

Justin I	518–527
Justinian I 'the Great' (Flavius Justinianus, Petrus Sabbatius)	527–565
Justin II	565–578
Tiberius II Constantine	578–582
Maurice (Mauricius Flavius Tiberius)	582–602
Phocas	602–610

LATER EASTERN EMPERORS (610–1059)

Heraclian Dynasty (610–695)

Heraclius	610–641
Heraclius Constantine (Constantine III)	Feb–May 641
Heraclonas	Feb–Nov 641
Constans II Pogonatus ('the Bearded')	641–668
Constantine IV	668–685
Justinian II	685–695

Twenty Years' Anarchy (695–717)

Leontius	695–698
Tiberius III	698–705

Justinian II 'Rhinometus' (second reign)	705–711
Philippicus	711–713
Anastasius II	713–715
Theodosius III	715–717

Isaurian Dynasty (717–803)

Leo III 'the Isaurian'	717–741
Constantine V	741–775
Artabasdos	741/2–743
Leo V 'the Khazar'	775–780
Constantine VI	780–797
Irene	797–802

Nikephorian Dynasty (802–813)

Nikephoros I 'the Logothete'	802–811
Staurakios	July–Oct 811
Michael I Rangabé	813–820

Amorian Dynasty (820–867)

Michael II 'the Amorian'	820–829
Theophilos	829–842
Theodora	842–856
Michael III 'the Drunkard'	842–867

Macedonian Dynasty (867–1056)

Basil I 'the Macedonian'	867–886
Leo VI 'the Wise'	886–912
Alexander	912–913
Constantine VII Porphyrogenitus	913–959
Romanos I Lecapenus	920–944

Romanos II	959–963
Nikephoros II Phocas	963–969
John I Tzimiskes	969–976
Basil II 'the Bulgar-Slayer'	976–1025
Constantine VIII	1025–1028
Romanus III Argyros	1028–1034
Michael IV 'the Paphlagonian'	1034–1041
Michael V Kalaphates	1041–1042
Zoë Porphyrogenita	Apr–Jun 1042
Theodora Porphyrogenita	Apr–Jun 1042
Constantine IX Monomachos	1042–1055
Theodora Porphyrogenita (second reign)	1055–1056
Michael VI Bringas 'Stratioticus'	1056–1057
Isaab I Komnenos	1057–1059